A KINGDOM KEEPERS NOVEL

THE RETURN

BOOK THREE
DISNEY AT LAST

ALSO BY RIDLEY PEARSON

WITH DAVE BARRY

For a complete listing of Ridley's published books
visit www.ridleypearson.com

A KINGDOM KEEPERS NOVEL

THE RETURN

BOOK THREE

DISNEY AT LAST

RIDLEY PEARSON

DISNEP • HYPERION

Los Angeles   New York

Copyright © 2017 Page One, Inc.

Printed in the United States of America

First Edition, March 2017
10 9 8 7 6 5 4 3 2
FAC-020093-17122
ISBN 978-1-4231-8433-1

This book is set in 12.5 Adobe Caslon.
Book design by Joann Hill

Library of Congress Cataloging-in-Publication Data

Names: Pearson, Ridley.
Title: Disney at last / Ridley Pearson.
Description: First edition. | Los Angeles : Disney Hyperion, 2017. | Series: Kingdom Keepers novel: the return ; book 3 | Summary: "The stakes are high—both for the past and the future. The finale of The Return series leaves the Kingdom Keepers with unimaginable choices to make"—Provided by publisher.
Identifiers: LCCN 2016044102 (print) | LCCN 2016058878 (ebook) | ISBN 1423184335 | ISBN 1368002102
Subjects: | CYAC: Good and evil—Fiction. | Time travel—Fiction. | Cartoon characters—Fiction. | Walt Disney World (Fla.)—Fiction. | Disneyland (Calif.)—Fiction.
Classification: LCC PZ7.P323314 Dj 2017 (print) | LCC PZ7.P323314 (ebook) | DDC [Fic]—dc23
LC record available at https://lccn.loc.gov/2016044102

Reinforced binding

Visit www.DisneyBooks.com
www.thekingdomkeepers.com
www.ridleypearson.com
www.kingdomkeepersinsider.com

DEDICATION

To Wendy Lefkon and Marty Sklar

SPECIAL THANKS TO

Genevieve Gagne-Hawes for her incredible editorial work. Dan Conaway and Amy Berkower and Writers House for their representation. And to Nick Perkins, whose idea this (The Return) was.

ACKNOWLEDGMENTS

To all the wonderful Keepers, another series comes to an end! Thanks for Keeper-ing the dream alive. Brooke Muschott as my Keeper of the Keepers Encylopedia, for her edits and patience. Jessica Kim and especially Jen Wood for driving the readership to new heights.

Chris Ostrander and Tim Retzlaff for all the connections within Disney and help getting the word out. Becky Cline and Kevin M. Kern for not only allowing me access to the Disney Archives, but for holding my hand through the process. Kim Irvine and all things Disneyland. The Imagineers, including Alex Wright.

Nancy Zastrow, Jen Wood (yes, again!), Miranda McVey, and Brett Ellen Keeler for their behind-the-scenes work with me in the office—their tolerance and patience. Tanner Walters, David and Laurel Walters—copyedit and editorial.

Marcelle Pearson for stepping so gracefully into a new role as my go-to office partner. Mary Ann Zissimos for building great book tours. This is KK book ten, perhaps the last, and each has been an unbelievable ride. I've been so lucky to live in this world.

Ridley

St. Louis, October 2016

A KINGDOM KEEPERS NOVEL

THE RETURN

BOOK THREE

DISNEY AT LAST

1

GRAY FINGERS OF DEAD TREES twisting toward the sky warned of just how far he was from civilization. The still water of the Mississippi swamp absorbed the tarry black of the night sky, creating a crater, a void in the earth's surface, bottomless and dangerous. It held secrets, whispered of curses and secret burials. Sticks rose like bones from its muddy surface. A slice of yellow moon, shrouded in wisps of rapidly moving cloud, proved too weak to throw shadows, yet strong enough to reveal the stark landscape.

The man riding in the black chauffeur-driven 1953 Buick Roadmaster's backseat looked away from the water, as if witnessing a secret act he had no business seeing. No business being here. Four hours from the airport, where his private plane had landed. Three hours of nothing but the occasional deserted gas station or dirt roads leading nowhere. He lit a cigarette and smoked it aggressively.

His driver consulted a large foldable map and then monitored the car's odometer, alert for an upcoming turn. It was 1955; handheld cell phones wouldn't be in use for thirty years; GPS wouldn't be in public use for another forty.

"When we arrive," he instructed the driver, "you are not to leave the car no matter what you may see."

"Yes, sir."

"Doors locked."

"Yes, sir."

"You know these parts?" he asked the man.

"I know *of* them, I guess you could say. Back a couple years—forty-eight, forty-nine it was—a young girl and her mamma went missing out this way. Canoe trip, I believe. God rest their souls."

"Are you scared?"

"I don't scare easily."

"Answer the question."

"I am. Yes, sir. Folks like us, like you and me, are not welcome here. These folks keep to themselves, to their ways. You might say they operate by their own laws. I've heard not even the po-lice travel out this far."

"No heroics."

"No, sir."

"You drop me. Come back in an hour. If you don't see me, leave as quickly as you can."

"Now that just goes against everything in my job description, Mr. Johnson."

The man in the backseat nearly chuckled at hearing

his alias spoken; he'd forgotten his personal secretary had hired the car anonymously for him. This was no typical business trip.

"You tell your dispatcher it was on my orders. My secretary will back you up."

"Yes, sir. I'll do as you say."

The car slowed; the driver flicked the turn signal, its dashboard indicator flashing red throughout the interior. It seemed as much a warning for those in the car as an alert for other vehicles. The car swung right down a potholed and puddled lane narrowed by encroaching vines and spiny brambles. A mile passed, the dirt track as tight as a throat, swallowing the car as it passed through.

"No one done come this way in a long, long time. You sure 'bout them directions?" The driver used the wipers to repel the tangles of spiderwebs and insect cocoons covering the windshield.

"The swamp water is what connects these people, not roads. It would have been faster for us in a boat."

"You wouldn't catch me dead in a boat out this way." The driver laughed. "I'm likely wrong 'bout that. Might be the only way you'd find me. Dead, I mean." He slowed the vehicle. The branches scraped the car's exterior, screeching like newborns. "I keep up like this, won't have no paint left."

"Another half mile."

"Won't be no road, another half mile."

"Just the same: another half mile." The man sat back patting the sweat off his brow with a neatly pressed handkerchief.

"Better be someplace to turn around. Ain't no way I can back up in this kind of dark. Feels like we've been eaten by a snake. Jonah and the whale. Know what I mean?"

Exactly half a mile farther they reached a spot where the vines and swamp grasses had been whacked short by a sharp blade. A long, rickety dock connected to a lazily erected tin-roofed shanty the size of a one-car garage. The smell of woodsmoke hung in musty air thick with mosquitoes. The passenger calling himself Mr. Johnson walked the dock's length as the car perfected a seven-point turn to reverse direction. The car waited, facing out.

The man walking out to the dock believed the smooth brown rocks, arranged like stepping stones alongside, to be a form of environmental decoration. When they moved, his breath caught. Humanoid figures stood up, men and women, silhouetted waist deep in the turbid lake. Their dark skin, yellowed by the light of the moon, looked sickly and grotesque. It took a moment to realize the figures were neither living nor dead, but in a suspended state between the two. Hypnotized, perhaps. Drugged? Or, more likely, long left for dead.

Together, the creatures strode toward the dock,

streaming wakes behind, blocking any chance of the man's return to shore. They pulled themselves up onto the squealing wood, dripping a dark goo too congealed to be water. The man quickened his pace, which only served to aggravate the twelve figures as they moved more urgently toward him.

A wizened, crippled thing appeared in the shanty's open doorway. He? She? It leaned upon a crooked hardwood cane, one shoulder higher than the other, knees buckled. Clumps of what had to be hair hung from its head, covering an animal-skin tunic. Hair beads clattered like dull bells.

The water-things advanced, now so close the passenger could feel cold breath on the back of his neck. A disgusting smell, like old hamburger left too long in the fridge, overcame him.

The beaded, bent creature waved its open palm. The water-things grunted and moaned—dogs denied a meal. They backed away and stepped off the dock, splashing into the water.

"Join me, if you will," said it with the cane. "Youse welcome to set a spell."

"I am—"

"Amery Hollingworth."

"Close enough. Astonishing." Amery Hollingsworth had not supplied his name.

"Youse gots youself three young 'uns, all boys, and a missus."

"Impossible!"

It smiled crookedly. "I'm a boastful sort. You must forgive an old man his small pleasures." The broken and bent thing indicated a well-worn stump stool, its wood polished by decades of human contact. Firelight caught shadow images on the bare walls in a rapid-fire slide show. There were six such stumps arranged around a small open fire at the room's center. Nothing larger than twigs crackled as they burned.

Hollingsworth took a seat facing the . . . man. Yes, an old, old black man with slate-gray cataracts for eyes. His voice was rougher than the skin on his hands.

"Your buggy left youse behind, son."

"He'll return in an hour," said Hollingsworth. "It has taken me three years to find you."

"Me, or a man *like* me?" The crippled man chortled.

"What kind of man is that?"

"Youse the one comin' here, no invite. Youse best tell me."

Hollingsworth nodded. "A man with a certain . . . reputation."

"Such as?"

"Reanimation," Hollingsworth stated bluntly.

"That right there, a big word. This right here, a simple man."

"You've turned sticks into snakes."

"So did Moses. Don't youse make me into no Moses. 'Sides, I done rocks into frogs, never no sticks. Them sticks ain't living. That right there no easy thing, son. Leave that to thems above."

"Any living thing?"

"Ain't right to go asking no question you can't handle."

"I can handle more than you might think."

"I don't do much that there thinking, son. Me is more just a part of things. The nature of things. Ash and water. Blood and wine." He reached into a shallow pocket on the tunic, hesitated, and then withdrew a four-foot water moccasin, still dripping wet. It could not have fit into that pocket.

He threw it at Hollingsworth, who erupted off the stump and slapped the thing to the side. It clattered to the wooden planks. A leg bone of some kind, bare and bright, no longer a snake.

The old creature chuckled. "Yep. Figured as much." He shuffled over, picked up the bone, and threw it into the water; a snake swam away on the surface. "Why you here, son?"

Hollingsworth sat down and wiped his brow with

a starched handkerchief. "I propose a partnership," he said.

"Why on God's precious earth should I listen to such poppycock? Mine is not a gift to be bought or sold. That would be sinful."

"Bartered then, negotiated."

"A trade? I think not. Youse come a long way for nothing, Mr. Amery. It is no short walk back down that there road. Your man not coming. I seen it in his heart."

"I offer you your own . . ." Hollingsworth searched for the correct word. "Circle, I believe it's called."

"I's work lonesome. No need no circle."

"A traveler," Hollingsworth said, "can always use sorcerers and sorceresses."

"Words. A man comes into another man's abode, he must be right careful with his words. I's but a humble servant."

Hollingsworth tugged at his suit trousers, unbuttoned his collar, and loosened his tie. "I can provide you witches, warlocks, maids, and servants. Your own kingdom. I can elevate your *reputation* from a shrimp-eating swamp priest to dark lord of your own kingdom. We work together, you and I. We achieve a greatness both of us want. A kingdom, if you will, never before experienced on this earth since the Dark Ages."

The old man's eyes rolled into the back of his head

in an expression of pure pleasure. "Youse keeps on talking, son. A poet, youse is."

"Imagined, but never realized. Conceived of, but rarely demonstrated. I offer you a kingdom, a circle, comprised not of those dead-eyed stumbling zombies out there, but witches with power, real power. The kind of power it takes centuries to develop. I lack the ability to control such fiends, even if I could create them, reanimate them. You, on the other hand, can do both."

"I's done no man's bidding but me own."

Hollingsworth took a long, calculated breath. "I don't venture into such an arrangement lightly. We'll take a blood oath, me and you. I'm aware you could . . . terminate me and our relationship. You won't kill someone who shares your blood."

The strange, bent man examined Hollingsworth, head tilted, clouded eyes roaming. "Youse done exaggerated your powers of persuasiveness, son. If I done wants, I kills you here and now."

"I could have gone to she of the desert or the great beast of the snows. I came here."

The man shuddered. "A mouth like yours is trouble."

"I had a feeling about you," Hollingsworth said. He met eyes with the Traveler for the first time, well aware he risked a spell being cast. "We travel to the edge of the great sea, to the city of the Angels."

"I's hears of this place," the man said contemplatively. "'Course I do. Whys you think an old bent soul like mine would bother, son?"

"You've dreamed of it," Hollingsworth said. "You've *seen* it in your future."

"My future, unlike youse, stretches far."

"You can see my future?"

"Youse think these old eyes give me vision?" He chortled again. "Youse one ambitious man."

"The Lost Angels."

"I heard youse."

Hollingsworth dipped his hand into a pocket and removed a straightedge razor. He unfolded the blade and it glinted in orange firelight. "Shall we?"

2

Two FOURTEEN-YEAR-OLD GIRLS waited in the steadily moving line at the turnstile entrance to Disneyland. The day was hot and glorious, the crowd excited. The air smelled of fresh popcorn. Children tugged at their parents, willing the line to move faster. Cast Members politely processed the tickets and passes of entering guests.

The two girls would never be mistaken for twins. One was taller and super thin with straight, almost white hair, invisible eyebrows, and nearly albino skin; her face was drawn long and tight; her chin pointed, her cheekbones high. She appeared older than she was.

The other was smaller and less put together. Her short hair looked as if she'd cut it herself. Her olive skin was a lush, dark auburn and her eyes nut brown. Those eyes were not cruel, but they were not all giggles either. They seemed to carry a tolerated pain, and an impatience with others.

This girl made eye contact with another girl two lines over, a Native American about her same age who stood chatting with a pair of boys, both of whom were trying too hard to look unimpressed. The girls nodded to each other. The mission was a "go."

"We're on."

"We are *so* on," said her skinny partner. "How exciting is this? Have you ever been?"

"No, of course not. We're a long way from Baltimore."

"The other side of the world, as far as I'm concerned."

"Nervous?"

"No! More like amazed."

They were both on one-day tickets, which meant their photos weren't part of the pass. If they left the park intending to return, they'd be hand-stamped when leaving. But they weren't planning on returning. Not after what they were going to do. Not today.

The two boys and the Native American girl entered the park through the tunnel to the right; the pair of girls, through the tunnel to the left.

The two groups of teens had been warned of the importance of timing. Tomorrowland was to suffer a power outage while (by hijacking the area's music speakers) a demented voice warned guests to flee. There was another plan for Frontierland and New Orleans Square. It was to appear a coordinated attack; their actions couldn't end up looking like coincidence or freak accidents. When those in charge of the parks looked back on the events of this day, they were to see a series of well-executed, perfectly timed *supernatural* events. They were to suspect and confirm the Overtakers were far from gone. Fear was their most powerful weapon.

Minara, the blond girl, made for the restrooms at Rancho Del Zolcalo, next to Thunder Mountain Railroad. Javelot, her companion, took up a position in the viewing area alongside the Rivers of America, in front of New Orleans Square. Both girls wore Zenton waterproof digital watches, supplied by their handlers. Their life skills coach, Mr. Abrahms, had ensured they understood the proper operation of the timepieces. The watches continued their relentless countdown: nine minutes to go.

Minara entered a stall in the restroom and began undressing. She didn't remember at what age the change had taken place; it had coincided with the other anticipated changes, as well as with being disowned by her adoptive parents and shipped off to Baltimore. Events swirled and blurred into a painful storm in her head. She'd been adopted from Romania at the age of two; she'd heard her instructors at Barracks 14 mentioning her heritage as if it might explain the change. They'd labeled her a shape-shifter, but that was too simple a name for a strange, sometimes dreadful process.

She stripped down to a matte black bikini that fit perfectly with her purpose. Crammed her shed clothing into a stuff sack and hung it from a hook on the back of the stall door. Now came the hard part. Since its beginnings, the procedure had confounded doctors, parents, her friends, even herself. It came from a place of wishing and wanting, of anger and hope, disillusionment and fear. It came not from concentration but from release, from turning herself over to an image she formed in her head. Always an animal.

Despite the pain, it felt surprisingly good. Delicious, even. As colorful lines raised like welts on her skin, her muscles began responding as well, pulling and bending her limbs, her bones, into contortions seen only at the circus. Here, in the tiny bathroom stall, browns and blacks crept up her legs, long gray hairs were drawn across her belly, forming what looked like fur; her back began to arch, her neck and head to invert. Her back bend continued until she threw her hands over her head to catch herself. Her pose looked like that of a gymnast, feet flat on the floor, hips and chest stretching high in a backward arch, head hanging, arms outreaching.

The stinging that covered her body cooled somewhat and she knew "the drawing" (as she thought of it) was complete. She began to move automatically as if she'd walked on all fours all her life, first hands, then feet, her back breaking in an upside-down arch. Immediately, there were bloodcurdling screams. The slapping of sandals on tile sounded like hands clapping; the girls and women rushed from the restroom in panic, fleeing the giant tarantula.

At first, the guests who saw the running and heard the screaming outside the restroom were entertained. This was Disneyland, after all. But the panicked cries seemed so . . . real, and the women doing the screaming, so . . . terrified.

The entertainment element passed as the King Kong of spiders arrived into the sunshine. It moved in all directions at once. Forward; to the side; spinning in sharp, quick movements. Children froze, paralyzed, as their parents scooped them up and took off running.

But it was the congestion and steady flow of park guests in and around Big Thunder Mountain that turned panic into bedlam, order into chaos.

Javelot heard the screams behind her and grinned. Minara could scare the tar out of you. Despite the vestiges of a smile, she maintained a kind of mental shield, keeping all thought and energy off her. It was like having a thick plastic bag or see-through helmet over her head.

Her attention was directed onto the silhouette of the captain of the *Mark Twain Riverboat* on the Rivers of America steamboat.

Her effort wasn't an effort at all, but a kind of wishful joining. Easily accomplished, she simply "wished to know." As long as that wish involved a living animal, she *became* whatever, whoever it was. The connection never lasted long, though she could return to it repeatedly. During the brief joining, it wasn't a matter of hearing the person's thoughts or memories. It was more like taking the steering wheel of a car from the driver.

It had started at the age of eight when the family dog ran into the street in front of a UPS truck. Javelot was there, in full empathy with the dog. It stopped and reversed itself as if tugged sharply by a leash. Her mother had seen the dog's impossible about-face and called it a miracle. And Javelot had, from that day forth, begun to think of herself as just that—a miracle, and that confidence drove her to bigger and more ambitious attempts at mind control. Her mother should have caught on when her grades went from Cs to all As.

The captain of the *Mark Twain Riverboat* never knew what hit him. One minute he was piloting the vessel as it circumnavigated the Rivers of America, clockwise, as always. The next, he'd pushed the throttle fully forward and aimed his paddleboat for the Sailing Ship *Columbia*, anchored away from the dock.

If the guests registered the change, they offered little initial reaction. Several visitors on the deck of the

Columbia spotted the giant paddleboat steaming straight at them and called out the alarm. By the time those aboard the *Mark Twain Riverboat* comprehended the physics involved—*a body in motion*—the collision was imminent.

It came as an explosion of wood, as people dived from both vessels into the languid water below. At the moment of contact, the captain looked down at his own hand on the throttle, seeing it as if it belonged to someone else. His only explanation was that he'd blacked out momentarily, an inexcusable and unconscionable act.

The terrified shouting that had begun with the sighting of the giant tarantula swept throughout Frontierland, through New Orleans Square, and as far as Critter Country. Guests helped panicked swimmers out of the water on Tom Sawyer Island and all along the park's shoreline. There were skinned knees and banged elbows, a few bloody noses, and more than a few guests suffering from shock. But no serious injuries.

As the collision of the boats drew everyone's attention to the water, the tarantula withdrew, nearly unnoticed, to the women's restroom. Moments later, a young woman was heard screaming from inside. She sprinted out of the restroom yelling, "*Spiiiiderrrrr!*"

She was tall and thin with a drawn face and exceptionally pale skin.

This girl was joined by a smaller, dark-haired girl with a bad haircut. They fled amid the hundreds of other park guests running in every direction. By the time these two girls reached Main Street USA, another flood of terrified guests originating from Tomorrowland was flowing toward the turnstiles. Thousands of them now.

One girl looked at the other. Both grinned devilishly. They joined hands and ran their hearts out.

While others cried in terror, theirs were cries of joy and accomplishment.

3

FINN WHITMAN WAS A LOT LIKE other kids,
only he wasn't. The same could be said for his friends,
Philby, Charlene, Maybeck, and Willa.

The five were gathered in a workshop backstage at
Disneyland. It looked like the inside of a garage but had
a whiff of mad-scientist. Contributing to the peculiari-
ties of the place was the obvious lack of anything modern. It was as if they were in a museum: the hand tools,
the lighting, the absence of any kind of plastic. It was
all metal, leather, and wood. Bare lightbulbs hung from
thick black wires.

The giveaway to the peculiarity of Finn's situation
was the wall calendar. It showed a full-figured girl in a
tight sweater standing alongside a sports car. The calendar carried the banner title JULY and, in smaller type in
the upper right corner, the year: 1955.

Finn stared at that calendar. He and all but two of
the others had been living in 1955 for ten days now. It
hit him hard that none of them would even be born for
another forty years.

Through a series of strange, though explainable,

events, the five had left the comforts of smartphones, smart cars, and Smart Water behind. They had boarded Disneyland's King Arthur Carrousel as holograms (yes: holograms!) in the time of Taylor Swift and arrived in the original Disneyland at the time of Elvis Presley.

The problem they now faced was terrifying: they lacked the technology to return to the future. Time travel was tricky, to say the least.

A Disneyland Cast Member about the same age, a nineteen-year-old guy named Wayne Kresky, had been helping them. He wore the same baggy khaki pants and button-down shirt as the other backstage Cast Members. His eyes looked gray indoors, but blue in direct sunlight. The artificial lighting changed his blond hair to sand.

"Here's the deal," said the redheaded Philby in a vaguely British-accented voice. "Obviously the technology available to us is a bit prehistoric in 1955. Color TV is barely on the scene, there's never been an astronaut—"

"We know all this!" complained Maybeck. "Talk to us about the Return!"

Maybe it was his being taller that made Terry Maybeck seem older than the others. Maybe it was his occasional reminders to the others that he was the descendant of great-grandparents who'd been slaves. He deservedly carried that chip on his shoulder, and somehow it made him seem more mature, more experienced than the other Keepers. Whatever the case, Maybeck had that "it" that made him cool. The "it" that made him stand out.

"I was simply explaining—"

"Well, don't! None of this is simple, and none of us care about the technology!" said Maybeck. "We don't need a Professor Philby moment. We *need* to know if you and Wayne have come up with a way to get us back to the present. To our families. Please tell me you have, because we already lost our real selves. We're stuck as holograms until the park closes, same as it's been each and every day since we got here."

"Some of us got here late," Willa reminded them, pointing out two others in their company. Jess and Amanda had followed them into the past and were currently in a state of partial shock. It was one of those it-seemed-like-a-better-idea-at-the-time things that now, by the looks on their faces, they probably regretted.

Jess and Amanda, both unusual and exceptional in their own ways, had plunged themselves into the past, each to deliver a message. They were, in fact, twin deliverers of impending doom, the kind of messengers no one wanted to listen to. For both, the idea of the Keepers taking on yet another *mission* was almost too much to bear.

"We were able to return an inanimate object," Philby said.

"English!" Maybeck demanded.

"You don't have to be such a Neanderthal," Charlene snapped. Maybeck listened to Charlene, paid attention to her and her cheerleader good looks. The two had a thing going—a more-than-friends thing, a romance thing—that kept Maybeck on a short leash. "He means an un-living object. Not a plant or animal."

"A Coca-Cola bottle cap," Philby supplied. "Small. Easily identifiable as belonging to now, 1955. We know it worked because it disappeared from the carousel and then reappeared about twelve hours later."

"That's huge!" Finn said.

Philby nodded toward him. "It is. But what we can't seem to pull off, at least not yet, is returning a *living* object and keeping it that way. We tried a green leaf, but we toasted it." He lifted a curled, blackened stem. "We know the Imagineers in the future received it like this because they sent it back with a note."

"We made adjustments, and sent across a beetle in a cage of toothpicks," Wayne said. "It's a dual test because the toothpicks are themselves formerly living matter. Golly, if even the cage can make the journey, it's a big step in the right direction."

Finn took this all in. Considered the leader of the

group, he found it better to listen than to express opinions too quickly. To be a decent leader he had to be right at least some of the time, and given that he barely understood the science of what Wayne and Philby were attempting, he'd kept quiet so far.

But a leader can't remain quiet forever. There was a much bigger elephant in the room. He knew who had to address it; it did no one any good to put it off any longer. But he also knew how unpopular he was about to become.

"The fact you've made any progress at all is amazing." Heads nodded in agreement. All but Maybeck's. A good start. "But we all know we're avoiding the bigger issue. Amanda and Jess have been here a week—"

"Eight days," Jess said, correcting him.

"Eight days!" Finn trumpeted. "Amanda warned us about Amery Hollingsworth being behind the creation of the Overtakers, and we've done nothing about that. Jess has had a dream about Jack Skellington burning bones. If that's also Hollingsworth's doing, then we have to act!"

Speaking the name Hollingsworth was like shouting "Satan!" in church, or "Benedict Arnold" in Congress. By 1955, Amery Hollingsworth, a former rising star in the Disney company, had become a traitor of the first order, a disgruntled employee intent on ruining Walt

Disney's company and the man's dream. Hollingsworth was said to be a brilliant but dangerous man.

Amanda's unusual looks—she might have been some small part Asian or Hispanic—her calming voice, and her wise-beyond-her-years confidence projected an authority few of the others ever challenged. She and Jess had shared a rough childhood that had cemented a friendship stronger than some sisters, and she carried that mystery with her as well. "I know none of you wanted to hear that Hollingsworth turns the villains against the parks, but it's true. I wouldn't be here if it wasn't true. He's responsible. He's the source—*the* creator, I guess—of all the awful stuff that we end up fighting in sixty years. The battle you guys face in the future started here, in 1955. If you—*we*, I guess—can stop it now, maybe it won't happen then. I'm not saying I know anything about time travel, but maybe we can prevent the tragedies, the destruction to the parks, the *darkness* from ever happening."

Her message cut to the hearts of the five Kingdom Keepers. They had given years over to battling the Disney villains in order to stop them from ruining everything Disney. The idea that all that horror could be prevented was nearly too much to process.

"Dillard," Finn whispered. Finn's closest neighborhood friend had died for the cause.

"We don't know that we can stop that!" Maybeck

spoke sympathetically and compassionately.

"We can hope," Finn said, his voice trembling. "Can't we? If the villains never rise to power, Dillard's never involved in any of this. He lives!" He caught the others staring at his trembling fingers and stuffed his hands into his pockets.

The workshop door rattled. "Kresky?" called a strident voice.

Everyone, including Wayne Kresky, froze as still as the spiral pillars in front of Snow White's Scary Adventures. Wayne pointed into the back of the workshop, to a narrow, open-ended storage area that held scrap lumber and odds and ends. All seven kids rushed to it like trained dogs. They scrambled in, some ducking, some climbing amid the racks. The idea was to get as deeply into shadow as possible. The teens ended up in groups of two and three, pressed into one another, and curled up as small as they could. Finn put his arm around Amanda and held her close; she leaned her head onto his shoulder and whispered.

"We can save Dillard. We're going to save—"

A conversation at the door cut her off.

* * *

"Yes? What is it? I'm busy here," Wayne said, appropriately testy. He faced two kids younger than him.

"My name's Shane," said the red-haired, square-shouldered boy in a wobbly baritone. It was as if he was trying to make himself sound older than he was: likely sixteen or seventeen.

"Yes, I can read that on your shiny new Cast Member pin," said Wayne. "I haven't seen you around before, so welcome to Disneyland. New, are we?"

"I'm Thia, like in Cyn*thia*." The young woman looked a year or two older than her counterpart. She had a solid, unflattering build and poor posture. Her face was round, with pink, puffy cheeks and beady dark eyes reminiscent of chocolate chips.

"We're your new trainees," said Shane.

"Gee willikers! What's that supposed to mean?" Wayne blinked, confused.

"We've been assigned to your team—"

"To learn the ropes—"

"To serve an apprenticeship—"

"To get the hang of, to get down cold, to get a look-see at what you do and how you do it," Shane said. "Exactly."

"I don't want to be mean, but I don't work with apprentices or any others. Mr. Disney himself gave me this assignment. I test new gizmos. I invent stuff. It isn't work you do as a group."

The two looked crestfallen, heads cast to the floor.

"Who arranged this?"

Thia spoke, her voice quavering. "Ah . . . Mr. Hawkins, Jim . . . Hawkins. Four weeks of apprenticeship."

"I'm sorry, I'm not familiar with Mr. Hawkins." Shane spoke, though clumsily. "He's at W.E.D."

"You don't want us?" Thia said, clearly hurt by Wayne's reaction.

"It's not that. Please. I'm busy, that's all. I work by myself."

"We could watch," Shane suggested. "We'd be quiet and all. It's only a few weeks."

"We could run errands for you." It was Thia's turn to try to convince Wayne. "Or stay out of your way. Gosh, this place is spiffy! What's all the wires and such on that table?"

"I . . . work . . . *alone*," Wayne repeated.

"If you don't want us, what are we supposed to do?" Thia asked, sounding on the verge of tears.

"Okay, cut the gas and listen up," Wayne said. "Write this down. It's a test. If you get it right, you can watch me work later on today. Don't bother coming back here until you have it solved. Ready?"

Shane prepared to write on his hand. Thia held a Disneyland notebook.

"Ready," she said.

"Write this down: There's a basket containing five apples. How do you divide the apples among five children so that each child has one apple while one apple remains in the basket? I'm not going to repeat it. Now, shoo, and don't come back until you've got it." He shut the door with a thud.

"You can come out now," Wayne said a full minute later. "They've gone."

"What was that about?" Willa asked. The quietest of the five Kingdom Keepers, Willa was also one of the smartest. She lacked Charlene's head-turning good looks, but she also put almost no effort into her appearance. Slightly mousy with unremarkable brown hair and a reddish nose that gave one the idea she'd been crying, Willa eschewed leggings for jeans and covered her top in layers of bralettes, camis, and *Bob's Burgers* T-shirts.

"I'm assuming you heard," Wayne said.

"I heard," Willa said, "but I also happen to have a mother who can't stop watching ancient TV shows like *I Love Lucy* and *Father Knows Best*. Jimmy Hawkins was—is, I suppose, given that it's 1955—a kid actor on *Annie Oakley*. That's a little too coincidental, don't you think?"

"She made up the name?" Wayne questioned.

"She said the first name that came to mind. I would

check if there's actually a Jim Hawkins in W.E.D.," Willa said. "I doubt it very much."

"Hollingsworth!" Finn said. "The hotel dorm. That group of fake Cast Members he keeps there. Those two are spies! Hollingsworth is trying to infiltrate your workshop."

Looking deeply troubled, Wayne took a moment to place a telephone call to Disney's W.E.D. team, the architects and engineers who'd developed Disneyland. He asked to speak with "Mr. James Hawkins." Then he hung up the phone slowly, looking bewildered. He studied the faces of the group of teens staring back at him.

"We've got trouble," Wayne said.

"No, no, no," Maybeck countered. "We've got opportunity."

4

As an artist, Terry Maybeck was brilliant. As a human being, he was sometimes a fool. The opportunity he perceived was straightforward.

"Amanda and I should follow those two. If they're Hollingsworth's agents or informers, they'll probably lead us to the others. Like bees returning to the hive." He received dubious looks from everyone else. "Maybe we even get Hollingsworth! We want to bug out, right? Go home. To the future. According to you two," he said, singling out Amanda and Jess—often called Fairlies, short for fairly human—"the Imagineers say we gotta stop Hollingsworth. So it's time to stop talking and start walking. They're getting away." He motioned to the door.

"No offense, Terry, but you kinda stand out," said Charlene. "I'm sorry to say it, but the only six-foot-tall teenage black guys out there are pushing wheelbarrows. You're wearing a suit."

The Keepers had crossed over in "Sunday school clothes" so that they'd blend in during Disneyland's lavish opening day celebration. Being projected images, they were stuck with those costumes; although when the park closed for the night things changed dramatically for the Keepers, it was currently daytime.

"I'm wearing this stupid dress," Charlene continued, "but it's a 1950s stupid dress, and a lot of girls are wearing them. And sure, Amanda's in skinny jeans, but thankfully someone thought to tie a bandana around her neck to give her the cowgirl look." In 1955 Disneyland, there was a lot of cowgirl going around. Westerns were all the rage in film and television, popularizing the look among children. Disneyland's Pack Mules, Shooting Gallery, Conestoga Wagon rides, and Disneyland Stages all played into the trendy theme. "The good thing for us is that we girls aren't much more than ornaments. No one's going to pay much attention."

"Of course they will," Finn blurted out. "You're both so beautiful."

Judging by his hologram blush (a technological rarity), he hadn't meant to say the words aloud.

"Go!" Willa said. "Follow them, but don't do anything stupid."

"This is me we're talking about!" Maybeck complained. "What happened to 'Black Is Beautiful'? It should be me out there!"

"You're about ten years early," Willa said. "Late

sixties." She smiled at him, though; Maybeck only rarely made a big deal about his African American heritage. The 1950s segregation was getting to him, Willa thought. She added, "Besides, Terry, you're gorgeous. All us girls agree about that."

Amanda and Charlene hurried out the door.

"Between Amanda's powers and Charlene's athleticism, they're the best choice anyway," said Philby in his dry academic way.

"What powers?" Wayne asked.

"That's right! You still don't know, do you?" Philby said in a kind of confused tone. "For now, it's better we just leave it. There's only so much any of us can handle, and you're not ready for Amanda."

* * *

"Ready?" Charlene asked Amanda. They had caught sight of the backs of the boy and girl near the Plaza end of Main Street USA. It was time for action. Their holograms were in color, and more rounded than Charlene's original two-dimensional variety. But while Wayne and Philby had improved the look of the projections, they were far from perfect. They looked the most convincing when pushed up against a wall, or another static background. Mixed into a crowd, they gave off a ghostly image—still solid looking, but not quite right.

"Remember to stay in sight of each other." Amanda cut across to the Tomorrowland side of the street. With a subtle motion of either hand she gently *and invisibly* nudged park guests aside ten feet in front of her, creating an open lane for herself. Those who felt themselves pushed turned around to complain, but saw no one; they had no inclination to attribute their being shoved to a girl still ten feet from them. Who would ever think a person could manipulate things with the simple motion of a hand?

When Amanda *pushed* a young girl out of her way, the movement caused the girl to drop her ice cream cone. With quick reflexes, Amanda directed a small *push* beneath the cone; it briefly defied gravity, floating in the air. The girl grabbed it.

"Did you see that?!" the little girl exclaimed to her mother, who shook her head.

Amanda passed her, already motioning aside others.

Shane and Thia circled the Plaza to the left, Charlene not far behind. They took the third asphalt path to the left heading toward the park's bandstand. The bandstand, an open-air, circular, covered stage, was surrounded by an ornate white railing. An American flag hung lifelessly from a flagpole atop its pointed roof.

Amanda paused in the busier Plaza area, noting that there was no landscaping around the bandstand other than a few orange trees and rows of benches beneath blue-and-white umbrellas. With no band currently playing, the stage and benches stood empty. If Shane and Thia had a meeting planned, it would be easily witnessed.

For her part, Charlene turned toward the benches, took a seat, and watched as the two Cast Members walked up the bandstand's steps to the floor. They wandered about, pausing to look at the castle and talk among themselves. Then they came around as a pair, forcing Charlene to lower her head. The two gazed out over the bench area.

Moments later, Charlene heard their footsteps descending. She kept her head down, concerned her hologram might have given her away. She counted slowly to ten and raised her chin as a shadow appeared at her feet and crept up her crinoline skirt. She found herself looking up at the boy, Shane.

"What's buzzin', cousin?"

Charlene didn't speak.

"You're one of the new kids, aren't you?"

She only stared. If he reached out to touch her, things would get weird. Her unstable hologram reacted to fear, turning solid and therefore vulnerable to attack, and she was currently fighting back a sense of panic.

"My advice to you, sister, is for you and your pals to

cop a breeze, fade out, put an egg in your shoe. And in case you didn't notice, Pinky's out of jail."

She instinctively cocked her head, given he was focused on her dress.

"Your slip's showing," he said.

"I'm not wearing a slip."

"The fluffy stuff."

"It's supposed to show." Charlene looked beyond him for Thia. Gone.

"Buzz off."

"You first."

"You gonna make me make you?"

"I thought Cast Members were supposed to be nice."

"Oh . . . yeah. Cool. Look, Dolly, fire it up and goose it. I'll clue you: your Clydes aren't wanted here, all your nosing around. Bug off, and don't come back."

"My friends and I love Disneyland . . . Shane," she said, reading his name tag. "We come here every day. Maybe I should talk to someone about how rude you're being to me."

"Later, gator. And no flapping your lips, you hear me? You do and you'll be eating a knuckle sandwich." He raised his fist.

The moment he did, he slammed to the ground. It wasn't like he'd fallen off-balance; it was like he'd been hit by a hurricane wind. He slid a few feet, eating a bunch of dirt that he spit out like a sputtering motor.

Amanda, standing a few feet away, held her palm out in a *push*. "There you are!" Amanda said innocently. "I've been looking everywhere for you."

Charlene hopped off the bench and hurried to join her.

"Thank . . . you," Charlene said. "Things were getting nasty."

"I noticed."

"The girl, Thia, disappeared."

"Not exactly," Amanda said. "When this bully headed over to you, Thia went around behind the bandstand and vanished."

"You were watching?"

"She never saw me. She got around to the far side, looked around, and then ducked. Vanished, but I doubt any magic was involved. More like a door of some sort."

"A hidden door."

Charlene heard the footfalls before Amanda did. She bumped Amanda aside, dropped to one knee, and stuck out her leg. Shane tripped and skidded painfully across the asphalt.

The girls took off running, eager to disappear into the crowded Plaza.

"He tried to warn me that we aren't welcome," Charlene said breathlessly.

"Whatever. I want to hide and watch him. I've got a hunch he's going to follow the girl wherever she went."

"Under the bandstand," Charlene said.

"Under the bandstand," Amanda confirmed.

5

"How dangerous is this for you?" asked the man walking beside Mattie. He had something of a belly and an odd walk.

"It's California Adventure," she answered. "How dangerous can it be?"

"That's not an answer."

"Think of me as a spy, then," she said. "I'm trying to get information that people want kept secret. It has its moments."

"So it's dangerous," he proposed.

"I'm very good at what I do. Not to worry."

He took a long look at her. "I don't doubt it."

The park, alive with thousands of visitors, stretched out under a canopy of background music and blue sky. The guests exuded excitement, walking faster than normal, talking louder. There was lots of pointing and families stopping abruptly. If you didn't look out you'd pile into someone.

"You don't get out much, do you?" Mattie asked. "Are all your Cast Member hours spent in Disneyland, or what?"

"I'm a Dapper Dan. Where would you expect me to be?"

"Point taken."

He didn't look like a Dapper Dan. At the moment, he wore chinos and a polo shirt, not his costume's red pants, white shirt, and red-and-white-striped vest. He had a weathered, jowly face with semicircles like kangaroo pouches beneath his eyes. He walked duck-footed, without bending his knees much. Mattie had trouble looking at him without grinning—which wasn't fair, so she didn't look over much.

"Let me ask you this," she said. "What are our chances of finding one of your brother's *associates*?" She placed emphasis on the final word.

"We'll find out soon enough," he said. "They're either here or they aren't. I either see them or I don't. You know, it seems you know more about me than I do you, Mattie. Judging by the red streaks in your hair, your torn jeans and combat boots, you're . . . how do I say this politely? . . . a person who enjoys her own company."

"A loner? A loser? A runaway?"

"I would never be so impertinent."

"Loner, yes. Runaway, yes. Loser, never. And you know why."

"My brother. Of course. We share a cause, no matter

how different we look." He paused, looking over at her as they walked. "What do you call it, that thing you do? What you did to me when we first met."

"*Reading*. I call it *reading* someone."

"What if they don't want to be read?"

"It doesn't usually matter. Most of the time they can't stop me."

"It's a violation, you know?" He sounded wounded. "Taking someone's thoughts without their permission. Without their *knowledge*. How's that possible?"

"I don't know," Mattie said solemnly. "I stopped trying to figure it out a long time ago."

"You don't like having an ability like that?"

"It's ruined my life—so far, at least. Being a freak is not so hot."

"I'm sorry for whatever my brother and his people did to you."

"I don't need your sympathy. I don't expect anything of anyone. Except myself. I expect things of myself."

"You once accused me of being a spy."

"That was Amanda, I think. Not me. But, yeah. You didn't deny it."

"And here I am, being a spy."

"Funny how that's worked out," she said.

* * *

Between the Tower of Terror, Ariel's Grotto, California Screamin', and Cars Land, this side of the park had long been a favorite of Mattie's. She was beginning to feel comfortable navigating her way around, knowing where the best food was, the nearest restroom, the good shopping.

"You must know what this is about," Mattie said.

"I can speculate easily enough. I'm assuming we're here because of all the trouble the other day. I can't think of a time the park was closed like that. Not that there was any choice. People were frightened. A few were hurt on the steamboat."

"It was awful."

"But couldn't you just read me and see the faces of the people who associate with my brother? It would seem you don't really need me."

"It's not as if I get a full download, you know?" Mattie's voice was softer now. "I pick up on what you're thinking. Usually I have to make it happen. You know, like giving you a prompt? I have to make you think about something if I'm going to *read* what I want to find out. Not always, but almost always."

"That sounds tricky. A bit risky, even."

"Yeah. There is that," Mattie said.

"I'm afraid I'm no good to you if I'm supposed to defend you . . . I'm slow and not the fighting type."

"No sweat." She reached out and thumped him on his generous belly as they walked. It was an overly familiar gesture she felt perfectly comfortable with—she'd seen inside this man and knew him to be good-natured, with a strong sense of humor.

Zeke Hollingsworth laughed heartily.

"You're the youngest Hollingsworth."

"I'm the middle son, Ebsy. The Cast Members call me Zeke. Amery's my older brother."

"Amery Jr."

"He's called that sometimes, yes." Zeke looked over at the top of her head. "Is it safe, what you do? This reading? Can it harm you in any way?"

"It's super disturbing," Mattie answered honestly. "Imagine getting inside someone else's head. When it happens, there's this moment where there's no me, no Mattie, just the target's thoughts. And then there're the *reachers*. I thought you were a *reacher* when I first targeted you."

"Dare I ask?"

"What I do isn't always a one-way street. Some people are able to detect my *reading* them. They reach back across. *Reachers*. I'm in their heads, they're in mine."

"That doesn't sound good."

"No," Mattie said. "It feels as if I'll . . . lose myself, you know? Like I'll just zombie out or something."

"Then why in heaven's name are we doing this?"

"I'm a Fairlie. It stands for *fairly human*. You're forced to take chances when you're the one with the 'special gift.'" She drew air quotes.

"How many of you are there?"

"That's a question you should ask your brother, Amery Jr."

"Baltimore," Zeke Hollingsworth muttered.

"Bingo," said Mattie.

* * *

Together, Mattie and Zeke walked around California Adventure for nearly two hours. He told her that *World of Color* was his favorite show. He spoke of the changes he'd seen here and in Disneyland with a degree of nostalgia. He talked of his brothers and him following their father around when the "old man" worked with Disney. Zeke had been too young to remember, but Junior had told him stories.

Mattie had no memory of her own father or mother. She'd spent five years in Barracks 14, and three before that living with her grandparents. For a few precious hours in California Adventure she felt as if this awkward man was kind of a dad. She somehow knew that once Zeke saw her in action and was reminded of her freakishness, his opinion of her would change. People didn't know how to act around those different from themselves. The trick was not to act at all; but some people failed to learn that lesson.

"There's one of my brother's guys," Zeke said under his breath. They'd come around the circle, nearing the entrance to Cars Land. "To your right, standing next to the vineyard. Dark slacks and the pale windbreaker."

"Got him," she said. "Name?"

"I . . . ah . . ."

"What's his name?" Mattie asked. "I need a name!"

"Billings? Or Bill Inis? Was it Bill? I think it's Bill."

"I need a name!" Mattie repeated. She saw the target join the stream of park visitors, heading in the direction of the Red Car Trolley route and the gates. "We can't stay together. He might recognize you."

Briefly losing sight of the target, she left Zeke. She moved quickly, but without breaking into a run. Caught sight of him again.

"Mr. Inis!"

The target didn't change his pace. Zeke had given her the wrong name.

"Excuse me, sir! Mr. Inis?" Mattie called once more. The target broke stride, turning slightly. A tall man with crow's-feet at his eyes and a thick, sand-colored mustache, he was celebrity handsome. He focused on her, his determined blue eyes enchanting and calculating. His lips parted as if to speak, but he said nothing. Instead, he squinted slightly, like the sun bothered him.

Mattie took his right hand firmly in both of hers. "It's so good to see you, Mr.—" She purposely cut herself off.

In that infinitesimal, immeasurable instant, a portal opened to the man's thought. His name was in fact James Calder Corwin. She saw a long hallway with discolored gray walls and a lightbulb burning; she saw a rapid-fire stream of faces, traffic, and groups of teens entering Disneyland. She forced the words *Fairlies, Barracks 14, Baltimore,* and *children* onto him. In the same mental image some of the teens looked back at her: she knew their faces! They were Fairlies! All of them!

Groups of Fairlies entering Disneyland? In trying to figure it out she'd let her guard down. Suddenly, she felt a crushing sensation like the early warnings of a massive headache. *A reacher!*

James Calder Corwin was using the same conduit to steal her thoughts. They entered into a polite battle of wills, both working hard to disguise their ability, an unforgiving heat filling her eyes. There was no letting go now. If she could win out, she might be able to push him into not remembering the *read*.

He gained. He possessed enormous power and knew how to use it. She resisted him, throwing out distracting images and false information. He, too, pitched a volley of worthless memories at her. She dodged them, letting them pass her consciousness. Mustering all of her strength, she blasted a sentence at him: *Of course I remember you, Margaret.*

"Of course I remember you, Margaret!" he said, looking bewildered.

Mattie instantly released her hold on him and apologized profusely. "Oh my gosh, I'm so sorry! You look so much like my biology teacher, Mr. Inis! Please . . . I'm so sorry! How rude of me!"

"Not at all." James Corwin looked a little bit like Mattie had punched him in the face. The spoken sentence had *blanked* him as she'd hoped. The microsecond that had felt like minutes lapsed.

It took a moment to untangle their wills.

"It's not 'Margaret,' is it?" Corwin said rhetorically. "It's Martha? No!" He focused on her face. "I *do* know you, don't I." A statement, not a question.

"I'm so sorry to have bothered you. My mistake." Mattie turned away.

If he had recognized her, it was from Barracks 14! She felt a pit open in her stomach, a sickening, nauseating sensation. She swallowed frantically to keep her food down. She'd just stood inches from—had made physical contact with—a man from her past. A man capable of capturing children. Of testing them like they were frogs in biology class. She felt dizzy and afraid.

She saw Zeke standing at the end of the bridge pretending to admire some potted flowers. Mattie walked past Zeke. "Keep your eye on him."

Moments later, Zeke Hollingsworth found her.

"He went into the Off the Page and didn't come out. Mattie? Mattie, are you okay?"

"He's a *reacher*," she said. "He can force his thoughts into you."

Zeke inhaled sharply.

"His name is James Corwin. He came after me."

"Corwin! Ah! Yes! I remember him well. He's close to Amery. A confidant, for certain. Did you . . . were you able to . . . you know—?"

"*Read* him? It was bad, very bad. He *reached*. We fought, and I won. He won't remember, but I was lucky this time. Adults never have that kind of strength." Mattie slowed and looked up into Zeke's face, wondering how much he understood, how much she should share. "It's complicated. I need to talk to Joe right away."

"Who knows if that's even possible?"

"We have to make it possible. There's going to be an attack, Zeke. An attack on Disneyland."

6

MIDNIGHT PASSED WITHOUT a clock tower tolling. No coyotes howled; nor did wraiths descend from the sky. Just another night in Anaheim, California.

Disneyland's guests had left three hours earlier, driving off in their four-door Chevrolet Bel Airs and Buick Skylarks. The cars were old and boxy, with white-walled tires and silver AM radio antennas. In all the Disneyland parking lots there hadn't been a Japanese or Korean, German or Italian car to be found. The few pickup trucks looked like Mater; their engines ran loud and bubbly.

With the closing of the park, Charlene and Amanda had transformed from weak holograms to mortal girls. Both had changed into the loose-fitting blue jeans and black T-shirts supplied by Wayne. Charlene was especially glad to be free of her crinoline petticoat for a few precious hours. Her blond curls were held off her face using bobby pins. If things got physical, she didn't want to be blinded even for an instant.

Squatting behind a bench in the last row from the bandstand, the girls pulled neckerchiefs over their chins and noses, hiding everything but their eyes. Their breathing was rough and rapid; they clutched hands for a moment. Both girls squeezed to signal companionship. They were in this together. Then they hurried to the back of the bandstand.

Amanda pointed out the two seams in the wood lattice, which ran like an apron around the bandstand's raised platform. Her fingers reached, searching through the checkerboard lattice. She made contact with a metal latch, deciphered how it operated, and pulled a small tab. The lattice popped open. The two bandits locked eyes, sharing a moment of silent glee.

Gently, Charlene opened the gate. Amanda ducked and stepped into the dark cavity beneath the bandstand's stage. The five-foot-high space forced her to duck her head. She nearly tumbled forward as her right foot dropped into place. A step.

She reached back, grabbed Charlene by the forearm, and pulled. Hesitantly, Charlene took the next step with her. Together, the girls descended three more steps. Amanda waved her arms, seeking purchase in the pitch black. Her fingers smacked into a metal grate. She ran her hands up and down it, at last connecting with a large hinge attached to a curving concrete hole.

"It's a big drain, I think," Amanda whispered. "There's a screen or lid, something that's raised. The drain is open." She dropped to her knees. "Found a handle, or maybe it's a step? Hang on." She felt around. "It's a step, a metal bar sticking out, but there's another below it."

A light came on, startling Amanda. Charlene was holding an L-shaped green flashlight. "I was a Girl Scout," she said, almost apologetically. "I got my silver award, but couldn't quite cut gold. Still, I learned to be prepared. Borrowed this from Wayne's workshop."

The light revealed a concrete hole three feet across. A wire hatch, opened and held up by a hook, came down from the underside of the bandstand stage. The hole was deep, perhaps eight or ten feet, with metal ladder rungs leading down. The bottom was dry, sand-covered concrete.

Amanda threw a leg over the edge and placed her toe on the first step. Then the next. She paused. "We're going down here, right?" she asked.

"Right."

"I knew you were going to say that."

A moment later, the two girls were standing at the bottom, the light shining into a four-foot-high tunnel. The sound of flowing water echoed ahead of them.

"Drainage," Charlene said. "Or maybe . . ." She didn't finish her thought.

"What? Say it! Please!" Amanda sounded frightened.

"Finn once told me that back in 1955—as in now—all the lakes and lagoons in Disneyland were connected. That was right before he and I dove into a pond and swam underwater and into a—"

"Pipe," Amanda said.

"You got it."

"So this—?"

"Has something to do with it, I'll bet." Charlene pushed past Amanda, leading the way. They stooped low and shuffled ahead for about twenty feet, at which point the pipe hit a T-junction, similarly sized tunnels running off in both directions.

The main tunnel felt like a concrete box with a trough in the center, carrying a large corrugated metal pipe about three feet in diameter. The narrow box allowed for a small flat ledge on either side.

"That's what Finn and I swam through," Charlene said, flashing the light onto the pipe.

"And this?" Amanda asked, indicating the narrow space.

"Storm sewer for rainwater. Access to repair the pipe. Typical Disney efficiency. Philby would love this."

"Which way do we go?"

"That way is Main Street, and the pond we dove into."

"And that?" Amanda pointed.

"I'm only guessing, but I'd say this is a tunnel to the castle."

* * *

Moving through the storm sewer conduit required the girls to lean against the pipe, with their bottoms rubbing along the concrete wall. It was slow going, as they had to maneuver around the occasional support bracket. Every so often, park light would filter down through an overhead street drain, allowing them to switch off the flashlight. The added light made the space less spooky, a welcome reprieve.

"Given that this is hardly easy," Amanda said, "why would anyone bother?"

"I'm not sure we'll know until we get there. At the very least, it's some kind of escape route. One thing's for sure: those two weren't ordinary Cast Members. They were lying to Wayne, just as we thought."

Their journey took less than ten minutes, though it felt like twice that. The pipe ended at a concrete wall and a second short access tunnel, like the one below the bandstand, to their left. The girls climbed similar built-in ladder steps, the pipe narrowing and reaching a manhole-size drain cover. It opened easily.

The two girls climbed up and out, finding themselves in a cavelike concrete space: the interior of the castle's southwest wall, possibly near the drawbridge. They followed scuff marks lit by the flashlight. Finally, they spotted a metal door set into the wall to their right.

"Whoa!" Amanda proclaimed.

"Yeah," agreed Charlene. "I love this stuff."

Amanda shook her head hard. "It's spooky."

"It's exciting." Charlene's eyes were alight in the dark.

"Maybe for you."

"I think you should go first in case we need you to push someone."

"Oh, thanks a lot!"

"It's late, Mandy. No one's going to be hanging around here."

"If that's true, then why would I have to push?" Amanda asked teasingly.

"Busted," Charlene said.

Amanda cracked open the door an inch and put her eye to the space. "Flashlight." Charlene passed it. Amanda aimed it into the crack, but almost immediately snapped off the light. "I saw movement. People near the back of the room," she whispered.

"That's good, right?" Charlene said.

"As opposed to a dragon's lair? Yes."

"Let's go."

"Why?"

"Why not? Charlene asked. "The scuff marks clearly lead inside. Aren't you at all curious?"

"The word *petrified* comes to mind."

"You're the one with the superpower," Charlene said.

"It's *not* a superpower. I don't know what it is, but it isn't that. I'm a freak, okay? I get it. It doesn't make me brave, only bizarre."

"You're brave. I've seen you in action, Amanda, remember?"

"I'd rather not hurt people."

"Is that what's bothering you?"

"What's bothering me is I don't mind *pushing* to defend myself, or helping you guys, but I'm not real excited about using it because we got ourselves into trouble."

"Well." Charlene paused. "That's admirable."

"You sound surprised."

"You really are made for Finn," Charlene said. "You know that, right? That sounds exactly like something he'd say. He can be so righteous!"

"We're breaking and entering. Trespassing."

"We're following a route used by two spies who lied to Wayne and tried to infiltrate his workshop."

"Well." Amanda twisted her lips, considering. "When you put it like that . . ."

"That's how it is, Mandy. It's us against them, period."

"I'm going first," Amanda said, her confidence swelling.

Charlene patted her on the back. "I'm right behind you."

7

THE COLORFUL PHOTOGRAPHS and art on the office walls gave a false sense of joy and celebration. The Disney Cruise Line ships. Mickey. Mortimer Mouse.

Joe Garlington had the original art, not copies. And he had a steely look in his eyes that contrasted oddly with his Hawaiian shirt, curly mop of hair, and surfer tan.

Mattie shifted, uncomfortable. She would have preferred a park bench near a playground. This felt like the principal's office. It felt like Barracks 14.

The personal risk represented by the information she possessed terrified her. She was opening a door to involvement, a door she wasn't sure she wanted to enter.

"How certain are you?" Joe's voice was somber and deadly serious.

"I knew them," she said.

"Fairlies."

"All of them. Yes." There it was, a sense of betrayal. This, despite her knowing better. The Fairlies had been family. How could she do this without speaking to them first, to the ones she'd loved?

"Here?"

"It could have been something he was imagining, you know? *Reading* a person isn't exactly science. Most of our abilities, our Fairlie abilities, shift and change. Maybe I *read* a memory." But she didn't believe her own words.

"How many, again?" Joe had a pen in hand. It had Mickey ears on top. That pen, writing something down, made her statement all too real. Mattie was ratting out the very people whose friendships had kept her going.

"Lots," she said quietly.

"As in?"

"I don't know. A dozen. Maybe more like twenty." How could she explain her *reading* to him? It wasn't like watching a documentary on TV. It was more like a dream/nightmare of images and voices, all mixed up in a swirling stew of someone else's thoughts. An uncomfortable invasion of privacy, like hiding in a closet and eavesdropping.

"Entering the park?"

She'd told him this enough times. It seemed like punishment to keep repeating herself. "Right. I didn't see that; he did. He thought it, remembered it. Maybe imagined it."

Even as she spoke, she despaired. No one understood her.

"And this guy Corwin. Any sense of where he is in regards to Hollingsworth?"

"I didn't see anything like that. I'm pretty sure he was in charge of the kids. The Fairlies. That makes sense with the way they ran the Barracks."

"But a *reacher*?"

"Yeah, that's the thing. Pretty sure he's one of us. A Fairlie, but an adult. I didn't think . . . What we've always said among ourselves, what somebody heard one time in Baltimore, was that our *abilities* weaken as we get older. They leave us after our early twenties. With Corwin, maybe not." She shrugged. "Maybe what I heard is true. But maybe it isn't. He tried to *reach*, to *read* me. That much I'm sure of. And he's no teenager."

"So maybe some of you retain your abilities. Does that scare you?" Joe asked.

"Are you my shrink now?" Despite her bluster, it did. It terrified her. If someone *read* her, they might learn everything about the Keepers, about Amanda and Jess. She'd be a traitor to her own team without meaning to be.

Joe stared across the desk at her. Mattie stared right back at him.

"I'm not your enemy," he said.

"Good. I'm not your daughter. You don't get to

know what scares me. You don't get to know the things they put us through."

"So what about your abilities?" Joe asked, raising an eyebrow.

"They're only getting stronger. So don't worry: he didn't *read* me, if that's what you're asking. But he tried. That's the thing: he tried!"

Silence. Someone was mowing one of the studio lawns. Mattie wished she could leave, could lie out in the sun, smelling the fresh-cut grass. She wished she hadn't shared anything with Joe. But her friendship with Amanda and Jess overcame all caution. She knew she had to do this, to help in any way she could.

"When he . . . you know, I made him say what I was thinking. That's a first for me. Pushing a thought like that. It made me tired, but it happened, which was cool." She regretted her words the minute they left her mouth.

"I'll bet it did. That's useful for me to know."

"Which is why I told you." Mattie paused, locked eyes with Joe. "Now, let me ask you this: What happens when I'm no longer useful to you?"

Joe nodded. "That's a fair question." He smirked, neither a smile nor a frown.

"Amanda, me, and Jess. We're tired of people using us. Adults using us. If it's a fair question, how 'bout you answer it?"

"No reason for that attitude."

"There's every reason. You want me to list them?" She gave him a moment. "If you please, sir," she said sarcastically, *"answer the question!"* Her voice rose on the last three words, echoing till it drowned out the lawn mower buzzing outside.

"We take care of our own. That's you, if you want it to be. Jess and Amanda, too. They're starting over, and we're helping them."

"Are you kidding me? You sent them back in time! We may never see them again! Are you *kidding me?*"

Joe lifted his chin and spoke carefully, as if he were working to stay calm. "This is a difficult time for all of us, Mattie. I need your help. Amanda and Jess need your help."

"Those Fairlies I saw inside Corwin's head? They're coming for you, Joe. They're coming to wreck your parks. Maybe against their will. I don't know. And maybe they're already here. If not, they're on their way, and they can do stuff you wouldn't believe."

"Oh, but I would believe. I believe you. And nobody but nobody's messing with my parks."

"Then we need a plan," Mattie said defiantly.

Joe's eyes warmed, and for a moment, Mattie felt like he could see into her soul. "That's more like it."

8

"SOME KIND OF BREAK ROOM, maybe," Amanda whispered to Charlene, "but pretty bleak."

Charlene tried to nudge her away from the viewing spot, but Amanda held her ground. "Empty?" Charlene asked.

"Three Cast Members sitting with their backs to us. I can't see their faces. No idea if they're Thia and Shane."

Charlene, the more agile of the two, positioned herself beneath Amanda and was able to get her ear to the crack in the door. "They're talking about Wayne's riddle. Must be them."

One of the seated Cast Members threw a glance over his shoulder in Amanda's direction. It *was* Shane. Amanda jerked her head back, cursing internally, as she yanked Charlene away with her. She signaled Charlene for quiet, index finger to her lips.

Amanda dared to steal a quick look. Shane was coming toward them.

"Go!" Amanda hissed, pushing Charlene down the tunnel. "Hurry!"

The two girls sprinted off, struggling to navigate the narrow space between the raw concrete walls in the dark. When a glow of light spread out behind them, Amanda tugged Charlene down onto the dusty floor.

"What's going on?" came a boy's voice from the break room.

"I don't know. I thought we shut the door. . . ." Shane's voice, much closer.

"Wind," said a girl who had to be Thia. "It happens."

The glow lessened as the door shut. Amanda and Charlene waited as muffled voices stirred from beyond.

"Phew," Charlene whispered. "That was—"

"—close?" Shane's voice, from down the corridor. He'd closed the door without going back into the break room.

Amanda and Charlene clambered to their feet and sprinted. But running blindly through the dead spaces inside a castle wall proved impossible. Both girls smacked into an unseen barrier. Charlene fell.

Shane came up from behind at a run. Amanda and Charlene could not allow their faces to be seen, could not afford to be easily recognized by whoever these people were. Instinctively, hating the necessity of it, Amanda raised her hands, palms out, and *pushed*.

She couldn't see what transpired, but she knew at least Shane was sailing through the air. In seconds, she heard a painful groaning. It made her sick; she wanted to run back and make sure her target was okay. Having such an ability wasn't always a good thing.

Bending, she helped Charlene up. They returned the way they'd come, soon reaching a slice of light that guided them forward. Both were fast runners. They put Shane and the darkened corridor quickly behind them. They climbed, finding themselves under the bandstand's platform. Reaching the shed door, they paused to crack the door to make sure they were in the clear and they ventured outside. They hurried to a distant bench and collapsed, winded.

Neither girl spoke for several minutes.

"What just happened?" Charlene asked at last, breathlessly. "Is that even possible?"

"Is what possible?" panted Amanda, equally winded.

"Think about it! If those two were trying to spy on Wayne—on us!—could they possibly be Cast Members?"

"Interesting."

"And the tunnel, the route they took . . . there's no way that's a Cast Member thing."

"Agreed," said Amanda. "But it could be a Cast Member shortcut or something that they use without permission."

"I suppose."

"I heard a boy's voice. Shane, maybe."

"Yeah, same." Charlene sounded puzzled and not at all pleased. "So they're Cast Members, but they aren't because they're spies. They're using what at best are unofficial secret routes to move through the park."

"Agents for—"

"Do not go there!" Charlene snapped. "I mean, this is 1955. They can't possibly be . . ." She didn't finish voicing her thought. She wanted Amanda to come to the same conclusion and, by doing so, to see things her way. To agree with her.

Amanda took a while to speak. At last, she breathed, "Yeah . . . I think maybe they're part of the Overtakers."

9

AMERY HOLLINGSWORTH JR. stayed away from the grave. An odd figure of a man with an upturned cleft chin, deep-set hollow eyes, and oversize, elongated ears, he watched from a comfortable distance as the digging continued. At 3:30 a.m., an overhead shroud of fog glowed yellow from the sulfur streetlamps down on Sunset Boulevard.

The hillside cemetery, less than a mile from the Chateau Marmont apartment building, occupied a small pocket of land on a terraced bench between two meandering cul-de-sacs. Virtually unknown to all except nearby residents, it suffered from a decade of neglect. Dry, auburn, waist-high weeds obscured all but the most ornate and ostentatious gravestones. The same grasses and vines had engulfed the rusting wrought-iron fence that had once majestically guarded the afterlife. Hollingsworth took care with his cigarette ash to avoid setting the lot on fire.

The Cajun Traveler stood nearby the digging, so still he might have been carved like some of the other statuary. A peculiar-looking thing in an ill-fitting, moth-eaten oversize brown suit with white pinstripes, the Traveler hadn't moved a muscle in well over forty-five minutes. He waited with the patience of a leopard, his eyes trained down onto the digging, awaiting the reveal.

The men shoveling glanced in his direction as little as possible, though they acted as if he were their foreman.

It was the second grave to be exhumed. The first held a coffin that contained a corpse embalmed prior to burial so that its prunelike skin still clung to its aged bones, looking a good deal like an overcooked Christmas turkey. The Traveler had waved off the diggers, moving them to this new plot.

The second coffin revealed itself a few minutes later and apparently looked promising to the Traveler. His lack of motion told the two to continue their work. Decades of dry rot left the wood coffin lid a mass of decay. Judging by the teeth marks around several of the holes, burrowing varmints and rodents had made a hotel of the place, and perhaps a snack shack as well. The two men tried to remove the lid, but it crumbled and fell in. A cloud of sawdust rose, driving the men backward to where one fell over while the other fanned the air with a thick, calloused hand.

The Traveler moved to the edge of the pit, avoiding the piles of sandy earth. He didn't exactly walk; it was more like a glide. Hollingsworth stepped closer himself, wanting to hear the Traveler if the man should speak.

"Youse tell me. Is dem dere bones done white as teeth?"

The worker still standing forced himself to peer down into the coffin. He called for his buddy to pass him a flashlight. It was a big device, with a large DC battery on a metal handle with what looked like a small automobile headlight mounted to pivot. When the man closest to the coffin switched it on, the light shot fifty yards or more across the pallid gravestones, throwing black shadows and illuminating sun-faded plastic memorial flowers. He tilted it down and it was like he'd set the coffin on fire.

The worker cussed and jumped back, throwing a beacon of light high into the dusty air.

"It's a mess. A nest maybe."

"A mess of dem bones?"

"Bones. White hair. A skull with no jaw." He cussed a second time.

Without looking behind him, the Traveler knew exactly where Hollingsworth was standing. The Cajun turned and nodded. Hollingsworth swallowed hard, his Adam's apple bobbing.

"Get those bones into the bag, boys," Hollingsworth said, "and pass them over here. Then fill her in. The other one, too. Then you're done for the night. And remember, I'm paying you to keep your mouths shut. You don't, and you're going to get a visit from my friend here. Nobody wants that."

The standing worker jammed his hands together at the crotches of his fingers in order to drive his gloves on securely.

With trepidation, he reached in and began digging out the bones.

10

THANKFULLY, NO ONE HAD thought to ask about the five teens, who'd not been seen in more than two weeks. The parents had been appeased, for now, with reassurances that their kids were safe.

The studio infirmary wasn't talked about much. Joe Garlington was one of only a handful of executives who had any reason to know it existed. Decades before, when the studio had been built miles from any reliable hospital, the company had constructed a small medical center to provide emergency care for their grips, electricians, and the occasional actor hurt while shooting a film. With the advent of better roads and better health care, the medical center fell into disuse; it had been kept clean and available for emergencies, but hadn't served any real purpose since 1987, when a worker had taken a nasty fall.

Joe nodded to the security guard outside the twin doors. Recognizing the head of Disney Imagineering, the guard made haste to unlock them.

"Anything to report?" Joe asked him.

"The nurses come in, the nurses come out. I verify their IDs against the list. That's all I know, sir. All I need to know. No unauthorized visitors."

"Okay. Good enough."

The guard checked down the hallway to make sure no one was watching, and admitted the boss.

Having never been modernized, the infirmary looked like something from a film set. Six beds, aligned in dormitory fashion along the opposing walls, were iron-framed, and raised and lowered by a hand crank. The overhead lights were 1960s tube lighting, the flooring powder-blue linoleum. The privacy windows were divided, the lower panes fogged architectural glass, the uppers clear. Alongside each bed stood a steel side table painted army gray. The room was overly warm and smelled of disinfectant.

"How are they?" Joe asked the female nurse. A male nurse worked a computer at the far end of the room.

"Stable. Steady."

"Active?"

"Yes, sir. We've seen a good deal of muscle reflex, ankle and wrist movement. Vitals are good."

Sleeping on top of five of the beds, wearing 1950s costumes, were two girls in crinoline skirts—Charlene and Willa—and two boys in work clothes—Finn and Philby. The remaining boy, Maybeck, had chosen a dapper suit. Side by side, the Kingdom Keepers slept not-so-peacefully.

A young woman in regular clothing occupied the sixth bed. Her vaguely Asian eyes and dark hair lent her an astonishing beauty. Amanda. Occupying a foldaway cot next to her was Jessica, or Jess.

All were connected to IV bags and an umbilical network of wires that monitored their vital signs. At times, their cheek muscles twitched, causing their lips to move. A shoulder flexed; a leg tensed. Joe found it discomfiting to watch.

"No bedsores?" he asked the nurse.

"No, sir. We're rolling them and moving them as per our instructions. So far, so good." The nurse was lovely to look at, no older than twenty-five, with rich brown eyes. But her kind face held an expression of grave concern.

"You can ask whatever you like," Joe said, seeing the desire in her.

"It's just . . . they've been comatose for two weeks now. I wonder if transferring them to a hospital isn't the proper—"

"They're fine, I assure you. The monitoring of their vitals is of critical importance. You and your team are doing everything just right. Thank you so much."

"Thank you, Mr. Garlington."

"I need you to set up another cot, please. I need to sleep here tonight."

"Here?"

"Yes, for security's sake. I'll be up and gone before the park opens. I won't need any medical attention, just privacy." He saw the woman's confused expression and felt bad. "I know this makes no sense to you. It's complicated, as we explained at the start. I can't go home, you see? A hotel is out. Should I by any chance extend my nap beyond the park opening tomorrow morning, should I go past the twelve-hour mark . . . well, at that point I might need some fluids, if that's what you think is right."

The nurse nodded, frightened despite her efforts to appear otherwise.

"That's not going to happen," Joe said softly. "An ounce of prevention."

The nurse inhaled, exhaled ever so slowly, and stood taller. "Yes, sir."

"That's the spirit," Joe said. "Now let's get that cot, shall we?"

Joe double-checked with the Imagineers on the location of the Return before going to sleep. The all-important fob was the key to his coming back from hologram to human. The computer imaging required to construct his hologram had taken ten hours the previous night and six hours of voice recording during business hours. He was ready for some rest.

He shut his eyes at 10:00 p.m., by which time both Disneyland and California Adventure were closed. At 10:17 p.m. he fell fast asleep—the first crucial step to crossing over as a DHI.

* * *

Joe Garlington woke on the warm concrete at the base of the Partners statue. It was a clear California night. The sky offered no stars, only a city glow and the red flashing sparkle of planes in flight. It took him a long moment to recall his mission and test his surroundings.

"I've done it," he eventually said aloud, his voice vaguely electronic, nasal. The computer rendering of his DHI had been rushed. Color definition had suffered; his clothes looked pale. And his voice sounded robotic. But it would do.

He came to his feet—though his hologram moved in jerky motions, it did move—squared his shoulders, and took a look around at the dark park. So this was what the Kingdom Keepers felt like when they crossed over. A tingling throughout, one's limbs glowing slightly. A dizzying sense of weightlessness combined with the ability to stand upright and move.

Joe tested his walking, reached out to touch a

bush. His glowing hand passed through the leaves and branches. He had no intention of taking the time to try to work with his hologram to perfect his abilities. He'd crossed over on a particular mission. He had work to do. And quickly.

Wayne Kresky's early efforts to bring holograms into the park at night had been largely inspired by a physicist's work at the University of Central Florida. The man had theorized that the realm of live-projected holograms would, by necessity, include the projected subject's ability to see into "the ether," defined by Merriam-Webster as:

> A medium that in the wave theory of light permeates
> all space and transmits transverse waves.

Wayne took this definition to heart. A firm believer that Walt Disney's characters would live forever, he believed them a part of the ether as well. He'd consulted physicists at Cal Tech and MIT, had spoken to theorists at Michigan University and Vanderbilt. Technologies had been tested. Success had come after seven years. Finn Whitman had proved the theories.

True to form, one of the early reports from Finn, the first boy to cross over as a DHI, was his ability to see Disney characters. The *real* characters, not the costumed actors park guests saw by day.

Joe Garlington was hoping to confirm these stories for himself, because he needed help. If he failed to connect with the real Disney characters, then Disneyland and California Adventure might be smoking ruins within a matter of days or weeks.

His jerky hologram stuttered down Main Street USA. Joe continued to work hard to grasp the feeling of weightlessness. Of nothingness. His mind-body wanted to convince him he was in a dream state; his mind-consciousness understood that being projected as pure light allowed him a material presence. He wasn't cells, but particles. He wasn't exactly human, but that didn't mean he didn't exist. He was here; he was just different.

In their relative innocence, he thought, maybe the teens had an easier time "going with it." For his part, Joe found himself resisting his condition. Then, as he calmed, a limb or part of his body would vaporize, light particles dislodging from his image like clusters of butterflies. Only by stopping and working to accept his condition could he attract the escaping sparkles of color back into his hologram.

"Interesting," he said to no one. *I have to believe to survive,* he thought. Then he laughed. *Walt Disney would have loved this!*

As Joe approached Disney Clothiers, he glanced to his right and saw a line of silhouettes atop the rooflines at the back of the terrace. Human silhouettes. Men wearing tams, holding . . . brooms. He moved toward them, passing tables with collapsed umbrellas at their centers. A hint of humidity hung in the air, not quite fog but working on it.

"Bert?" Joe called up.

One of the figures moved. "Oi! Who's asking, then?" He slid down the roof tiles, caught his broom head on the gutter as he fell, and landed in some shrubbery as softly as a robin on a lawn.

"The name's Joe."

"Good solid name is Joe." Bert extended his dirty hand for Joe to shake.

"I welcome the greeting, but you see . . ."—he swept his hologram through Bert's hand—"I'm not quite all here, in a manner of speaking."

"Light on your feet," said Bert, amusing himself to no end. He whistled and waved an arm. The ten or so sweeps shot down the downspouts and joined him.

"I could use some help," Joe said. "Mr. Disney, too. It's that important."

"You need say no more, friend! A kite? A flying car?"

"An introduction to Mary," Joe said. "And Mickey. The Mad Hatter. The Fairy Godmother. I need them all, Bert. I need to call a meeting, a secret one. The villains must not hear of it. Mr. Disney wouldn't want that."

"And a big meeting it would be, your lordship!"

"I'm no lord. Far from it. But a gentleman, I hope. You see, we're under threat, Bert. We're kites in a storm, all of us. But if we can act as a group . . ."

"As to that," Bert said, "I can point you in the right direction, tell you where to find my Mary. But you see, friend, the animals and us . . . We tips our caps to 'em, me boys and me." The sweeps nodded in agreement. "We's cordial and such to all of God's creatures."

"Except them bats!" one of the sweeps called out. "Them bats comin' out of the chimney!" The others laughed along with him.

"We dance and we make merry. Sure we do! But as to what you might call any real conversation twixt them and us, 'tis few and far between. Ain't a real lot a sweep has in common with a chipmunk reared up on its hind legs."

"Or a dog with ears as long as its tongue," cried another sweep.

"But you could get word to them?" Joe asked.

"I could try, I suppose," said Bert, "but it might just be that your efforts would carry a ways further than my own. As to where you'd find them, well, it isn't so difficult this time of night. They tend to carry on down to the Troubadour Tavern."

"And the villains?" Joe asked.

"Was a time they was organized, something to be

afraid of. Not so much anymore. Them kids took care of that. Them that's left's a sorry lot, all scattered about. You find 'em picking food from the rubbish. I might feel bad for 'em if I didn't dislike 'em so much!"

His boys crowed and cheered. Several patted Bert on the back.

"Let's make it the Fantasyland Theatre in an hour," Joe said. "Can you spread the word by then?"

"My Mary's the one who can fly, friend Joe. She, Tink, and Peter can cover this park in no time. Let's see what we can whip up."

11

HE NEEDED A MOMENT to collect himself. Taking a deep breath, Joe looked out from the stage beneath the Fantasyland Theatre tent top onto a gathering of Disney characters.

These weren't Cast Members, he reminded himself, not employees, not people with families and bills to pay or places to get to, but Disney characters—living, breathing Disney characters. Mulan strode in from offstage and took a seat out front, as did Pocahontas. He saw Sulley and Tiana sitting with Elsa. Ariel moved gracefully in from backstage, too, followed by Mickey and Rapunzel, each part of the "Mickey and the Magical Map" show. A dozen rats from *Ratatouille* chatted with Ewoks. Chip and Dale and Flik sat with Stitch.

"Hello, everyone. Allow me to introduce myself!" And Joe did just that. He gave a short explanation of the Imagineers, tying its creation, like that of the characters, to Walt Disney. He spoke of the Kingdom Keepers, who received a standing ovation, and showed his audience how he, too, was now a hologram. After briefly describing the DHIs' final battle with the villains, an event none of the characters would soon forget, he extended his explanation into something larger.

"You are some of the most beloved characters of all time. You've won worldwide admiration from your films and your representatives in the Disney parks. You've made millions of children happy, and that is some of the best work anyone could ever do. But in the same way Walt Disney helped create you, the Imagineers, of which I'm one, have come to realize there is a single human being, a man who is responsible for the unhappiness and destructive nature of the Disney villains."

A chorus of booing rose and died like the tent taking a giant breath.

"This man has built himself a human army, an army of children with special talents, children he and his people have treated cruelly and unfairly, an army willing to do as they are told because they fear what this man will do to them if they don't."

Joe let the wave of murmuring subside before he spoke again.

"These children—teenagers, actually young adults—possess an assortment of powers that range from starting fires just by looking at something to reading minds. No two are the same. All of them are dangerous. We Imagineers do not have enough people inside the parks, especially young people, to search out these intruders. I've called you together to ask for your help. Your Cast Member characters are able to see so much. That will help us. But we know you wander the parks as well. We would like you to watch for trouble in ways we cannot. We ask only that! We do not want you interfering with these young people. In fact, we advise against it: they could very well mean you harm."

More conversation erupted.

"But we do need your help. Adults talk about how 'real' it all is, and we've long believed that much of that can be attributed to your interaction with the guests, however it's accomplished. Now we need that interaction more than ever. We need your eyes. Your senses. We need to know if we're under attack and by whom."

"We're with you!" shouted a character from the crowd. Joe thought it was Jasmine, but it could have been the Fairy Godmother behind her.

"Over the coming days, we will have more Plaids than usual in the parks—Cast Members wearing blue-and-red-plaid vests. Please, share any suspicions or sightings with them. We can ill afford another catastrophe like those that happened near Thunder Mountain and in Tomorrowland."

Loud muttering. A lot of nodding.

"We must stop that kind of trouble before it occurs. For that, we need you."

He faced row after row of princesses, overgrown mice, and stunted forest creatures. How useful could such an assembly be? Joe wondered. To face the evil intentions of Amery Hollingsworth Jr. with a band of the sweetest characters ever seemed like a fool's errand.

"What's the meaning of this?" bellowed the voice of a security guard standing at the back of the pavilion.

The characters jumped up and scattered, tripping, falling, hurrying to the exits.

Joe froze, panicked. Normally he had the clearance to be here, but if he stuck around, he risked being identified as a hologram, something he feared for a variety of reasons. His mission was to make the Disney characters allies of the Imagineers. There was no question of their loyalty to the Keepers, but what about adults wearing name tags?

For Hollingsworth's Fairlie attack to succeed, the man would need double agents in Disney security. His crime was therefore not only the physical threat he presented to Disneyland and California Adventure, but the seeding of distrust between characters and Cast Members. Joe needed to quiet the security guy before the man ruined things. In order to do that, he needed to lead him away from the pavilion and the characters—and quickly.

Mind made up, Joe moved offstage and into the wings. He located the stairs and descended.

"You!" the security man called out, having nearly caught up to Joe in record time. Joe felt tingling in his arms: fear. Fear was his enemy. He ran as fast as he could, darting beneath the colonnaded overhang of the gazebo that fronted It's a Small World; emerging out the other side, he veered right. A Return fob had been placed at the base of the Storybook Land Canal Boat lighthouse.

Trouble was, the guard was only a stride or two away from tackling him—or trying to. The Imagineers were on record as having shut down the hologram development program following the completion of Version 2.0, a model of DHI not yet introduced to the parks. Any discovery that the program was up and running could be disastrous. If the security guard attempted to physically stop Joe, the secret would be out.

Joe heard a *whoomph* and glanced back. He gasped: the security guard had been knocked to the pavement, and a large striped tiger—Tigger—was rolling past him. Tigger came to his paws and hurried away, leaving the security guard reaching for his hat.

Without thinking, Joe tried to step over the fence surrounding the red-and-white miniature lighthouse. But his hologram moved, ghostlike, right through the divider. Joe worked his way around the cylinder, searching for the small key fob. At last, he spotted it in the grass and bent to pick it up.

The security guard, having turned on his jets, reached the replica lighthouse only a few steps behind Joe. He hurdled the fence and hurried around the structure.

No one. The man he'd been chasing had . . . vanished!

There was an overriding sense that something strange and unexplainable had just happened. The guard frowned, turning in useless circles. How was he supposed to explain this? His fellow workers would think he was going crazy. No, he wouldn't mention this to anyone.

Not even to his dog, Steamboat Willie.

12

A TWIN PROPELLER TWA airplane grabbed the attention of Jess's hologram as she worked her way down the narrow backstage passage that paralleled Disneyland's Main Street USA. She found the grinding roar of the plane easier to take than the blast of a jet.

Cars, on the other hand, made far more noise in this time. Radio music was scratchier, but thunderstorms had stayed the same. From what she'd seen so far, living in 1955 was slower, its people friendlier and less worried, the sky clearer.

The last to arrive into the past, Jess had acted on impulse. She'd not thought to dress for 1955. The clothes she'd been wearing when she'd gone to sleep in the present comprised the outfit her DHI now wore each and every day. Thankfully, for her Imagineering internship, she'd had on black jeggings and a vintage orange Walt Disney World T-shirt. To Cast Members in 1955, her leggings looked like tights—very Fantasyland —and her T-shirt like something from Tomorrowland (since no one had heard of Walt Disney World).

As she walked, Jess received smiles, nods, and tips

of the hat from some of the men. The occasional sparkling of her hologram worried her—until it was met
with outright grins of enthusiasm from passersby. The
beautiful thing about Cast Members was their openness
to fantasy and creative expression. Rather than look
confused by her, they looked somewhat envious.

Jess's Fairlie ability had been thrust upon her:
she could future-dream. Dubbed by the Fairlies a
"Dreamer," Jess seldom knew which dreams were actual
visions of things to come, and which were her nocturnal
imagination. Over the past few years, she'd honed her
ability considerably. The haunting images of a graveyard
at night had been real. They possessed her. So did her
dream of the night before: she and a boy at the Plaza
Pavilion restaurant. In the dream, a smartly dressed
mother of two at the next table asked a gentleman for
the time. "Two o'clock on the button!" the gentleman
replied spryly.

In her dream, the boy's ice-cream float filled half the
glass—a real drinking glass, not plastic. So she and the
boy had been there at least long enough to buy drinks,
sit down, and dip into them. It was currently 1:35 p.m.
Jess had heard the Keepers complaining about their first
week or so in the park, how their projections had been
two-dimensional. Philby and Wayne had overcome
that limitation, so Jess now projected fully. However, in

certain zones within the park, the projections weakened or disappeared. Wayne called these the "dead zones." Philby was in the process of mapping them.

Added to this very real concern, bright light threatened their 1955 holograms. Jess and the others looked decent in sunlight and terrific after sunset, but any kind of glare cut right through them—a reflection of sunlight off water by day, a bright flashlight or car headlight by night. Such highlights overexposed them, rendering their images an obvious projection. With this in mind, she stayed vigilant, trying to spot reflective surfaces. Oddly for someone consisting of nothing but light, she feared it.

Entering the terraced seating area in front of the Pavilion restaurant, Jess carefully examined her surroundings, trying to match her dream with reality. She had to be extra careful not to connect with any of the white wrought-iron chairs or tables, as they would pass through her hologram and bring unwanted attention. Life as a hologram was a whole lot more complicated than it had once sounded.

She stopped in front of an empty table, the *only* empty table on the terrace. Before someone else grabbed it, she allowed herself to think of the graveyard dream. Briefly made solid by the thought, she quickly sat down, ducking beneath the open umbrella at its center. Despite being a hologram, her heart beat wildly in her chest. She closed her eyes and focused on her hands. Her fingers tingled. She tentatively reached for a red plastic catsup bottle, which was paired with a yellow mustard one. She touched it, *felt it*, and watched as the bottle dented with the contact. She thought she must have looked odd to people watching her, but at least her finger had not passed through it.

Nearby, small gray birds challenged one another for table crumbs. A bold seagull sat perched atop the roof of the Pavilion. Jess waited. And waited. Heat rose from the pavement. Car horns sounded from an unseen intersection.

Then a thin guy of medium height wearing thick black-rimmed glasses approached. His dark hair was parted to the side and oiled, his face long and thin, like the rest of him. He had a square chin and kindness in his eyes. When he smiled, as he did at Jess, his cheeks creased more on the left than the right, as sharp as an arrow, but his dark brown eyes never wavered or squinted. They remained fixed on her and deeply interested. Intense, without feeling threatening.

"If you don't mind my saying so," he said in a thick New Jersey accent that reminded Jess of old gangster movies, "you look incredible." His eyes darted around to the other tables. He lowered his voice. "And I think you know what I mean." Again, he smiled from nose to chin.

She spun the catsup bottle for him.

"Impressive. Really, super-duper." He wore a blue button-down and khaki chinos. His brown shoes were polished and laced tightly.

They didn't speak for a moment. The nondescript birds fluttered at their feet and around the tables. At last, he said, "The name's Marty. Marty Sklar. I'm a newspaper man. Was in college, anyway. The *Bruin*. UCLA. Now, for the company. That's what I do. The *Disneyland News*. Some publicity and marketing, too."

"O . . . kay? I'm Jessica."

"So I keep my nose to the ground. I make it my business to know what's going on in the park as well as outside of it."

"Sure," Jess said.

"And I'm buddies with Wayne. So when I started poking around about the stuff guests were saying, I ended up with Wayne. Basically forced him to tell me something about you and your friends."

"I didn't know that."

"What I believe, what I don't believe. No never mind. Nothing to worry about, kiddo." He drew his lips closed, like pulling an imaginary zipper. "Tight as a drum. But I came across this piece. One of those giveaway rags. Police blotter sensational stuff. Still, I'm a curious sort, so I read everything I can get my hands on. Wayne tells me one of these kids he's helping has dreams. That would be you."

"That would be me."

"He says on occasion these dreams have the feel of our own Esmeralda. She's our fortune-teller."

"You could say that, yes."

"Said you told your friends about a dream involving a graveyard."

"Did he?"

"I'm sworn to secrecy here, doll. To the company. To Wayne. To you. Nothing leaves my lips. On that, you can depend."

"You talk funny for a writer."

"I probably write that way, too! Who knows why Mr. Disney asked me to run his paper?"

"I think you're being modest."

He shrugged. "I'm just trying to be Marty. Nothing more. Nothing less."

"So . . . what's the point, Marty?"

"Direct! I like that."

Jess liked his smile a lot. She felt in no hurry to go anywhere—a rarity.

"So, there's this." He reached into his pants pocket and produced a wrinkled sheet of paper. He unfolded it and slid it across the patio table. The right column of the small newsprint page held ads. The printing method left the letters fat and rough. Marty called it *mimeograph*; most of the cheap "giveaway rags," he said, were of similar poor quality.

A GRAVE SITUATION

Residents of Hollywood Hills report vandalism and desecration at a local private cemetery that dates back to the 1920s. The little-known resting place, on a hill west of Laurel Canyon Boulevard, has been the source of vandalism in the past, but "never on this scale," says LAPD officer Sam Self. "At least two graves were disturbed. The possibility that one or more of the dead may have been exhumed is under investigation."

Marty produced a second page from a different paper. It, too, contained an article about a graveyard being vandalized. Jess reread both pieces and pushed the second sheet back to him.

"Ring any bells?" he asked.

"Breaking apart gravestones . . . not that one. But this one?" She tapped the first. "Yes, I'm sorry to say."

"Sorry? It's uncanny! Incredible! I'd think it'd thrill you!"

"Not exactly. I used to get excited about 'coincidences' like this, yeah, but that was a long time ago. In another world. I have a history of this, Marty, and that means I'm about ninety percent sure this article is right. There were two well-dressed men there. Two more digging. It was foggy, or maybe smoky."

"Thursday? Yes! Dense fog all along the hills!" He paused to appraise her like she was some sort of science project. Jess sighed. She was used to it. "Did you know that about the weather?" he asked. "You didn't, did you? I can tell by just looking at you!" He smirked. "Gee whiz! Isn't that something?"

"Oh, it's something, all right. But not anything you'd want, believe me."

"May I . . . may I ask the nature of your dream? If I'm not being rude."

"You're not, Marty. It's fine. Look, I tend to dream of stuff that's threatening, you know? To me, my friends. A lot of the time, I'm personally connected somehow. Other times, I can't figure out the connection until much later. Does that make sense?"

"I have no idea if it does or doesn't," he said, still sounding excited. "I've never spoken to anyone who can dream the future before!"

"A little quieter, please." Jess had seen a few heads turn in their direction.

Marty cupped his mouth. "So sorry!" He studied her long and hard, clearly impressed. "So, what's next?"

Jess paused, thinking. "Research. That's what Philby calls it. I'd say it's more like investigating or spying, but that's Philby. He's the scholar of the group."

"I think I'd like to meet him."

"Yeah, you two would get along for sure."

"You're different," Marty said, "but then, we all are, Jessica. For gosh sakes, don't let it get you down."

"I don't know how much Wayne told you, Marty, but different doesn't begin to describe me."

Marty lowered his voice to beneath a whisper. It sounded more like a soft breeze. "You're from another time."

Jess matched his volume. "I don't expect you to believe it."

"Why not? I'm in Disneyland, after all."

"I'm a girl from the future, in the past, dreaming the future. You want to talk about confused!"

"Well, I'd rather talk about the process."

A guy in 1955, Jess was realizing, didn't necessarily understand expressions from the 2000s. "The process is a mystery. Like so many mysteries, it just stays unexplained and unexplainable. I guess when it happens to you, you eventually accept it. First you deny it; then you tolerate it; then you accept it. That's the real process."

"Oh, I see. Not exciting, then." He sounded apologetic and contrite.

"It's okay. Really! That's how everyone sees it. But to me and my friends—other friends, not the ones here—it can feel like we're dwarves in the circus."

"The bearded lady, that scares me," said Marty.

"I don't get that so much because you can't see what I do. But my friends, for sure."

"Where are they, these friends?"

"A long way off." Jess wondered if Marty believed any of what he was hearing, or if he was just going along with her. People couldn't wrap their minds around time travel. She'd experienced it, was living it, and even to her it felt more dreamlike than real.

The Plaza teemed with hundreds of people dressed in oddly formal clothes—pressed trousers and shirts, dresses and skirts, hardly a sneaker in sight. The park guests seemed less in a hurry, though no less excited and fascinated by their surroundings. The lack of mature landscaping, the absence of anything plastic, smartphones or FitBits, made her feel like she was on a film set, absented from real life.

The sky was perfect, too, not a speck of air pollution. When the breeze blew from a certain direction, it carried the scent of fresh oranges. Jess breathed deep; she felt both thirsty and hungry.

"You look like you're a long way off," Marty said. He was looking at her thoughtfully. "Can you do anything with this information? What d'you mean by research? And when do I get to meet this Philby character?"

"I'll talk to the others." He was a stranger. Could she really trust him with their plans?

But she knew all too well what they were.

The Keepers were going to visit the graveyard.

13

D<small>UE TO WHAT</small> P<small>HILBY CALLED</small> "limited transmission distance," the 1955 holograms disappeared a short distance outside Disneyland. This vanishing threatened their survival, so as holograms, the Keepers remained within the confines of the park. To leave, they had to wait till closing time, at which point they lost their holograms and gained their real bodies.

* * *

A day, a night, and another day had passed since Jess's meeting with Marty, hours spent by the Keepers organizing and planning. By the time the group piled into Wayne's old pickup truck that night, the air blew chilly on a light wind, car exhaust filled the streets, and apprehension cloaked the Keepers.

Wayne drove them through a Hollywood of yesteryear in his red Ford pickup. The three boys were in the truck's open bed, hair whipping, eyes wide open. If Disneyland was the G-rated 1950s, Hollywood's Sunset Boulevard was off the charts. Older women dressed as schoolgirls in short plaid skirts and white kneesocks leaned against buildings. Young women the same age as the Keepers wore scoop-necked party dresses and black patent leather shoes with ankle socks. The men, young and old, had on suits, fedoras, and boater hats. The boys their age had buzz cuts and deep tans. People of all ages smoked cigarettes and laughed loudly.

Bushy-topped palm trees lined one side of Sunset Boulevard. A fire-engine-red city bus with a white top choked along behind them. Cool old cars—old only to the Keepers—drove slowly, windows down. A pair of mangy-looking dogs crossed the street; the Keeper boys heard Wayne tell the girls, inside the cab, that they were coyotes.

Most of all, the signs stood out. Big, small, electric, neon, hand-painted. Everywhere, signs. If they could have spoken, it would have been a cacophony. They competed for one's attention at all elevations, barking out brands, begging for business. Bikini-clad women and T-shirted, muscular men pushed products of every kind: movies, watches, liquor, cigarettes. Restaurants and businesses shouted their names in colorful fonts, trying hard to impress. There were NO PARKING signs, street signs, and speed limit signs. The onslaught of visual noise reminded Finn of Las Vegas or New York's Times Square in modern days.

Finn didn't want it to end, but the moment the

truck turned into the hills, the visual noise went silent. There wasn't a sign in sight. Just small houses, windows dark, palm trees, and plants of every variety—flowers, vines, shrubs, cacti—swarming wild or held back by a gardener's vigilant trowel. The smell of fresh-cut grass battled the perfume of bougainvillea. Within a block, Sunset Boulevard might as well have been miles away.

Wayne ground a few gears, chugged the pickup up the hill, and turned left into a street marked DEAD END. Deader than most people knew, Finn thought; the Keepers' destination was a certain private cemetery.

* * *

The suffocating silence enveloped Willa. Though a city hum wafted up the hill from Sunset like a thin fog and the occasional confused or angry dog released a volley of complaints somewhere in the distance, none of this could dispel her sense of this place's emptiness. Pale lamps burned from inside a few houses, but these seemed more like set decoration than signs of life. It felt as if an evacuation order had been issued, that residents had fled suddenly and perhaps permanently.

"Do we know where, exactly?" she asked Philby.

Wayne had killed the headlights, leaving Philby to study his crinkled road map, using the truck cab's faint interior light. The pickup was parked at the side of the road, under a canopy of tree limbs and vines. The Keepers had agreed that it was essential to stay hidden.

Philby pointed to the end of the narrow lane and down the hill into an inky reservoir, jet-black and unnerving.

"Not really . . ." Willa said.

"Afraid so."

The Keepers gathered their equipment from the back of the pickup: flashlights, two shovels, a cloth tarpaulin. The shovels were made of heavy oak and iron, the flashlights bulky and cumbersome, both different from those sold in the future. Maybeck collected three road flares, the phosphorus kind that looked like sticks of dynamite. Wayne carried a portrait-size mirror, saying only, "I hear ghosts don't like mirrors." Philby hung a length of chain around his neck like a long scarf. He told the others he'd read a series of books called Lockwood & Co. in which chains were used as boundaries between ghosts and mortals. It couldn't hurt to try.

"Just because Jess dreamed it," Willa said, "doesn't mean we're going to run into trouble. But the newspaper articles supported this. If Wayne's right about the weather, then her dream is in the past now."

"It's a cemetery, Willa. Think about that. People,

digging in a cemetery. What do you think is the *best* that can happen?"

Willa nodded. "Yeah, okay. Every precaution. I get it." Being a Keeper had shown her that anything was possible.

* * *

The group descended a steep hill of knee-high dry grass. Willa slipped, but Philby caught her. Maybeck and Charlene trekked hand in hand. Amanda and Jess held hands too, steadying each other. Finally, they reached a once decorative, now rusted, wrought-iron fence encircling an area about the size of a baseball diamond. Wayne flooded the area with light.

They stood on a flat section of ground, a small grassy meadow. Below and to both sides could be seen roofs, a chimney on one, a lighted window or two. The houses were quite close, easily within earshot.

Inside the fence, the grass gave way to sprays of wilted weeds, tipped over like bowing children. Interspersed among the clumps, the old gray gravestones struggled to stand. A tree had taken root in the nearest corner, so long ago that it absorbed part of the fence, which ran through its formidable trunk and emerged on the other side.

"Freaky," Charlene whispered.

A gate hung open to their right, clinging to one remaining hinge.

"This is the place," Wayne said. "Let's go."

"Might I suggest," Philby said, "that two of us work with the chain? Finn and me. We will stay inside it as much as possible while the rest of you stand guard, two on each of the three remaining sections of fence. We'll use the flares only if necessary, as there's a huge risk of wildfire. Whatever happens, if you light a flare, do *not* drop it. Keep hold and stomp out any hot ash that falls."

Finn blinked. He wasn't leading, at least not for the moment. It felt odd, as if Philby had borrowed something without permission. He, Finn, was the one who made most of the plans, and though he didn't mind sharing responsibilities, a degree of competition always hovered between him and Philby. He briefly recoiled. Hopefully nobody saw.

Nobody did but Amanda, who saw everything to do with him.

"The shovels and tarps?" Willa asked, holding one of the tools.

"Once Finn and I find the graves that were messed with, we'll decide what to do. First, we make sure this place isn't haunted."

"You're getting carried away," Wayne said. "Such imagination!"

"We've seen things you wouldn't believe," Philby replied. "We take nothing for granted."

Wayne nodded. The flashlight beam dipped along with his head and caught two yellow eyes peering back at them from the middle of the fenced area. Charlene let out a kind of squeaky scream that sounded like a dog getting kicked. The eyes vanished, and everyone heard an animal scampering away.

"Coyote," Wayne said. "And that's all!"

"Let's get this over with," Philby said.

Everyone split up to assume his or her post. Philby and Finn created a semicircle of chain inside the gate, stepped into it, and redistributed the links into a full circle in front of them. They moved this way into the heart of the cemetery, careful to keep their bodies contained within the circle of iron.

"How do you know this Lockwood book you read was right?" Finn asked.

"I don't," Philby said. "And I don't believe in ghosts either. But you know . . ."

"Yeah, believe me: I know."

"There's fresh dirt closer to me," Amanda said, shining a flashlight.

"Some over here as well," Maybeck called in a hushed voice. "Looks like a grave."

Jess stood a few yards from Wayne. He blinked,

concerned by her rigidity. "You okay, Jessica?"

When she failed to move, he tried again, a little louder.

Jess moved her head slowly in Wayne's direction. "He's like Jack Skellington, only human and way creepier."

"I don't know him."

"He oversaw the digging," she said, very confident. "It was him and at least two others."

"Are you okay?" he repeated.

"I'm having a moment."

"I'm not sure what that means," Wayne said. His eyes were wide and frightened.

"I can see him out there," Jess said. "Faintly. Not like a ghost; more like the kind of thing you see when you shut your eyes after a bright light. You might call it an afterglow."

"Energy," Wayne said.

"Yes! Energy. Like that. Psychic energy, I'm thinking."

"Doesn't sound good."

"It wasn't vandalism," Jess said. "Not like we read about. What I'm seeing is so close to my dream. But it isn't the same. Not exactly. And I think that means it happened. I think it really happened."

"Guys!" Wayne called out, slightly louder. "Jack be nimble. Easy does it. Jess here is having a moment."

Philby waved. He and Finn had reached the area of disturbed dirt spotted by Amanda. It was a full grave of heaped, raw earth. Philby bent down and picked some up. Freshly dug, it crumbled in his hand, still a bit moist.

"This is not right," Philby said.

"No kidding," Finn agreed. A chilly breeze swept across his skin, raising gooseflesh. "You feel that?"

"That would be: yes."

"What do you—?"

"Incoming!" Maybeck called out sharply. "Tree!" He muttered a string of bad words.

Philby and Finn bolted back, eyes darting up. The towering tree was only a few yards away. It looked to Finn as if a branch was loose and swaying in the wind. *Two branches*, now that he looked more carefully. No, *four*, he realized.

There was no wind.

"Legs," Finn whispered dryly. Not that he meant to speak softly; his voice wouldn't go any louder.

"Interesting," Philby said.

"Really? That's all you've got? 'Interesting'? How about 'freaky'? The cold is no coincidence."

"Agreed."

The legs belonged to two figures—men? Finn wondered—sitting on a lower limb. Swinging their legs. Along with the chill came a putrefied smell that reminded

Finn of the time his father had found a dead rabbit, a wild one, in a pile of lumber in their backyard. It was just splotchy fur and the shape of something that resembled an ear. Another something was most definitely a rabbit's foot, all out of luck. It was the smell of something scary and sad, something gone and something else remaining. It was death, he thought, or a particular thing that came along with it, like how a long shadow follows a light.

The two men came out of the tree with the ease of mountain lions, nimble and weightless as they hit the ground. But from there it was all awkward, stiff-legged movement, as if they were wearing knee braces and their arms were wrapped tightly to prevent the elbows from bending.

"Chain," Philby said, never taking his eyes off them. He toed the metal links, pushing out and extending the circumference to give him and Finn and the Fairlies more room inside. "Check where the ends meet. Make sure they overlap."

Finn did. And he raised his shovel like a weapon. "Excuse me, but do you see any eyes?"

Philby answered with his flashlight. Both Philby and Finn screamed at the same time. Then they turned and ran out of the chain circle, not in the direction of the gate but precisely 180 degrees away from the two . . .

"Zombies!" Finn shouted.

"Flare!" called Philby.

"Catch!" shouted Maybeck. Despite his terror, he vaulted the fence and ran toward his friends.

Philby missed the flare. It landed in the weeds to his right. "Dang!"

Finn stopped, hesitated a moment, and then sprinted back to Philby's side. He dug through the weeds to Philby's left.

The two strangers walked stiffly forward.

"No eyes, right?"

"Right," Philby answered. "And dirty as all get-out."

"Grave diggers."

"You said that, I didn't."

Red-white light flashed all around them, defining shadows and turning the landscape surreal. Maybeck had lit a flare and was holding it out like a sword aimed at the two men. The disgusting things trudged on toward the three boys as if an enormous weight pushed down on their shoulders.

"No teeth." Finn.

"I noticed." Philby.

Maybeck swore.

Philby located the missing flare.

"What if they aren't afraid of fire?" Maybeck asked.

"Then we burn them," Philby answered, "and hope they reconsider."

14

"ARE THEY . . . ALIVE?" Maybeck asked. "How is that even possible?"

"Technically," Professor Philby replied, "I think Finn nailed it. I believe the correct term is *undead*. Soulless creatures. Zombies."

"Stop!" Finn shouted at the two approaching figures.

They didn't. Finn swung his shovel and hit one of them. Hard. The *thing* stumbled to one knee, but got up again, unfazed.

"This is not good," Maybeck said. He thrust forward with the fire-spitting road flare.

The two men stopped.

"That's better," said Philby, and lit the flare he'd recovered as well. "Now we're getting somewhere."

The two things stood ten feet away, unmoving. Unblinking.

"They . . . aren't . . . breathing," Finn muttered.

"Get back! Go away!" Maybeck said, lunging bravely forward with the flare. The undead did not move. "They don't exactly seem terrified," he said to Philby and Finn in a low whisper.

"Well, I am," Finn said. He was the only one without a flare, and felt the absence powerfully. "Did you see how hard I hit him?"

Philby addressed the two figures. "You're guarding the graveyard?"

One of the two undead groaned. It sounded almost as if he were trying to speak.

"I'll take that as a yes," Philby said. "For whom? A businessman?"

The man Finn had struck shook his head no.

"A skinny man in a dark suit!" Jess shouted. By now everyone on the other side of the fence was leaning forward, straining to hear every word.

The other undead turned toward Jess.

And then he started moving through the grass toward her.

"Stop!" Philby shouted. The thing was unresponsive.

With Finn's attention divided, the other weirdo grabbed hold of the shovel and yanked it from Finn. Maybeck attacked, waving the flare. The flame touched the silent man's clothing. Nothing happened.

"Dude," Maybeck said in a panic, "I think he's fireproof."

The grave digger tossed the shovel aside.

Philby, out in front of the undead staggering around

the fence, drove him back with the flare. The creature wailed, still focused on Jess.

Charlene and Willa jumped the low fence and boldly closed in behind the *thing* threatening Finn and Maybeck. The girls barked rude comments, trying to distract it. Maybeck used the moment to try to set fire to the creature. Again, to no effect.

Jess shouted, "Who did this to you? Who changed you? The skeleton?"

The grave digger roared, chin to the sky.

"Let's get out of here!" Philby cried.

"Immediately, if not sooner," said Wayne, who'd raced back down the hill as the flares turned the treetops orange.

The Keepers backed away from the grave diggers in unison.

"On three," Finn directed. Even in the midst of chaos, it felt right to be leading again. The confidence was clear in his voice. "These things are slow. We turn and hightail it to the truck. Pair up! No one flies solo," he said, nodding at Maybeck. "And no one gets left behind."

He waited for someone to argue. When there were no objections, he began counting. "One . . . Two . . ."

15

"**I** HAVE THE SUPPORT YOU NEED. With your help, we can rid the park of what I'm calling the radical Fairlies."

Joe had come around from behind his desk. He wore a blue-and-gold Hawaiian shirt, shorts, and leather sandals. A faded friendship bracelet hugged his left wrist, right where most executives of a large international company would have worn a watch. "Your support team will need some instruction and leadership, but I think you'll find there's no lack of confidence among them. You won't need to be too rah-rah."

Mattie sat silently, admiring the South Sea island souvenirs and collectibles on Joe's desk and walls. His office was like a weird museum. He was waiting for her answer. She muttered and looked away, trying to make it clear she didn't like the idea. She worked better alone.

"I suppose all that can wait," Joe said. Mattie smiled slyly. That was better. "The characters I have in mind for you aren't going anywhere. I can see that your earlier suggestion has merit." She smiled more widely. "Truthfully," he said, "I would rather know their plans, understand their intentions and hierarchy, than simply get rid of them. Gathering information beats potential violence any day. The chance to learn something is always better than being heavy-handed. So, yes, I think we should consider your plan."

"I'm glad." Mattie chose her words carefully. She didn't want to sound pushy, but she also didn't want to be a pushover.

"There are complications. Always complications." This last bit Joe said to himself in a disgruntled, irritated manner. "We have internal processes for the implementation of our DHIs. Committees. Subcommittees. It takes time. And I know for a fact we won't receive approval for what you have in mind. Version 2.0 in-park guides are about to be brought on-line again. At present, all the resources for that technology are fully committed. I can't possibly pull any of my team. We don't have the luxury of time, do we? No! We must act, and act now. If we do this—and I'm only saying 'if'—it will need to be done in absolute secrecy, and we will have to settle for Version 1.6, which has its drawbacks and limitations. I should know! I've tested this myself."

"I don't understand most of what you just said." Mattie gave him a sly smile. "I stopped listening when you said you liked my plan. What about your testing it yourself?"

He chuckled. "I crossed over, Mattie. The problem with version 1.6 is that it makes you prone to fear and emotions. For reasons not yet understood, emotion weakens the hologram and gives you a material presence. You become more solid, more human. More vulnerable. You can be hurt, wounded. You can feel pain. And you can be caught, which is probably the more dangerous side effect. If they can capture your DHI, your sleeping body is stuck at the time of crossing over. The kids call it Sleeping Beauty Syndrome."

"The Syndrome." Mattie nodded. Chills ran down her arms. She'd heard the stories. Maybeck and the other Keepers had nearly been lost for good that way.

"In 2.0," Joe said, "you can more easily direct when to be material. Anger can trigger it. That would benefit you, since you need to physically touch a person to use your gift."

"My ability."

He nodded. "To *read* someone."

"The anger's not a problem for me," she said. "I'm angry most of the time."

"I don't like hearing that, Mattie."

"Try living at Barracks 14 for a few years. You sense you're a prisoner, but you never can really figure out if it's true or not. They feed you. They compliment you. They make you their friend. They make you feel special.

Then you escape and discover it's all a lie. You're the same freak you were all along. The anger . . . You can't believe that kind of anger."

"To have a chance, you will need to control it. Can you do that, Mattie?"

Mattie frowned. She liked Joe, grudgingly, but still. She didn't appreciate the parental tone he took with her, though. Grown-ups thought they knew everything. They mixed lies with truth when convenient and then preached about how you should never do that. They invented random rules that made their lives easier. They were hypocrites.

"I guess we'll find out," she said. "Won't we?"

16

CREATING A DHI FOR MATTIE took two excruciatingly long nights. During working hours, for fear
of being seen, Joe couldn't risk using Soundstage 6, the
Studio's green-screen stage, so Mattie started work at
8:00 p.m. and continued until 6:00 a.m. A process that
typically took several weeks was reduced to a few basic
movements and an abridged script.

Donning a skintight green leotard, tights, hood, and
gloves, all with action sensors affixed, Mattie performed.
She walked, ran, sat, jumped, kicked, and squatted in
front of a string of synchronized video cameras. When
she grew too tired, she read scripts into a microphone,
nonsensical phrases and word combinations intended to
train the digital processor to speak like her. Then it was
back to the soundstage, sometimes repeating actions like
picking up a glass or mug, sometimes nodding or shrug-
ging her shoulders. She jumped off a low box, a higher
box, a wall. She somersaulted and she fought. She
fought and she fought and she fought: with dummies,
with a martial arts expert, with a woman her own size.

When broken down into individual events, the

movements of the human body turned out to be insanely complicated. Mattie had to walk slow, fast, casually, intentionally, angrily. Each was slightly different from the others.

And yet, Mattie was told, this endless series of movements equaled approximately one-tenth of the program for the Keepers. Once she was crossed over, Joe and his team—all of whom were sworn to secrecy—reminded her that she would need to move slowly and deliberately. There had been no time to program subtlety or nuance into her DHI. The computers projecting her three-dimensional image were able to fill in some, but any quick motion that had not been recorded would cause blurring, or even brief invisibility.

Joe explained it in simple terms. "If you get into trouble, just remember, you will reconnect with us once you're asleep."

"Only if I can fall asleep!" Mattie said.

"The point is that you'll be the real Mattie during the day. You can spy for us, learn what you can. Then, at one a.m. each night, we will cross you over. That way you can seek help from us if you need it: at any time, your DHI can leave wherever you are, even if you're captive."

Looking nervous, he cleared his throat. Joe Garlington nervous? Mattie blinked. Not good.

"Though we've never tested it, we believe your DHI is capable of defending your sleeping self. You will cross over at the Hub, like the Keepers. That's how the system is programmed, and there's no time to change it. We will have a contact person there watching for you. Whatever your situation, we can help. We have a number of plans and strategies in place. For this first test, if you're okay when you cross over, then we'd like you to locate the Return and end the projection. Your sleeping body will behave normally—you can be awakened, for one thing. Does that make sense?"

"You're saying if I'm okay, I will look for the Return and use it. If I'm not, you guys'll help me."

"That's right! Now, for the bigger question: Are you ready to try it out? Are you ready to test being crossed over?"

Mattie smiled. "Are you kidding me? I've been waiting for this for a long, long time."

* * *

Falling asleep wasn't easy. Mattie's heart rate was elevated in response to her adrenaline and excitement. Her 11:00 p.m. bedtime stretched out indefinitely. She would later tell the Cryptos (an elite group of Imagineers who worked in a secret basement lab in Disney Studios, under Joe's direction) that her mind ran wild, that she was thinking too much about falling asleep to allow it to happen. She experienced short but vivid dreams—not unusual for her—and awoke abruptly to see that only a few minutes had ticked off the clock.

During other periods, she ran through lists in her head, thinking of things she'd forgotten to do. Her eyes would pop open, and the clock in her small room above the Studio's theater would reveal that only twenty minutes had passed. She'd get angry, which made falling asleep yet more difficult.

So when she dreamed she was coming awake on the sidewalk in front of the Partners statue in the middle of the Plaza in Disneyland, she turned her head to the side to look at the bedside clock.

Instead, she saw a mangy calico cat with half a tail and a serious chunk of its right ear missing. Its fur stood up, as if it had bitten a live wire; it had anime eyes and ridiculously long white whiskers.

Her first thought was that it was an illustration, so she looked to the other side. Bushes. Back again: cat. Bushes. Cat.

She sat up. Partners statue.

Cat. Bushes.

Statue.

No clock.

Concrete warm to the touch.

* * *

The cat was gone. The bushes were there. The statue was still there. The concrete was still warm.

The castle rose behind the statue.

Warm concrete, Mattie thought. Tingling hands and feet.

Tingling? Tingling!

No lights on in the castle.

No lights down the street.

Main Street USA! Castle. Concrete warm to the touch!

"Cross over," she said aloud. And she started laughing. Her chuckling grew to guffaws, to howls, to tears streaming down her cheeks. She lifted her hand, but there was nothing wet to wipe away. Maybe not tears, but the feeling of tears. Maybe not her, but the feeling of her.

"Oh . . . Em . . . Gee," she spoke to no one. "You have got to be kidding me!" She gave a short squeal, followed by more laughter. And finally, a test.

Carefully, she swung her arm toward the low concrete wall that surrounded the Partners statue. Her hand and forearm disappeared; only her elbow showed. She pulled her arm out. Her arm was whole. She tried again, and again her arm disappeared into the concrete.

She was a hologram!

120

17

Philby assigned the Keepers, Wayne, Amanda, and Jess to the task of collecting specific items—Wayne, phosphorus flares and digging tools; Maybeck, small pieces of ironlike nuts and bolts; Willa and Charlene, swords; Finn, lengths of iron chain. He was taking his reading of Jonathan Stroud's Lockwood & Co. series as the actual "How to Battle Ghosts" manual—*despite*, Finn thought wryly, *that the books are fiction.*

No one questioned the assignments, a rarity for the Kingdom Keepers, who were prone to long discussions and never short on opinions. Though no one said it, they all knew that they'd be returning to the graveyard as soon as preparations were made. After midnight, if possible.

On everyone's mind—also unspoken—was the danger involved. The two grave-digging zombies haunted them. No one wanted to face those two again, much less the contents of the disturbed graves. But if they didn't figure out what the enemy was up to, then they might face an adversary armed with the element of surprise. Definitely a bad practice—they'd lived through countless versions of it when facing the Overtakers. If they didn't learn from their own mistakes, then, according to Mr. Woodward, Philby's senior history teacher, they were destined to repeat them!

This time, the team was reduced in size. If they were caught and arrested, at least it wouldn't be all of them. Wayne would drop them off and pick them up, but not be part of it himself. Charlene and Maybeck, by far the most fit, were the first to volunteer. Finn would lead the group; Jess, whose dream had led them there in the first place, felt she had to attend to confirm (or not) their findings. As for Willa, Amanda, and Philby? They were reluctantly staying put.

Wayne moved them to the wood shop in the Opera House, as it wasn't currently in use. Shane and Thia's snooping had put Wayne's workshop off-limits to all but Philby. He and Wayne were continuing to make progress on a variety of DHI transmission issues, in an effort to allow the visitors to return to the future.

The team of four was dropped off at exactly 12:30 a.m., under a light but warm drizzle. Maybeck lugged a pickax and two shovels. Finn carried some heavy lengths of chain to ward off the zombies; Charlene had bits of iron and a ten-pound bag of rock salt for the same purpose. All carried phosphorus flares tucked into their waists, a flashlight with red film over the lens, and curving, steel-bladed Arabic swords Wayne had pilfered from the Disneyland costume shop. The sword blades were sharp and hung from the waist to the knee, making it dangerous to walk. Jess carried the sword but swore she would not use it, having little tolerance for unnecessary violence.

"I hope Philby's author guy, Lockwood or whoever, knew what he was talking about," Charlene whispered to Finn. "Otherwise, we're carrying a lot of junk around for nothing."

"Authors do research," Finn replied. "At least the ones I've heard speak at school."

"You sure that wasn't nonfiction?"

"Fiction, nonfiction, what's the difference?"

On the way down the hill, they split up. Charlene and Maybeck headed directly for the graveyard. Finn sprinted ahead, and Jess peeled off to the left, remaining outside the rusting wrought-iron fence. The light rain made their hair and shoulders damp, but softened the grasses to silence.

They approached slowly, as if they were walking in six inches of snow. Finn switched on his red-lens flashlight, throwing a dull beam just a few feet ahead. It was enough to see by, but only for a few feet.

Jess, who had circled around near the tree, waved

with two arms: she didn't see the grave diggers up in the branches. She bravely approached a small shed beyond the graveyard and offered the two-arm wave again. *Clear!*

Finn went to work—at this wedding, he'd be the flower girl. From the moment he passed through the tilting gate, he sprinkled nuts, bolts, and rock salt to either side, making what he hoped would be a ghost-proof lane.

Their first target was the recently dug grave in front of the wide-limbed tree. As Maybeck and Charlene waited, Finn spread more of the collected iron bits and salt, forming a path to the second stirred gravesite. When he'd completed the alleys, marked by the dissolving white salt, he created circles of chain from which to begin digging.

When he'd finished, Charlene and Maybeck entered warily. Maybeck walked carefully straight ahead; Charlene veered to the left.

"Do we happen to be missing something?" Maybeck whispered to Finn, who was, by design, inside his own chain circle at the branch of the two lanes, sword out and at the ready. "How much does this place remind you of somewhere else? Take out the weeds and put it on a slight incline. See any similarities?"

The artist of the group, Maybeck saw things differently: in shapes and designs, colors and forms. But with this hint, and even by the dim red glow of his flashlight, Finn saw what had previously eluded him. "The Haunted Mansion's graveyard."

"Bingo."

With its odd headstones, some upright, some sagging, the plot closely resembled the small patch of make-believe in front of the Disneyland attraction. There was a dried-out animal topiary and, to the left, a stone carving of a squirrel.

"That's bizarre," Finn said. "I thought it was supposed to be in New Orleans."

"I don't think death follows state lines," Maybeck said.

"A pet cemetery?"

"I think it's more like 'mixed-use,'" Maybeck said. "If those ones that were dug up are pets, they had to be bears or lions. A small horse, maybe."

"You're disgusting."

"I try."

"Get digging," Finn said, looking over toward Charlene, who was throwing dirt like a dog after a bone. "We're wasting time."

In the ensuing minutes, Finn heard the steady bite and toss of the shovels. He kept his eye on Jess, who remained outside the iron fence, near the sprawling tree.

Hardly close enough for Finn to see, Jess nonetheless projected an intensity, a heightened alertness that reminded Finn of the two undead grave diggers. Finn didn't believe in zombies, didn't believe something could be undead, but for the moment he had no other reliable explanation for what they'd seen.

Jess clearly sensed, or at least anticipated, trouble of the worst kind. She craned forward, constantly lifting up onto and lowering off her tiptoes, messing with her hair. Her twitching, combined with the gloomy setting, put Finn on edge. He, too, kept watch in all directions, especially toward the shed, which Jess had not dared enter. He watched the gravestones and the areas of disturbed dirt where Charlene and Maybeck were working themselves into a sweat. He expected the unexpected, feared the fearsome. Something strange and horrible had happened here—people tampering with graves. By repeating that act, he and his friends were asking for trouble.

The thud of a spade's blade hitting something solid but hollow rang out through the graveyard. Finn shivered as he looked in Charlene's direction. She looked back at him, as if apologizing for succeeding. Finn moved toward her, taking great care to remain within the confines of the protected path. His active imagination had him straying outside, being collared by some unclean spirit, and pulled beneath the raw earth, gasping and fighting for air.

He snapped out of it. Charlene's shovel had scraped dirt from the top of an old, rotting coffin.

"It isn't very deep," she said. She'd barely dug down more than a foot. "Not even covered up, really."

"They were lazy," Finn said. "The grave must have caved in as they removed the coffin or something."

"So what now?" Charlene asked, dread choking her throat.

"We open it," Finn said. "And maybe see what they were after."

"There's no 'we' in that," Charlene said, stepping back.

Finn glanced up beyond the trunk of the tree to Jess.

"Fire," she said, recalling her dream. "Something to do with fire."

"Maybeck!" Finn called hoarsely.

"I'm kinda busy over here," said Maybeck, shoveling more quickly now.

"I'm going to help him!" Charlene said. "Good luck!"

"No!" Finn called, poking the coffin with the tip of his curved blade. "You're going to hold the flashlight." He redistributed the length of chain into an oblong. "And if you're smart, you'll stay inside this with me."

"That's a little cozy for my taste."

"According to Philby's author, the chain is a stronger defense than the bits of iron and salt, but suit yourself."

Charlene looked around the ground nervously, and then resigned herself to moving inside the closed length of chain. "This is insane, just for the record."

"There is no record," Finn said. "This is all brand-new to us."

"Jess," Charlene called to her friend. "Remember what I said."

Jess gave her a thumbs-up. "Got it!"

"I'd appreciate it if you told him not to do this," Charlene said.

Jess, a dark shape in the limited light, shrugged.

"Yeah, that's what I thought," said Charlene. "Some friend you are."

"No question it's been opened," Finn said, scraping away dirt from the sides of the coffin and training his dull red beam on it. He kept the sword in his right hand, passed his flashlight to Charlene. "You ready?"

"No," she said, her hand shaking so violently the red orb of the flashlight's glow danced on the earth-encrusted box.

Finn tried to open the casket from within the ring of chain, but his leverage was all wrong. He stepped outside of it.

"Finn! No!" Charlene's voice cracked.

Finn couldn't speak. His chest pounded, his heart throbbed, his hands sweated and trembled. Behind him, Maybeck continued his vigorous digging. Finn heaved up the heavy lid a crack, the only sounds that of the damaged wood decaying and crumbling. Another inch. Yet more, the lid now open nearly a foot.

"Aim it here!" Finn called. But Charlene had looked away. Finn set down the sword and pried his flashlight from her grip, straining to hold the lid open with his left hand. He trained the light inside. "Oh my gosh!"

He dropped the lid down with a bang. Leaving it askew, he sprang back, and landed on his bottom.

Charlene leaped to the edge of the chain circle. "What the heck!" She sounded angry.

"Did you see her?" Finn asked, his voice weak.

"I didn't see anything! I wasn't looking!"

"You okay?" It was Maybeck, leaning on his shovel to catch a breather.

"Dandy," Finn called back loudly, wondering why it had to be his job to open the coffin. Privately, he spoke to Charlene. "A skull with hair like cotton candy. Leathery little ears. But nothing on her face. Just bone."

"Her?"

"A grandmother's dress, all rotten and torn. Her hands. Her feet. It's so disgusting!"

He called over to Maybeck that there was nothing interesting. Finn closed up the coffin, working delicately not to destroy the lid in the process.

"Let's leave it like this until we see what Maybeck's looks like," he suggested to Charlene.

"Sure," she said, in no great hurry to start moving dirt again. "What do you think this is about?"

"I think Jess's dream means something. I suppose they always do, but this one's a keeper, no pun intended."

"Got something," Maybeck called, his shovel also banging against an object as he stabbed it down.

"So do I," called Jess from beneath the tree.

Finn whirled, eyes darting to Jess. "What?"

"The shed," she said warily. "The shed. Maybe those same two from last time. But more with them. Ghosts, like the others."

"You . . . dreamed that?" Finn asked.

"I . . . I touched the fence and I just *saw* it. It came and went, like that time in Epcot."

"Were we in what you saw?" Finn asked, his throat dry.

"Yeah. We were . . . And it wasn't pretty."

"Fighting?" he said.

"Yes," she confirmed.

"The shed," he murmured. Jess, like the Keepers,

knew when to answer and when to be silent. The Keepers could finish each other's sentences, guesstimate a fellow Keeper's thoughts, anticipate a reaction and change the way they worded something because of it. They could feel what the other person was feeling.

Finn might have believed once that none of this was possible, but he'd seen it so many times, had been part of so many strange happenings in the company of this small group, that he knew it was theirs and theirs alone. They belonged to a club that wasn't any other kind of club, a group that only acted like a group by themselves. Jess, like Amanda, was as much a part of them as any Keeper.

"Those clouds," Jess said now, pointing into the yellowish night sky, "were in my vision. Whatever I saw—and I'm not saying it means anything!—happens tonight, when those clouds are a little bit farther to the left."

Finn hustled toward Maybeck's grave, minding the passageways. "We need to hurry. Jess has seen something . . . bad."

Maybeck, already working furiously, took offense to being rushed. He used some creative language to suggest Finn borrow Charlene's shovel. However, Charlene arrived at nearly the same moment and pitched in. In a matter of minutes, she and Maybeck had uncovered the casket. Once painted with shiny black enamel, it was held together with brass hardware gone green. The moist soil just beneath the surface was a perfect habitat for earthworms and banana slugs, all of which adhered to the coffin's exterior in a slow-moving tangle, giving it the appearance of movement. The thing looked animated, writhing slowly before them.

"Eww," Maybeck said.

"I second that," said Finn.

Galvanized by Jess's confidence, Charlene dug deep and found her determination, pushing back her earlier wariness. She stepped forward, her shovel on the ground, her sword in hand. "We have to hurry, you two. Really!" She placed the tip of her sword on the first of the coffin's three fasteners. "It's been opened. These have all been pried loose. And recently." She forced the blade into the gap where the coffin lid met the main section and leveraged it open, grabbing the lid with both hands. "A little help?"

Finn joined in. Together, he and Charlene hoisted up the lid, Charlene's flashlight at the ready. The casket contained dirt, more than a few spiderwebs, and the same overpopulation of worms, some stretched, some compacted to small blobs that didn't look like worms at all. Some of these swam in and around anatomic holes in the bony face; others could easily be mistaken for a pattern on the black suit. Most definitely a man's, complete with what had once been a white pocket square, blue tie, and belt with a silver buckle. The shoes—black with leather soles—had rotted away. Most distressing, and impossible to miss was—

"No hands," whispered Charlene.

"Noted," said Finn. "No left arm from the elbow."

Charlene used the tip of her curving sword to pull back the right sleeve. "Make that a pair. Why just the forearms?"

Both skeletal arms were missing from the elbow. Finn's sword stirred the dirt, looking for the missing appendages. Charlene did the same on the left side.

"Look at the color of the breaks at the elbow," Charlene said.

"Not as yellow as the outside of his bones," said Maybeck the artist. "That's called white."

"As in: recently broken," said Finn.

"Someone broke off both arms at the elbows?" Charlene asked skeptically. "It's not as if there were fingerprints to steal."

The skeleton was just that: a skeleton. All bones. Picked clean.

"Besides," Charlene said, "why *his* arms and not *hers*?" She meant the other skeleton.

"I think you'd have to be the one stealing bones to know that."

"Guys?" Maybeck whispered, his voice implying great concern. "I'm getting the high sign from Jess. I think we have company."

18

ONLY AMANDA KNEW Jess's best-kept secret, that her ability to dream the future actually frightened her. The kids she'd lived with in Barracks 14 had real powers: moving objects with their thoughts, displacing water with a wave of the hands, like Moses. She had dreams. So what? Where others showed real courage, she had dreams. Where some were brave, she was not.

Yes, at certain moments she could reach deeply inside herself, discovering a resolve and defiance that surprised her. But most of the time her instinct was to run the other way.

Like now, for instance: looming in silhouette atop the incline where Wayne had dropped them was a lanky man—at least, she thought it was a man—with perfectly square shoulders, a pencil neck, and legs like circus stilts. After the shock of seeing him, Jess's first thought was his clothes were draped over a frame as insubstantial and thin as that of a prisoner of war. Or a skeleton. She often made such snap judgments of people based on their dress, flattering or unflattering, and though she wasn't proud of judging a book by its cover, it served her well most of the time.

But the man's oddly thin frame was nothing compared with the luminous aura surrounding him. There was no light up there to create the illusion of a silhouette, Jess realized. The halo surrounding him from the waist up was emanating from *within* him. It was like walking into a blindingly bright room only to realize there were no lights anywhere. Maybe, she thought, there's no one there. Maybe it was just another of her visions.

No such luck. The figure lifted his arm and gestured toward the shed.

Jess felt like a drain had opened in her heart, in her nerves, her confidence. It was as if she'd gained a hundred pounds in an instant. She had called to the others only a second or two before, but now her head wouldn't move, her neck wouldn't turn, her jaw wouldn't open, her vocal cords wouldn't sound. She wasn't sure she was breathing.

That motion of the aura threw something through the air. If she could have seen other wavelengths of light, Jess was sure, she'd have witnessed a contrail drawn from the lanky figure to the shed, and from him to her, to the cemetery. It would have been as red as fire or blood, yet feathery and fast as a snake's tongue. It would have burned the skin or cut a hole through stone.

From the shed they came. The figure on the hill had *called* them; Jess felt certain of it! Whether or not a door opened, Jess couldn't be sure, which made the appearance of the figures all the more troubling. She had seen wraiths sixty years into the present whose entire purpose of being was to absorb the living into their smoky forms. The specters emanating from the shed looked no different, except for the burial clothing that tagged them as residents of a graveyard. Suspiciously transparent hands and heads, open mouths like dark caves.

"Gate!" Finn shouted. "Swords and flares!"

Jess found she could move again; she raced to the gate, closing herself in with the others. "It's an iron gate. This is where we test Philby's theory," she hissed.

Among the dozen or so undead walking toward the plot, Finn spotted the two grave diggers from the Keepers' earlier visit.

"Corpses or ghosts?" Finn called out to Charlene.

"What?" Even in the limited light, it was clear she'd gone ashen.

"Heads or tails. One or the other. Take your pick," he said.

"Ghosts!" Charlene said.

"Corpses," called Jess.

"I'll take shortstop," Maybeck said. Whatever that meant.

"I'm with Charlie," Finn announced. "Jess is going

to figure out what the missing arms mean. Maybeck, you're in the middle. Whoever needs him most, holler."

Finn tugged Charlene by the arm and ran with her toward the oncoming ghosts, the wrought-iron fence the only barrier between them. Finn spoke in a whisper, half prayer, half statement. "I sure hope Philby was right about the iron."

Charlene answered in a gravelly voice that sounded nothing like her. "I think we're about to find out."

19

Jess heard the fizzing of flares, and the night came alive. Shadows jumped and shifted with each burst of flashing yellow light. She heard the clanging of shovels and swords, shouts and calls.

But she could not allow herself to be burdened by such distractions. She'd learned from the Keepers that each member of a team had to keep to their assigned job. To deviate from your role was to place the whole team in jeopardy. So Jess tried her best to block out the battle being waged behind her, to block out the ugliness of the open coffin's contents, and do what was being asked of her.

Determining why the arms were missing was no easy task. Had the dead man worn a wristwatch or gold jewelry, or something else of value? Perhaps, she thought, the skeletal arms had been removed and discarded once the treasure was bagged. Or maybe the grave robbers sought to identify the deceased by evidence of prior bone surgery or disfigurement, even DNA. The possibilities seemed endless.

She understood what Finn needed her to do. She just didn't know if she could do it.

Their situation demanded that she hurry. Hesitation was her enemy; the others were waiting for her, defending her so she could get the job done. Jess leaned over the grave's earthen wall, feeling the dirt crumbling beneath her knee, and grabbed hold of the broken elbow. The bones were cooler than the air, dry and porous like stone. Her stomach lurched. She willed herself not to throw up, not to faint and fall into the grave herself.

Whatever was going on behind her, the fight was drawing closer. Repulsed by touching the skeleton, she let go and closed her eyes, hoping for a waking dream or image. Nothing.

She slid off the edge and into the grave, far enough down to align both hands with the protruding bones. She took a deep breath of stale, fetid air. She grabbed hold. She shut her eyes.

The glow on her inner eyelids softened—one of the flares had burned out. Finn and Charlene were shouting. Maybeck was calling out inappropriate names for their attackers. Jess blocked it all. Though it was Mattie who read people's thoughts by touching them, Finn had wanted Jess to try touching the skeleton in an effort to future-dream it as well.

Nothing. She kept her hands clasped tightly on the snapped bones. *Come on!* she thought. *Tell me what happened to you!* she demanded mentally.

It was the wrong question. Instantly, she felt a pang in her chest like an explosion. *She saw a room, an apartment, maybe, at a sharp angle. She was falling.* More correctly: this man she was holding on to was falling. *Falling dead of a heart attack.* Jess let go, her chest aching painfully. She felt surprised, horrified, curious, and frightened. The man had died of a heart attack. But that wasn't the answer she wanted. She grabbed hold again. *Think!*

What recently happened to your arms? she thought, eyes closed.

The figure up on the hill appeared before her eyes, that same unexplained glow surrounding him. His image comingled with the face of one of the grave diggers from the night before. He raised a shovel like a scepter and lowered it sharply.

Jess buckled with the blow: he'd hit the right elbow first. Then the left. She felt it. With both forearms in hand, the grave digger turned, offering the separated limbs to someone standing at ground level.

"Jess! Jess!" Finn's voice.

She snapped out of it.

Finn, Maybeck, and Charlene stood with their backs to her, swinging their swords. The last flare sputtered, about to go out.

Finn shouted, "Jess! We gotta go over the fence. It's iron! It's our only hope."

"Right now!" Maybeck shouted.

She felt a hand grab the neck of her shirt and haul her to her feet. Charlene, Finn, and Maybeck turned and jumped over the open grave. Maybeck hoisted Jess up and dragged her behind him. She scrambled up the far wall of the grave, and they ran as a group for the iron fence enclosing the graveyard.

"It's spiked!" Finn said. "Be careful!"

Maybeck was tall enough to get over easily. Charlene vaulted without a problem. Finn and Jess took longer and required some help.

A ghost caught up to Finn and tore his shirt as he leaped over. But the ghost and his menacing army stopped at the fence, though the terrified teammates hardly noticed.

They were too busy getting as far away as possible.

20

MATTIE HAD BEEN TOLD to let them come to her.

Joe had arranged the sudden employment through the store manager, Teresa, who had quickly trained Mattie to run goods between the stockroom and the store floor. Mattie was assigned the hours that no one wanted: in the morning and late at night.

With the store closed, she and another girl, Jaanavi, restocked and neatened shelves, following the lists generated by the cash registers of what had been purchased during the day. Jaanavi, a vibrant girl with a headband braid and gorgeous skin, had six months of experience on the shop floor. She took the chore of neatening the piles and racks of clothing, while Mattie brought product up from the stockroom, wheeling carts, racks, and dollies loaded with sweatshirts, Mr. Potato Heads, and Elsa dolls.

The stockroom, underground and beneath the store by one level, was roughly the size of a football field. Its narrow, crowded aisles blocked out a good deal of the spotty overhead tube lighting. The abundance of clothing absorbed all sound, like a forest blanketed by a deep snowfall. Mattie didn't mind being down there during store hours with the other Cast Members, but alone, at night, it wasn't pleasant. The thousands of dolls, toys, and plush animals looking out from plastic bins brought on a sense of gloom and spookiness. Adding to that was the fact that the far end connected to an underground trucking dock and recycling station. Although Disney security controlled the trailer trucks coming and going, Mattie's imagination had people sneaking in on foot.

Mattie's attention ticked in that direction as she rolled a dolly along an aisle of hanging T-shirts and Elsa costumes. As she passed a pair of four-foot-tall white plastic Stormtroopers, the helmets of the soldiers moved with her. Hearing something, she stopped and glanced back, wondering if the heads had been angled like that a moment earlier. She took two more steps and pivoted, trying to catch them moving—nothing.

Wary now, Mattie moved ahead more slowly, clicking the talk button on the wire of her radio headpiece.

"Th . . . at -ou?" came Jaanavi's scratchy voice. Reception between the floors was far from perfect.

"Yeah. Just checking. All good."

"No problem."

As Mattie moved ahead, concentrating on the list and

sorting toys and clothes into specific bins on the dolly, she missed several snakes, three-foot Kaas, which slithered off a shelf, their pink tongues flashing, and oozed silently to the concrete floor. They glided toward her, maintaining a perfect S shape. The two Stormtroopers stepped out of their boxes, snapping the twist ties holding them to the cardboard like tissue paper.

A rattling sound ahead stole Mattie's attention and kept her from looking behind—it sounded like a million sticks being dumped out of a truck.

There were no deliveries scheduled at this hour. She reached for her headset wire, but decided against it. She'd checked in with Jaanavi only a minute before; she didn't want to seem like a little kid.

Maybe the sound wasn't wood at all. Plastic? Metal?

She spun sharply, sensing something. Two Stormtroopers marched toward her, three snakes behind them.

A girl's figure appeared, far down the same aisle. Not a child; she had a woman's fuller shape, was possibly Mattie's age or slightly older. No face or distinguishing features were visible in the dim aisle.

"Hello?" Mattie called out. A Stormtrooper raised his right arm, and she jumped to the side as a beam of light shot from an E-11 blaster rifle. A plastic duck on the shelf beside her head disintegrated in a puff of smoke. One of the snakes raced for her ankles, and Mattie scrambled awkwardly upward, using the shelves as a makeshift ladder. Another blaster fired at her, and a plush Mufasa's whiskers shriveled.

The ethereal woman's arms moved like a . . . a *conductor's*. She was orchestrating this!

"What do you want?" Mattie cried.

No answer.

A *whoosh* of wind snapped her head around. At first, she couldn't comprehend what she was seeing. But combined with the clatter she'd overheard earlier—wood? plastic? metal?—it made sense: hangers. Plastic hangers.

There were racks holding *thousands* of them at the far end of the room, and they had taken flight like wayward boomerangs. They came at her, birds with plastic wings and thin metal necks; the loophole heads were hooks, trying to snag her hair and clothing. Mattie was so stunned that she failed to defend herself from the initial attack. A chunk of hair tore from her head; her shirt popped its top button as her left sleeve ripped away.

She covered her eyes and ears with both arms, dropping to the ground—the snakes were on the move. She heard another blast and felt her leg burn wickedly. Her shirt was nearly torn off, and still the hangers kept coming, stabbing and hooking.

"STOP IT!" she cried, to no avail.

Desperate to cover herself, she pulled down a pile of Monsters University sweatshirts from the shelf. To her relief, the pecking briefly subsided. She jumped down and raced ahead, wary of the snakes and Stormtroopers. To her astonishment, she saw the hangers diving, moving in a wave to scoop up the fallen sweatshirts and lift them back onto a rack. Could that be the answer?

Mattie started pulling clothing from the shelves and throwing it into the air. The hangers dove and caught the garments, racing to land on a hanging rod. Pile after pile, all the way down the seemingly endless row, she launched costumes, sweaters, and shirts as high as she could throw them.

Another round of blasters nearly hit her. She'd had enough. With the hangers frantic as fleeing cockroaches, she dared to do something she'd never pictured herself pulling off. Frozen in place, she waited, breathless, for the snakes to advance. As they closed in, she slammed her foot down, first behind the head of the one to her right, and then, in an awkward stretch, the one to her left. She snagged the right snake from behind the head and held it out in front of her just as the next blaster round fired.

It zapped the snake, removing its head. She dropped the lifeless body and did the same for the one on the left, enduring two bad stings before singeing the head of the remaining snake. Two more piles of T-shirts kept the remaining hangers busy while she calculated how to handle the advancing Stormtroopers.

Without any hint or prompt, she understood what had to be done. Street-savvy and worldly-wise, Mattie was not one to dawdle. She'd faced pain like this before. Moving swiftly now, she ran to the end of the aisle and turned left. The air filled with the sound of something tearing loose; the Stormtroopers spotted their target and fired almost simultaneously.

On either side of the two towering toys, smoke rose. They fired again. And then the one to the left dropped in a pile of melted plastic. The second fell on its heels, taking a blow to the chest, its legs still trying to walk.

Ahead of them in the aisle were Mattie's head and feet. Between these parts of her was a shiny rectangular mirror emblazoned with the words: HAVE A MAGICAL DAY! AND LOOK YOUR BEST! The light blasts from their E-11s had been redirected to self-destruct.

The older girl at the far end of the aisle, who had been following along in the wake of the battle, clapped anticlimactically.

"Well done. Very well done! So you are who we think you are? No normal girl could think like that, react like that. Two words you will speak to me. Only two, mind, or you'll never see me again. Are you ready?"

Mattie had to slow her breathing, collect herself, and process everything she'd just been through. To her surprise, she wasn't burned. Her skin was only red and irritated where the blasts had landed. She pulled her shirt closed slowly and buttoned the two buttons that remained. Then she grabbed one of the Monsters U sweatshirts and slipped it on, wanting to make the woman wait.

"Ready," Mattie announced.

"Baltimore!" the woman called down the aisle.

Mattie felt the twitch of a smile curl her lips. "Barracks 14!" she shouted back.

The Stormtroopers stopped moving. Hangers fell to the floor as if strings had been cut.

She'd made contact.

21

*P*INOCCHIO SITS ATOP A TABLE. *Not a wooden table, but something gray and smooth, almost like concrete. There are no puppets hanging above him, none clinging to the wall. Whatever light floods him is not sunlight from a window but something bluer and higher; his shadow spills out beneath him like a black skirt. He is not in the company of other puppets, but is alone and sad-looking. Geppetto is nowhere to be seen.*

No, wait; he isn't sitting on the table at all. That's an illusion: the boy puppet is lying flat. No, not that kind of lying, for his nose is its proper size. He is thin, so thin he appears to be part of the table itself.

Suddenly hands—could they be Geppetto's?—come into frame, wearing thin white gloves. When Pinocchio is lifted off the table, he's translucent, making a curiosity out of the shadow visible just a moment earlier. Was it the shadow of a head, looking down at the transparent boy?

A burst of light suggests the passage of time. Short or long? Impossible to tell. The transparent puppet boy flaps slowly, like a small flag in an inconsistent wind. The light behind him, coming through him, is suddenly orange and flickering, and there is no mistaking it: it is a flame. And the boy is headed straight for it.

As he nears, his edges curl and melt; in an instant, he catches fire, blue flame with curling red edges. He is released into it. He vanishes. There is laughter, or chanting, or both, a mixture of languages, tones and mirth.

* * *

Jess bolted awake. Blinking woozily, she stared across a darkened pillow. Her eye caught the worn edge of her sketchbook, which she'd left jammed between the bed frame and mattress, a pencil at the ready. A battery-operated reading lamp clipped overhead completed the setup. She sat up, switched on the light, grabbed her notebook, and began to draw.

The puppet boy on the table. In the fire.

In trouble.

She'd come to feel when a dream represented an actual event in the near future, instead of a mind wandering in sleep. She wasn't always 100 percent right, but she was close.

This was one of the real ones. This was important.

22

AFTER CLOSING UP FOR THE NIGHT at 1:00 a.m., Mattie was supposed to ride a city bus two stops to a waiting van, which would return her to Burbank, a long tedious drive, but one Joe deemed necessary. When she failed to arrive at the van, Joe was awakened and informed; he sent the driver back without her.

Joe lay awake a good part of the night, not out of concern for Mattie, but out of excitement: she'd made contact.

Escorted by the Fairlie she'd met in the stockroom, Mattie arrived behind the Hollywood Backlot Stage. "I'm Antonella," her escort said. She wore a leather coat with a dozen shiny zippers. Her chinos suggested that beneath the leather was a Disney Cast Member costume. Two silver studs, likely magnetic, shone on her nose. At the moment she looked tough, her hair parted severely and asymmetrically on the left. But, Mattie thought, it was a look easily changed to fit the Cast Member code.

"These kids up here," Antonella said. "You may know some of them. I wouldn't make a big deal of that even if they do."

"Okay."

"For the time being at least, no one's going to trust you."

"That's comforting."

Two girls and three boys about her age met her there.

"We recognized you," a boy said. He didn't say who "we" was; Mattie knew. He had exceptionally straight, broad shoulders, a narrow waist, and flat abs. His running shoes were worn-out at the heel and scuffed on the toe. He looked like he shaved, probably daily, and wore contact lenses that irritated his eyes.

"I know you," Mattie said slowly, disregarding Antonella's advice. "You're Humphrey. We took that class on self-control together."

"Melinda? No! Madeline!" With the recollection came a smile, and with the smile, a tilt of the head, as if he saw someone different from the girl he'd recognized.

"It's Mattie. It's been a while."

"You escaped. She escaped!" he told the others. "Thanks to you, we all had a bad couple of weeks."

"Sorry about that, I guess. I took what you might call an indefinite leave."

"Because?" one of the girls asked Mattie.

"Some friends needed me."

"That was a big risk to take," Humphrey said.

"Look who's talking." Mattie raised an eyebrow. She

had to appear naive. It wasn't in her repertoire. "How many of you made it out? How? And why here? So many questions! That must have been some breakout!"

To them, this had to appear like she had taken their presence in the park as a coincidence. It was something no Fairlie fully believed in.

"Actually . . . no," the boy said. "We didn't escape."

"What's that supposed to mean?"

"Where are you living?" a thin, sickly-looking girl asked. *Osanna?* Mattie thought she remembered the unusual name.

"Who wants to know?" Mattie answered, stiffening her shoulders.

"She does," she said, motioning toward Antonella. Younger sister, by the look of her.

Mattie nodded but said nothing.

"We're here on a mission," Humphrey interjected. "Twelve of us."

"Twelve?!"

"Maybe lucky thirteen, if you come on board."

"Me? No. No mission for me, other than lying low and avoiding recapture." She and Joe had agreed: she had to make them work for it.

"You're not part of another cell?" Humphrey asked.

"Cell? You mean the Barracks *sent you here?*" She made herself incredulous.

"That's enough!" Osanna told Humphrey, who silenced her with an angry look.

"Are you supposed to be spying on us?" Humphrey crossed his arms defiantly. "Making sure we're sticking to the program?"

"Let me get this straight," Mattie said, leaning back and raising an eyebrow at him. "I escaped nearly two years ago and came clear across the country just so I could be in place to spy for the people I escaped from? Are you nuts?"

"That's not an answer," Osanna said.

"Why are you here, anyway?" Mattie asked.

"We told you," Humphrey said. "A mission."

"We told her too much," Antonella said. She held Mattie firmly by the arm. Mattie winced, intimidated by a girl who had made toys move and hangers fly. What kind of ability was that? she wondered, curious and slightly afraid. Even Amanda couldn't use her telekinesis in such a controlled way.

"No more names," Osanna announced. "No more explanations." To Mattie: "You're spending the night with us."

"Am not!" Mattie protested.

"Blindfold her," Antonella told the others. "Osanna, tie your belt around her head."

Mattie pretended to try to shake loose of Antonella's

formidable grip. She wanted the girl to grab her by the forearm and make skin contact. If they touched, Mattie could *read* her. . . .

"Come on!" Mattie complained. "What the heck?" She pulled and twisted, but Antonella was too strong.

"We appreciate our privacy," Antonella said melodramatically. "We aren't going to hurt you. We just want to protect ourselves until we know what's going on."

"If you turn me in, if they take me back to Barracks 14, I'll be put in 13. I'll go bonkers. You know I'm right!" Mattie's heart raced, her palms sweating. In theory, Joe and the Cryptos could and would prevent any such thing from happening. All Mattie had to do was fall asleep in order to cross over.

"That's up to you," her escort said bluntly. "What we do and don't do is up to us. And that has *nothing* to do with you."

"Nothing," Osanna echoed.

"You're bounty hunters?" Mattie said. She had no problem sounding afraid. "They let you out, give you some momentary freedom for returning past escapees?" It was a bluff. She and Joe thought they knew why they were here: to destroy the park.

"It's none of your business."

"What's my roommate supposed to think? She'll call in and ask where I am."

"You'll be back at work tomorrow," her escort said. "Don't get all in a twist. Right now you're an inconvenience. Don't make yourself into a problem. You wouldn't like being a problem."

23

For THE SECOND TIME, Mattie awoke as a hologram in front of the Partners statue. An orange moon occupied the granular sky, the air damp and heavy like a bathroom after a long shower. The lights of an airplane flashed and sparked. Slowly, she sat up and tried the arm-through-the-concrete again. Yes, she was a hologram.

A woman waved. A grown-up. She sat on a low wall in front of Sleeping Beauty Castle. She wore navy blue pants and a deeper navy zip sweatshirt with the letters *WDI* stitched on the front. Mattie approached and sat down next to her.

"I envy you," the woman said. "I've never done that myself."

"It's amazing."

The woman chuckled and nodded toward a small palm tree, recently transplanted, judging by the four wood supports. "In case you don't remember, that's where it is. The Return. That's where it will always be." It was tucked deep between the upper leaves of the transplanted tree.

"I've made contact," Mattie said, trying to keep the tremor from her voice. It wasn't easy. Her arms tingled, and when she purposefully touched the stone, she couldn't make her hand disappear inside. Fear.

The Imagineer pulled out a notebook and pen. She fiddled with her phone. She was recording their conversation now. "Go on. Tell me."

Mattie explained the bizarre events in the stockroom, the meeting in California Adventure, being blindfolded. She named Antonella, Osanna, and Humphrey.

"Do you know where you spent the night? Where they took you?"

"Not exactly. Maybe the tower over Carthay Circle? Inside Grizzly Peak? Someplace high and not too far from the Hollywood Backlot Stage. I took two hundred and fifty-four steps before I started climbing stairs."

"Impressive. They called it a mission? Their words?"

"Humphrey said that, yes. Those words. I think it was Antonella who didn't like him letting that slip."

"And right now you're asleep where?"

"That sounds so crazy, doesn't it?" Mattie drew back for a moment, mulling her situation silently. How had the Keepers trained themselves to think of this as normal? "They locked me in a closet. Sleeping bag. I'm not in any kind of danger."

"They let you use a washroom before going to sleep?"

"They did."

"Big or small?"

"Interesting! I hadn't thought that would be important, but I can see how it might limit the possibilities!"

The Imagineer waited her out. Then she repeated herself carefully. "Multiple stalls or just a single toilet?"

"Toilet and sink. No stall. The paper dispenser, it wasn't automatic or anything."

"Tile floor? Color of the walls?"

"You're good at this."

The Imagineer winced, attempting patience.

"Cement floor," Mattie said.

"Concrete." The woman made a note.

"Gray floor, white walls. Boring. It wasn't a public toilet, was it? So, what, I'm backstage? They, these Barracks Fairlies, are backstage somewhere. You think?"

"I'm just the one asking questions. People smarter than I am will discuss it."

"Analyze, you mean. I'm a project now." Mattie had been a project most of her life. She didn't like the feeling, and wondered anew how she'd put herself in such a spot.

"Don't get too wonky about it, sweetheart," the Imagineer said. Her eyes were kind. "Everyone here has your best interests at heart. You and your safety are all we care about right now. This other stuff is an afterthought."

"Nice of you to say."

"Joe wouldn't have it any other way. Trust us. It's a process, that's all. A means to an end. You snap your fingers, we will snatch you up and get you out of there."

"But you don't know where I am. And you won't hear me snap my fingers."

"Right. So back to it." The woman gave Mattie a moment to focus. "How many stairs? Do you recall? Did you count?"

"They carried me for some of them. I think they did it to mess me up, so I couldn't count, you know? I'm not sure if it was a single flight or a lot more. We went up, we went down. We went back up."

"They're careful." She made another note.

"Paranoid, more like it. And I think Antonella and her skinny sister are either in charge or threatening Humphrey to take charge. Humphrey was pretty nice and chill about everything, but he had a way about him. I think he would have answered my questions without pressure from Osanna. Princess Charmless."

The woman chuckled. She made another note, then asked, "Are you afraid for your safety? I want you to think clearly about that before answering. It's important. It's all that's important."

"I'm good." She paused. "Seriously, I am."

The Imagineer regarded her thoughtfully, then

nodded. "If you're sure. Mattie, I need you to count stair steps next time. Remember everything you can. Sounds. Smells. Especially sounds inside and out."

"Okay."

"You can pass a note to Teresa."

Mattie blinked, stunned. "She's one of yours?"

"Ours. Yes. She will pass along anything you want us to know. Spoken or written."

"Will it be you, tomorrow night?"

"If you're still at it. If Joe doesn't call it off. Cancel your DHI."

"Why would he do that?" Mattie questioned indignantly. "I made contact! That's what I was supposed to do." She wasn't saying what was really on her mind: she wanted to experience the thrill of crossing over again; she didn't want Joe taking away her DHI. She was just getting into this. Being a hologram was such a different sense, a magical, almost invisible feeling. She felt important, mysterious, but without the baggage of her ability. She felt connected to the Keepers. How could Joe even consider taking that away?

The woman's eyebrows flared in a way Mattie didn't think she meant them to.

"Twelve of them," Mattie said. "That's what worries you. It's a lot, twelve abilities. As someone who knows what she's talking about: that's a lot. But it's not the threat to me that should concern Joe, it's the threat to the park. Those Fairlies and their abilities are all the more reason to worry. Joe needs to know what they're up to and who's behind it."

The woman said nothing.

"Please. Talk to him."

"None of that's up to me," the woman said. "I'm just the messenger."

"Not really. That's *my* job. *I'm* the messenger. You mess up delivering the right message and this park is going to come undone. And that's going to be on you. Not me, not Joe."

The woman looked like Mattie had slapped her.

"So deliver the right message."

24

Jess's description of her Pinocchio dream left Amanda and the Keepers puzzled. What was its significance? No one dared suggest that it might not mean anything, but Jess could see doubt in the faces surrounding her, concern in their sideways glances as they strived to connect with each other.

"I know it sounds weird," she said, "but I'm sure it's one of the real ones."

"Me too," said Wayne, coming out from behind his workshop table. "There's a Pinocchio project under way. A moving puppet. Mechanical. Golly, I was asked to help on that, but I skipped it. Feels silly, I guess, now that we're here. But I know a couple of the guys, good fellows. I'm sure they'd give me a peek."

"You think there's a connection?" Finn glanced over at Amanda. Despite everything, despite the chaos around them, he couldn't stop thinking about her jumping onto the carousel to join them. What courage that had taken. What a risk. They had barely talked, just the two of them, since her arrival, and things were beginning to feel strained between them as a result. He didn't want that. He only wanted that look she'd just given him, wanted it in his mind like a photograph.

"They told me they were wanting to work from the acetates, the cels, but that someone had misplaced them. They needed folks like me to dig through the vaults up at the Studios. No such luck! Not for me, bub, I'll tell you what! I'm perfectly happy here where I am."

"Misplaced, as in missing?" Philby asked.

"Yeah, so?"

Philby stared down Jess, long and hard. "So? How does Jess dream about something that's gone missing, unless—" He let it hang there for the others to consider. "Right?" he asked.

Finn nodded. Maybeck looked a little lost. Charlene was raising and lowering her heels, as if ready to sprint, her mind elsewhere.

"Acetate is highly flammable," Philby said softly.

"Wait!" Maybeck said a little too loudly. Wayne startled. "Philabuster, are you saying someone stole these acetates and that Jess dreamed about whoever it was?"

"And that whoever it was, for reasons unknown, was setting the acetates on fire? Yes. That's exactly what I'm saying."

"Hollingsworth," said Willa. As was often her way, she'd been hovering on the outskirts of the conversation. "Remember what Nick told us about the man's grudge with the company? Hollingsworth was fired for—"

"Stealing animation cels," Philby said.

"Good grief," Wayne coughed out. "I know all about that. But . . . I mean . . . Jess's dream is connected to *that*? That's impossible, isn't it?"

"Nothing is impossible," Finn said, stealing a look in Amanda's direction, wishing she would glance over at him again.

"It's impossible they *aren't* connected." Professor Philby sounded as if he'd stepped up to the whiteboard. "Mathematically speaking, I mean. But it's entirely unrealistic to believe two such identical incidences, both connecting to the disappearance of the cels, could nonetheless be unconnected."

"Did anybody get that?" Maybeck asked.

Philby continued, his voice suddenly tentative. "Jess dreams the future. So, Hollingsworth is going to burn an acetate of Pinocchio sometime in the near future. We don't know when, or why. But it's going to happen."

"We need to know what's going on," Willa said softly.

"All of that is well and good, but someone please explain why people are breaking the arms off corpses with shovels," Finn said. "Jess had a vision of that happening as well. Can we take one dream at a time?"

Wayne was pacing back and forth, thinking furiously. "Do we actually believe the two dreams are connected? Jess dreamed them both, but . . . Yes, we know Hollingsworth is guilty of the theft of the cels. But we have no proof he's also connected to the graveyard and morgue."

"You haven't been at this as long as we have," Charlene said.

"Feels like sixty years," Maybeck said.

The group burst into laughter.

25

MATTIE AWOKE, SITTING UP HARD, as if someone had punched her in the gut. She blinked in the dark, taking a moment to identify the thin slice of light at the bottom of the closet door in front of her. The *locked* closet door.

Her heart raced, her body overly warm; she felt as if she'd run a long-distance race. She lay back down, the thin sleeping bag the Fairlies had provided barely cushioning the hard floor. It took a while for her to find sleep. Later, when she awoke again, she heard noises in the hallway, more activity than previously. She pounded on the door, tried to shout through it, but the sounds passed and faded, replaced by an uneasy silence.

Mattie crossed her legs yoga-style, and waited. No stranger to the dark, she nonetheless felt claustrophobic and agitated, reminded of her captivity at Barracks 14. Life in the Barracks had taught her to manage expectations, to not set unrealistic goals, to keep a measure of acceptance balanced with her dreams of what was possible.

By the time her door was unlocked and open she

forced back her anger and stayed in character. "Look," she said to Antonella, "I work at the Disney store today. I need to show up. I need to do my job."

"They want to see you," was all the girl said. She blindfolded Mattie and led her through faint voices in the hallway and, far in the distance, muted traffic sounds. Mattie stumbled quite by accident and, as she did, made contact with Antonella. She *read* the girl—it was as if a movie streamed through her: bits of conversation, faces, a gate, stairs. By the time Mattie found her balance, she knew what this girl had eaten for breakfast—oatmeal; what the girl looked like in front of a mirror—more ribs than flesh, pale skin reddened by mosquito or bedbug bites; that she'd recently stood on a balcony with a view of a parking lot and a piece of Space Mountain. Mattie saw a group meeting where Humphrey and a girl stood before the Fairlies like generals. She *read* that this girl had a crush on Humphrey.

"What do you think of Humphrey?" Mattie asked. She had the edge now.

"He's okay."

"Just okay?"

"Smart. Fair. I like him."

"Osanna?"

"She's my sister. What do you want me to say?"

"Do you think they'll let me join you guys?"

"You work for them. Disney. We could use some-one on the inside. But I should warn you: this is bigger than any one of us."

"Meaning?"

"We're here for a reason." This time Mattie tripped intentionally, hoping Antonella would be thinking about that mission. As the girl steadied Mattie, and the images flashed through Mattie's mind, she saw the Disneyland entrance jammed with guests trying to get out, Central Plaza with a massive amount of wild fire-works exploding above the castle *in the daytime*, a map with six oversize handwritten numbers on it, one of them—number 6—the Matterhorn.

Then, nothing. Her mental canvas went blank.

Mattie was led into a neatly ordered room where the girl Fairlies outnumbered the boys two to one. She counted ten in all, so two were elsewhere. Humphrey came over to her.

"I need to get to work," Mattie told him. "I'm going to be late!"

"We all do. You go when we say you go."

"Then please say it soon or I'll be late."

Humphrey glared at her disapprovingly.

"Look, I'm glad I found you guys, or you found me," Mattie said. "We're family. Yahoo. But I've got a good job and I want to keep it."

"We all have good jobs. Yours will depend on what you're willing to do for us."

"What's that supposed to mean? Do what?"

Humphrey explained, "We need you to *read* someone for us."

"For me to what?" Mattie gasped.

"You *read* Antonella just now, didn't you? Look, we need you to prove yourself. Maybe *read* a higher-up in the company. Maybe get that minute-by-minute schedule of theirs. Something like that."

Mattie felt as if she'd been punched in the throat. She coughed.

"Don't sweat it. We'll let you know when the time comes. And just so we're clear, I'm not worried about Antonella. She doesn't know enough to harm us by your *reading* her. But you're not touching me, and if you try again, I'll know you're a traitor. You got that? Curiosity? I understand. But you're on notice. Wear these, or we'll lock you back in that closet." He pulled a pair of black knit Minnie Mouse winter gloves from his back pocket. Mattie pulled them on, trying to appear as if she didn't care about the requirement. In fact, she was devastated.

"I've got to get to work," she said, caustically.

"Wait here." Humphrey left the room.

She considered searching through the belongings on the floor, but it wasn't worth the risk. If she remained part of their group, she'd find out everyone's name soon enough.

When Humphrey returned, he blindfolded her again, passed her off, and someone—Antonella?—led her downstairs. She counted nine landings as she descended. Once outside, Mattie could tell by the quiet that the park hadn't opened yet. That put the time before 9:00 a.m. She was still wearing her World of Disney costume, a look that wouldn't cause concern.

Mattie counted 317 steps to reach what she took to be an exit from one of the two parks. That, combined with the 254 steps last night, might allow her to triangulate a location for where they'd locked her up. Outside the park, they moved to the left, in the direction of Downtown Disney. That meant they'd exited California Adventure, not Disneyland. She continued to count steps before realizing Antonella had let go of her arm.

"Hello? Are you there?" she said, standing perfectly still. She repeated it more loudly this time. "Hello? Are you there?" The sound of running. The park had opened.

"Is who there? There are a lot of us here."

Mattie reached up and tentatively—so carefully!—untied the knot of the blindfold, expecting Antonella to stop her. She found herself face-to-face with a Disneyland guest, whose excess weight stretched out the red Mater T-shirt he wore.

"What's with the blindfold?" the man asked. "That looks like fun!"

"Not so much," Mattie said, stuffing it into her pocket. "Do you happen to have the time?"

"Eight forty," the man reported.

"Late," Mattie said. Thanking the man, she hurried off to World of Disney.

* * *

Mattie was in the midst of getting chewed out by a Cast Member for the horrendous condition of the storeroom when her supervisor, Teresa, intervened.

"It wasn't Mattie's fault," Teresa told the man. "Besides, it's being cleaned up as we speak."

"I can help clean," Mattie offered.

"Please."

Fifteen minutes later, a tired-looking Teresa joined Mattie in the disaster zone stockroom.

"He means well," she said. "It was a mess and he blamed you."

"Which is accurate! I'm sorry. I left in a hurry and didn't have time to clean up."

"Never seen so many hangers on the floor."

"Funny, right? I'll pick them up, promise," Mattie said. She looked around.

There were still several hundred hangers scattered

about, caught on clothing, on the walls, the floor. Mattie lowered her voice. "If I give you a note?" She waited, her heart pounding. This would confirm whether Teresa could be trusted.

A Latina, today with a waterfall of gorgeous hair, Teresa looked pretty even when deadly serious. She nodded faintly, barely dipping her chin.

Mattie didn't know whether to scream or faint or call 911. "Oh my gosh!" she whispered. "I need a pen."

26

Hollingsworth followed the Traveler down a well-lit, nondescript corridor. The vinyl tiles beneath their mud-caked shoes were marked with green and blue directional lines. At the end of the green track, two oversize swinging doors opened into a reception area.

The Traveler's fleshless bones propped up his baggy brown suit, making him look like something that should have been hanging from a line in a department store window display. He walked up to the woman reception-ist and waved his hand. For an instant, the air seemed oily, like the Traveler had opened a window to swirling water deep under the sea. Then it shifted, as powdery and misty as a chalk eraser banged against a blackboard. The woman's expression never altered.

"Thank you," the Traveler said, though the woman had not spoken. She had not moved or even blinked. Without bothering to check if Hollingsworth was trailing him, the Traveler pushed through a sec-ond set of swinging doors. "Lights, please," he said. Hollingsworth's trembling finger found the switch.

The room held an abundance of stainless steel. Plastic

tubes led from tables into drains, each one illuminated by a powerful lighting fixture. It was cold and quiet.

"Supply and demand," the Traveler said in his deep Cajun growl. "Ain't that the rule of law in these parts?"

"It's a law of free-market economies," Hollingsworth said. "Good old capitalism."

"Same thing, as far as I'm concerned. I demand, they supply."

"What did you do to that woman?" Hollingsworth wasn't sure he wanted the answer.

"Best stop your sniveling and get to work. We have fires to feed. We need us some kindling."

"Will she survive?"

The Traveler spun around, fast as a flash of lightning. "If I'd wanted her spirits to pass, then they'd 'a passed, friend. If I'd wanted you asking nincompoop questions, then I'd 'a told you so. You best learn to accept what you gone and asked for. Ain't that right? Yes, sir. You answer me: Yes, sir."

Hollingsworth wasn't in the habit of answering to anyone that way. But he was in no mind to test this creature's powers; he had a feeling he'd only seen a small sample of what this monstrous man could do. "Yes, sir."

"A vehicle set in motion stays in motion. Ain't that right?"

"Not exactly," Hollingsworth said.

But the Traveler didn't want an answer. He didn't want Hollingsworth speaking at all. The sticklike man slid open a heavy steel drawer and took hold of a cold, limp hand. A loud *snap* echoed throughout the room. Hollingsworth looked away, fighting to keep himself from throwing up.

"Fingers keep us alive, ney? They is what makes our fire come to life, youse see?" said the wraith. "In life there is death and in death there is life." Another loud *crack*. "Find me some shears," he instructed. "I'm going to need a snip here and there if I'm to collect us our kindling."

27

MATTIE'S THIRD DAY with the Fairlies went much like the first: blindfolded, released before opening hour so she could work, meet back up with an escort after work. Each night around 1:00 a.m., she found herself lying near the Partners statue. With little to report, she typically spoke briefly to the Imagineer waiting for her, and then returned. The return jolted her awake, shook her to the core. But she was getting used to it, even enjoyed it. She'd come to accept and understand what was happening to her instead of questioning it. She was a DHI. In her own way she was now a Kingdom Keeper. With this mystique came a responsibility. Joe had put her into the parks for a reason.

"If you're going to keep treating me like a prisoner," she told Humphrey on the morning of the fourth day, "I'll take a pass. Don't bother sending anyone for me tonight. I'm sick of this."

"We had to make sure no one was watching you. That we were safe. No one person can jeopardize the team."

The last part sounded memorized or programmed, like Humphrey had been hypnotized before being sent.

Mattie wondered if that might explain the team, as he called it, and their willingness to go after Disneyland. That, in turn, caused her to question if there wasn't some small piece of each Fairlie that objected to the mission.

"Why are you here, anyway? What are you doing?" she asked him, trying to sound naive.

"We're doing what we were assigned to do, and that involves not asking questions."

"Is that right?"

"That's right."

"So the Barracks are forcing you to use your abilities just like they always have."

His face screwed into a knot. "It's not like that." He didn't sound convinced.

"So what is it you're supposed to do for them?"

"If you want answers like that, if you want to join us, you will need to prove yourself."

"I don't want to join you. Who said I did?"

"I think you do or you wouldn't look around for one of us at the end of work each night."

"I like having company, it's true. I've been alone for a long time. So what? I like that I know a couple of faces here. It's comforting. But why would I want to join something I know nothing about? Why won't you tell me?"

"Prove yourself and I'll tell you about it."

"Don't go all Maze Runner on me, Humphrey! You know I have abilities just like everybody else in this place. Test me? Prove myself? Let me take off these gloves and I'll prove myself."

"Not on me," he said. "On someone else."

"Who?"

The coffeepot's hot tray spit, sounding like a snake. A Fairlie came in and opened the refrigerator and found a bag of carrots and chewed loudly. He looked at Mattie and Humphrey and, feeling the tension, left the break room.

"Do you know a man named Joe Garlington?"

"Never heard of him." She tried not to look too freaked-out.

"Kim Irvine?"

Other Fairlies passed outside the break room in the hallway, and Mattie had the feeling if she made a run for it, she'd be caught within seconds.

"Everyone knows Kim Irvine! Not to speak to. I don't mean that. But I know who she is, what she looks like."

Humphrey lowered his voice. "We want you to *read* her."

Mattie barked laughter. "You want me to *read* Kim Irvine? I don't even know Kim Irvine! You think I can just touch someone and download every thought they've ever had? It doesn't work like that, Humphrey! It's very specific. Surgical, you might say. Believe it or not, it's tricky looking into someone else's brain."

"Master key," he said. "Your search string for Kim Irvine is 'master key location.'"

"Is it?" Mattie said, failing to disguise her surprise. The Barracks Fairlies wanted a master key to the park's locked doors: stores, utilities, security, administration. That couldn't be good.

"Do you have a problem with that?"

"I . . . suppose . . . not. And if I get it, when I get it, then what?"

"You'll report back to me."

"You sound like them, you know that? Remember when you first came to the Barracks? How weird and military it felt? The grown-ups ordering us around. Making us file reports. All the exercise and stuff? Making us stand in lines like little soldiers? The way they kept reminding us how special we were and how no one understood us the way they did. Remember that?"

"Your point being?" He sounded upset.

"They conditioned us!" She heard the sorrow in her own voice, but couldn't stop it. "You. Me. All of us! Why do you think I had to escape? Because I didn't want to end up like you, Humphrey. I didn't want to end up talking and acting like them."

Humphrey looked away, as if there was something to see on the break room's blank wall. The vein in his neck pulsed rapidly. He blinked repeatedly.

Mattie said, "Look, I'll do this for you. But then that's it. No more blindfolds, no more treating me like this. I escaped the Barracks for a reason. I won't live like this."

"We all paid for your escape. Don't forget that."

She recalled how the community had been treated following Jessica and Amanda's escape. The supervision. The questioning.

"Yeah," she said, "well, I'm sorry about that. But I'm not spending another night in that locked closet. If that's not part of our deal then you can look for the master key yourself."

Humphrey grunted. Mattie took that as acquiescence.

"Kim Irvine," Mattie said. "This isn't going to be easy, you know?"

28

"**W**HY NOW, SO LATE?" Nick Perkins followed Ezekiel Hollingsworth through a Cast Member entrance from South Harbor Boulevard into California Adventure. As a growing eighth-grade boy, Nick , who had once befriended Jess, Amanda, and Mattie as a research expert on all things Disney, needed a few inches before high school. He also needed twenty pounds and a new wardrobe. The chinos and polo shirt gave him a chess club look. He came off as somewhere between ten and fourteen years old; with a mop of brown hair, he was thin and handsome and looked like he belonged in a Harry Potter movie.

"Because we're meeting some friends. As to why you: I think you may know the enemy better than I," Zeke replied.

"Enemy? Like your brother?"

Zeke continued without breaking stride.

Nick waited, then spoke. "Let me just say this, I think you need me."

"That's modest of you."

The backstage area resembled a light industrial

warehouse park. The attractions occupied three- and four-story, flat-roofed, aluminum-sided rectangular monstrosities. Scattered on either side of the access road, cream-colored house trailers served as small offices and break rooms. There were maintenance sheds, buildings for refrigerated food storage, and gas generators in case the electricity failed. Everything was neat and orderly and surprisingly clean.

Zeke knew his way around, suggesting he wasn't strictly a Disneyland Dapper Dan Cast Member. He was likely more experienced in the world of Disney than he let on. His father had been part of the company's beginning. His brother was attempting to be part of its undoing.

"You're Ezekiel, the son of Amery, brother of Amery Junior. Your father—"

Zeke cut him off. "My father killed himself. He was humiliated, despondent. Only my brother still holds a grudge. Rexx and I see the situation more for what it was. Our father stole Disney acetates—animation cels. They had little or no value at the time, but he stole them anyway, and they fired him, as any employer would do. From then on, his life went downhill. We kids lived through it. He couldn't let it go.

"After my father's death, Rexx moved to India and started a new, prosperous life. I joined the company—

I love everything about Disney! It's just my brother Amery who can't move on. He seems to believe he owes it to our father to continue what Father started. Call it retribution. Avenging Walt's curse on him. It's a fool's errand. And I'm sick and tired of our family name being dragged through the mud."

"Does that have anything to do with why we're here?" Nick asked, looking bewildered. "Your mother was Bethany Blair Longfellow. She left you and your family after your father lost his job with Disney. That may have contributed to your father's . . . condition."

"You mean suicide. Astonishing!" muttered Zeke. "You're wrong. Our mother left us to take the only job available to her at the time. She supported us. All of us! Mother defended Father to the bitter end. Failure like that, for a man of those times . . . it proved too much, that's all. It was his undoing. Our family's undoing. Amery, being the oldest, saw the most. It scared him. Scarred him. Permanently."

"Apologies," said Nick.

"Here we are," said Zeke, as if their brief conversation had not taken place. "A Bug's Land."

Despite all the lights flooding the Tower of Terror's exterior, Nick and Zeke were enveloped by darkness as they entered the nearby jungle area of A Bug's Land.

"Can I ask a stupid question?"

"Keep looking straight ahead." Zeke spoke so softly his words were nearly lost on the breeze.

"That ladybug thing back there. I think she was looking in the other direction a moment ago."

"We're being watched. That's Francis. Be respectful."

Nick stuttered. "B-but she's p-plastic. Her head can't move."

"Is she? Are you sure? We're to wait here," Zeke explained, "under the only four-leaf clover." The clovers were the size of streetlamps.

"Let's hope it brings us some luck, because I think we could use it."

Anticipation is a kind of venom. It seeps into your bloodstream like a toxin, either charging you with the adrenaline of excitement or the poison of dread. Over the course of the next few minutes, Zeke and Nick shuddered with each rattle of palm fronds, every revved engine out on the street or swoosh of birds overhead. A cat crossed in front of them. Nick jumped.

"Did you see that? That's bad luck, not good!"

"It was a gray cat, not black."

"Whatever. It crossed our path!" Nick paused, looking behind them at the tall attraction. His rattled nerves forced him to speak. "Did you know the Tower of Terror was inspired by a TV show?" Zeke said nothing. "Also, there are stories that the TV show was based on a freak accident in the early 1950s. Lightning and—"

"Nick, *please*." Zeke, too, appeared on edge, or expectant.

Nick was hearing things. *Squeaking or voices.*

"Be on alert," Zeke said.

"Do you really think th—"

"Shh!" Zeke had had enough.

Not squeaking, but voices. Definitely voices. High voices, almost too high to hear. But heard they were.

"Is that them?"

"Who's the boy? Do you recognize him?"

"Do we trust them?"

"The boy looks trustworthy."

"You and boys!"

"Quiet, please, everyone!"

All different voices. Nick wanted to tell them to shut up. He wanted to run. Zeke was smiling. The voice they heard ask about trustworthiness was that of a young woman. An agreeable, almost familiar voice.

"Stand still," Zeke said. "No sudden movement. No overreaction."

"What's going on?"

Nick did not move. Zeke seemed poised for the unexpected.

When it finally happened, Nick nearly screamed.

29

Nick rubbed his eyes. He'd heard stories about the Kingdom Keepers. He'd seen plenty of weird stuff since meeting Amanda and Jess, but seeing Anna appear from the shadows off the terrace stole his breath. Anna, of all the characters! She was one of his favorites—he loved *Frozen*. Now she wore a green fur-trimmed vest over a white shirt and forest-green leather pants.

"How can I see them?" Nick asked. "How can *you* see them? I thought only DHIs could!"

"I'll let you in on a little secret: if they want you to see them, you'll see them. But it isn't often they do."

"Hello?" Nick said, unsure if an animated character could hear him, if Anna was real or an apparition.

Anna stepped aside, revealing the incredibly tan Nani, from *Lilo and Stitch*, who wore a lime-green crop top and blue shorts. Nani waved and Nick waved back timidly.

"Are you seeing this, too?" he asked Zeke.

"Son, tonight you will see and do things you'd never believe were possible. And you won't ever tell a soul."

Flynn and Aladdin were next. They stepped out of

some thick bamboo. Flynn's biceps strained the shirt beneath his dark blue leather vest. He had more facial hair than in *Tangled* and an air of strength and impertinence that seemed to say: *Go ahead and try.* Aladdin, by contrast, looked wimpy and smallish, which surprised Nick.

Zeke stretched himself taller and cleared this throat, obviously preparing to speak. He appeared apprehensive. Nick gave him his full attention.

"I'm Ezekiel," Zeke said, addressing Flynn, "friend of the Apprentice and the Scullery Maid. You will please introduce me to them."

The change in Zeke's bearing, his formality, and the tone of his pronouncement created a moment of heightened tension. He continued, "You must inform them at once. There is no time to waste! This comes directly from Mr. Garlington."

Flynn and Aladdin stood a bit taller.

"You will please wait!" Flynn said. He nodded to Aladdin, who took off back through the bamboo. Anna and Nani stood by, though Anna had raised her open palm toward Nick. He didn't believe she had the power of Elsa, but he wasn't about to test her.

"Son," Zeke said to Flynn, "you do not want to treat us this way. You do not want Mr. Garlington looking upon you unfavorably. I have a job to do. We all have a job to do. In a couple of minutes, we're going to be working together anyway, so this stance of yours isn't helping."

"What will we be doing together?" Nick asked.

"Mind yourself," Zeke said harshly, only for Nick's ears. "Stop ga-ga-ing, Nick. This is serious. It's business."

"I'm talking to characters from my favorite movies, and you're telling me to get serious?"

"Yes, I am."

Nick rocked impatiently from toe to heel. "Okay."

"Halt!" Flynn called out as Nick took a careful step toward Zeke.

"Let him pass!" a squeaky voice called from the direction of the bamboo wall.

Looking in that direction, Nick saw silhouettes. Vaguely familiar silhouettes. Silhouettes that made the childish glee nearly jump out of him again. But he kept in mind Zeke's caution. Aladdin was one of the shapes. The voice had been all Mickey. The idea that Disney characters—living, breathing Disney characters—could possibly exist caused him to try to wake himself up. He had to be dreaming. But he wasn't! Unable to help himself, Nick released a gasp of incredulity as Mickey Mouse emerged from the thick jungle. He wasn't the tuxedoed Mickey Mouse who hugged kids and signed autographs in the park; he had a smaller head and a longer, more pointed nose. His eyes weren't the size of soccer balls, like the park Mickey. This was a four-foot-tall mouse standing on his hind legs. He wore a deer-hide shirt and black capri pants covering his fur. Nick had studied archival photos of Disneyland on opening day, of the odd-looking Mickey and Minnie, more ratlike than cute and huggable. But the Mickey in front of Nick wore fire-engine-red shorts that rode high on his waist, yellow shoes, and oversize white gloves. He seemed slightly older but not elderly, curious yet composed. He projected a sense of calm control, but his eyes were deliberately searching, as if he saw more than others.

"Who called for me?" Mickey asked, giving them an oddly shaped mouse smile.

Nick was surprised to hear Mickey's voice. The park Mickey never spoke, and even rumors about the Keepers, and Amanda's and Jess's accounts of the events, said that the real Mickey never spoke. The other characters had always served as translators. Perhaps Mickey had changed his mind about not talking, or the technology shift had somehow led to more people believing in him talking, fueling his speech. Whatever the reason, Mickey and Zeke carried on a conversation like it was the most normal thing in the world. "I did," Zeke said. "Mr. Garlington would appreciate the help of you and the other characters. There is trouble in the Tower. A girl, a human girl, has been taken captive."

"The Witches?" Mickey said, cocking his head to the right.

"Humans. Youngsters. Agents of a menace. This is Nick, who knows the girl and something about the group who may be the ones who've taken her."

"Hello, Nick," said Mickey.

"He . . . llo." Nick's voice cracked.

Zeke addressed the mouse, who maintained a careful separation from them, with Aladdin and Flynn in between. "Nick is the right age and look to be our agent."

Am I? Nick thought, though did not say.

"Nick will establish the location of the captive and estimate the enemy's numbers. Your group will block the exits. No one leaves without my permission," Zeke said.

"That's agreeable, Ezekiel. Gee whiz, isn't this exciting?" Mickey announced loudly, "It's okay, everyone! Come out, come out!"

When nothing happened, no one showed, Nick looked to Zeke for some kind of explanation. But before Nick spoke, the unthinkable happened.

30

W HEN MARTY SKLAR, editor of the *Disneyland Daily News*, chased down Wayne, he had no idea of the events he set in motion.

As a collector of news, Marty had come across a quirky story.

"You and your friend Jessica asked me to keep an eye out for any more graveyard vandalism," Marty told Wayne as they nibbled on strawberry snow cones. They sat comfortably, taking in the view of the Plaza. Since opening day three weeks earlier, the crowds had only grown. Women and young ladies wore dresses or skirts with blouses; young men donned shirts and ties, and their fathers were in sport coats and ties. Lines formed at the ticket counters for each ride, with sometimes a wait as long as twenty minutes. The sound of guns popping carried from the Shooting Gallery, while calliope tunes battled in a conflict of melody and volume.

"I sure did," Wayne said. "Did someone raid another graveyard?"

"Not exactly." Marty slid a folded newspaper across the metal table. "Third column, down at the bottom."

It was a city paper with ads for Studebaker con-
vertibles, Jiffy Popcorn, and Lucky Strike cigarettes.
Wedged between the ads were a number of small
stories.

BIZARRE BREAK-IN
CONFOUNDS POLICE

MARTHA STANDLER

Los Angeles Police are investigating a break-in at
the morgue of Pacific Hospital, where it is alleged
two men subdued a receptionist and subsequently
defaced a number of cadavers. Motivation for the
crime is unknown and also under investigation,
according to sources. A detective who wished to
remain anonymous suggested the crimes could be
the work of the occult or Communist activity.

"It may be some kind of ritual or political statement. We ain't sure at this time," the detective said.
"The investigation is ongoing."

Wayne read the piece twice. Then he pushed the
paper away.

Marty said, "I thought it of possible interest on
account of the grave and everything. It mentioned the
occult and dead bodies and such."

"Yes! Thank you," Wayne said.

"You okay, Wayne? You lost a shade or two."

"What do you suppose they mean by 'defaced'?" Dust rose from a sparsely planted garden as a dust devil took wind. The not-unpleasant scent of horses followed the passing of the wagon circling the Plaza hub.

"Maybe they drew crosses on them. Something like that."

"Do you happen to know this reporter?"

"Nah. But I'm pretty darn sure I could give her a jingle for ya. What's the plan, Stan?"

Wayne furrowed his brow, thinking hard. "Maybe she's heard rumors but couldn't print it without witnesses. It's worth asking. I'd like to know what she means by this defaced business." The buzz of the go-karts from Autopia carried from a distance like flies on the inside window screen dying to get out.

"I can check for you. No sweat, Chet."

"If you can't get her to talk, Marty . . ." Wayne paused, locking eyes with the shorter, stockier man. "You might try telling her the bodies are missing forearms and hands."

"How's that?"

The buzzing of the go-karts grew louder, or maybe that was just Wayne's sensitivity.

"Yeah. Hands. Just tell her you're trying to confirm

it was the hands that were taken. If that doesn't pique her interest, nothing will."

"And why would I say that, Wayne? How would I know something like that? 'Cause she's going to ask. She's a reporter. You understand? Reporters ask questions."

"Tell her a cousin of yours works on an earth digger, and the police used it to excavate the coffins of that graveyard thingamajig."

"Exhume, not excavate." Marty paused, narrowing his eyes at Wayne.

"If that doesn't get a rise out of her, I'd be surprised."

"Sure got a rise out of me," Marty said.

The two young men stuffed their faces into the paper cones, tongues seeking out more sweet ice.

"Hands?" Marty said at last, licking his sticky lips.

"You didn't hear it from me," Wayne said.

31

FROM AROUND CORNERS of buildings, behind hedges, and out of darkened doorways came a remarkable cast of characters: Dash and Bob from *The Incredibles*; Stitch and Kristoff; Rapunzel and Jasmine. The Blue Fairy appeared with Mulan. Last to step forward, more beautiful than a crystal lake or a field of roses, was Cinderella. Though dressed in her work clothes, a simple brown dress, she seemed to attract all the light and quiet the wind. Nearly everyone released a sigh of contentment at the sight of her.

All but Mickey, whose twitching nose and whiskers appeared to be catching a scent.

Nick couldn't take his eyes off Cinderella. "Aha! The Scullery Maid," he accidentally spoke aloud.

Sounding impatient, Zeke explained things to Nick. "A girl named Mattie—do you know Mattie?—is being held captive inside the Tower of Terror, by the residents of Barracks 14. We both know who owns the Barracks."

Nick nodded. "Your older brother, Amery."

"Correct. You're of an age and size where you can blend in with these kids who are holding her. At least briefly; long enough for you to confirm her location."

"You're repeating yourself. I got this when you talked to Mickey."

"I wasn't sure you were paying attention."

Nick paced in a tight circle, mind working furiously to put the pieces together. "Kids? Fairlies? There are Fairlies in there?"

"Yes. Rebel Barracks Fairlies with unknown, perhaps dangerous powers." In contrast to Nick's frantic movement, Zeke was very still, perhaps gauging Nick's nerves. "We will devise a plan to get her out once you've established the layout and Mattie's whereabouts."

"So the characters are backup?" Nick said, still puzzled.

"Gosh! I believe that question is meant for me," Mickey said, stepping forward. He gave Nick a grave nod. "You are friends with the Children of Light. We are indebted to them. We will always be indebted to them. Of course we will help."

"So once you have this plan," he said to Zeke, "what makes you think I can pull it off alone?"

"You don't have to!" The boy's voice came from over Nick's left shoulder. "I'll help you."

He was younger, with both an air of innocence and yet confidence about him. He moved in a shuffle, his shoes worn on the inside of his arch. Despite his substantial girth, Dillard didn't throw a shadow. His face, round and pixieish, was too large for his thin arms and legs. He looked like a balloon that needed more air, almost transparent at certain angles.

"Who . . . what . . . are you?" Nick asked.

"My name's Dillard. And Finn is . . . was . . . my best friend."

Nick stepped closer and offered his hand to shake. Dillard lifted his as well, but Nick's hand passed through it without even a whisper. The boy looked transparent for a reason! He was—

"A DHI?" Nick said, astonished.

Dillard smirked. "Don't hold it against me." He looked behind and called out to an empty pathway, "It's all good!"

From around the corner stepped Mattie.

32

"I DON'T MEAN TO BE RUDE," said Zeke as he stepped up to Mattie, "but this entire arrangement is being made on your behalf. We've all gone to a great deal of trouble to rescue you. And yet, here you are, in no need of rescue. I, for one, need an explanation—and possibly, along with my friends here, an apology." He motioned to the league of Disney characters.

Mattie's lips parted, her mouth opened, but before she could speak a word, she just shook her head and stepped through Zeke like a phantom. The man spun around, brushing his front as if he'd spilled something down himself. He looked thoroughly and utterly confused and frightened.

"Sorry," Mattie said. "It seemed easier to show and not tell."

"You too?" Nick said, hurrying over to her.

"I'm in there," Mattie said, pointing to the Tower. "My real self." She took in all the characters, astonished and impressed, and asked Nick, "Why are they here?"

He explained the plan to her.

Mattie addressed Mickey and Cinderella, and spoke

reverently. "I don't think I can even explain how I'm feeling right now, but I want you to know I'm a huge fan." She gave them a wide, warm smile, and then turned so everyone could hear her. "Of all of you! I can't believe you would do this for me."

"For you and for Mr. Garlington!" Mickey said.

Mattie looked quizzically at Nick, who said, "I'll explain later."

Mattie's DHI went solid as she hugged Mickey. She curtsied—quite well—to Cinderella, who nodded at her regally. "Again," she said, "thank you all for being here."

After a short huddle between Zeke, Mattie, and Mickey, the plan was settled. Mulan, Flynn, and Kristoff, along with Dillard and Nick inside, would divide into two teams.

Mattie pulled Zeke aside and explained. "The Barracks Fairlies' leader, a guy named Humphrey, assigned me to . . ." She didn't have time to explain her ability. "To *ask* Kim Irvine for the location of a park master key."

"She won't tell you that."

"I can be persuasive. Let's leave it at that. I was being watched, monitored, but I managed to let her know what I was doing—who I was doing it for. I assume she let Joe know and that's why you're here."

In fact, Mattie had *reached* the thought, planting

it into Kim Irvine while simultaneously *reading* the woman for the location of the park's master key. "She knew someone was going to try to steal it. The attempted theft was prevented, and security might have caught the Barracks Fairlie, except it was Minara, a shape-shifter who turned herself into a snake and got out of there before they figured out what had happened. Are you following this?"

"I am. You provided inside information and someone you're calling a Barracks Fairlie nearly got caught."

"I'm being heavily supervised. They can't prove that I had anything to do with Minara almost getting caught, but they're suspicious. They don't want to let me leave the tower, even for work. If I escape on my own it will look one way. If someone rescues me, it's something different. That's about all I can say." Mattie pointed to the Tower of Terror. "And that's why you're here—at least I think so."

"You're in trouble," Zeke said, "and Joe wants you back."

"The thing is, you won't catch all of them. No way. They're Fairlies. It's not going to happen. I think Joe's probably using characters to help out so that it doesn't look like security is involved. He wants it to look more organic."

"I wouldn't know about that," Zeke said.

"Look, Joe doesn't know what he's up against. These particular Fairlies have been brainwashed, the same way we all were, but even more so. They'll hurt the characters, maybe worse. Mattie noticed a change in the man, the look of a major realization overtaking his face. "Something I said?"

"The Disney characters will guard the exit and entrance. That's all. That's how Joe wanted it. Nick's assigned to find you and get you out."

Mattie nodded thoughtfully.

"You have a problem with that," Zeke said.

"Joe sent Dillard's DHI as backup. That tells me he knows it'll be rough going for Nick. I want out of there at some point, don't get me wrong! And Joe wants it to look like two of my friends are trying to rescue me. I get that."

"But . . ." Zeke said.

"But it's dangerous." Mattie hung her head. It wasn't a move she'd modeled for the computers, so the motion was jerky and disconcerting to Zeke. "I have another plan, the only real way I think we can stop these guys. And yes, I need to be rescued in order for it to work."

Mattie paused, thinking of Nick. He was a little too animated for her liking. She understood that being in the presence of real, living Disney characters—ones that walked, talked, and were now joining him as allies in a possible confrontation with wayward Fairlies—was a lot to process, especially for the first time. He was bubbling over, running at the mouth like a rock star's fangirl.

It made sense. This was Nick, a boy who'd devoted years to researching the threat posed to Disney by the Overtakers and Amery Hollingsworth. Nick, who now realized the stories were true. In his time working with the Keepers, he'd met some mean kids inside Cars Land. But Mickey Mouse? Anna? Not the costumed variety, but the real things?

Mattie excused herself and moved over to Nick. "Are you sure you're up for this? You look a little freaked-out."

"A little freaked-out? Yeah, for sure. But I'm okay," Nick replied. "Zeke gave me this lecture already."

"It's not a lecture. The Fairlies in there," Mattie said, "I know what they can do. It's weird but extraordinary stuff. Like being a supernaturally fast runner. There's a kid who can overheat energy sources, like lightbulbs. Explode them. They're freak shows. I oughta know. But remember, Nick, most of their abilities are more thought than action. I've never fought them. I wouldn't want to. If they try to fight, distract them. Their abilities require extreme concentration. Don't give them any time for that."

"If that was supposed to be a pep talk, it failed miserably," said Nick.

"I've got this," said Dillard, listening in. "I can do what he can't."

"What makes you think so?" Mattie asked.

Dillard waved his arm. It swiped through Mattie's hologram.

"That's nice at parties, but it won't help Nick unless you can channel it. Look," she said, "the giant spider that messed up everything over by Thunder Mountain? That was a girl named Minara. The shape-shifter. The blackout in Tomorrowland? Santiago, the one I was telling you about, the guy who can mess up energy sources. Fairlies don't do party games. Jess, Amanda, and me, when we were at Barracks 14, we knew the grown-ups were lying to us. They said we were under government observation. Sure! I'm sure they made it all up, made so many of us feel special. Made us feel important to someone. Anyone." She paused and took a deep breath, her eyes suddenly distant and searching. "Somebody tell me this: Why do we always want to be different? What's so special about that? Because I'm telling you, when you're as different as I am, all you want to be is like everyone else."

Then Mulan moved toward them with the gracefulness of a dancer. "We are all set," she said.

"Getting in there won't be easy. They have guards posted all over the place," Mattie said.

"Nick?" Zeke asked. "Any secrets about the ride?"

"Sure, but you're not going to like them," Nick said. "Have any of you heard of the pit?" He won blank stares from the group. Addressing Dillard, he asked, "Can holograms climb?"

"Light as air, fast as light," Dillard said, beaming.

"Yeah? Well, not me," said Nick. "I'm going to need some help."

"Why?" Mattie asked.

"There are cameras all over the place, including the elevators, and a security room with a bunch of screens on the ground floor."

"These Fairlies will know that," Mattie said. "They'll be monitoring."

"Exactly! The stairs are out because of cameras. And anyway, the doors on the ground floor are locked," Nick said.

"So?" Mattie was clearly annoyed with Nick. "There is or is not a way in?"

"Fun fact: the doors on the upper balconies are *not* locked."

"And you know this for sure?" Zeke asked.

"I do. One of our two teams can get in by climbing the outside of the Tower to a balcony. The other team . . . it's a little tricky, but doable. I'll take that group."

Mulan spoke up. "Kristoff and Dash will join us. This gives us both speed and strength. And I will have my bow," she said, reaching over her back and hoisting up her weapon.

Zeke touched her bow in wonder, but then motioned her to put it away. "No one is shooting anyone tonight."

Mulan seemed disappointed. She signaled Kristoff and Dash, who both joined the group.

Mattie focused on Zeke, who looked at Nick. "We need two plans," Zeke said. "Two teams. If we fail, it puts Mattie—the real Mattie—at serious risk. Divide and conquer. Double our odds."

Nick blinked and swallowed. "Mattie, I'm going to need some insider information. Fairlie stuff." He took a deep breath. "You're not going to like this."

33

THE TEAMS OF FLYNN, Dash, and Dillard jumped a low fence and hurried toward the gift shop. Flynn provided a leg up for the two, and, using a downspout, climbed up and over and dropped onto a flat roof. Interrupted by enormous ventilation ducts, the flat roof held two sets of metal bars, like jungle gyms, to which were affixed massive theatrical lights. Their beams were trained on the attraction's lightning-struck facade. Both light stands had stepladders alongside.

Flynn moved seamlessly, as if he had planned everything. Grabbing and adjusting the nearest stepladder, he placed it beneath the section of Spanish-tiled roof that pointed up toward the hotel sign. He motioned for the others to move quickly. They climbed the ladder and pulled up higher, ascending the slippery heights. Flynn offered his interlocked hands as a step. Dash, then Dillard made quick work of it, using the balcony's rungs. They were moving as a team now, two balconies, three. Higher and higher.

"This is the fifth floor," Dillard whispered. "The light deck, like Nick said."

Flynn crossed and tested a doorknob. It twisted. "He was right!" he called back. "Not locked!"

The hallway was dark, with simple vinyl flooring and bare walls. It looked like a school basement or hospital emergency room corridor. Dillard's hologram moved silently. Dash and Flynn followed.

Soon they reached the door to the stairs. Inside, Dillard pointed out an abundance of muddy shoe prints. They could have belonged to Cast Members, but Cast Members didn't let things get dirty. The mud implied non-Disney intruders. The idea was to figure out which floor the Fairlies were using. At that point, they would get Dillard into place. Once Mulan, Nick, and Kristoff were established as backup, Dillard would attempt the rescue.

"We follow the prints," Dillard said in an electronic whisper.

"What about the cameras?" Flynn asked, not knowing what a camera was. But he'd heard them mentioned as a reason not to take the stairs.

"Ground entrance only," Dillard said. "We couldn't take the stairs from the ground entrance. We're good." Down they went. Lower and lower. Darker and darker.

34

ALL SOUNDS BECAME CLOSE; Nick could hear his own breathing as a raspy pulse, like sandpaper at work.

Five stories below ground level, he, Mulan, and Kristoff reached the bottom, a bunker-like area that smelled of motors, electricity, and oil. Nick coughed. Mulan slipped past him. From the start, she'd assumed the role of leader.

Unlike the two Disney characters, Nick understood the danger of entering an area controlled by agents of Amery Hollingsworth Jr. These Fairlies would have been handpicked to disrupt and destroy Disneyland. They were powerful adversaries. The first attacks—the spider, the ramming of the *Columbia*, and the power outage—had proven as much.

Mulan made about as much noise as dandelion seeds on the wind. An extremely faint light shone from somewhere overhead, turning the air chalky. Nick caught up to her and followed her down a short set of concrete stairs.

"The pit," he said, looking straight up. "That's the bottom of one of the ride elevators."

In some distant part of his brain, he marveled at the sight; he knew kids who would drool to be in his shoes.

"It reminds me of the dungeon in Arendelle Castle," Kristoff said. "An area my dear friends know nothing about."

"Let's skip the nostalgia," Nick muttered. He didn't like the thought of a dungeon.

Mulan's bow, worn across her back, scraped the wall, the sound like Styrofoam stuck in a cardboard box. The three froze, waiting expectantly for someone to hear. Nothing happened—though their eyes adjusted and their heartbeats slowed back down. At last, Mulan pointed out a service ladder, built into a wall. Her shifty, abrupt movements as she approached it made her look like an insect.

"Hold off," Nick said. Mulan shot him a look of confusion. "Too dangerous."

Mulan didn't like being told what to do, but she returned to his side. To support his claim, Nick indicated an electronic control box mounted to the concrete. Then he pointed up. "That ladder on the wall provides access to the elevator repair. There's no escape hatch on the bottom. The bottoms of all the cars are sealed and fireproofed. The ladder will only get us as high as the bottom of the car. This box controls the two elevator cars in this shaft. The cars don't stop here at the bottom—they unload at ground level. But they do fall this far, and they do pause before racing back up. So that's our chance."

"Our chance?" Kristoff questioned.

"See those pipes on the bottom of the car?" Nick said. "That's our way up."

"You think you can hold on, mountain man?"

"Do you two have issues, or what?" Nick asked.

"She is always on Elsa's side," Kristoff said dismissively. "Not one of Anna's greatest admirers."

"That is not true at all!" Mulan burst out. "Do I love Olaf? Yes! Sven? You must ask? As for the two girls . . . so much fuss! I know plenty of girls."

"Issues," Nick said, nodding.

Something invisible and more toxic than burning electricity hung in the air, as thick as fog. Nick sensed it, could practically taste it: it wasn't his new character friends. No. They were not alone.

35

Dash stopped Flynn and Dillard as they faced a long hallway.

"The kitchen is down there on the right," Dash said. "It's a corner room with windows that look into the hallway. If we stay low, we can slip beneath the windows and keep out of sight."

"What about the two guards?" Dillard asked.

"Past the kitchen on the left, there's another corridor. The two guys are down there."

"No sign of the others? Nick's group?"

Dash shook his head, his hair flopping. He squinted his eyes shut inside his mask. "There's a stairway at the end, though. Hang on." Dash zipped away, only to reappear two seconds later, not even slightly out of breath. "Another stairway at the end of this hallway, too. FYI: the movie's just about over. If we're going to do this, it has to be now."

"So let's get going," Flynn said. "Once we get upstairs, I'll keep our line of retreat open. It'll be up to you and Dillard to find the girl."

"Good plan," said Dash.

Dillard looked a lot less certain. "How is it that you guys are so heroic and optimistic? There's a dozen of them. Three of us. And they have such bizarre skills that we don't even know what they are, much less how to counter them."

"Look, in my story I get the girl," Flynn said, "and Dash's family beats Syndrome. It's just the way we roll. And when Dash says 'now,' he means now."

Dillard nodded, clearly shaken.

"Relax," Dash said, trying but failing to put a friendly hand on the older boy's glowing shoulder. "You're a hologram and we're . . . well . . . us. What could possibly go wrong?"

"I can think of a few things—a dozen to be exact."

36

"DID YOU ARRANGE THIS?" Amanda asked. The 1955 night sky over Anaheim glowed a dull yellow, but stars peeked through in ways that didn't happen in the present.

"What, exactly?" Finn said, returning a question with a question, something that he knew annoyed Amanda.

"You and me. This," she said, as they walked toward a toolshed.

"Oh, that," he said.

"That's not an answer."

"I might have arranged it. Okay, yeah, I did. Why does it matter?"

She smiled at him out of the corner of her eyes. "To me it does."

"In a good or a bad way?"

"Oh, good. Very good." The air felt cool. Finn was boiling.

"I've . . . you know, missed you," Finn said. He cleared his throat awkwardly.

"That's also good. You're on a roll."

"I can't lie, your . . . ability . . . might be useful. So technically I'm using you."

"Happy to be of service, though I hope we don't need it." Amanda gave him one more smile, and then her tone became more businesslike. "Who's this Marty guy?"

"Friend of Wayne's. He does the park newspaper, and he knows all sorts of stuff about what's going on. Some of it he can print, some he can't."

"This Pinocchio thing," Amanda prompted.

"Right. That's from him. An oversize Audio-Animatronic. Nose grows. The whole bit." Finn made a point of staring at the workshop shed across from them. It looked like a single-car garage that had been plopped down absentmindedly.

"But we happen to know that a physical Pinocchio never shows up in an attraction for thirty years. So . . . ?"

"Think how many zillions of things Disney started or dreamed about but were never finished, Amanda. Especially back then. *Now*. The fifties and sixties. I'll bet Walt had a million ideas. His team, too. And some of them really never were finished, and some were put on the back burner for thirty, forty, fifty years. But it was Pinocchio going up in flames in Jess's dream, so we can't not follow it up."

"How could Pinocchio ever be an Overtaker?" Amanda asked. She sounded sad.

"No one's an Overtaker yet. That's what we're here to prevent. Don't forget: you and Joe were the ones who told us to stay and stop Amery Hollingsworth."

"Junior. Yeah. Are you mad about that? You sound mad." Amanda twisted her hair nervously.

"I'm just saying: we already took care of getting the ink to Walt's special pen." Finn didn't mean to sound so defensive. "The pen is going to be in One Man's Dream so that we'll be able to find it there in sixty years, as stupid as that sounds. We've accomplished what we came to do."

"It doesn't sound stupid. Not when you know what's coming a long time from now. Jess and I made you all stick around," Amanda said, leaning back a little, as if trying to see the effect her words had on Finn.

"No one made us do anything. You gave us information and we're here. End of story."

"But you're mad," she said.

"No, I'm worried."

"You're always worried."

"Well, that's true," Finn admitted. "But this time it's . . . *personal*. It's about us: you, me, and the Keepers."

Amanda stopped speaking and took Finn's hand, and he wondered what genius allowed him to feel like a human being after closing hours, because this wouldn't have been the same as a hologram. His hand felt warm, which meant hers was not warm, which meant that she'd kept her cool and he had lost his, and he felt conflicted about that.

But more than anything, he didn't want to let go of her hand. He felt connected to her, and dare he even think it: *whole*. It wasn't about wanting to kiss her or hug her or any of that stuff, it was about *connecting* on a level the two of them rarely reached.

He thought about how long he and Amanda had known each other now. How much they'd shared, how close they'd grown. He thought about the color of her hair and her eyes and how he could see them even with his eyes closed. He thought about what a good person she was, how she'd come through so much and yet carried herself like her life had been charmed. He thought he didn't just like her, he admired her. He thought she mattered.

"Here's the thing," he said. "Philby, and Willa, too, has this random idea, a theory I guess you'd call it, about what happens if we stop Hollingsworth."

"If? There's no question about that. We have to stop him. Think of Dillard, of Wayne, of the fires, all the destruction."

"Yeah, well, that's the thing, isn't it? That's *exactly* the thing. Their theory goes that if we stop Hollingsworth, and if what he's doing is creating the Overtakers, then they never happen. And if they never happen, Wayne never needs to stop them, and if Wayne never needs to stop them, then maybe he never leads the DHI Project. So maybe we—the five of us—are never recruited as models for park guides. *Maybe we never meet at all.* That includes—"

"Me and you," Amanda said breathlessly. Her mouth hung open in astonishment. She stared at Finn as if the theory was his fault.

"You haven't thought about that?"

"No," she admitted. "Not like that. Not in those terms. I guess I figured . . . I thought . . ." She looked pale. Sick, maybe. "You know, fate, or whatever."

"Fairy tale," he said.

"What?"

"*We all* get hung up on the fairy-tale ending, right? That things always work out. But Philby, Willa? They say no matter how you tweak the past, if you even *can* tweak the past, that the present will work itself out anyway. It'll just find another way to accomplish the same present."

"You mean fate." Amanda's eyes were so bright in the dark.

"Like that, but not exactly," Finn said. "I mean, the other side of the argument says that if you mess with the past, if you even visit the past, the present can't possibly be the same upon your return. By going into the past, you change the present forever. Period. Every human deed has an impact."

"I kind of like that, actually," Amanda said. "The last part."

"It doesn't work out so well for us, though, Amanda. You, me, Jess, the Keepers. If we've changed the present by getting onto that carousel, and if we fix things now so the Overtakers never exist, then we'll never meet, we'll never work together, know each other."

"I get it. But if it's fate, it's fate." She sounded almost happy about the idea.

"You want it to be fate? You trust the fairy-tale ending? When have you *ever* seen a fairy-tale ending in your life?"

"Are you kidding? I see them every day! I'm looking at one!"

She was looking right at him.

"This isn't an ending," Finn complained. "It's just beginning!"

"See?" Amanda's voice quavered. "That's what I'm talking about."

She stretched forward and kissed him gently. So gently he wasn't sure they had even kissed. But there was a faint taste of strawberry or something sweeter on his lips, and he knew he hadn't put it there.

"This may never happen," he whispered.

"Interesting, because it's happening right this second." She leaned forward again and kissed him on the cheek. He awkwardly tried to aim for her lips again, but bumped her with his nose and she stepped back, laughing. "I'm not laughing *at* you," she said quickly, "but *with* you."

They were still holding hands, Finn realized, and she was squeezing his, which probably meant something but he didn't know what. He was stuck revisiting his clumsiness, how he'd whiplashed her with his nose.

"I am so lost," he said, almost apologetically.

"It makes you unbearably adorable."

"Is that so?" Suddenly he felt slightly more confident.

"That is most definitely so," Amanda said.

Reaching the shed, they used Wayne's master key to let themselves in. Finn shut the door quietly, but quickly. With no windows on any wall, he switched on the light, and he and Amanda drank in the organized chaos of the space.

Worktables were built along three of the four walls, reminding them both of Wayne's shop. A central workstation formed a kind of kitchen island in the room. Odd-looking tools and parts lay strewn about; glass jars filled with nuts and bolts, screws, and washers lined the back of each table.

But it was the three nearly life-size Pinocchio mannequins that held their attention. Never mind the electric fan the size of Big Ben in the far corner.

"That's creepy," Amanda whispered. The mannequins had been modified with power tools, the limbs cut at the joints. Wires protruded from the middle mannequin and ran every which way; he'd not only been cut apart and reassembled, but the arms, waist, and legs carried long scratch marks, as if a lion had attacked.

In all three of the life-size puppets, the faces had been carefully dissected, leaving a hole where the nose should have been, empty eye sockets, lines at the sides of the jaw, and drilled holes where eyebrows would eventually be fitted. The dead stares served as reminders of the graveyard.

Finn continued to look around the shop.

"What exactly are we looking for?" Amanda asked in a hushed whisper.

"One of those animation cels, maybe, like Jess dreamed about. Something that doesn't belong. All this stuff is so ancient looking," Finn cautioned, "that none of it looks like it belongs. Face it, 1955 was prehistoric."

"There's so much stuff," Amanda said, turning over papers, digging through mechanical parts. "I'm not sure I'd know it if I saw it."

"I hear you."

They stood on opposite sides of the small shack, rummaging through the contents of the workbenches, metal wire milk crates, and toolboxes. Finn found a pile of designs covered in scribbles, spilled coffee blobs and oil stains.

"What if we plugged him in and turned him on?" Amanda asked abruptly.

Finn spun around and stared at the three mannequins. "What would that tell us?" he asked.

"No clue. Just an idea."

"Interesting."

"Stupid, I suppose."

"Not necessarily," Finn said. "There's a speaker attached." He pointed to a workbench on the left. "So they're making him speak. That might tell us something. *He* might tell us something."

Amanda nodded eagerly. "Let's find out."

Finn crossed the shop, traced some cords from the back of the wired boy. They led to a box, which connected to a tape recorder and a small amplifier and speaker. "This box must move the motors in his jaw. Philby would get all this, I'll bet."

"And these?" Amanda held up a bundle of wires as thick as her forearm.

"Movement. Motion, I imagine," Finn said. "Nothing in his legs. It's all head and arms."

Finn switched on the tape recorder, the small box with the wires, and the amplifier. "That's all of them, I think." He hesitated, his hand on a silver lever on the top of the tape recorder.

"Did you turn down the volume?" Amanda asked.

"Good point." Finn did, wondering anew where a girl like Amanda had come from, how she could possibly like someone like him. "Ready?"

"As I'll ever be, I suppose."

Finn moved the lever.

37

A PROJECTOR SWITCHED ON, beaming an image of the animation-Pinocchio onto the standing mannequin. Finn and Amanda both startled back.

"Not cat scratches," Finn said after he caught his breath.

"What's that?"

"I thought those lines on his waist, his neck, looked like cat scratches. But I think it's more like the work of a chisel." Finn frowned, stepping closer to the mannequin. "This guy's been *carved* to fit the projected Pinocchio perfectly. That is so Disney, to make him so true to the movie."

"No kidding." Amanda was also closely examining the fit of the projection to the mannequin. "What a ton of work someone went to. It's exact, down to an eighth of an inch."

"*Are you my conscience?*" said the four-foot-high mannequin suddenly, his jaw moving, the tape recorder playing.

"Oh, that is weird," said Amanda. "That looks so—"

"Real," said Finn. "Yeah. It's nuts."

"I'd rather be smart than an actor," said the boy mannequin with the missing nose.

"That's from the movie! That's when he doesn't want to be a puppet any longer," said Finn.

"Finn! That's it!" Amanda said.

But the eyeless boy interrupted.

"He's my conscience. He tells me what's right and wrong."

"What's 'it'?" Finn asked, but the tape kept running, and the mannequin kept speaking.

"You're right! He doesn't want to be a puppet any longer. Did you hear what he just said?" she asked. Quoting Pinocchio, she said, "'He tells me what's—'"

"I'm real. I'm a real boy!"

"I don't like it," Finn said. "When does anything Disney think it's real?"

"Finn! It makes so much sense!"

"It doesn't to me!"

"A fire! That's it! A great big fire; lots of smoke!" The mannequin's head moved side to side and his right arm raised. For a moment it appeared he might start walking. Both Finn and Amanda stepped back.

"I . . . don't . . . like . . . this!" Finn hissed, more urgently now.

"It all fits!" Amanda repeated. "He's quoting movie lines. He wants change. He wants to be real. He wants a fire. Well, Jess dreamed of a cel burning. The projector could cause that. A person could cause that."

"Quick, some wood! We'll make him sneeze!"

Finn hadn't noticed the other wires until that moment. Sometimes things just happened that way. His attention fixed so intensely on one thing that he failed to notice others. It had been hard enough to decipher the connections between the sawed-up mannequin, tape recorder, and amplifier. With the workshop as cluttered as it was, what was another bundle of wires?

"Problem," he said, as a string of clicks and hums filled the far corner of the room. The same corner of the room that held the enormous fan.

"Finn, in the story, Pinocchio makes the whale—"

"Sneeze . . ."

The fan blades looked like they'd been salvaged from an airboat. With a diameter of eight feet, that sort of fan was capable of propelling an eight-thousand-pound boat across a swamp at over twenty-five miles per hour. However, in this case the fan was powered by an electric motor, not gasoline, and it was bolted to a concrete floor. Pieces of information came back to Finn in a rush: the motor had been purchased from a movie special effects company and could generate hurricane-force winds of over fifty miles per hour—or roughly the equivalent of a whale sneezing. It was intended to be the big moment of the Pinocchio attraction.

"The sneeze blasts him and Jiminy Cricket out of the whale! That's us!" Amanda said.

"Yeah. Oops!"

Finn grabbed Amanda's hand. But they made it only a few feet before the fan blades spun up. The first indication was the paperwork—plans, notes, receipts, litter—lifting and heading aloft like frightened birds.

"I'm real! I'm a real boy!" crowed Pinocchio, the projected image making him into something too believable.

Next came the wood-handled tools, like screwdrivers, handsaws, and drills. Then, midstep, Amanda and Finn lifted off the ground, suddenly light as feathers. For the tiniest of moments, no more than a fraction of a fraction of a second, they floated unmoving, neither forward nor back. Then the full force of the blast struck them like a boxer's punch. The wind batted them across the shed, pinning them against the far wall. Finn's body was held, twisted to the side. Amanda's pose was more like a five-pointed star.

It is said that in such threatening moments time slows to a crawl. But the Keepers knew that was a lie; the more apt analysis was the well-worn expression "Time waits for no man."

Perception, on the other hand, is another thing altogether. Finn saw the flying contents of the workshop coming at them: every tool, bolt, piece of wire, switch, washer, pencil, fastener, roll of tape, tape measure, magnifying glass, Coke bottle, ball of string, candy wrapper, scrub brush, toothbrush, paint can, oil can, bobby pin, and clip-on bow tie traveled at half speed in exaggerated three dimensions, like rocks in a comet's tail. Finn found himself able to quickly identify which of the objects would succumb to his particular gravity. Those, without a doubt, were going to hit him. A few others, including a sharp-toothed handsaw and a pane of flat glass, might or might not impale him.

Amanda understood immediately the degree of her exposure. Finn was slightly twisted; she was not. And now she hung on the wall like a pin-the-tool-on-the-Amanda party game.

Flattened against her will, she first marveled at the astounding quantity of objects in the workshop. With each in its place or lying on a countertop, the tools had appeared ordered and not all that many in number. With every last object aloft, there barely seemed any air left in the shed for them to fly. She assessed the potential danger, rapidly determining that she might come out of this bruised or broken but alive.

Finn was another matter.

Of the several hundred airborne items, it wasn't the pencil or the sharp shards of tin, the coffee mug or the spinning hacksaw blade that troubled her. It was a wood chisel, a bevel-ended tool that looked like a hefty screwdriver, its short flat blade sharp as a razor. Its trajectory, like an arrow, aligned with the center of Finn's chest.

Through a fog of adrenaline, the panic of being pinned to a wall, and the terror induced by a hundred dangerous tools and machine parts hurtling toward her, Amanda focused. She struggled to lift her arms against the wind; it was no use. It took all her concentration to spread the little finger of each hand. Next, the two ring fingers and middle fingers, at which point her hands rolled of their own accord, the backs of her hands slapping the wall. All of this took approximately half a second, though her senses placed it at half a minute.

Afraid to close her eyelids for fear that the wind would seal them shut, Amanda widened her eyes instead. And she *pushed*.

It was one thing to *push* an object. A clock, a lamp, or a chair had significant surface area to be caught by her powers. Aerodynamic but with enough mass to gain good speed, a chisel traveled like a throwing knife.

Amanda slowed and then stopped the bigger items. As neutrality was reached between the forces, the winds offset one another. Items reaching this equilibrium fell to the floor, pulled down by gravity. The pencil, some bolts, a screwdriver or two . . . and still the chisel did not stop.

It took a deeper reservoir, another level of commitment for Amanda to *push* hard enough to interfere with the basic properties of physics and aerodynamics: *An object in motion stays in motion with the same speed and in the same direction unless acted upon by an unbalanced force.* Newton's first law. She knew this stuff. The plaster behind her hands cracked, indenting and turning the wall to dust. Her head, hips, and heels followed, crushing the wall. She'd made a static snow angel.

And still the chisel came at Finn.

Amanda had never used her power to its fullest. She'd come close, but mostly a small release of energy, a burst, was enough. It was even sometimes *too much*— hurtling furniture, slamming doors, knocking people off their feet. But this small item, a bit of metal and wood, took everything she had. She'd hoped to stop it. She'd have to deflect it instead.

With nearly all her strength, she managed to rotate both wrists in unison. She launched a pulse of energy. It wasn't enough.

A pencil she'd missed stabbed Finn in the thigh; Amanda watched in slow motion as it pierced his pants and dug into his leg. Watched, as Finn's face contorted and he tried to cry out, but the oncoming wind filled his mouth, billowed his cheeks, and choked him.

Finn's injury was the trigger. Amanda's final reserve of energy fled from her out-turned hands like a demonic spirit, a wave of pent-up anger and unbridled resolve. Not only did the chisel alter its course, it jerked away as if it was on a tight string. So did each and every other airborne item. All the flying debris responded as if to a shock wave, lurching three feet counterclockwise.

Amanda had nothing left, not an ounce of strength.

The reversed debris slowed as it neared the powerful fan, but did not stop completely. For a moment, it was almost as if one side of the workshop remained in the hurricane, while the other hit a physical limbo. Then the lead objects on the counterclockwise side slipped past the halfway mark and whipped into motion, caught by the force of the fan. Everything in the room began spinning, slowly, almost reluctantly at first, but soon the spinning motion became more ferocious. It evolved from tropical storm to hurricane to twister.

Finn inched to his right, Amanda along with him. Again he tried to speak; again the wind forbade him. The two were pulled violently from the wall and hurled into the tornado of debris. Every item from pushpin to chair was captured in the counterclockwise stew. The mass rotated slowly at first, perhaps at the speed of a vinyl album. Then it accelerated to the speed of a washing machine on spin cycle.

As Finn and Amanda completed their third revolution, buttons began tearing from their clothes. Finn's pants button popped free; his zipper strained; the buttons on Amanda's shirt exploded randomly until they were all gone, exposing the T-shirt beneath. Desperately, she took hold of a large wooden spool, using it to advance her through the mass of swirling objects. Only when she reached out to take Finn's unsuspecting hand did she let go. He turned his head, startled by the contact.

"Won't . . . survive!" he managed to cough out.

She shook her head, tears streaming. "I'm . . . sorry."

"Saved . . . me!"

"Started . . . this."

Finn, a Weather Channel devotee (the only channel he and his father could agree on), had seen so many stunning videos of Midwestern and Texas twisters, had watched a mile-wide funnel cloud lift a barn, cattle, and trees into its vortex while phone poles, lawn mowers, and car doors flew from its outer extreme.

"Door!" he managed to scream. It sounded closer to a whisper given the roar. "Spin you!"

Revolution number seven, speed forty-five miles per hour, face distorted. Finn used every muscle in his body to spin as violently as he could, whipping Amanda around him like an orbiting moon. Smart enough to understand his plan without explanation, she stretched for the workshop's doorknob. Too high. Missed.

Revolution number eight. Another miss. Revolution number nine. Speed fifty-seven miles per hour, hard to breathe, nearly impossible to see. Amanda caught the doorknob. She and Finn formed a line of stretching arms, their bodies strung from the doorknob like a kite tail.

"Can't . . . turn . . . it!" she cried.

Finn flexed, pulled, and managed to hook elbows with her. Debris collided with their bodies, pounding him, striking and cutting them both. "Hold . . . tight!"

They met eyes. Magically. Only a moment's worth, but a connection. An all-or-nothing exchange, an implicit understanding that Finn was counting on her and she, him.

Then Finn sucked their elbows into his side and spun a pirouette like a figure skater or ballerina, his body parallel to the floor.

The doorknob rotated. The door's latch released; the phenomenal wind found an outlet, and the door blew away from the structure at sixty-three miles per hour, taking the two teens with it.

Amanda let go of the door, but not of Finn. Together, they flew. With the dissipating wind behind them, they soared aloft like Wendy and Peter Pan, hand in hand, hair streaming away from their faces, their bodies soaring over the contour of the earth below.

Finn spotted a possible landing and hunched forward to propel them downward. Amanda resisted, though only for an instant.

Together, they crashed and splashed into the waters of the Jungle Cruise, their landing softened by a light push from Amanda.

Together, they bobbed to the surface, no longer holding hands.

Together, they paddled and turned, watching as a Disneyland workshop exploded into a nighttime tornado, a cloud of debris lifting the shop's roof forty feet into the air and the whole of it—tools, mannequins, litter, splintered wood—sinking equally fast. The vortex left the pavement strewn with junk. A few odd pieces splashed alongside Amanda and Finn, causing both to raise their arms as shields.

They swam to the edge of the river, climbed out muddy, their eyes wide.

And then they did something completely unexpected: they laughed.

38

MULAN PUSHED THE green button and hurried to join Kristoff and Nick, who were waiting at the bottom of the elevator shaft.

Thick steel cables whined against pulleys. The elevator floor, as large as a two-car garage, *fell* toward them, growing in size. Technically, it wasn't falling but being pulled faster than gravity itself. The three standing directly beneath suffered a moment of silent apprehension. If Nick was wrong about how the attraction operated, they were about to get squashed like bugs.

Kristoff reached overhead, like he could stop it and save the others. As if.

"You're safe," Kristoff told Nick.

Nick didn't feel safe.

"Or is it you I should help?" Kristoff asked Mulan.

"Don't trouble yourself. I'll see you up there!" Mulan was crouched on her toes, ready to spring forward.

The elevator stopped abruptly, raced up, and was sucked down again, stopped. The pattern was random and unpredictable. To the three immediately beneath, it looked like the head of a hammer dropping on them.

"I . . . do . . . not . . . like . . . this!" Mulan hissed.

The car braked, stopping mere feet overhead. With perfect timing, Kristoff took hold of one pipe, and Mulan hooked a leg over another, coiling around it like a snake. Nick entwined his fingers around a third pipe and locked his grip.

"Hold on," Kristoff said.

With a tremendous jolt, the car lifted, flying up at an absurd speed. Nick's fingers, wrapped around the metal bar, went white. Then the random movement of the attraction began: the car braked, dropped, rose, braked, rose, and fell toward the bottom of the shaft.

Nick lost hold of the pipe with one hand. He swiped for the bar but missed. Mulan reached down and caught him just in time, locking their forearms.

"Hang on!" she shouted, swinging the boy. "Legs!"

With the pit rushing toward him as the car fell, Nick bent his knees and tucked into a ball. The car braked and stopped only feet above the concrete. Nick felt Kristoff wrap an arm around him and pull.

"Let go!" Mulan chided Kristoff.

"Give him to me!" Kristoff argued. "I've got him."

The two played tug-of-war with Nick, Mulan not letting go of his arm. Then, as fast as it had fallen, the car shot back up the shaft at supernatural speed.

Nick's arm strained. His shoulder felt like it was

pulling out of its socket. Kristoff's tight hold squeezed all the wind out of him; he couldn't breathe. The elevator car plunged downward as Mulan and Kristoff continued to wrestle over Nick. Now they held him with a view down the shaft. The hurricane-force wind flapped their clothes and stood the hair up on their heads.

"Look out!" Mulan shouted.

The other drops had been child's play. Whatever the car was doing now, it seemed to be doing it on its own. It raced for the pit, the concrete coming at them at lightning speed. Nick saw where this was going. He elbowed Kristoff in the ribs and punched Mulan on the arm. As they released him, he swung up and hooked his legs, making himself flat against the pipes.

The collision didn't go well for Kristoff. The burly mountain man had little time to react. He made a smart move: letting go completely, dropping to the bottom of the pit, and lying flat as the car screeched to a stop. Mulan entwined herself into the pipes like Nick. The car blasted off the bottom. Nick's stomach lurched.

"No . . . no!" Kristoff, flat on his back, called out, seeing Nick's open mouth.

Nick spit up—or down, to be more accurate—the foul mess splashing onto Kristoff like water from a burst water balloon.

The car raced up five stories in less than two seconds

and glided to a merciful stop. Kristoff, the size of a bug at the bottom of the shaft, scraped the slop off his face and chest, flinging it to the ground.

Nick climbed hand-over-hand across the pipes toward a maintenance cage recessed into the wall, Mulan behind him, scurrying like a squirrel on electrical wire.

"Now what?" she said, breathing hard, studying the tight confines of the maintenance cage. The elevator car fell away with a *whoosh*.

"Now we find the Fairlies," Nick said.

39

ONCE OUT OF THE CAGE, a short hallway led Nick and Mulan into a longer corridor, its floor covered with debris. The overhead ceiling was riddled with gaping holes as if hit by . . .

"Sky fire did this," Mulan said.

"Lightning," Nick whispered, nodding, "and an earthquake or two." Faint music and voices flowed down through an overhead hole. "I think we're on the wrong floor."

"I suggest we find out." Mulan effortlessly slipped the bow off her back, allowing it to run down her arm and into her hand.

"That was cool," Nick said, flashing her a wide smile. "But remember, I'm going alone. You're backup. Please, follow the plan. If I'm in trouble, Dillard will help. And Dash should be around here as well."

"The villains are full of witchcraft and trickery," Mulan warned. "They can shape-shift, throw curses, cast spells. You must take care."

"Actually, these are more like human villains," Nick said, "young kids with weird powers. But no sorcery."

"I understand little of what you say," Mulan said. "But I will do as you ask."

And with that, she hoisted Nick, who scrambled through a burned hole and up a level.

Nick was working with what Mattie had told him about where she thought her room was. He'd made it only a few feet before he spotted Dillard, coming from behind on his hands and knees.

A movie was showing in the break room, Dillard explained in whispers. Nick told him about Mulan waiting a floor below.

Then the two boys inched forward. Nick tested the door and found it locked. "Your turn," he told Dillard.

Dillard stuck his hologram head through, then disappeared inside. A moment later, Nick heard the boy shouting.

Dillard reappeared. "She's sleeping, and I can't wake her."

"She hasn't returned," Dillard said. "Something's messed up. As long as she's a hologram down there with the characters, she can't wake up here."

Nick looked around.

"If we wait," Dillard said, "the movie's going to end and there are going to be Fairlies everywhere."

"I need something to pry open the door," Nick said.

"Dash!" Dillard called. A blur shot toward them, and there stood the small boy.

"You rang?"

"Something to pry open this door. *Quickly!*"

"I understand 'quickly.'"

"One-thousand one, one-thousand two," Dillard counted. "One—"

Dash zoomed to a stop, a tire iron in hand. "Sorry . . . it was two blocks away."

"Fast enough," said Dillard, "though I *was* getting worried."

Nick pried open the door. The door jamb splintered. The door swung open.

Dillard said, "I sure can't carry her."

"I can try." Nick was noticeably smaller than Mattie. He scooped up her lifeless form, her head and feet dangling awkwardly from his arms. "I don't know about this."

"Come on!" Dash yanked open the door.

40

THE MINUTE THEY STEPPED into the hallway, a Barracks Fairlie cried out from behind them, "Hey! You two!"

Nick found the strength to run. Dillard found the courage to face the Fairlie. "It's a medical thing!" he yelped, trying for the distraction. "We could use some help!"

The Fairlie tried to push Dillard away, but his hands swiped through the hologram and he fell off-balance. "Transparency," Dillard said. "My ability."

Showing off, he offered the Fairlie a hand, surprising the Fairlie when they again failed to make contact. All the while, Nick continued running down the hall.

"I don't know you," the Fairlie countered.

"You guys actually think you're the only group inside the park?" Dillard laughed artificially. Nick was close to the big hole in the floor. The Fairlie caught him looking.

"ESCAPE!" the Fairlie shouted.

Kids came piling out of the movie room. Nick felt his legs go out from under him—and he was still far short of the hole in the floor. He'd been *pushed* by a Fairlie.

Mattie's lifeless form crashed onto him. But in the next second, one of the Fairlie boys grabbed for his leg, from which an arrow protruded. A girl shrieked as a second arrow pierced her arm. And Mulan appeared from the shadows at the end of the hall.

Mattie sat up from atop Nick and climbed off him, onto all fours.

"You're awake!" Nick said.

Mattie blinked and shook her head. She spotted Mulan at one end of the hall, a few wounded Fairlies near them and more at the other end, ready to fight. She had only seconds to assess the situation and make a choice.

Mattie called to the Fairlies, "Help me!"

"What?" barked Nick.

The temperature dropped instantly, the work of a smallish girl with sky-blue hair, her eyes closed. Mattie searched her memories of the Barracks for the girl's name . . . Mary Ann! She'd been dyeing her hair like that for years.

Mattie's limbs ached. Her rapid breathing left steam clouds hanging in the subzero air. Mulan fell to the floor and coiled into a tight ball. A shivering Flynn appeared and dragged Mulan away with him.

The tips of Mattie's fingers glowed a bright red. Then, with horror, she watched as a brown-black stain spread toward the first knuckle on every finger: frostbite. All around her, most of the Fairlies weren't doing much better.

As Dillard—unaffected by the cold—approached to help her, she saw Zeke in the clutches of several Fairlies. How had they caught Zeke? Jaw set, Mattie crawled away from the hole in the floor, toward the Fairlies. Dillard attempted to help her, but his arms passed through her.

"Go," she whispered to Nick. "Take Dillard."

"What? No!" asked Nick incredulously.

"Now! Don't be stupid."

"Whatever!" Nick dragged himself toward the hole and slipped over the edge and dropped to the floor below. Dillard lingered a moment longer, but then followed down the hole.

"They're gone! Stop it!" Mattie pleaded to Mary Ann. The hallway slowly warmed.

Reading a person, a difficult task under any circumstances, was incredibly difficult for Mattie during chaos. In such situations, the human brain shuts down most thought, relying on established channels of instinct to strive for survival. Not only did Mattie's targets shut down, but she had to battle her own brain to allow avenues of thought to remain open while her more basic self was trying to close them.

Mattie reached Mary Ann, then touched her, *reading* her for "mission."

Mattie saw four faces, a flash of a parade or World of Color, a brown double-doored fence gate, an image of long pipes and of a fluted wheel.

She looked back toward the hole in the floor, wondering if she'd made a great mistake by gambling on her own plan.

41

"WE BOTH LIKE MATH," Willa said.

"Agreed." Philby's voice sounded apologetic, as if he were embarrassed by the admission.

"The Transitive Property of Equality," Willa said. "If A equals B and B equals—"

"I'm not stupid," Philby said, "I passed sixth grade, so what are you trying to say?"

"We need to do something illegal."

"Technically we're not breaking the law, because in 1955 we haven't been born yet."

Willa smiled at him. "Good point. Look, Jess dreams of Pinocchio burning. That's our 'A.' Finn and Amanda go all Wizard of Oz in the workshop where Pinocchio's a mannequin *and* there's an animation cel projected onto him. That's 'B.' Pinocchio's story was about becoming *real*. 'C'—a Disney character becoming real. Sound familiar?"

Philby's face tightened with thought, and Willa watched the realization hit him, washing his features with fear. "The Overtakers."

"Exactly! Maybe that shop has less to do with

Imagineers, and more to do with Cast Members like Shane and Thia."

"I'm listening. We still haven't broken a law that I know of."

"The mannequins appear to be part of the early development of Audio-Animatronics. So you add up Jess's Pinocchio dream, everything Finn and Amanda discovered in the workshop, and the fact that it proved dangerous. You throw in that the Pinocchio story is all about the boy becoming human—then his mannequin becoming human! Joe approved Amanda and Jess coming back here to warn us about Hollingsworth, to get us to stop him from creating the Overtakers. So . . . do you remember why Walt Disney fired him in the first place?"

"Stealing animation cels!" Philby shouted it. "Oh my gosh! You have got to be kidding me!"

Willa felt like she was floating. Philby not only understood her theory, he bought into it. He had jumped to the same conclusion.

"There are two . . . tangible pieces of evidence in all this. The stolen animation cels, and the mannequins, which could easily have something to do with this. If we want to follow actual hard evidence . . ." She left it hanging, hoping Philby would bite.

"We're going to break into the mannequin company's building."

* * *

The following night, after Philby and Willa had transitioned from hologram to human, while the small city of Anaheim slept peacefully, Finn, Maybeck, Amanda, and Charlene escorted them to the Manaheim Display Manufacturing facility. A single-story concrete block building, the plant had tall windows that were covered by burglar-proof wrought iron. Its metal-reinforced front and back doors and four padlocked loading bays made it look like an urban fortress. Prominently displayed signs warned that the property was guarded by Holmes Electric Protective Company, of Bakersfield, California.

Maybeck, Amanda, Philby, and Willa studied the building from directly across the street.

"Check for skylights," Maybeck said, addressing Charlene, who nodded and took off up an exterior water pipe, climbing like a monkey. She disappeared onto the flat roof. A moment later, she reappeared at the edge, her arms crossed in an X. She followed this with a punching motion.

"What's that about?" Willa asked.

"Can't you read sign language? There are skylights, but they don't open," Maybeck said. "We could break them, if necessary."

"No," Philby said.

Maybeck stepped out of the shadow briefly and

raised his arms into an X. They saw Charlene descending the same downspout only moments later.

"We'll never get in the front door or any of the windows," Philby said.

"I have an idea," Willa offered. "Did you guys see that store called Five and Dime back there? It was still open."

"Yeeeeaah," Maybeck said, drawing the word out, wondering where she was going with the idea.

"So Wayne gave Finn some money." Willa smiled and raised an eyebrow. "What if Finn goes and buys a padlock that matches the ones on the garage doors?"

"Okay," Maybeck said, but inquisitively.

"Amanda uses her ability to *push* one of the locks open."

"Is that even possible?" Maybeck asked.

"Worth a try. Let's say she can push one open. It's broken after that. So—"

"We replace it with the one Finn buys," Philby said excitedly. "When they open tomorrow, there'll be no evidence anyone broke in."

"But the combinations won't match," Maybeck said, shaking his head slightly. "They won't even be able to open it."

"Which won't make any sense," Philby said, "but it will probably seem to them like the stupid padlock failed, not like someone broke in."

250

"Genius!" Maybeck said, looking squarely at Willa, who smiled uncharacteristically.

"Wait!" Amanda said. "What if those garage doors are on the same alarm system? I mean, why wouldn't they be?"

"We'll know once we open one," Philby said. "But at least we can open one!"

"That's a big risk," Amanda said.

"We've got to try." Philby was fully on board now. "If the alarm goes off, we replace the lock and book it out of here. If not, me and Willa will go inside."

"And what if no alarm goes off? What if it's a silent alarm?"

"Was there such a thing in 1955?" Maybeck asked. "I'm serious! I don't know the answer."

"Let's hope not," Philby said. "We're here. If there's information, it's in there."

"It's simple math," Willa said, grinning.

The plan took less than two dollars and twenty minutes to carry out. Amanda *pushed* the existing padlock open like it was made of paper and opened the garage door two feet. No alarm. Philby and Willa crawled through. Amanda lowered the garage door and returned to her post.

* * *

Inside the building, the skylights admitted enough street light for Philby and Willa to avoid running into the lathes, saws, and drills. At the same time, the faint light turned wooden mannequins into an army of life-size ghosts. Some were headless, some without arms or legs, some in a woman's figure, some in men's, dozens standing, dozens more stacked on shelves, like the dead piled high in the catacombs of Gothic cathedrals.

"I don't like it here."

"Well, that makes two of us," Philby agreed. "Office?"

"Up there." Willa pointed to an area along the wall. A tree house platform with a deck and railing had been constructed of bare lumber. The two hurried upstairs, where three small offices stood side by side. Through sliding glass doors facing the shop floor, Willa and Philby saw paperwork, posters, and calendar girls cluttering the desks and walls. The center office, which housed a long section of filing cabinets, attracted their interest.

"If we're going to find a connection between the mannequins and Hollingsworth, we'd better get to it."

"Agreed," Philby said.

Willa took the filing cabinet drawers marked *G-H-I*, while Philby dug into those marked *D-E-F*.

"If Nick Perkins were here," Willa said, her fingers flying through the manila file separators, "I'll bet he'd know the name of Hollingsworth's company."

"Too bad we can't text him."

"Too bad texting hasn't been invented yet."

"We should have thought to put a message on Jingles." The carousel horse had been used to send notes to the present time, sixty years ahead.

"Yeah, hooray for hindsight!" She sounded angry. "Nothing under *Hollingsworth*."

"There's a Disney file here. Looks like they order about six mannequins a month. I don't think that helps us much."

"Wait!" Leaving the cabinet drawer open, Willa sat down at the desk and took hold of a rolling card file. The surface was inscribed with the word ROLODEX. Turning a knob on the side rotated one business card at a time, some typed, some handwritten. "Old-school," Willa said, spinning it to the *H* tab. "Darn it! Nothing."

"Surprise."

"Hang on!" Willa left Philby alone to inspect the next office. It had a bigger desk that wasn't as messy.

More importantly, its Rolodex was twice as big.

* * *

Charlene's adrenaline level peaked on the roof of the Manaheim Display Manufacturing plant. Back at ground level, assigned to guard the place in the dark, she began to feel sleepy and lazy. Boring. Boring. Boring.

She preferred activity to sitting around any day—or night.

Something about a pair of fast-moving headlights on the next street over sounded an alarm in her brain. It was the second time she'd noticed a car in the area. Given a split second to decide if the car was a concern to Philby and Willa, Charlene opted to be on the safe side. She reached the back door and pounded three times.

By the time she was running away, the headlights had turned toward the building. Charlene whistled, signaling danger.

She heard the same whistle repeated, moving around to the front. That would be Finn, she thought.

The team was warned.

* * *

Willa started at the sound of the distant knocks. Having just worked her way to the chair side of the industrial-gray metal desk, she leaned toward the bigger Rolodex.

"Come on!" Philby stood in the doorway, his whole body practically humming with tension. "Hurry! No time for that!"

Alphabetical tabs divided the Rolodex. As Willa spun the side wheel, the letters rotated backward— *O, N, M, L, K, J, I, H.*

"Wait! I've got it!"

"Forget about it! We'll come back!"

But Willa knew they wouldn't. It was now or never.

* * *

Amanda, out front, regarded the headlights as the ultimate threat. She would never have imagined the existence of a silent alarm in 1955. But maybe the fifties weren't as prehistoric as she'd thought.

The replacement padlock they'd bought warmed in her hand. The plan had been to replace it after Willa and Philby were done. Currently, the garage door had no lock on it at all. Images of her friends being arrested swarmed through Amanda's brain. Two kids with no past, no residence, no family. Not good!

But if she could manage to lock the garage door before whoever was in that car started looking around, maybe she could avoid a whole pack of trouble.

With the headlights approaching fast, Amanda made her move, crouching as she raced for the set of delivery doors. On her belly, she locked the padlock on the door and waited, not daring to move, as a big blue Buick pulled onto the bib of the parking lot. The driver turned off the vehicle and switched off the lights.

On the side of the car was written HOLMES ELECTRIC PROTECTIVE COMPANY.

Amanda hesitated, not moving. The guard checked

the front door. Finding it secure, he headed for the far window. Amanda belly-crawled into the shadows.

A minute later the guard stood exactly where Amanda had lain. He checked all three loading bays, showing no signs of concern.

Amanda gave herself a gold star. And then . . .

Five long minutes later, he reappeared at the front. Amanda waited for him to get back in the car. Instead, he withdrew a cluttered key chain that chimed dully as he sorted through his choices.

Then the guard opened the door and headed inside.

* * *

HOLLINGSWORTH, AMERY read the hand-typed contact card. With no time to copy the information, Willa pulled it from the Rolodex and pocketed it. She caught up to Philby, who in the limited light looked a little sick.

"Somebody's here," he gasped. "Shaking the doors, checking the windows. We're cooked!"

"I got his info. They had a card on Hollingsworth! We were right, Philby!"

"That won't matter if we're caught." He grabbed her hand and pulled her down the stairs with him. At the very moment they reached the shop floor, the front door opened. Philby pushed her behind a standing mannequin. He ducked behind another.

A flashlight's beam strayed across the ceiling, the floor, and some of the machinery. It flashed across the two mannequins, behind which the kids stood frozen in place. It found more machinery, more mannequins. It found the stairs to the offices and led the way up them for the man who held the light.

The second he entered one of the offices, Philby pushed Willa closer toward the front door, this time hiding behind fully dressed mannequins meant as sales displays. It was an entire family: mom, dad, and two children.

The door was only a few steps away. Philby eyed it longingly. With the guard upstairs, they might reach the door without being seen. . . . He caught Willa looking in that direction as well. The thought was annulled by the rapid descent of shoes on stairs.

The flashlight burned in their direction and lingered on the family of four. Onto the front door. Back onto the family. Philby dug into his pocket and retrieved a coin—a penny. He tossed it high and hard. It clattered to the floor a few feet away.

The guard moved in that direction.

The light turned away, and Philby hand-signaled Willa to move. They reached another set of mannequins and hid.

From across the building, the light raced back to illuminate the family of four. Philby watched from a few yards away as the guard returned to inspect the clothed mannequins. He was maybe twelve feet from Philby and Willa.

Philby slowed his breathing. Willa looked at him calmly, as if trying to tell him it was going to be okay. She pointed carefully to a piece of machinery the size and height of a Ping-Pong table. It took Philby a moment to spot the open space beneath the heavy steel platform, to understand her plan. He nodded.

The light streaked across the crowd of mannequins. Shadows leaned and slanted. For a moment Philby felt off-balance, as if he wasn't standing straight. The light went to the floor.

The guard was coming in their direction.

Willa held up three fingers. Counted down: three, two, one.

In unison, she and Philby shifted one mannequin closer to the piece of machinery. Their movement caught the attention of the guard, but he lifted the flashlight too late; they were already posed behind a different pair of mannequins, out of sight.

But the guard clearly had a keen sense about him. He moved toward the grouping of a dozen mannequins in which the two were hiding. With no order to the formation of the dummies, the guard was forced to walk among them to look for his burglars. The steady stream of light moved around, painting mannequins and the floor alike in a narrow white beam.

Willa and Philby watched each other and, as the guard neared, they slithered around to the opposite sides of their mannequins. It was like hide-and-seek, a crazy, nerve-jangling ballet. The only advantage Willa and Philby had was the telltale movement of the flashlight's beam. The man walked right past them and, turning, forced them both around to where they'd started. When he put his back to them, Philby darted to the piece of heavy machinery and slipped into the empty space beneath, finding himself inches deep in sawdust. Willa followed, tucking herself into a ball. Philby wrapped his arms around her from behind and held her.

The flashlight moved around the area for the next several minutes. Then it went dark. The door could be heard opening and closing. Philby began to extricate himself from the cramped space, but Willa grabbed his arm, stopping him, and pressed her lips so close to Philby's ear that she practically kissed him.

"Remember the trick played on Charlene and Amanda?"

Philby nodded, relaxed, and stayed where he was.

A full five minutes passed before a long sigh filled the work area, followed by the sound of the door opening and closing a second time: the guard had faked going out, just as Shane had surprised Amanda and Charlene in the secret wall of the castle.

"Phew," Willa said.

"Good call."

"Thanks! I think I was about to have a heart attack."

They heard the guard's car rumble to a start and motor off.

"Think how surprised he'll be when we trigger the alarm on our way out!" Philby sounded excited by the prospect.

They repositioned themselves in the middle of the shop floor, waiting for the signal to leave.

"Show me," Philby said.

Willa produced the card. "It's Hollingsworth's phone numbers and addresses." Together, they studied it by the light of a window.

"Incredible," Philby said. "Excellent work!"

"Looks like his company is something called *Renatus*," she said. "It's in Fullerton. There's an address, phone number, everything." Willa looked toward the door. "It's been long enough. Let's get out of here."

"No!" Philby said.

Boom! Boom-boom! A pattern of three knocks echoed in the air: all clear.

"There! You see? We can go now!"

"The first files we were looking at? They were

deliveries. Orders. Hollingsworth wouldn't have a card unless he was a customer!"

"O . . . kay?"

"What if there's a file under his *company* name?" Philby asked. "You go outside and collect the others. Be ready to move. I'm going to check the files."

"No way! I'm not doing that! It will trip the alarm again, and besides, I'm not going anywhere without you. So, go! Hurry."

Philby did the strangest thing, then: he kissed Willa on the cheek. Before she had time to react, he took off, running upstairs. He probably thought she was going to be mad he'd done that, but she wasn't. She'd even liked it, just a little. Willa was glad it was dark, so he couldn't see her blush. If she resented the kiss, it wasn't for the kiss itself, but for the distraction it caused. She could hardly think, much less focus.

She moved closer to the window, tucked away the contact card, and peered outside, fearing the car might return. It was dark out on the street; her friends were out there but she couldn't see anyone. A calico cat slunk past, skittish and afraid. That pretty much defined her as well: jittery, concerned, hyper, nauseated.

Philby came bounding down the stairs and nearly tripped near the bottom step. His face and eyes were alive with that ginger, boyish glee he occasionally allowed to show. At times of such excitement, his former British accent seeped through, as it did now, while waving some onionskin paperwork at her.

"Three shipments, the most recent scheduled for delivery tomorrow!"

"To Renatus?"

"The order is written up for Renatus, but it's not being delivered to Fullerton. It's heading to Eighty North Harbor Boulevard, Anaheim. Same as the other two deliveries."

"Here in Anaheim?"

"It's got to be just ten, fifteen blocks away."

"What are we waiting for?" she gasped.

"Ladies first!" Philby said, mimicking a sweeping, gallant gesture toward the door.

But Willa turned him around, pointing to the back. "I'd rather not take chances."

* * *

The group walked in silence, heading for North Harbor Boulevard. Amanda said something about getting the lock onto the bay door in time; Willa laughed about jumping around between mannequins, while acknowledging that it hadn't seemed funny at the time; Philby applauded Willa's mental toughness in pursuing the Rolodex while "under fire"; Finn listened;

Maybeck chided and mocked where appropriate.

Seven blocks later, when headlights shone onto the side of a building, the teens scattered without any kind of signal.

The car that drove past—slowly, deliberately—was a police car. It couldn't be coincidence. The security company had reported a break-in.

Five minutes later, the Keepers scattered for a second time. This time the car belonged to the Holmes Electric Protective Company, the driver familiar to Amanda, Philby, and Willa.

When they'd regrouped, Finn took charge. "We pair up and take different streets. We meet at the shipping address in no more than ten minutes. Stay out of sight."

The pairs blended into the shadows and disappeared, coming together again, eight minutes later, at 80 North Harbor Boulevard.

Finn double-checked to make sure they had the correct address. "We should have known, I guess," he said. "In some weird way, we should have expected this."

They'd arrived at the front entrance of a building that towered above them. Abandoned. Deserted—or so it looked from the outside. Finn knew differently. Some of the other Keepers did, too, including both Fairlies, who would live there sixty years in the future.

It was an old, dilapidated, all-too-familiar hotel.

42

JOE GARLINGTON'S DHI flickered occasionally, either the result of a weak signal or the projection limitations inherent in Version 1.6. He faced Mickey, Mulan, and Kristoff across a table inside Club 33 in New Orleans Square.

Young Nick Perkins sat next to Joe. The empty dining room's rich wood furnishings, tile, and leaded glass windows lent it an old-world feel. The linen-covered tabletops held plates, silverware, and glass goblets.

Joe had listened to a recap of the events in the Tower of Terror the night before. "It doesn't explain why Mattie stayed behind," he said.

"She must have been captured for a second time," Mickey said. "Poor thing."

"She chose to stay," Nick said. "She told us to leave her."

Joe frowned and shook his head.

Mulan said, "It was so cold. She must not have been thinking clearly."

"Ezekiel?" Joe addressed Mickey, his voice pleading. "Was Ezekiel with you?"

Mickey shook his head, deeply troubled. "He wanted a view of the group climbing the building. That's all I know."

A lot of head shaking followed. Nick raised his hand timidly, like an elementary school student. "I shouldn't have let her stay."

Joe waved him off. "You did as she asked."

"Another raid?" said Mulan. "We know where we are going now. That makes us stronger."

Joe studied the others, including Nick. "If the Fairlies have taken Ezekiel hostage, we can't go barging in there."

"Our numbers are many," said Mickey, "our powers great."

"So are theirs," Joe reminded him. "The Fairlies must have abducted Zeke for a reason, part of a bigger plan. They need him for something. And—hear me out—if they've been keeping an eye on Zeke, they may know about him and Mattie. And she won't know that."

"Meaning she's in even more trouble than we thought," said Nick.

"She's a woman," said Mulan. "Have any of you considered the obvious?"

"There's nothing obvious about Minnie," said Mickey. "She's always surprising me!"

"Exactly!" said Mulan. "Precisely my point! Mattie

stayed behind *on purpose*! She has a plan of her own. We should be asking ourselves what that plan is, and then determine how we can help her."

"If only we could cross her over again we could talk to her," Joe said. "The question is, with Zeke captured, is her plan any good?"

Nick said what everyone was thinking. "Or did she just mess everything up?"

43

DAYLIGHT. MATTIE'S WINDOWLESS room didn't tell her the sun was up. The scent of coffee and sound of footsteps coming through the door did. She was human again. In the same lifeless room, with the same lousy smell and lighting. She tried the door. It wasn't the same! It was unlocked!

"Good morning," Humphrey said. He appeared to have been waiting for her. Mattie used the washroom and returned. He had a cup of tea ready and steaming.

"Gloves, please," he said, indicating a pair of white cotton gloves on the table. Mattie slipped them on, then added three sugars and some cream to her tea. The small kitchenette smelled like coffee and breakfast cereal.

"Where is everyone?" she asked.

"Out. Working."

"On?"

"Cast Members have to work."

"True enough."

"That was a big decision you made last night," he said.

"I thought the quickest way to get rid of them

was to pretend I was going with them. It worked."

"Why'd you choose to stay? It's not like we've been treating you so great."

"You have to ask? I lived in the Barracks longer than most of you."

"You *escaped* the Barracks."

"You know what it feels like in there! Turns out running away isn't so great. It's been hard for me out here alone," she lied. "Finding you all—or I guess technically you found me!—scared me at first. I do not want to go back there."

"And him?" Humphrey pointed through the kitchenette's windows, which looked onto the hallway, indicating the closed door across the way.

"I was going to ask you," Mattie answered nonchalantly. "Amery's brother, right?"

Humphrey didn't answer right away. He played with the spoon in his cup of tea, watching it swirl. "He was the prize."

"Excuse me?"

"Did you think we were that interested in a disloyal, ungrateful former resident of the Barracks? We've been watching you. You must have figured that out once we decided to show ourselves. Come to find out, you'd been spending time with the traitor brother, a man who doesn't recognize his father's cause, his *family's* cause."

"I was . . . bait? You *used* me?"

"Does that bother you? You've helped us, Mattie. We couldn't have done it without you."

"Bother me? As a person, yes, of course it does. I do *not* appreciate being used!" Her head swam. She'd led them to Zeke. Had they watched as Zeke had summoned Mickey and the others? Did his ability to round up the good characters give them something they lacked? "I don't know why you care about Ezekiel Hollingsworth all of a sudden."

Though Mattie's expression didn't change, inside she was livid. She cursed the gloves. How she'd have loved to read Humphrey's thoughts at that moment. Philby or Willa could have figured it out, she thought irritably. Some kids were smarter than others; some had more powers.

A dreadful thought hit her—a kiss would be as good as wrapping her fingers around a wrist or arm. Humphrey had that drooling boy look, the kind that told a girl to look out. He was the kind to touch your cheek or brush shoulders or—heaven forbid!—kiss your knuckles, acting like he was a prince and you a princess.

Back in the Barracks, he'd been that annoying boy who thought he was God's gift to girls. It worked on some people—Mattie remembered that one of the Fairlies here seemed to have a crush on him—but to her, he was repulsive, arrogant, and pushy. A boy who saw himself as a leader, took the place of said leader, but never really understood how to lead.

"Who said it was all of a sudden?" Humphrey asked. Mattie blinked, trying to remember what they'd been discussing. *Ezekiel Hollingsworth.*

"I'm not saying you could possibly know why you'd been ordered to capture the man's brother," Mattie said slowly. "I didn't mean to embarrass you. Who could know that?"

"Embarrass? We're getting him out of the way, Mattie. We're protecting him."

"Of course you are," she said in a disbelieving tone. "Not that you'd tell me the truth anyway! I mean, all I did was blow off my chance to escape." She paused a second, trying to confuse him. "I suppose you're the leader because of your ability, right? 'Cause this is *not* an easy group to convince to follow you. I remember, at the Barracks, that was something they counted on: as long as we didn't come together behind a leader, we were no threat to them. But here you are, Humphrey, and you're the obvious leader . . . along with Mary Ann."

Even though Mattie was playing Humphrey, she found she was nervous. She knew psychological manipulation, and yet she didn't know how to make herself attractive to boys. It just seemed to happen sometimes.

In movies, the girl could control it, could manipulate the boy, make him like her if she wanted. In real life it was a lot trickier.

But Humphrey was blushing, so she thought her comment about him being one of the leaders had worked. "Leaders are strong," she added. "Powerful. In command. I happen to like that, for what it's worth."

He clearly appreciated her comments.

"So that would make your ability . . . what? Did you drop the temperature last night?" She knew it had been Mary Ann, but asked anyway. "No, I don't think so. Your ability's bigger than that. You can change your voice? Maybe it's something like you can identify the last person who touched an object before you? No. Those are useful, but not quite leadership material. Invisibility? Yes, that would do nicely to establish one's leadership. You could spy. Pry. Surprise. Is that it, Humphrey? Can you make yourself invisible?"

"Games? Tricks? You think?"

He was playing along. What next? Mattie wondered. How to draw him in, so he'd confess his ability? To know one's strengths meant you also knew his weaknesses.

"You know what I think I'd find out if I *read* you, Humphrey?"

"No, but I think you're going to tell me."

"I think I'd find out you want to kiss me." She let the sound of it bounce around the room. She'd never said such a thing to a boy before, but these were special circumstances.

In truth, the thought repulsed her. Humphrey was far from ugly, but hardly her type. If she could have put Finn and Philby into the same boy, that was the boy she'd want to flirt with.

Humphrey looked . . . embarrassed! Mattie decided to strike fast as a snake. "For someone, anyone, to lead this group, he or she would have to have an ability that went way beyond impressing the others. We were all impressed at the Barracks."

He leaned forward. "So if I tell you, I get to kiss you?"

She had him. "On the cheek."

"On the lips."

"But just a peck. A quick kiss. Nothing mushy. Agreed?"

"Agreed."

"Let's hear it. But if I don't believe you, the deal's off." Mattie already regretted it. In the old days, she knew, girls used to sell kisses at county fairs. She'd seen it in movies. And sure, she'd watched the *High School Musical* movies, with all their mushy kisses. But she wasn't about to do it. Not with Humphrey, that was for sure!

"I enhance other people's powers," he said, boldly and proudly.

"What? Seriously?" She'd never heard of such an ability.

"If your power is hearing things at long distances and I focus on you or touch you, that distance just got a mile longer."

"No way."

"Way!"

He was so blinded by her offer of a kiss that he didn't understand what he'd walked into. If this was true, his ability meant that when they kissed, his ability would magnify the depth of her *reading*. Likewise, she thought, her *reaching*. What thought could she push into his mind that would help the Keepers and Joe long term?

And then, she had it, right there in the forefront of her mind. On the tip of her silent tongue. A thought to bury deeply, so that it might bubble up days later and he'd take it for his own.

A girl walked past the kitchenette. "Show me on Shelby," Mattie said.

"You don't believe me."

"I don't believe you," she said, toying with him.

"It's complicated with Shelby. Hang on." He summoned the girl, a brunette with a bowl-cut bob, large brown eyes, and puffy lips. Her chin was broken out, her ears a bright red as the two talked. After a moment, Shelby nodded.

Humphrey ran down the hall excitedly and returned with a pair of binoculars. "Okay!" he called. "Come on!"

He led them to the end of the hall and out onto a side balcony overlooking the park.

Mattie's heart leaped. They were high up, at least five floors. The park sprawled out at their feet. Off in the distance, Mattie could see Disneyland, the Grand Californian. Buena Vista Street cut a line from the entrance to the Carthay, separating them from Soarin' over the World. The Hyperion stood to her right, the edge of Hollywood Pictures Backlot directly below. Tower of Terror, Mattie realized. In Humphrey's excitement to show off, he'd given away their location.

"Pick a person," Shelby instructed Mattie.

"Anyone?"

"Anyone."

Humphrey giggled, unable to contain himself. He sounded about seven years old.

"Okay. The girl in the gray yoga pants. Light blue top. V-neck. She's—"

"Reading the ice cream menu. Got it!" Shelby declared, studying the girl carefully, then closing her eyes. "Mickey Premium Ice Cream Bar," she said.

"That's the last item she read, the one she considered for the longest time."

Humphrey passed Mattie the binoculars. The girl in the gray pants ordered something. A moment later the Cast Member at the stand handed her a Mickey Premium.

"Lucky guess," Mattie said. "Everyone loves those." She'd never heard of a Fairlie being able to see through another person's eyes.

"You, of all people, should know better," Humphrey said. "Okay. Ready for the eight-cylinder version?"

"The what?" Mattie asked.

"Never mind!"

"Pick another," Shelby offered, clearly offended by Mattie's doubt. "Someone just looking around, not at anything too close."

"Okay. The guy with the dreads. Wide shoulders." Mattie offered the binoculars back to Humphrey, but he motioned for her to keep them.

Shelby did the same study-and-squint routine. "He's looking up the street. There's an Asian girl wearing a Nike volleyball jersey. Number twenty-seven."

Mattie searched for the volleyball player through the glasses. "Impressive."

"Check this out." Humphrey placed his hand on Shelby's shoulder. "Same guy."

Shelby did the squint routine and smiled. "Nice! Double reflection. The glass behind the girl, then a reflection off a window across the street. There's a popcorn stand with a blond astronaut girl doll cranking the popcorn."

Mattie focused the lenses, saw the perfect reflection in the glass behind the Asian girl, then refocused to see the reflection in the next window. There, sure enough, was a faint, tiny blond doll wearing an astronaut's plastic bubble helmet.

"You could know that already," Mattie complained. In fact, she was hugely impressed with Humphrey's boosting of the girl's ability.

"Could I also know," Shelby said, "that the guy behind the doll is wearing sunglasses and has a short, dark beard?"

Mattie checked the binoculars. And when she pulled them down from her eyes, Humphrey kissed her on the lips without warning.

In that nanosecond she was flooded with his thoughts—some of which she would forget as quickly as possible! Most of them she simply filed for later study. She then *reached*, transferring her thought to him, burying it as quickly as it took for her to lean away.

"No fair! No warning!" She wiped her lips with her forearm.

Shelby laughed hard. "He got you!"

"You would have played coward!" Humphrey said.

It was true; she'd already been working out a plan to avoid the kiss. "Would not have!"

"Would, too!"

"Okay. Okay. So, I believe you. Your ability. It's impressive. You too," she said to Shelby, who nodded back at Mattie.

"We all got what we wanted," Humphrey said.

If you only knew, thought Mattie.

44

TWO LONG DAYS HAD PASSED. Nearing midnight of the second, and the end of the stakeout's third shift, Maybeck and Charlene found themselves losing patience. While Charlene kept watch on the old hotel's side door, Maybeck stood across from the front entrance, reading the evening newspaper.

POLICE REMAIN BAFFLED IN GHOULISH THEFT, MORGUE CLOSES TEMPORARILY

TANNER WALTERS

Anaheim police chief Robert Lawson had few updates on the ongoing investigation into the theft of body parts at the city morgue in Pacific Hospital. The case continues to baffle authorities, he said.

The city's district attorney, Francis Slague, meanwhile, received a court order to temporarily close the morgue.

A source close to the investigation said necessary arrangements are being made through the Jamerson

& Whimfeimer Funeral Home while law enforcement officials continue to search for answers.

The news matched what Wayne had learned from Marty Sklar. The information, plus their raid on the mannequin warehouse, had led the Keepers to divide into two groups. They were rotating surveillance responsibilities, one pair keeping an eye on the funeral home, the other—currently Maybeck and Charlene—watching the abandoned hotel. The remaining two Keepers rested and then rotated in.

Philby, the odd man out, continued to work with Wayne to extend the range of the DHI holograms to effect the return. They claimed they were making headway. The trick, according to Wayne and Philby, was to find a broadcast platform that could transmit data outside the parks. Once again it was Marty, who knew a guy at an AM radio station in town, who came through. The radio's transmitter was not used after the station went off the air at midnight: an opportunity.

And now the midnight hour was fast approaching.

Lost in his thoughts, Maybeck didn't notice the police car until it slowed and stopped at the curb next to him. The officer in the passenger seat, a white man, rolled down his window. "Help you, boy? Ain't I seen you earlier, this same spot?"

"Just enjoying the fresh air, officer," said Maybeck, bristling at being called *boy*.

"Plenty of fresh air everywhere, son. It's late. Why don't you just move along and get on home before there's trouble."

"I'm just appreciating the architecture of the old hotel, sir."

"Sure you are, boy. Why don't you just appreciate it from someplace else?"

"Because the hotel happens to be there, sir."

"You talking fresh with me, *boy*?" That time there was no mistaking the man's tone—or his use of the word. Maybeck caught himself as he made a fist.

"No, sir. I wasn't aware of any curfew."

"I said: move it!"

"Yes, sir."

"Watch your mouth with me, boy! And don't let me catch you back here, you hear? You stick to the orange groves and shoe shining with the Mexicans and the other coloreds."

"Excuse me?" Now both fists were clenched.

"You got ears, boy? You need to be told things twice? My partner here . . . we got nothing to do. You want us to bring you in and teach you about listening?" He checked with the driver. "We are more than happy to oblige."

Maybeck had read about the 1950s in America, how African Americans—"coloreds"—had suffered racism and prejudice across the country, including in Los Angeles. He'd seen it depicted in plenty of movies and TV shows. But it was completely different when the words you'd read about were being said to you by some blotchy-skinned former high school football team bully.

"First of all, as to the teaching part: you two, and who else?" The policeman didn't like that one bit. He and the driver exchanged a long, meaningful look. "Second, I don't mean any trouble, and I will gladly move on, but, third, I have the patrol car's license plate memorized and your badge number."

"And fourth," came a girl's voice. Charlene! She approached the passenger window with the walk of a fashion model. There were times she could look thirteen, and others, more like twenty. This was one of the latter. "My friend and I have the utmost respect for men in uniform." She didn't even sound like Charlene, her voice all buttery and soft. "It's just a little school project, that's all. We mean no harm. But if you two come around later, I for one certainly won't complain. On the other hand, if my friend leaves, then I have to leave, too, and I won't be here when you return. And that would be a crying shame."

"You're with him?" the policeman asked.

Charlene measured her audience. "I don't appreciate the way you phrased that, officer. Do I look like I'm *with* him? Please! But as to the school project, yes, very much so." The Kingdom Keepers had been using the school project excuse for years. Charlene felt entirely comfortable in guessing Maybeck had used it. "I believe they're calling it *integration*."

The policeman stared at her too hard. She felt sick. "Please," she said.

The dashboard radio spit static. A woman's nasally voice blared from the small speaker, *"Calling all cars. Three-Adam-Two requests backup in pursuit of two male suspects on foot, currently heading north on North Lemon Street in the vicinity of La Palma."*

"We won't be long." The policeman grabbed for the radio microphone and rolled up his window. The car drove off. Charlene released a deep sigh.

"That was not fun," Maybeck said.

"Which part?" she asked. "The police, or the fact that I saved you?"

"I had it handled."

"Sure you did."

"Maybe I should take the alley for a while."

"You think? I'll be right here."

Maybeck crossed the street and turned the corner into the alley. Less than a second passed before he jumped around the corner once again. He pointed and mouthed silently for Charlene. She couldn't read his lips, had no idea what was going on.

Seeing her confusion, Maybeck raised index fingers on either side of his head; he was either mimicking an alien or . . . the devil . . . or . . .

It took a moment to figure it out, and once she did, she nearly screamed. *Villains! Overtakers!*

45

FIVE MINUTES EARLIER, Willa and Jess had occupied two park swings across the street from the Jamerson & Whimfeimer Funeral Home, a sprawling Colonial with white clapboard siding and gleaming black trim. A full half of the building was surrounded by a wraparound porch. Four brick chimneys pointed into the glowing sky.

"One hour and we're on rest. We can finally sleep," Willa said.

Neither girl was swinging, just sitting there, the toes of their shoes dug into the soil below. Nighttime insects and frogs threw up a chorus of chirps and cheeps, the sound so loud and so close at times that it made both girls uncomfortable. "What a day! Between watching the hotel and here it's like we never get a rest."

"Don't remind me. Bor . . . ing!" Jess said.

"Hey!" Willa said in sharp whisper.

Across the street, two slender guys, who from a distance looked about the girls' age, appeared out of some tall bushes alongside the funeral home.

"Look!" Willa pointed down the street to a slow-moving police car.

When the two guys saw the police car, they took off running. The police car sped up, racing past the park. It traveled a full block before skidding to the curb, a solo red light flashing atop its roof. A policeman jumped out and took off on foot; the patrol car's red light continued to flash.

"Oh no," Jess said. "That doesn't look good!"

"I know." Willa found it hard to take her eyes off the police car's flashing light. "They came out right by the funeral place."

"Not that, Willa!" Jess said. "Over there."

She was pointing to a long, fancy black car parked on a side street. It was almost directly across from them. Two men, nearly indistinguishable in the dark, came out of the curbside back door. One was hefty, in long pants and a polo. The other wore a sport jacket. They moved up a driveway, headed for the back area of the funeral home.

"What the hayseed?" Willa said, exasperated. "What's that about?"

"That's called a diversionary tactic," Jess said. "Those two guys coming out of the bushes? Their job was to make sure the policeman followed them. That way these other two—"

"Know the cops are busy."

"Bingo!" Jess said. "And I'm probably wrong about

this, but the thicker guy looks like a guy we called the Dogcatcher. If that's who it is, he's one of Hollingsworth's guys, and he's no one to mess with."

"If two Hollingsworth guys are breaking into the funeral home," Willa said, pointing to the back of the building, "this can't be good. Reminds me of the grave-yard and the morgue robberies."

"We're supposed to get a good look at them and remember every last detail." Philby held out hope that Jess might be able force a dream, but Jess wasn't optimis-tic. "But let's not forget: there's also a driver in the car."

"Yeah." Willa paused, working out a plan. Jess could practically see the gears in her brain turning. "How about this: we take off together like it's nearly curfew and we've got to get home. Once we're out of sight, we cut around the building and get a better look at the back door *and* whoever comes out."

"That works for me," Jess said. "Philby didn't want us going inside."

"Thank goodness for that! You ready? We're going to act casual, just two *adorable* girls heading home for the night."

"Wish we were."

"Adorable or heading home?" Jess asked.

"Take your pick," said Willa.

* * *

"Did you see her face?" Charlene asked. "The woman who was just escorted out of there?" She and Maybeck held fast to the corner at the alley.

"Not exactly," Maybeck said.

Charlene was incensed. "Because you were too busy hoping her robe would fall off."

"Was not! But I kinda don't think she's wearing much else."

"She's not. Nothing else." Charlene's eyes flashed in the dark. "That's Lady Tremaine, you blockhead! And you can bet her two escorts are bad people."

"*The* Lady Tremaine? As in the evil stepmom from *Cinderella*? Are you kidding me?"

"They're putting her in that truck." It looked like an ice-cream truck, with a forward cab and a big square box stretching over the rear axle. Painted sea green, with no distinguishing marks, it was the kind of truck that wouldn't be noticed or remembered. And at any moment, Lady Tremaine would be riding in the back with two nasty Cast Members—who probably weren't Cast Members at all.

"We'll take it from here." Finn's voice caused Maybeck to jump.

"Sheesh! Don't do that!" Maybeck complained. "You can't sneak up like that, dude!"

"It's Amanda's and my shift. You two rotate to the funeral home."

"No way! This just got interesting!" Charlene said hotly.

"You mind?" Finn took her place, peering around the corner and down the alley. "They're putting her inside, all right. Too far to see her face."

"Yeah? Well, I saw her face," Charlene said, "and it was Lady Tremaine."

"That can't be, right?" Amanda asked. "I mean, it could be a Cast Member or something."

"If she's a Cast Member, I'm the Black Widow!" Charlene's excitement tested the limits of what might be considered a reasonable volume for spies. Finn shushed her softly.

"I'll tell you what," he said, addressing Maybeck. "If you and Charlene can wait around, Mandy and I will check it out."

"But you can't cross over out here. You'll be vulnerable. Granted, I know Philby and Wayne are trying that radio station test tonight, but that's later. At the very least, we should wait till then."

Finn blinked. He didn't think of Maybeck as a guy who waited—but here he was, showing measured caution.

"This is our gig, our assignment," Charlene said. Again, her voice rose to a complaining pitch. "We should be the ones to go in there. We were here when all this went down."

"I've been inside the hotel more than anyone," Finn countered, "and Amanda lives there—in sixty years, but still. Besides, there's no better defense than having Amanda with me to *push*. We'll check it out and report back, and then we can all decide who does what next."

"And we leave Willa and Jess hanging," Maybeck pointed out.

"You'll be a few minutes late at most," Finn said. "Amanda and I are not planning to hang around in there. We'll be in and out."

"And if you're not?" an irritated Charlene asked. "What then?"

46

A LARGE STEEL BIN stenciled with the name DEMPSTER DUMPSTER occupied the back corner of the funeral home's parking lot. It provided excellent cover for Jess and Willa, as it allowed views of both the facility's back door and the side of the building.

"We should call the police," Jess said.

"Using what, exactly?"

"Oh, yeah. I forgot. No cell phones."

Willa was quiet for a moment. "There must be a phone inside."

"Hollingsworth's guys are in there," Jess said.

"To break off more fingers. Just like the cemetery and morgue."

"So creepy. FYI: we are not going in there."

"We aren't, but I could. I could find a phone and call the cops."

"Don't be ridiculous."

"I'm not. Let's say it's Finn and Maybeck here, not us. What are they going to do?"

"That's not the point."

"Of course it's the point! If I—"

"We . . ."

"Call the police, and they catch those guys *in the act*, that's called evidence. Please note: there are no phones out here."

"There must be a pay phone somewhere."

"And you have some change in your pocket, do you?"

"What is it with 1955? Nothing works!" Jess couldn't look at Willa.

"You don't go in with me! I need a lookout. You see that piece of wood behind that wheel?" She pointed to the nearest Dumpster wheel, which was held in place with a small chunk of wood. "Anything strange happens out here, pull it away and push the Dumpster. Believe me, I'll hear it rolling! It'll sound like a freight train."

Jess nodded. "I don't like you going in alone."

"Just give me five minutes in there. Count to three hundred or something. If I'm not out by then, roll the Dumpster and head around with a view of the front."

"Why the front?"

"The Dumpster will get the driver out of the car. I'd rather not run into him."

Jess nodded. Her eyes were wide. She looked frightened. "Five minutes. Got it."

"Starting now," Willa said, crouching and aiming for the shadowed wall of the funeral home.

47

THE FIRST TIME FINN had walked through the alley entrance to the hotel, he'd been met with the smell of urine, the sight of litter, and the sounds of voices looming from somewhere within. That had been sixty years in the future from his current attempt, explaining why the paint on the door looked richer, and the smell was more tolerable.

He briefly considered taking the stairs, which had once led him to the lair of the Overtaker Kids posing as Cast Members.

"Where are we going?" Amanda asked, reading his mind as always. He appreciated their connection more than ever; she knew what he was thinking before he did.

"There's a hotel dining room, ground floor," he said. "It was, is, a dinner theater—you watch a play while you eat dinner. I can see a room like that having a projector. Can't think of where else."

"It's a start."

That was the other thing he loved about Amanda: her encouragement. They could be standing together on a twentieth floor, about to jump to their deaths, and she would say something about the view, or how she'd always wanted to fly. She seemed to have an inexhaustible supply of optimism.

"It's this way." Finn used his knowledge of the hotel as an excuse to hold her hand and lead her down a series of dusty hallways, through swinging doors, and into the lobby, which was stuffed with Victorian armchairs, sofas, and an abundance of red velvet.

Amanda whispered close to his ear, "It looks *exactly* like the lobby in Tower of Terror! I can't believe it!"

Finn nodded. "That's because it will be, a long time from now." He nodded across the open space. "Dining room's that way."

"Finn!" Amanda let go and rubbed her fingers against her thumb as if she'd lost feeling in them. "Tingling."

He'd thought what he was feeling had to do with his holding Amanda's hand. But now that she mentioned it, he felt it in his toes and ankles, too, in his forearms and shins. His scalp. "We're crossing over!"

"Philby and Wayne."

Finn closed his eyes, pushing away all worry and concern. The sensation flooded through him suddenly, as if a valve had been opened. He stepped up to the registration desk and dropped his hand toward it. His hand, wrist, and forearm passed through the wood without disturbing the skim of dust on its surface.

"They've done it!"

Amanda moved her hand toward the desk as well, to the same result. "But shouldn't we be asleep?"

"I think we're all clear," Finn said, referring to a DHI state that he'd been able to accomplish in Version 1.6. "We're here, but we aren't. It's incredibly unstable, but useful. Maybe they didn't know what to expect."

"Or maybe it's the best they can do."

"Exactly," Finn agreed. "And who knows if it'll last? But this is perfect for us. We've got to take advantage of it. Come on!" He reached for her hand again, but their projected hands failed to touch. They both seemed impressed but uncomfortable with the result.

Finn shook his hologram hand, weirded out. "That's so bizarre!"

"And here I was thinking I was the only one who felt that way."

48

WILLA WAITED IN THE SHADOWS of the Dumpster, her full attention on the car's driver. When he cracked his window slightly and reached into his top pocket, she predicted what would come next. The driver lit a stick match and placed it beneath the tip of a cigarette dangling from his lips. Momentarily blinded by the brightness of the match's flame, he had no chance of seeing her slip inside the funeral home.

Inside, Willa stood for a moment, getting her bearings. She stood in a long, luxurious hallway with green carpet, seashell molding, and blurry watercolors on the walls. A small table held a guest book and a rack of business cards. Farther down stood a sideboard, which held a box of tissues and some pamphlets about grief and prayer. The two rooms she passed, the Grove and Sequoia, looked like miniature chapels. The sight gave her chills.

Moving fast, Willa followed a tasteful sign to the office, in search of a phone. The door was locked, but an old black phone paired with another box of tissues perched on a table at the end of the hall.

She made it about three steps in that direction

before she came upon a pair of leather-padded swinging doors, beyond which, in the distance, were voices. Male voices. Two of them.

If . . . we . . . witness what's going on, Willa could almost hear herself saying, *then the police have witnesses.*

With the utmost care, she eased one of the swinging doors open. She heard heavy doors opening and shutting at a distance. She pushed through and eased the door shut behind her.

Rarely in an action role with the Keepers, Willa had never given a lot of thought to what the boys and Charlene went through at moments like this. The panic of adrenaline thumping in your ears, the hot skin, dry throat, and stinging eyes. How all your senses heightened until you lost familiarity with yourself. Was she actually smelling weird chemicals, or was that her own sweat? One of the voices sounded East Coast. The other, a little like a cowboy. She wondered if either was the Dogcatcher Jess had mentioned.

Inching closer to yet another set of swinging doors, Willa took small, cautious steps, her head swiveling like a bobblehead doll's.

When she turned back, a rag clamped over her nose. She swooned and lost all strength.

She was sleepy. She welcomed the idea of a good dream. She could see the waves, the setting sun.

Way, way back in the recesses of her mind flashed the image of an old-fashioned telephone. But she had no idea why it might be important. She seemed to remember something about Jess, but no; she wasn't even sure who Jess was.

A man's firm hand led her through the set of swinging doors and into a pantry that smelled of disinfectant. They passed into a kind of kitchen or science lab, with a long stone table at its center. The table had drains and tubes that led down into rusted buckets, which didn't make sense to her.

Her feet bumped into a small wooden stepladder, knee height.

"Up here."

Willa climbed the steps willingly, eager for the promised sleep. The bed looked more like a drawer, but she knew that couldn't possibly be. Awkwardly she climbed in, feetfirst. She felt her ankles and wrists being tied, but she didn't mind one bit.

"Pleasant dreams," the deep voice wished her. "Eternal dreams."

She felt the bed sliding and, as it did, a darkness close around her. It *was* some kind of drawer, and she was being closed inside. Locked inside. Locked into the extreme cold.

A latch clicked. Willa reached out in the darkness.

The space, the drawer, was no bigger than a coffin.

49

At the double door entrance to the George Hansen Ballroom, Finn hesitated.

Seeing his hesitation, Amanda said, "Look!" A sign read: BALCONY DINING.

"Brilliant," he said.

Together, they scampered up the stairs, entering a curving balcony area with enough room for a half dozen round tables and several smaller square tables along the railing. The place was in disarray—chairs knocked over, table legs missing, a layer of dust as thick as a tablecloth built up on all the surfaces.

The room below had once been grand, if small. Gold pillars flanked a curved stage. Tattered maroon velvet curtains hung like wind-whipped flags. Equipment occupied the center of the stage, vague and ghostlike amid the lack of light. Only a few tables out front were lit, dimly at that, by short dining lamps with small pleated lampshades, their cloth faded and shredding. Sitting at one of the tables was a well-dressed man, notebooks open in front of him, papers spread about.

Finn tested his hologram once again—still there! A faint blue outline along his arms confirmed it. Philby and Wayne had pulled off some kind of miracle.

Amanda cupped her pixelated hand to Finn's ear.

"Electric cables."

Finn spotted an elephant trunk of fat wires running offstage from the equipment. He could not make out what the purpose of the equipment might be. Philby would have known in an instant.

"See that in the air?"

"Dust?" Finn inquired.

"More like smoke."

"That's where Philby would say 'You're welcome,' I think."

She smiled and he thought in the real world the entire hall might have filled with light. He put his hologram lips to hers and kissed her, though neither he nor she felt it. And yet they did feel it, deeply, in a place holograms couldn't reach and never would. His heart felt as if it might stop, or break, or explode; he was light-headed and giddy.

"Thank you for that," Amanda murmured. "That's the safest kiss I'll ever have."

Voices broke the quiet. A man, just arriving. He carried what looked like a purse.

"It's him!" Amanda said, recognizing the tall, skinny form of the man.

"The one on the hill at the graveyard," Finn whispered. "I wonder if that's Hollingsworth? The guy with his back to us." The big man sat at a table with a machine in front of him. Some kind of old projector? Finn wondered.

A pair of teens entered the stage, carrying something at their sides like two firemen might carry a ladder.

"The kids onstage look way out of it."

"You think?"

"They're moving like robots. Been there, believe me! I'm guessing hypnotized, but with Mr. Skellington down there, who knows?" She crouched down, and Finn crawled behind her, the two peering over the wooden rail.

The hideously thin man in the baggy suit wasn't African American, or Latino, or Italian. He certainly wasn't Caucasian or Asian or Norwegian. Even at a distance his skin, a rich bronze, shone like polished metal, his teeth a glaring white; his hair, black as asphalt.

A girl their same age followed the two boys onto the stage.

"So he hypnotized stagehands to move his stuff around?"

"Possible."

"Or?"

"He's created his own 1955 version of the Fairlies.

Kids possess more power than adults. He could use them for targeted stuff."

"That's about as weird as it gets." Finn cut himself off as the two boys hoisted what they were carrying.

They stood a mannequin up onstage.

50

WILLA HEARD THE PURR of a fan and smelled stinky chemicals. She felt sick to her stomach, but at least she was breathing. Her wrists and ankles were bound, so she couldn't move, couldn't pound the walls for help.

The bad taste in her mouth turned out to be a disgusting rag stuffed down her throat. It tasted like an old sock or, worse, a used handkerchief. She couldn't concentrate. She had no recollection of the chemical-smelling rag being forced over her nose and mouth, no recollection of the hand leading her into the room with the cold metal bed.

All she knew was that she hated small spaces. Both her elbows touched cold metal, and if she tried to sit up, she hit her head almost immediately. Her situation created unimaginable terror. The men who had put her here had no intention of taking her out. She was clearly going to die in this box.

Adding to her fright, her memory was fuzzy. She couldn't remember exactly where she was or how she'd gotten here. She smelled trash, but only for an instant.

Was it real or a memory? It was as if her brain had emptied. She knew of Finn, Philby, Maybeck, and Charlene, thought of them as close friends, but couldn't place them. Were they also in dark boxes?

She felt impossibly tired, her limbs heavy.

She closed her eyes.

51

A MAN WHOM FINN THOUGHT OF as Amery
Hollingsworth switched on the machine. It was in fact
a projector. Under the watchful eye and direction of the
Traveler, it took at least a minute for the three teens to
adjust the female mannequin to his wishes. As they did,
the image from the projector joined it. A plain white
human-size wood figure became something altogether
different.

"That's . . ."

"Witch Hazel," Finn said. "She's in some early
cartoons—she tries to help Huey, Dewey, and Louie
when Donald Duck pulls one on them. Crazy powers;
she has control over witchcraft and black magic. It's so
weird how real she looks, projected onto the mannequin
like that."

Amanda was shaking her head vigorously. "I don't
like the sound of that."

"I don't get what's going on. Are they going to paint
the mannequin, or what? Why project her?"

"Left arm!" the man behind the projector called out
loudly.

Finn immediately recognized the man's voice. "I thought so . . . that's definitely Hollingsworth. We . . . ran into him when we were after the ink for Walt's pen. That's him, for sure!"

Hollingsworth shouted to the kids onstage. "Right knee! Let's get it correct, please! We don't have all night."

The teenage girl approached the mannequin. She wore a black apron that blended into her clothes. She withdrew a hand tool and what turned out to be sandpaper.

"What's she doing?" Amanda asked in a whisper.

"You remember the marks on Pinocchio?"

"Like fingernail scratches."

"I think she's a sculptor."

As if on cue, the girl worked a sharp chisel by hand, shaping Witch Hazel's arm. The girl sanded the same spot. The Traveler inspected her work. He pointed to the mannequin's knee and the girl sanded it, too.

"Not that I understand why, but I think they're trying to perfectly match the mannequin to the projection," Finn whispered.

"You're right! But why that kind of detail?"

Finn did not answer. Instead, he observed the man from the graveyard's acute attention to the work being done. He directed the teens with long, skeletal fingers, like a conductor working an orchestra. *A little more. Not too much. Just right!*

"Why bother?" Amanda said, nearly repeating herself.

"Lady Tremaine," Finn answered. "Jess's dream. The projection in the workshop. Now here. You see?"

"You're not saying . . . ?"

"I am. That's exactly what I'm saying! Hollingsworth is creating the Overtakers!"

"Then we've got to stop them."

Finn was about to reply when Amanda spun around, her hologram arm already lifted. A teenage girl stood where the stairs emptied onto the balcony. The girl opened her mouth—to sound the alarm!—but Amanda's *push* hit her so hard that her cheeks billowed out. Her clothes pushed against her like a second skin. Amanda kept her arm raised and moved slowly toward the girl, who skidded back and hit the wall. Without looking at Finn, Amanda spoke to him.

"Gag her. A napkin. Tablecloth. Whatever."

Amanda thumped the girl against the wall. Finn sprang into action, the fear spiking through him, making it no problem for his hologram to grab hold of things. He stuffed a dust-encrusted linen napkin into the girl's mouth, tied her shoes together by the laces, and used her own belt to secure her hands behind her back. An old waitress apron gave him the last ties he needed to hog-tie her so she couldn't move. They laid her down.

"This'll only buy us a few minutes," Finn said. "We're going to have to act fast."

52

JESS HAD WATCHED FROM BEHIND the Dempster Dumpster as the driver of the car entered the funeral home. She'd pulled the piece of wood out from the wheel and pushed hard. But the Dumpster hadn't moved. Not one inch. She put all her effort into it; it rolled silently for an inch or two and stopped. How was she supposed to warn Willa?

She came around to the front of the Dumpster and heaved on the heavy metal lid, which was divided into two halves. She could barely lift it. She tried again, managed to raise it a few inches, and let it go.

It sounded like a car crash. Jess bolted for the bushes and hid. No one came out of the building. Nothing happened.

Five more minutes passed. Six. Seven.

Her mind was racing so fast it was almost impossible to really *think*. She wanted to call the police. The closest phone was inside that building. Willa was inside that building. Three men were inside that building.

She rose to her haunches, wondering if she had the nerve.

53

"JESS? WAIT! SLOW DOWN! What about Willa?"
Philby cupped the telephone's heavy receiver after a second or two of frantic conversation. "Jess has lost Willa," he told Wayne, "somewhere inside the funeral home! Doors are locked. Jess borrowed a nickel to call from a pay phone near the park. Thinks she should call the police. She's asking me to do it for her."

"Is she sure Willa's in there?" Wayne asked.

Philby repeated the question to Jess, listened, and reported back. "She says Willa's in there, but that she'd have to break a window to make sure."

"Maybe she wouldn't," Wayne said.

"Hang on," Philby spoke into the receiver, again cupping the mouthpiece. "What do you mean?" he asked Wayne.

"Let's consider the possibilities," Wayne said. "One, Willa is hurt or injured inside the building, possibly locked up somewhere. Two, she's fine, but breaking a window, setting off an alarm, involving the police will get her—maybe all of us—in trouble. It will lead to a lot of questions that have to be answered. Questions not easily answered by you or any of your friends."

"That's not encouraging," Philby said. "I don't see how that helps."

"Sure you do," Wayne said. "You're just not thinking about what makes this night special."

Philby's face lit up. "Holograms! The radio signal!"

"We don't know if we've been successful, but we've sent the codes for Finn and Amanda. What if we added Jess and Willa to the signal?"

"Where are you, exactly?" Philby asked Jess. He snatched a pencil and scribbled out an address on the bench top. Wayne observed and shook his head. "Hang on!" Philby told Jess as he awaited Wayne's comments.

"It's farther," Wayne said. "It will require more power to the antenna for a decent signal. But I say yes. Jess becomes a hologram, and she walks right through the door. Finds Willa. They walk out without ever involving the police."

"There's no way to tell Finn and Amanda," Philby said, reminding Wayne. "Their projections could weaken, break off, even. They might go into SBS—Sleeping Beauty Syndrome—if that happens."

"Would you rather call the police?" Wayne asked.

Philby un-cupped the receiver. "Jess? Listen up. We have a plan."

54

Willa could no longer think. The confinement in the cold metal box had her in a state of utter panic.

The fan was not simply blowing. It was refrigerating. If she didn't stop shaking, her limbs were going to disconnect from her body. She felt tired, terrified, and defeated.

That's when she heard something! It sounded like a familiar voice trying to shout into a pillow from the other end of a very long tunnel. She could not make out the words, or how far the tunnel might be, only that the voice sounded anxious. Desperate. Maybe it was her own voice reverberating in her ears. Maybe she'd been tied up in an echo chamber.

No. *Couldn't be.* Her voice was hoarse from crying out for the past thirty minutes. She tried once more, but nothing came out. It was like her voice box was frozen.

The girl's voice sounded again, closer but still indistinct. Willa wanted to put a name to it, but it was no use. Her head felt stuffed with cotton.

She was never getting out of here. She was going to freeze and die in this box.

55

AMANDA TOOK THE LEAD, heading downstairs
from the dining theater's balcony. Coming to an abrupt
stop on the final tread, she threw her arm out to stop
Finn, held up three fingers, and pointed toward the
lobby.

Three guards!

She moved her fingers like someone walking and
then shook her head. *We're not getting out that way!*

Finn nodded, considering the possibilities. He, too,
walked his fingers, but he motioned *around*, suggesting
they avoid the lobby.

Amanda rotated a make-believe crank by her ear.
Projector!

Finn nodded, then shook his head and walked his
fingers, indicating silence. Then he held up his palms
and separated them like *curtains*. He was suggesting
they tiptoe through the dining theater, go backstage,
and escape the building there.

Amanda nodded. Peering around the edge at the
three men in the lobby, she counted down with her
fingers. Three . . . two . . . one!

They slipped through the dining room entrance and held tight to the wall, moving ever so slowly. Those onstage were partially blinded by the projector's light, and Hollingsworth had his back to Finn and Amanda. They made it a good distance.

Now came the tricky part: they were even with Hollingsworth. From where they stood to the open backstage doorway a few rows ahead, they'd be exposed, easily spotted.

As Finn considered a way around their predicament, a girl's voice rose from the balcony.

"HELP! INTRUDERS!"

All eyes turned to the back of the hall, including those of Amanda and Finn. Then Finn leaned his shoulder into Amanda and nudged her toward the stage door.

The girl they'd tied up was standing now, calling down from the balcony.

"Two kids! Watching from up here! They got away!"

Finn and Amanda slipped backstage into darkness, thin blue lines glowing around their invisible holograms.

56

As soon as the three men drove off from the funeral home, Jess made her move to the back door. Her body felt as if it was sparkling like a fizzy drink. Philby's plan to turn her into a hologram was apparently working. She stepped up to the door, closed her eyes, and . . . *stepped through.*

So this is where people go once they die. It gave her the weebies.

The funeral home's hallways were designed to impress, to imitate a grand mansion, to make the visitor feel comfortable. It was like a stage set, someplace special but sad, lovely but godforsaken. A chill ran up her spine, through her shoulders, and out her arms. Her fingers felt cold and tingly.

She reached down and dragged her finger across the smooth, polished wood, only to recoil. With the brief contact, she felt her chest implode with grief and sadness. Tears sprang from her eyes. She staggered, unable to walk properly, weeping uncontrollably, moaning. It was the grief of hundreds of loved ones standing at the table while being consoled for their loss. Jess saw faces—old and withered faces with staring, bloodshot eyes; young disbelieving faces; men, women, boys, girls, Latino, Caucasian, African American, Asian, all gripped with the horror of death and loss. All crawling around inside her head like her future dreams, but these weren't dreams at all, and they weren't in the future. This was the past. The present.

She struggled to her feet, wanting to turn off the images, the deep-seated emotions and the pain. But she bumped into a table, and they all came flooding back.

Her toes tingled as well. Her entire body felt different. She lost her balance, fell toward an overstuffed chair—and *passed through it.*

The faces vanished. Now she saw only her current surroundings: a small sitting area with a couch and chairs, a coffee table, and two boxes of tissues. She took a deep breath, so glad, so eternally glad the faces were gone.

It took her longer to readjust to being a hologram.

57

Now backstage, Finn moved purposefully toward a thin rectangular frame of light surrounding an exit door into the alley. Partway there, Amanda stopped him. It didn't occur to either of them that if she could stop him, if she could physically touch him, her hologram had failed.

Instead, Finn focused his attention on the stage, where Amanda was looking. Seen from the side, the Witch Hazel mannequin divided down the arm, half projected color, half wood-white. At her feet, a low metal dish, shaped like a wok, contained a fire of brown grasses and small twigs. A table close by appeared to hold X-rays—oversize sheets of plastic film. Finn tried to absorb it all, to memorize it. His state of panic didn't help him any.

"You see?" Finn said. "Do you get it?"

"Maybe not," she admitted, "but really, we have to go!" This time, Finn pulled her, tugging her off-balance and hurrying her toward the door. Again, he missed the significance of that physical connection—missed as well the absence of the glowing blue light at the edges of their bodies.

He aimed for the door, but it really didn't matter—their holograms could transfer through anything material.

Amanda was dragging, holding herself back. Inches from the door, Finn skidded to a stop. "We can't be afraid. We need to be all clear for this to work."

Amanda pursed her lips and nodded.

"Pleasant thoughts. Like pleasant dreams."

She nodded again.

"Keep right there, eyes closed. Hold on." Finn stepped forward and banged into the door. He stumbled back, pulling Amanda down with him, and grabbed for his head. Back home in his own time, the words he spat out would have gotten him grounded.

Reaching over for Amanda, he touched her face.

He . . . touched . . . her . . . face!

"Finn!"

"Something's happened," he mumbled. "Philby. Our DHIs. I guess that's kind of obvious."

"Are you all right? There's a bump . . ."

Finn felt the egg on his forehead but shrugged the pain away. "Follow me," he murmured. Staying on hands and knees, he slipped across the far back of the stage, threading through the ancient props, sawhorses, and set decorations. Amanda followed on his heels like they were playing some kind of train game.

Voices. Finn lay flat; Amanda lay flat. They heard

the clear sounds of people approaching—a guy and a girl by the door behind them. They were panting; clearly they'd been running.

"We lost 'em," the boy said.

"We don't *know* we lost them," the girl said. "And by that I mean, the door *is* locked."

"Let's go!" shouted Hollingsworth from the dining room. "No more distractions!"

By the way the two teens hurried back, Finn gained a respect for the degree of discipline Hollingsworth instilled in his people. Discipline . . . or fear. The man was no one to mess with.

Aiming for a side exit, which would hopefully be unlocked, Finn stayed on his belly and crawled, Amanda close behind. She grabbed his ankle as a chorus of chanting rose, echoing throughout the theater. Not pleasant chanting, not choirboy material, but edgy, primal rhythms pulsing out toneless melodies. The kind of chanting that ran gooseflesh up both Finn's arms and tickled the back of his neck.

The large backdrop, a white screen like a giant bedsheet, hung between Finn, Amanda, and whatever was going on out on the stage. The projector threw an enormous silhouette of the Witch Hazel mannequin onto the screen, fifteen feet high and six across at the shoulders. Added to the silhouette was a low orange flickering. Open flame. Three smaller figures reached out and placed their hands on the looming figure.

"What if they're like us? Like Jess and me and Mattie? Early Fairlies?" Amanda inquired.

"This is 1955!" Finn said, objecting.

"So?"

"So I liked your hypnotism explanation. Let's stick with that." Finn shook loose Amanda's hold and belly-crawled as fast as a lizard toward the far edge of the backdrop. He eased his head around carefully to steal a look.

On the screen, the silhouette's arm jerked and bent at the elbow. Amanda sat up and clutched her knees to her chest, biting into her arm to keep from screaming. The silhouette's left arm moved. Amanda lost her breath. She felt as if someone was suffocating her. *How is this possible?* she wondered.

Finn's actions told her everything. He backed up, away from his view of the stage, his face chalk gray. His mouth hung open; he wanted to speak, but like her, he couldn't yet breathe. Crawling again, he reached her quickly.

"We gotta get out of here . . . now!" he wheezed, still struggling for breath.

"Finn?"

Eyes glazed, pale face sweating, he looked deathly

sick. "The skinny guy . . . Skellington . . . he put some kind of curse or spell . . . all the chanting . . . He burned the cel, just like Jess said. Witch Hazel . . . the mannequin's alive, Mandy! *She's alive!*"

58

CROSSING OVER LATE AT NIGHT wasn't a choice for Mattie, but a matter of course. Like it or not, when she fell asleep, Joe and the Imagineers had control of her.

It didn't sit well. But she didn't have any choice in the matter.

She awoke once again on the concrete at the foot of the Partners statue. Instead of the woman Imagineer she'd come to expect, she saw Joe tucked beneath a banana plant.

She ran toward the small palm tree that hid the Return, Joe fast on her heels. Behind them the castle lights shone on its rising spires and darkened roofing.

"Wait!" he called.

Mattie did not want to wait or talk, to plan or scheme. Joe's very presence told her this was serious. Joe did not wait around after midnight for chitchat.

If she could only reach the Return in time, she wouldn't have to deal with him. How could such a short distance seem so far? How could she feel threatened by Joe, of all people?

"Mattie, please!" He had guessed her plan.

"Stay away!"

"We got a message! The Keepers!"

She skidded to a stop. The Return was stashed a yard or so to her left, Joe three yards to her right. "There's something I have to do." A light breeze fluttered the plants. They seemed to be waving at her, inviting her to join them.

"Philby got a bug—an insect—to cross from the past and back again. Alive! He asked for some more gear. The Cryptos tell me it's for radio transmission. They think Philby may have figured a way for them to return."

Mattie glanced toward the bushes. Back to Joe. Back to the bushes and the tempting waving of the leaves.

"They're going to come back," Joe said. "It's over, Mattie."

"Over? It's not over! The Barracks Fairlies have Zeke Hollingsworth, Joe. They *used* me to get him. You're talking about responsibility and worry and all that. What about Zeke, the OTs? The Fairlies? They're trying to ruin this place. They *will* destroy it if we—if *I* don't do something to stop them."

"The police can raid the Tower. Zeke will be all right."

"Are you listening?"

"There's only so much any one of us can do. That includes you, Mattie."

"You know that's not true. This was your idea!" She cried, balling her hands into fists at her side.

"A bad idea, as it turns out. It's too dangerous."

"Who got to you?"

"Mattie, be respectful."

"I *read* a guy named Humphrey. It's bad, Joe. They're going to rip the park apart, and they're going to blame it on Zeke. I have to go back. I have to stop it. I *can* stop it!"

"I can't let you, Mattie. Not alone. Not by yourself." He took a step toward her.

"I'm not alone!" She lunged for the bushes.

Joe dove for her ankles.

59

MATTIE HAD ONLY CROSSED over and returned three or four times. The first few experiences had been so dreamlike that she couldn't say absolutely that they'd happened.

When she awoke on her bed in the Tower, missing her left shoe, she sat up and stared at her own foot, wiggling it, bending her ankle. Joe. Joe had stolen her running shoe right off her foot.

Finn had told a story about waking up after his first return to find a burn on his arm, a burn he'd received while crossed over. The other Keepers had shared similar stories. But Mattie found it totally different when experiencing it herself. A mixture of disbelief and realization combined into doe-eyed astonishment.

She was messing with a world she knew little about. What if Joe was more worried about her crossing over than what she did here? What if the technology was compromised and he'd been afraid to tell her? Why had she been so eager to return without hearing him out?

And how was she supposed to explain a missing shoe

to the Fairlies? She was Cinderella, but in reverse—she needed that shoe back!

She undressed quickly and slipped into the musty-smelling Hello Minnie sleeping bag the Fairlies had provided. They weren't locking her room anymore, but the wing of the Tower where they slept was guarded through the night. Humphrey was no idiot; he'd spread the Fairlies over several floors.

She tossed and turned for the next several hours, unable to sleep. When she heard some bumping around and smelled coffee, she threw her clothes back on and headed into the break room, shoeless.

It was Antonella, thin and dark-eyed, and suspicious by nature.

The best offense is a good defense. Or is it the other way around? No matter!

"Have you seen a shoe, a running shoe, anywhere?"

Antonella didn't answer, only glanced down at Mattie's stocking feet. "Unless you give us something useful, you're no use to them, to us. You understand that, right? And if you're no use to us? Well. You know what happens to things that aren't needed." Her eyes ran up Mattie's body in a way that chilled. "Put your gloves on. Right now! You know the rules!"

Mattie did know. She would have given anything to *read* a girl like Antonella. "Oh my gosh! Hang on!"

She returned to fetch the Minnie gloves and brought her lone running shoe along with her. "It's like this one. Gone! How could that happen?"

"Exactly," Antonella said. "How could that happen? The room has no windows. You must have been wearing it on your way in."

"Why would someone take one of my shoes? That doesn't make sense."

"No, it doesn't."

"Just like this mission of yours."

"Excuse me?"

"Have you thought about what you're doing? Other than getting out of the Barracks."

"I don't know what you mean."

"You—all of us—are being used in the exact same way they used us in Baltimore. Don't you see? I don't know about you, but I grew up loving Disney. Everything about it! Why would I want to wreck that? I wouldn't. But they do. Do you know why? Do you know the history of this thing?"

"It's none of my business." Antonella's eyes darted left and right, as if she were searching for an escape.

"You don't want it to be your business because they offered to get you out of the Barracks," Mattie said. "That's all that matters, right? I *understand* that, but it's not all that's at stake! The guy who owns the Barracks, who runs it . . . his father stole from Walt Disney! That's what this is about. He stole from Walt Disney, and Walt fired him. That's all this is, a son trying to mess up the guy who fired his father, except they're dead, his father *and* Walt Disney both. So what's the point, Antonella? It means *nothing.*"

"That can't be right."

"No? Okay. So you tell me why the people running the Barracks allowed a dozen Fairlies, all with abilities that can be used to scare people or physically destroy things, to be sent to Disneyland. Because it wasn't for vacation!"

Antonella might as well have been slapped across the face. She reeled back, putting her hands against the counter as if for support.

"Consider this," Mattie continued. She was a little breathless, but she had to do this, had to build up the idea she'd *reached* into Humphrey. "If you, or any of us are caught, we'll be arrested. Do you think the Barracks is going to bail us out? You think they care? Do you think they give a rat's tail what happens to any of us?"

She caught her breath. Antonella was staring at her like at a car wreck, like she couldn't look away.

"No, they do not. They want us to do what they can't, and they want us to be blamed so they're not. Not to mention how selfish you—all of us!—are being!"

"Selfish? We're living like homeless people, girl. Don't go there. That is just plain nonsense!"

"Really? Then answer me this, Antonella. What's going to happen when a bunch of teenagers *who have special powers* are blamed for damaging, maybe ruining, 'the happiest place on earth'? We, the Fairlies, go from being freaks to bad guys. We're the juvies, the criminals, the kids you can't trust because they're so strange to begin with! We wreck it for every kid out there who's growing up wondering why they're so different. How can we do that? How can *you* do that?"

Antonella's tears told Mattie she'd connected. The tough girl stood there, shoulders slumped and loose, not looking so tough anymore.

Only as she tasted salt on her lips did Mattie realize she was crying, too. Not for herself, but for the young kids with abilities. She'd been there; Antonella had been there. They understood.

"I have a little sister," Antonella gushed. "Fire. Pyrokinesis."

"Three Fairlies in one family? That's—"

"Rare."

"Unheard of. No one has ever . . ." Mattie blinked, trying to take it all in. "I *have* heard that if it ever did happen, both abilities would be more powerful than others'. Are your parents—?"

"Dead. Both dead. If they had abilities, they never told us."

"And your little sister? Antonella . . . you cannot go to jail. You have got to get this figured out, and soon!"

"You don't go against the Barracks."

"Agreed," Mattie said, clearly surprising Antonella. She waited for the expression of bewilderment to leave the other girl's face. "You don't go against them. It's suicide. Some of those kids in 13 never looked right to me. You get put over there, part of you goes missing. Permanently."

"You're not making sense." Antonella was angry, or embarrassed by her crying, or both.

"I can't do it. You can't do it. But *we* can. One of us, two of us, three of us try to go against them, we end up in Barracks 13 or worse. But if we all go against them together? If we turn our abilities back on them . . ." She left time for Antonella to imagine the possibilities. "Instead of them seeking revenge for some dead guy, *we get our revenge on them*! How sweet would that be?"

Then, knowing when to end a tease, Mattie muttered, "I wish I could find that darn shoe," and walked out of the break room, leaving the tear-streaked Antonella, unflinching, and unmoving.

60

JESS TURNED A CORNER and faced a wall filled with a dozen oversize drawers. She didn't like the look of the drawers or the table at its center, or the power tools on the wall and countertops. This was a butcher shop. This was someplace horrible.

She swallowed dryly while trying to grab hold of a drawer handle. But her hand passed through the metal. On her third try, furious, she suddenly made contact. She pulled the heavy drawer open, revealing a black bag and the gag-inducing chemical smell. She fought the urge to vomit.

Her hologram hands trembled as they hesitated over the zipper. She did not want to open the bag; did not want to look inside.

She heard a voice. Close!

She called back as she frantically opened a drawer.

She screamed. An old guy with yellow, puckered skin.

She slammed the drawer shut.

She fell off the footstool.

Willa's head—*only her head!*—stuck out of the next drawer over. A rag was stuffed into her mouth.

"Willa?"

Tears squirting from her eyes, Jess concentrated and tried to remove the rag.

"A little help?"

Jess felt faint, having no idea what to do. She was half laughing, half crying as Willa wiggled her hologram farther out. "This hurts," Willa said, slipping back into the drawer.

Jess slid open the drawer. Willa, lethargic and dulled, scrambled to get out of there. Her panic fluctuated her between a hologram and a mortal girl. Hugging her, Jess pulled her out and laid her onto the concrete floor. She tried to let go, but Willa wouldn't let her. The two girls hugged while Willa cried, sobbing, "I've never been so scared. Pitch-dark . . . this fan . . . They wanted me to die in there."

"You're here now. You're okay."

"We're holograms."

"How about that?" Jess said. "I called Philby. It's all Philby."

"Dell?" Willa said, using her boyfriend's first name.

"Uh-huh! Philby saved you."

Willa's sobs evolved to a slow, personal laughter meant only for herself. She continued clinging to Jess. "You saved me. Philby just pushed a few buttons."

"Details, details," Jess said. This time, the girls laughed together.

61

Less than a minute later, pain shuddered through Jess and Willa like a seizure. They'd made it all of two steps trying to get out of the funeral home's room of death drawers before being stricken.

"Wh . . . at's . . . ha . . . ppen . . . ing?" Jess moaned, her limbs twitching. Her face cramped like she had lockjaw, making talking excruciatingly painful.

Beside her, Willa's hologram face was a mask of horror, her cheeks moving as if small animals beneath her skin were trying to find a way out. Her eyes bulged, and Jess had to look away; it was so disgusting. Worse yet, she knew her face was the same gruesome vision.

The girls flapped and convulsed for a minute or more and then lay still, breathing as if they had run hard and fast.

"What was that?" Jess asked, her voice pinched by the remnants of suffering.

Willa spent a moment contemplating before speaking. "I'd suspect it's our projections. A problem on Philby's end."

"Sorry I asked."

"Do you think you can stand?"

"I'm not sure I can move. I'm afraid to try."

"I feel the same. Our fear may be in opposition to the holograms. Maybe the spasms are part of that." Willa tested the movement of her ankle. "Nothing," she said. She sat up. "It's over."

Jess kneeled, moving carefully, afraid.

Willa waved her arm toward the leg of a stainless steel table. She hit it, and it hurt. "Uh-oh," she said.

"What?"

"I've lost my hologram."

Jess reached out and touched Willa. "Me too. Is that what that was?"

"I don't know. We've always returned smoothly. Being here, in 1955, it's all different. Our sleeping selves are sixty years in the future. Crossing over and returning when we're here is so strange. So different."

Both girls stood, assessing their condition by moving and flexing.

"Have you thought about that?" Jess asked. "If what we're doing here has anything to do with the present?"

"I have."

"I'd like to hear that sometime."

"Yeah, same here," Willa said.

"Right now, I think the others need us." Jess explained the situation at the old hotel. "Philby didn't know what was up with Maybeck and Charlene. They were supposed to rotate over here."

"So they could be outside looking for us." Willa sounded strained.

"I suppose."

"If we've lost our holograms, we can't leave without setting off the alarms. So once we leave, we don't come back. We head straight to the hotel."

"But whoever was in here will know we were in here, too," Jess said. Her brow furrowed the way it did when she was thinking.

"Are you saying what I think you're saying?"

"We need to look around, Willa. It's probably our last chance. We need to know what those men were doing here."

"I think we know."

"So, we need to confirm it, then. Prove it."

"You'll excuse me if I'm not exactly thrilled with the idea of looking in these other drawers." Willa counted a dozen total—four across, three high.

"Yeah, I get that, but it has to be done."

"And fast," Willa said. "If we've lost our holograms, we can be pretty sure the others did as well. And that can't be good for anyone."

62

"THIS DOOR'S CHAINED, TOO," Finn said, getting a closer look at the nearest exit.

Amanda remained balled up, frozen.

"Mandy, we're going to be all right." Finn moved over to comfort her. "I know how horrible what they're doing is. For me, too. But this is why you came to 1955. This is what it's all about. This, right here. We've got to stop them."

"You're repeating yourself."

"I'm pumped."

"I guess," she groaned.

They both knew what was scaring them both: the skin-and-bones man orchestrating the transformation. Hollingsworth was calling some of the shots, but it was the Traveler, the man they called Skellington, who had turned the mannequin into a living witch.

"This is when it happened," Finn said. "Today. Now. This is the start of the Overtakers. This place. These people. I can't believe we're actually here."

Against the white sheet, Witch Hazel's eerie, elongated shadow jerked and twitched. Her movement was growing smoother. A craggy, grating voice spoke, quiet at first, but increasingly loud and confident. She was speaking. The words began as malformed, indecipherable grunts, but soon began to take clearer shape.

"We're outnumbered," Amanda said. "Skellington has powers that we've never heard of. We need to get out of here and organize. We need help, Finn."

All the while, behind them, the three smaller shadows reached out and connected to Witch Hazel's shadow.

"We can't take time to get organized. This is *happening right now.*"

"The kids are obviously being manipulated by Skellington. Hypnotized into pushing knowledge and maybe emotions into her," Amanda said. "I swear, this is not only the start of the Overtakers, it's the start of the Fairlies. So what if he hypnotizes us? Puts a spell on us? He's turning a piece of wood into some*one*, instead of some*thing*. How are we supposed to stop that?"

"No clue," Finn said, his mind calculating. "But if we don't do something fast there's going to be even more dark magic than the scarecrow in here, and we can't allow that. This is the part of history we came to change. You don't get second chances at things like this, trust me!"

"We can't fight that guy!"

"Mandy . . . we don't have a choice."

63

"WHY AREN'T THEY OUT YET?" Charlene asked
Maybeck. "Something's happened."

Maybeck stared down the long alley. "We're supposed to be relieving Jess and Willa at the funeral home.
This isn't our shift. We should get out of here."

"Seriously?" she said. "We cannot possibly leave!
We should go in there."

"Finn didn't want that."

"Who cares? You didn't care a few minutes ago."

A calico cat crossed the alley. A lonely car horn
sounded someplace far away. "Are those bats up there
flying around?" Maybeck asked.

"Terry, come on. Get serious for once."

"Ouch! Okay, hear me out. Finn knows the place.
We don't. He has Amanda with him. She can *push* anything. I'm not too worried about them."

"You are. I can tell you are."

"Yeah, well . . ." Maybeck trailed off, then cleared
his throat and said, "How do we find them? It's huge!
And what do we do if Finn doesn't want us in there?"

"Terry, they haven't come out."

"Noted." He hadn't taken his eyes off the sky. "I'm pretty sure those are bats."

"We can't just sit here."

"We're standing. But agreed. We belong over at the funeral home."

"We're going inside," Charlene announced.

"No, we're not!"

"Together. We're going to look around."

"And if we're caught?" Maybeck asked. "If we wreck things by prowling around in there?" He lowered his head. "I hate bats."

She huffed, annoyed with him. "Then I guess we mess it all up. But we mess it up trying to help, not sitting around. Since when do you sit around?"

"Since Finn told us to hang back," Maybeck answered.

"Since when do you care what Finn says?" she asked.

"Yeah, good point. Okay, then we do this my way. But listen, if there are bats in there, count me out."

64

"FINGERS," JESS SAID. "Missing . . . fingers, basically like the graveyard. I'm going to be sick." She descended the small metal stepladder, which led down from a top drawer. Running to the nearby sink, she unloaded, rinsed out her mouth, and wiped her face with a paper towel. "Oh, ick. Eeww."

Willa heaved a lower drawer shut, having barely opened it. "Enough! This is so disgusting. Why are they doing this?"

Her face pale with illness, Jess faced Willa and said, "There are Fairlies, like Mattie, who can *read* things—but for them it's objects instead of people. They touch something and they get an image in their heads. A couple times, I've been able to see stuff like that without being asleep—"

"Epcot. I remember."

"Yes. Epcot. And one or two times after that. Out in the hallway a few minutes ago."

"What's up, Jess?" Willa stepped toward her friend, suddenly concerned. "You don't look so good."

"At the graveyard . . . Finn asked me about the arms.

And I saw the past, Willa! I've never seen the past, only the future. In all the confusion . . . And then the next dream. Pinocchio. I wasn't there. You weren't there. It was Finn and Mandy, so we don't know exactly what they saw."

"I'm a little lost."

"You think *you* are! Don't you get it?"

"Apparently not," Willa confided. "Which kind of upsets me, honestly."

"The past, Willa! I've been taking all my dreams as future-dreams because *I dream the future*. But we're in the past! And I'm dreaming—"

"—the past!" Willa reached to balance herself.

"Which means *all* my interpretations are *wrong*! I can't help the way I see things, but I filter it—I know I do—because it's always the future. And I've filtered these recent ones wrong."

"Jess, you're kind of freaking me out."

Jess was pacing now, twisting her hands together. Her face looked frenzied, almost wild.

"In the graveyard I was interrupted. But now I know what I have to do, Willa." She paused, locked eyes with her friend. "I need you to help me, support me, whatever."

"Jess, no!" Willa said, stepping up to block her approach. "You're not going to do that again." Jess wrestled at her, trying to get past. "That was Finn asking you to do something he should have never asked you to do."

"He can't dream the future, can't *read* the past, which I just did five minutes ago out in the hallway! There was a reason he asked me. I've got to do this," Jess said.

"Don't, please!"

Jess saw tears in Willa's eyes.

"I have to. The fingers . . . what if I can see what's going on with them? That's important!"

"There must be another way."

"Apparently, I can sometimes dream, or *read*, the past instead of the future. Who knew?" Jess took a deep breath, steadying her voice, and said, "Now, please, step aside."

65

JESS PULLED THE DRAWER OPEN. Seeing the older lady lying there gave her a sickening chill.

"Jess, don't."

Willa's prompt had the opposite effect. Jess looked once, just enough to know where to grab hold. Then she jabbed her hand toward the spot and looked the other way, closing her eyes.

It belongs to a man. His grip is firm as he takes hold of her finger. There's the sound of something cracking, like garden scissors on a stalky weed.

Jess squints more tightly, pushing past the sound, into the man doing this.

An almond-shaped darkness. It takes her a moment to visualize, to realize she is tiny, hovering above a satchel or purse. She has never felt so small, so claustrophobic.

She's the broken finger as it moves into the satchel and, as the light changes, she's faced with not one, but a half dozen others.

Jess wants this to stop. Struggles to let go of the dead woman's hand.

Willa sees Jess's eyelids flutter frighteningly. She calls for Jess to let go.

The darkness clears. Other fingers are being stacked atop a pile of . . . hair or fur, or both. There's something like a movie screen behind it all, and other material under the hair, shreds of fabric, dried husks of crayfish, insect shells, and what looks like red cotton balls. A match is lit by the same long fingers; the cotton balls come alive with a twist of gray smoke. Something colorful and blurry comes between the fire and her eyes, not fully in focus until it lights upon the uprising flames.

It's Lady Tremaine. The woman melts, dissolves, and joins the coils of black soot.

Jess's eyes pop open. She releases the old lady's hand. Willa catches her as Jess loses her balance. "I know what they do with the fingers," she declares.

66

WILLA EASED JESS TO THE FLOOR, ran to the sink, gathered water, and lightly splashed her face. Jess blinked and sat up, breathless.

"It's a ritual," Jess said. "The fingers, the cels. They've done this before."

"The hotel. Of course! The mannequins. Like what happened with Pinocchio!"

Jess appeared to be in a haze, utterly exhausted by her vision. Willa propped her up, speaking in a whirl of words as the pieces fit together in her head.

"Jess, it all makes sense to me. The mannequins being shipped to Hollingsworth's company at the hotel. The Pinocchio mannequin. We have to warn the others! Look at the time!" She pointed to the wall clock. "Let's hope Maybeck and Charlie are outside waiting, because if they're not, if they're late . . ." Willa offered Jess a hand and pulled her up. "Can you do this?"

Jess nodded weakly. "I'm good."

"Liar."

"I'll be fine. Let's go."

"Without our holograms, we're going to set off the alarm. Once we do, the police."

"I saw the guy, the same skinny guy from the graveyard, up on the hill. Him. I don't think he's imitation anything," Jess warned. "He's some kind of sorcerer, or one of those spirit dwellers."

"A shaman."

"Yes! Exactly! It's like his eyes have no irises, just big black pupils. They don't blink. They just stare into the flames. It's like he's talking to the flames. Willa, I think he's the Devil."

67

MINARA, THE SHAPE-SHIFTER, was showing off in front of the gathering, first transfiguring into the giant spider she had used to terrify Frontierland, then into an enormous spotted lizard. Now she was a green stick-bug.

Humphrey stood among the few leaders up front, as did the girl, Antonella. But it was Mary Ann's moment, her blue hair covering her left eye, her lips stern.

A dozen or so Fairlies looked on, all dressed in their Cast Member costumes. Mattie, wearing her World of Disney outfit, could account for all the Fairlies but one—probably a door guard keeping watch. If her count was accurate, no one was guarding Zeke, though he was locked in his room and she had no idea who had the key.

Mary Ann stepped up to address the group. "Today, all the practice comes to an end. No more make-believe."

"Nice one!" a guy shouted.

Mary Ann seemed to choose her words carefully. "We go about our Cast Member jobs just like it's any other day. We give away nothing. All it takes is one of us to mess this up. They're looking for us. You understand?

Disney is looking for kids who messed up the park earlier in the week. Us. We can't give them anything to suspect."

"Finally!" a girl called out. "Been waiting for this!"

"Yes, we all have," Mary Ann said. "We will fail if we don't do this together, if it isn't timed just right. We've worked long and hard. Our housing has not been great."

The small group laughed.

"But we can put all that behind us now. Today, we prove what we can do."

Mattie tuned out the talk about how they were going to change things forever, her focus on Humphrey standing alongside Mary Ann, and on Antonella, who was in the crowd with Mattie, almost close enough to touch.

Through the crowd, she locked eyes with Humphrey and cocked her head in a curious, indulgent manner. Her gaze made it clear that his silence exasperated her. A similar connection with Antonella, who stood only a few feet away, followed. Heart in her throat, Mattie silently egged on Humphrey, urging him to say something.

As Mary Ann's blah-blah-blah continued, Mattie suddenly heard, "During a parade. Some of you will still be working. Others will have gotten off shift. In either case, we go at exactly five minutes past the start of the parade, when the guests are crowded around the route, and the attractions aren't as busy."

"Go? You mean attack!" some guy called out. The small crowd liked that. A modest cheer rippled somewhat pathetically through their midst. As the excitement built, Mattie slipped off her gloves and pocketed them. The morning briefings that she'd overheard from her room had ended with the sounds of slapping high fives all around. She intended to use the celebration as an opportunity.

"There's something else to consider," Humphrey called out, winning silence. Mattie suppressed a smile of satisfaction, rubbing her bare hands together to warm them. Humphrey cleared his throat. "When has the Barracks done anything for us? Until now, when have they offered anything? Even a field trip beyond the fences they built?" He stepped forward, his voice rising. "When have they done anything but use us?"

"Shut up, Humphrey!" a boy called.

"Let him speak!" cried Antonella. A giddy feeling rose up inside Mattie; she fought to keep her face still. "The answer is never! They trained us in that wretched place—but it was just to study us. They deprived us of sleep, food, one another's company, and for what? To study us again."

348

"Exactly," Humphrey said. "I'm not telling you what to do. I'm not speaking for anyone but myself. But have any of you asked yourselves what happens if things go wrong today? What if two of us are caught? Eight of us?"

"We fight our way out!" another voice proclaimed. A wave of support and hooting washed through the bunch, but it was meager at best—a few daringly vocal souls.

"Right. Us against Tasers and nightsticks. Now, there's a fight I want in on!" Humphrey's voice oozed sarcasm. "Your fight is going to last about five seconds, at which point you'll be in a police station. And here's the thing: How many of us think someone from the Barracks is going to bail us out, associate with a bunch of freak-show kids who tried to mess up Disneyland? I don't!" He took a breath. His fists were clenched at his sides. "The more I look at this mission, the more I think the whole purpose is to have us do their dirty work. Why? Because we're expendable."

He was looking right at Mattie, who blushed and lowered her head.

"This is what they trained us for, like Mary Ann just said. Today! Tonight! If a few of us *freaks* end up caught or hurt, so what?"

Judging his crowd, Humphrey risked a long pause. There was silence, then a chorus of voices.

"So what?" "Coward!" "Hear him out!"

"What now, Humphrey?" The last came from Antonella.

"Yeah," Mary Ann said, "what now, Humphrey?"

Humphrey stabbed an inquisitive look at Mattie, who relayed it to Antonella.

Antonella raised her voice. "We turn it back on them! We know who they are. We see them in the parks, watching us. Anyone gonna deny it?"

"Think to yourselves. Think *for* yourselves," Humphrey challenged loudly. "Are those Barracks spies there to protect us—or to watch over us, like prison guards?"

The hush that fell over the gathering was longer this time, which Mattie took as a good sign. She watched Mary Ann's eyes dance across faces, assessing opinions, measuring support. In that instant, it became obvious that Mary Ann was no one to mess with: in addition to her deadly ability, she had the instincts of an adept politician.

"Leadership will consider this," she said, weighing her words carefully. "For the time being, we head to our jobs as usual. Await the signal. It'll be given near the top of the hour. If it's two long, one short, we follow the plan; if it's two and two, we turn our abilities onto Hollingsworth's spies. We will want them all together in one place. We will need that bargaining power. Maybe, just maybe, this is the end of the Barracks. If not, it's the end of this place and all the stupid joy it represents."

Mattie anticipated dissent or objection. The Fairlies she had left behind at Barracks 14 were not known for taking orders well. But this group appeared far more disciplined, a condition she found troubling.

"Okay," Mary Ann said. "We're out of here."

The Fairlies turned to high-five. Mattie collected herself, raised her right hand, and moved through the snarl along with the others. In a fraction of a second, she had to decide to *read* for the location of the key to Zeke's room, or for whatever Mary Ann had meant by "the signal." With the former, she'd be *reading* to save a single man; the latter, the entire park and everything the Keepers had worked for, as well as the end to the system that had caged her and others like her for years.

She managed to slap three hands. Then she followed the Fairlies out of the Tower.

68

"*P*USH THEM!" FINN WHISPERED. He and Amanda were crouched in the darkened wing of backstage. Before them, the Traveler, the three kids, Witch Hazel. From out among the empty tables, Hollingsworth sat behind the flickering projector.

"We are locked in here, outnumbered, and we have no idea what kind of powers any of them have."

Finn laid out his plan. To his surprise, Amanda did not fully object.

"You've done this kind of thing before, Finn. I get that. But never like this. Never with a guy like that . . . that thing onstage."

"In case you didn't hear me the first time: this is the start of the Overtakers," Finn said. "Mannequins of Disney witches coming to life right before our eyes. Lady Tremaine. Now, Hazel. Right? We can end all of this—all the evil they do—before it starts. End *them* before *they* start. That's why you and Jess came back in time to warn us. This moment, right now. How many times do I have to say this?"

"It was more of a concept at the time."

Finn kissed her on the cheek, after which he said, "Sometimes it's nice not being a hologram." He paused, plotting their course. "Okay . . . Do it!"

69

Finn UNDERSTOOD THE LAW of unintended consequences, "That which one cannot foresee will outmeasure that which one can." He filed this one under: *It seemed like a good idea at the time.*

In the years Finn had known her, Amanda had grown up more quickly than he had. They'd been through rough times. Tedious and trying. Bodies changed. Brains stretched. Hearts widened. Her ability had developed along with the rest of her. The kind of *push* that would have once exhausted her had little to no effect now. The top limit of the force of a *push* had multiplied with each passing year; now she was more than a force. She was a danger. A weapon.

Face steady, hands fixed, Amanda fired her weapon across the dinner theater stage like the stream of an invisible fire hose.

Amanda's *push* toppled the Witch Hazel mannequin, sending it to the stage with a satisfying *crack*. The three kids onstage and the witch doctor flew off their feet and slid across the stage, limbs flailing, forming a pile that looked like a rugby scrum.

The problem? It came as the result of air currents, force vectors, and the collision of two interrelated masses—a possible law of physics about which Finn knew nothing. The *push* scattered the fire—*fingers* of fire—into a lush orange blaze of sparks and flames that fanned out like the rays of the sun.

Those that touched Witch Hazel set her aflame.

As Finn and Amanda charged through a swinging door into the multilevel dining area, Finn split off, aimed for Hollingsworth's table. Amanda looked back. The Witch Hazel mannequin stood up, her left arm and part of her head on fire. She appeared to be wood, or perhaps part flesh, part wood, and moved independently, in an eerily painful ballet. The witch, whose flaming left arm was also broken at the elbow, made a stirring motion with her hands, as if manipulating an invisible bowl in front of her. This was followed by a thrust so violent that a flaming chunk of wood dislodged from her arm and flew offstage, igniting a tablecloth.

With that thrust, a half dozen round dinner tables flipped onto their edges, becoming giant wheels. The legs of forty-eight folding chairs came alive, or at least grew flexible enough to walk and run in concert. The tables paired up, making three sets of two, and, like giant hands clapping, slammed together and pulled apart while rolling ahead—two pairs aimed at Finn, who was heading for Hollingsworth, and one for Amanda. Like well-trained soldiers, the chairs fanned out quickly and, as they did, began snapping their backs to their seats like oversize angry clams.

The speed of both tables and chairs was inconceivable. Amanda turned to run, catching a last glimpse of the spindly man, pulling himself up, his face a twist of menace.

The three Fairlies she'd *pushed* were also coming to their feet.

"Finn!" she shouted, dispersing her power toward the pair of rolling tables closest to him. They seemed ready to squish Finn like a tomato between two cymbals. The tables pivoted; the second pair headed directly for him. Amanda's cry alerted not only Finn, who held up a chair like a lion tamer, but Hollingsworth, who hadn't seen Finn coming.

In the next instant, snapping chairs attacked both teens. Finn fought back with a chair of his own, Amanda using small *pushes* to maintain a semicircular force field around her body. Some of the chairs bit each other, prompting reprisal. In what felt like seconds, many of them were fighting among themselves like a pack of wild dogs, leaving Amanda to *push* others out of her way. With the distraction of her efforts, she failed to notice Finn's situation.

Threatened by the approaching pair of crushing tables, Finn reached for Amery Hollingsworth, hoping that by making him a target, the tables might back off. He was wrong. The tables rolled and opened, enveloping both Finn and Hollingsworth.

"You fool!" Hollingsworth sounded resigned to their shared fate.

Finn remembered stabbing Maleficent and seeing her dissolve, revealing Dillard, his best friend. Saw Dillard fall dead. *Dark magic,* he thought. Wayne had left them in Toontown, there one minute, gone from this mortal earth the next. *Dark magic.* Finn understood clearly that his fate was at that moment linked with those of Wayne and Dillard, knew the end had come.

An instant of terror like none he'd ever known was followed by something more mysterious: infinite patience, the faces of the Keepers laughing, his mother hugging him, his father slapping him on the back. He experienced the warmth of triumph at seeing Hollingsworth's unfathomable panic. In the fraction of a second they shared—a piece of time that stretched out to minutes in Finn's mind—Hollingsworth was futilely looking for a way out where none existed. The tables had separated. Seeing Hollingsworth's realization made Finn feel all the better.

The tables closed.

Finn felt pride that he'd ended this horrible man and his ruinous scheming. That with any luck he'd ended the creation of the Overtakers before they'd barely started.

Hollingsworth's astonished eyes found Finn, who grinned slyly.

Hearing Amanda cry out his name, Finn turned his head. She was running toward the closing tables, leaning into it like a sprinter for the tape.

Finn's finish.

He and she met eyes. This, he thought, was how he would remember her: bold, defiant, thinking to the last moment that she could change things. He felt confident she would—this girl would become a woman; that woman would continue what he and the Keepers had started.

He closed his eyes, wished for her a perfect life, and with a stab of pain in his heart, whispered a silent good-bye.

70

TWO OF THE THREE FAIRLIES Mattie *read* told her Mary Ann held the key to Zeke's room. No big surprise. The third high five revealed a recognizable face, one of the hallway guard guys. Nothing more.

She'd spent the last twenty minutes getting little done in the storeroom. She'd moved a few bins around in order to look busy.

When Teresa approached her looking concerned, Mattie put a bin down and took a deep breath.

"You okay, Mattie?"

The thing about lying, Mattie realized, is that it never gets easier or better. Only worse and worse. "Actually, I'm kind of freaking out. Mary Ann, one of the leaders, told us all to listen for . . . I thought it was maybe Morse code. Longs and short."

"What exactly?" Teresa motioned for Mattie to join her in the open elevator car. But the car was just another cage, like her room in the Tower. Like the Barracks. Everyone wanted to decide things for her. Everyone wanted to lock her up.

"Please," Teresa said.

Mattie stepped inside. The doors closed. She felt herself begin to melt down.

Teresa tripped the stop button. "There's a security camera in this car, but no microphone. Stand in the corner by the buttons and no one can read your lips."

"Soundproof?" Mattie said.

"Right."

"This woman told me I could trust you."

"You can. But it's not easy, that kind of trust."

"No." *Not when Joe tries to drag you away,* she thought.

"Better to trust someone than no one."

"I suppose."

"Oh, it is. You'll have to trust me on that one."

They laughed together, Mattie somewhat sullenly. She couldn't remember the last time she'd laughed wholeheartedly.

Teresa said, "You're trembling. Are you sure you're okay?"

Mattie battled back tears, nodding. "I can't do this. Not now. There's too much to be done. The code is going to be 'two longs and one short,' or 'two longs and two shorts.'"

Teresa worked her phone, trying for a search engine, but the underground elevator prevented reception. "Darn!"

"I already looked up Morse code, if that's what you were going to do. In International Morse code, two longs and one short is the letter *U*. Two longs and two shorts are the letter *Z*. But the thing is, this code is going to be heard all across Disneyland." She took a deep breath, trying to convince Teresa how serious this was with her eyes, her voice, her whole body. "Either way, you need to tell Joe today's the day. He'll understand. Can you do that?"

"Of course." Teresa's eyes found the stop button.

"You were told . . . You're supposed to bring me in. Joe wants you to bring me in."

Teresa locked eyes with her.

"'Not easy, that kind of trust,'" Mattie said ironically, repeating Teresa's words back to her.

"Mattie . . ." Begging forgiveness.

"These Barracks Fairlies are going to wreck the park, maybe forever. You understand? And they're going to blame it on a Cast Member. An older guy. They may hurt him. For all I know, they may kill him! There's nothing Joe can do to stop it. It's too big, too well planned. Think of me as an undercover agent, Teresa. For the time being, I'm one of them. I have access. I can stop this. *We* can stop this. But if you kidnap me—and that's what you're doing, by the way, because this is *against my will*—then . . . that's it. All hope is lost. I have one chance, and it's today. If you delay me, even by an hour, it's over."

Again, Teresa eyed the stop button. But now Mattie did as well. Teresa had made a mistake: she hadn't selected the second floor. If Mattie could release the stop and hit the door-open button quickly enough . . .

Both girls' eyes left the panel and found each other's. It was to be a duel. Who was going to control the elevator car?

Mattie reached for the panel.

Teresa bumped her hard against the wall, knocked Mattie's hand away, and clamped down on Mattie's forearm, keeping her at bay. As Teresa touched her, Mattie got exactly what she wanted: she *read* her for "the code."

In the next instant, she punched her store manager in the chest, drove her shoulder into Teresa's midsection, and propelled her across the elevator car and into the wall.

You don't mess with a girl from the Barracks, Mattie thought proudly, reaching blindly for the panel and releasing the stop, then tripping the doors open. She glanced back, pushed 2, and jumped through the opening doors as Teresa unfolded from a ball on the floor in the far corner.

The adversaries entered a staring contest.

Mattie verbalized what she'd read. "The train whistle. You think the code will be given by the train whistle."

The doors began closing, time shrinking down to nothing. Teresa's surprised expression confirmed Mattie's *read* of her.

"Have a team ready," Mattie said. "When the whistle sounds the code: the Tower, fifth floor." The closing elevator doors had but a foot of space remaining. "He's in the room diagonally across from the break room. You must . . ."

The doors closed; Mattie shouted, unsure if Teresa could hear, "Free Zeke Hollingsworth!"

71

MATTIE BELIEVED IN DEMOCRACY. She also saw the need for oversight committees—a group of well-rounded individuals who could make the tough decisions faster than results could be achieved by a vote. But it wasn't lost on her that throughout history such committees had gone against group conscience, citing information or intelligence known only by a few—or to personally enrich those on the committee in question.

Nor was it lost on her that individuals wishing to thwart the decisions of such a committee had found their aims corrupted, too. Power corrupts; soda loses its fizz; reruns are boring; kittens grow into cats.

In this moment, Mattie lacked the time to weigh heady considerations about the moral implications of her actions. She would do what she felt was right and live with the consequences. "Right" meant leaving Joe out of it. "Right" was running to the Disneyland entrance, waiting impatiently, and finally cutting the Cast Member line. "Right" meant hurrying up the stairs to the Disneyland Railroad station and, seeing no crowd, guessing the train had left in the past few minutes.

"Right" meant a steely determination to outwit security and avoid being seen by Fairlies and Barracks officers, all of whom she knew to be in attendance. She used the backstage Cast Member entrance to get out of the tangle of guests and *ran*—ran hard. She was no Charlene, but living in the Barracks had trained her to marshal her strength, to summon up every advantage she possessed. She'd learned to run at her fastest, to lift her chin instead of slouching her shoulders, to carry her knees high into her chest and allow her ankles to drive her off the surface.

She ran past the Indiana Jones show building. Drawing surprised looks from other backstage Cast Members, as well as a few smiles, she pushed on, driven by the sound of the train and the clock running in her head.

Await the signal. It'll be given near the top of the hour.

Mickey's Soundsational Parade began around 3:00 p.m. With the parade providing distraction for the guests and work for the park's security team, it was a good time for the Fairlie sabotage. "The top of the hour" was only ten minutes away.

As Mattie cut through a small parking lot, yet

another enormous backstage structure looming to her right, something quick and sharp pierced her heart. Though it was an uncommon feeling, she understood immediately it had to do with the Keepers: Willa, Maybeck, Charlene, and Philby. She pushed herself for a fifth name—wasn't there a fifth Keeper?—but could not dredge it up. She repeated the four names yet again, unable to think of the fifth.

Were there only four? Could she get a number like that wrong? Running faster, harder, she tried to bring an image of the fifth Keeper's face—girl or boy? Latino? Asian? White?—into focus. But there was nothing.

Angry at herself, frustrated, she sprinted toward the train station, which was now in sight, the train just beginning to move. The sensation of loss propelled her. Her heart held on to the pain, convincing her that something—someone—had been lost. It was as if she'd *read* a person bearing the weight of a tremendous, unshakable grief.

Scrambling up an incline, Mattie reached the backstage side of the New Orleans train station, with its wooden platform and station buildings, including a post office. She charged along parallel to the last few departing train cars with their green-and-white awning tops, fire-engine-red siding, and black-and-white-striped railings. A female passenger saw her and waved her finger, admonishing Mattie, telling her that she'd missed the train.

Mattie caught the final car, took hold of the rail, and, with the platform running out, jumped.

72

Joe Garlington pounded the desk so hard some coffee spurted out the top of his mug onto the papers beneath.

The desk did not belong to him; the office was not his. He'd been offered it by Kim Irvine, who was in China on a project. Teresa stood before him solemnly, head slightly bowed.

"What exactly does she have in mind?" he bellowed.

"I'd prefer not to say, Joe."

"You'd what?"

Teresa said nothing.

"You think you're *protecting* her? From *me*? Do you understand the idiocy of that? I'm on her side, Teresa! Your side!"

"She told me to tell you about the Tower. The hostage. That we had to wait for the signal."

"She disobeyed me. Do you understand? She directly went against my instructions, instructions that had to do with her safety and ultimately the safety of the four . . ."

"Joe?"

"I . . . it's a number thing . . . Four? I can't seem to . . . Never mind. The point is that the teenagers apparently working for Amery Jr. are a threat to this park and its guests. Mattie has been playing a dangerous game."

"But I thought you and the Imagineers—"

"Yes, well, we changed our minds. Putting her undercover was irresponsible and more dangerous than we'd imagined. Now Ezekiel's missing as well, and you bring me this information, and I'm supposed to wait for some signal you won't describe? I have a responsibility to act on this information. His life could be in danger!"

"You have to wait for her signal. It'll be heard across the park."

Joe squirmed in his chair, half stood up. Sat down again.

She said, "It's a one-if-by-land, two-if-by-sea kind of thing. That kind of signal. Going after Zeke Hollingsworth early could trigger something bad. Mattie was adamant about that. A different signal maybe? Something more radical? We could backstab her."

"*I* could, you mean?"

"Joe, I think—I *know* that Mattie felt strongly about this. She has one chance, maybe the only chance, to make the park safe. To help us rescue Zeke."

"We know things you don't, Teresa. About Mattie,

about these other kids. I appreciate your concern. I certainly do."

"Yes, sir." Teresa's change from the informal did not go unnoticed. Joe stared at her long and hard. She said, "Please, sir, she trusts us."

73

GUESTS ABOARD THE DISNEYLAND Railroad grunted and complained as Mattie climbed over them. She reached the aisle and hurried forward, toward the front, where a small fire car separated the passenger cars from the locomotive.

Mattie practically dove into a seat as she saw the profile of James Corwin, the adult *reacher* she'd encountered with Zeke. James Calder Corwin, the man whose internal thoughts had shown her the familiar faces of Fairlies being used as park saboteurs.

She tried to follow Corwin's line of sight. He'd *reached* her when they'd made contact. A *reacher* could easily "force" the conductor to send whatever whistle signal Corwin wanted to send. But why a grown-up and not a Fairlie—unless . . . Mattie scanned the other passengers, frustrated she could see only the backs of heads.

Why send a *reacher*?

Why an adult like Corwin?

Then it hit her: Hollingsworth was taking no chances. What if he'd gotten word of the Barracks Fairlies revolt? He'd sent Corwin to make sure it never happened.

So what was Corwin's exact role?

And then Mattie saw it more clearly. How could she have been so dense? Corwin wasn't there to *reach* the engineer himself. He wasn't going to be identified as the guy who crawled up to the locomotive and interrupted the conductor. Let someone else get in trouble for that. Someone like a Fairlie.

No, he was there to subversively instruct whichever Fairlie was supposed to make the conductor send the signal. Only it would be *Hollingsworth's* signal: two shorts and a long. Destroy the park.

Corwin was there for the same purpose as Mattie— to force a particular outcome.

It made her realize she and Corwin were both looking for *a forcer*: a Fairlie whose ability was to cause the target to perform a physical act of the *forcer's* choosing.

Mattie knew only one such Fairlie. She scanned the passengers yet again. A girl named . . . And there she was: *Deajha!* A stunning girl of Indian descent with the most beautiful skin and dark lashes, Deajha had won the nickname Deja Vu at the Barracks. She sat in the middle of a three-person row a few rows ahead of Mattie.

Corwin, bigger and stronger than Mattie, was a practiced *reacher*, though as an adult, he likely had weakened abilities. Mattie had to decide whether to go after Deajha or Corwin; she couldn't get to both in time.

The decision was made for her. Deajha touched the woman next to her on the shoulder. The woman moved her legs somewhat mechanically, allowing Deajha to slip past.

Corwin stood. He wore a loud Hawaiian shirt, shorts, and flip-flops, the prototypical tourist attire.

Mattie waited, understanding the effectiveness of the surprise attack. *Reachers* fared better with touch *and* eye contact. Mattie needed only to touch her target.

"So remember: for a safe trip, you need to stay seated, keeping your hands, arms, feet, and legs inside the train. And please, watch your children," came a recording over the loudspeakers. It was the Disney park voice—not the engineer's—that was heard on wait lines and buses throughout the park. Mattie spotted a small video monitor mounted close to the train's engineer; he had initiated the playback of the recording.

Corwin took a step toward Deajha as Mattie closed in on him from behind.

The recording played for a second time.

An angry passenger shouted, "Come on, sit down!"

Mattie touched the back of the man's hairy neck. Disgusting! At the same moment, Corwin stopped. His head pivoted, seeking eye contact. But Mattie looked down at her feet and moved with him in order to stay behind him. An awkward ballet.

The touch was a jolt, the element of surprise hers.

In the first few nanoseconds she managed to *reach*—still a developing ability.

Two long, two short. Two long, two short. Two long—

Corwin mentally pushed back against her, like they were in a sword fight. Mattie's *reach* extinguished; she pulled her hand away, but Corwin caught her by the arm, maintaining physical contact—something she could ill afford.

She felt herself about to explain to him the Keepers' time travel, Joe's plan, and her own infiltration of the Fairlies. But this was Corwin's *reach*, telling her what to do, and she fought it. Her best defense was to *read*, to clog his effort to shove thoughts into her brain. She *read* for "colleagues," causing him to pause his *reach* and try to block her. That pause was all she needed: a flood of names and faces filled her.

With all her mental concentration, Mattie *reached* one final time—*two long, two short*—and broke his grip on her. She shoved him, before her *reach* had time to dissipate.

Corwin stumbled forward and into Deajha, not the sneaky attack he'd planned. Deajha didn't appreciate the contact, or the interruption. Nervous and irritable, she placed her hand on Corwin, who immediately sat down atop a fellow passenger. Complaining, the passenger squirmed into the middle part of the bench seat.

Deajha recognized Mattie. She raised her hands, to keep Mattie at bay.

The train's recorded message, asking passengers to stay seated, played for a third time.

Deajha scrambled out onto the fire car. Guests murmured disapprovingly. The engineer glanced back, clearly not knowing what to do.

Corwin fought the lingering effects of Deajha's *force* while also getting a look at Mattie. He finally made eye contact and offered an ugly snarl.

Ahead of them, the engineer straight-armed Deajha as she climbed into the cockpit, his other hand reaching for the walkie-talkie microphone. By trying to block her, he played into what she wanted: contact.

He dropped the radio mic. It danced on its coiled cord. His jaw trembled as his arm rose overhead to the whistle. He pulled: one long, a second long; one short . . . a second short. He waited, Deajha now the one maintaining contact with him. He repeated the same signal.

Mattie would never know if she, Corwin, or Deajha herself made that signal go out across the park. She would never know what the Fairlies might have done regardless of the signal. Perhaps they'd intended to revolt against the Barracks from the moment Humphrey stood up and explained things.

In any case, that's exactly what they did.

74

"**F**INN!" AMANDA FROZE as she witnessed the two tables converging on Finn and Hollingsworth. Distracted, her attention slipped and a chair bit her on the leg, like a snapping turtle, and held on.

Amanda cried out and fell, still fighting to maintain eye contact with Finn. The tables smashed together. She stumbled, losing consciousness. Black-purple shapes invaded the edges of her sight. As a curtain pulled across her vision, her hearing, her breathing, shutting out the horror of what she'd witnessed, she reimagined Finn's face. Grinning? At her? Unafraid? Proud, even?

She hated him. Felt betrayed by him. Abandoned by him just as she'd been abandoned by so many before him. Anger fogged what little thought remained. The pain in her leg couldn't compare to what she felt in her chest. Maybe her heart had stopped. Maybe she was dying along with him.

Then, a faint spark of what remained of her consciousness flickered like a candle when a door opens and closes too quickly. She hated him. She loathed him.

She loved him.

75

THE MOMENT THE ENGINEER released the train whistle's pull chain, he yanked the brake. Passengers screamed. The train slowed; a prerecorded warning alerted travelers to stay in their seats; the conductor knocked Deajha to the side.

Mattie was among the first to disembark, jumping from the car's lowest step onto a steep hill of soft grass, tumbling and rolling to the bottom. She ran toward the Haunted Mansion, trying to get her bearings: Rivers of America straight ahead. With the Central Plaza as her immediate destination, she suddenly felt miles away instead of only a few hundred yards.

Her sense of distance resulted from two unexpected situations. First, the relative emptiness of New Orleans Square, given the draw of the impending Soundsational Parade. It made sense to her that distances might stretch out if she battled crowds, but the effect was quite the opposite; seeing all that empty pavement increased the distance tenfold. Second, the sound effects, or more precisely, what Mattie first took to be sound effects. She'd tolerated thunder and lightning as a kid, but in more recent years, when she'd often been homeless, she'd come to be terrified of big and small booms—booms and gunshots, as she'd come to think of them—on the streets of Baltimore. She cowered with every pop.

Not bombs.

Not gunshots.

Fireworks.

In the daytime.

Not right! Not at all.

While some of the incendiaries raced into a blue sky, exploding and whistling, expanding into unseen chrysanthemums and invisible starbursts, other shells had been purposely aimed at Sleeping Beauty Castle, ricocheting off the walls and glancing out into Central Plaza. Some, Mattie saw with a burst of horror, had set parts of the castle ablaze.

As Mattie reached the Hub, she saw hundreds of guests fleeing smoking streamers as they skittered along the pavement, and blinding pulses of white phosphorus. She recoiled; the percussive explosions were intended to be hundreds of feet up in the air. At first enchanted, even diehard park guests backed up, turned, and walked briskly away, trying their best to obey the rule of no running.

In that moment, Mattie believed the Fairlie leaders had pulled a trick on her and Joe by reversing the meaning of the train whistle. None of what she was witnessing—including more fireworks going off behind her from Tom Sawyer Island—could possibly be part of a plan to attack the Barracks personnel. No, it had to mean she'd gotten it wrong; she'd forced the engineer to sound the full-attack alarm, exactly what she'd tried to prevent. The thought that she might be personally responsible for triggering an attack on Disneyland infused her with guilt, remorse, and unbridled anger. She could not, would not, allow her legacy to be "The Girl Who Destroyed the Park."

A group approached her at a full run, a group she recognized, a group she'd been expecting. If it hadn't been for the danger and chaos of the misfired fireworks, Disneyland guests would have swarmed this group, surrounded them so eagerly that they'd have prevented them from moving. Dash was in the lead, followed by Nick Perkins, Mulan, Kristoff, Pocahontas, Tiger Lily, Anna, and a dozen other characters. At the back of the pack, huffing and struggling to keep up with the rest of them, came the Minnie and Mickey she'd met in A Bug's World, with their pronounced noses, matted brown fur, and beady eyes.

"What the heck?" shouted Nick, dodging a smoking ball that zigged and zagged and zigged again, nearly hitting his running shoe.

Mattie blurted out that she'd messed up, obviously sending the wrong code.

"Dash! Tell her!" said Nick.

"I ran the park. Nick told me to. It's bad in Tomorrowland—more fireworks. Toontown. Tom Sawyer Island. The two entrance tunnels are blocked by parade floats, trapping us all in here."

"That would be the schedule details they wanted," Mattie muttered.

"Who?" Mulan asked.

"Never mind. It's no help to us now."

"But Madeline," Mickey said. He spoke calmly, even though he was winded. "Minnie and I witnessed more than one grown-up being held down by Cast Members."

It took Mattie a second to process what Mickey had said. "Were the Cast Members teenagers?"

"Yes," said Anna.

"And did you recognize the grown-ups? Were they Imagineers? Disney people you've seen around the parks?"

"Now that you mention it, no," answered Anna. "They were all men. All dressed up in suits. Not familiar at all."

"It wasn't me!" Mattie said ebulliently.

"Say again?" said Kristoff.

"I sent the right signal! Those teens you all saw were Fairlies!" Her mind sped up, as it often did when *reading* a person. "The Barracks—or worse, someone much more powerful—must have been planning the fireworks attack all along! They must have had a plan to disrupt the entrance, too!"

Having no idea where such things came from, Mattie heard herself barking orders to *the real characters of Disneyland*! Her, a runaway Fairlie, a pretty much friendless girl fighting for a cause that belonged to a bunch of missing time travelers. More surprising yet: the characters listened! Obeyed! Groups of five or six peeled off from the whole, running toward Tomorrowland or Toontown or Town Square.

The group diminished until it was just Mattie, Nick, Mulan, and . . . Mickey Mouse. Mattie felt the mouse's celebrity in a way that made her self-conscious and suddenly unsure. She wanted Mickey making the plans, but that clearly wasn't how he saw it.

"The tunnel," Mickey said. "That is," he continued bashfully, "if you think that might be a good idea."

"Tunnel?" Mulan asked.

"It's a transportation tunnel," Nick explained. "A road that connects the two parks backstage."

"If we don't stop the spies from the Barracks, they'll destroy the park and blame it on the Fairlies."

"I can shut down the pyrotechnics," Nick said, winning puzzled looks from Mulan and Mickey. "The fireworks!"

"Ah!" Mickey said.

"They must have commandeered the control room to have this much going on. We need to win it back. I can't do that alone."

Mulan loaded an arrow into her bow. "Lead the way, Nick. They'll surrender to me, or they'll pay dearly."

"Can you spare us?" Nick asked.

"Go!" Mattie said, with the conviction of an army general. Mulan and Nick took off running in the direction of the Ice Cream Parlor.

"I guess that leaves us as buddies!" said a wide-eyed Mickey, his little front paws worming nervously in front of him.

"I guess it does," Mattie said, shoving Mickey aside as a whirring, smoking blast of fireworks nearly engulfed him. The mouse thanked her. She tried not to think about having just saved Mickey Mouse—*the* Mickey Mouse!—from going up in flames.

"Best view of the park, Mickey?"

"Gee whiz!" He rubbed his black, wet nose with both hands and squinted. She'd never seen something so cute. "It's not Beauty's castle," he mumbled to himself. "Not the Small World tower. I know! Tower of Terror!"

"This side. Disneyland."

Back he went to rubbing his nose like it was a crystal ball. "Splash . . . Thunder . . ." His eyes popped open, suddenly electric. "I know!" He pointed across the Hub. "The Matterhorn! There's a deck on top."

"Yeah . . ." Mattie said, heart sinking. "So I've heard. A friend of mine was nearly killed up there."

"Golly!"

If there hadn't been a dozen flaming, streaking, screaming fireworks spinning and exploding all around them, Mattie might have found a moment to hug Mickey.

"You . . . are . . . so . . . cute!" she cried out. To her surprise, Mickey engulfed her in an enormous hug, nearly choking the wind out of her.

"Are we climbing the Matterhorn, Mattie? Because if we are, it just so happens I know a route that our guests used to take—years ago!"

"Climbing?" But no, Mickey was right: if they tried to reach the top through the inside of the attraction, they were likely to encounter Barracks personnel or guards. If they could win the advantage of surprise . . . "From up there, can a person see the whole park?"

"From up there," Mickey said, "a person can see the whole world! From the Indian Teepees to the World of Color."

Mattie realized these boundaries defined the only world Mickey knew, the only world he belonged to. She saw the flicker of flame from the burning castle in his shiny eyes and thought his world, this world, was approaching a very sorry end. She couldn't allow that.

"Yes, Mickey, we're going to climb."

76

MAYBECK AND CHARLENE took a few seconds to try to comprehend what they were seeing: a dimly lit room; a growing fire on the far stage; animated dinner tables colliding like clapping hands; folding chairs snapping themselves together like jaws; and a skeletal man onstage, running toward a flaming mannequin.

There was no time to make sense of it all. Charlene, ever the athlete, took off toward Amanda as Maybeck called out her name. Unable to spot Finn amid the chaos and the rising haze of smoke, he turned his attention to the Traveler. The man was on his knees, stacking sticks with bare hands. When the pile was tall and burning—a pyre—he waved a necklace over it.

From Maybeck's right came one of the teen guards, a guy about his size. He looked zoned, zonked, zombiefied.

Maybeck was not the most academic of the Keepers; like Finn, he preferred to leave that stuff to Willa and Philby. But he was by far the most street savvy, confident, and fearless. You won girls by being funny, or failing that, by stealing them from their boyfriends. And sometimes? You won fights by cheating. He snagged a chair, spun it to increase its speed, and released it—a projectile shooting through space.

It stopped, midair.

The guy's hand was raised, pointed at the chair, palm out. The other arm lifted. Maybeck dove, pulling a table down with him. The table froze in place, too.

Maybeck rolled to the next level of dinner tables, eyes open and searching for . . . what?

The guy "released" the chair, and it fell. He "released" the table; it rolled and overturned. Crawling, Maybeck intentionally pulled a tablecloth off in a cloud of dust; it stopped, as if suddenly frozen.

Maybeck threw another chair. It lifted. Stopped. Fell. A vase holding dust-encrusted plastic flowers flew up. Froze. Fell.

Humans exist within a framework of patterns. A fighter will throw two rights and a left jab. This guy worked right hand, left hand. Maybeck knocked over a table and stood behind it, straining to hoist it while keeping a chair in his left hand.

He felt the table stop and released it two feet off the floor; it didn't fall. Almost in the same motion, Maybeck stepped around the table and hurled the chair directly at the guy.

The moment the chair stopped, Maybeck charged

like a football player. The guy had both hands engaged. The surprise attack froze him, and Maybeck took him down hard, hit him across the jaw, and thumped his head onto the floor.

Suspend that, he thought.

77

Mulan arrived on the legs of a gazelle, neither winded nor sweating. From far behind came Nick, looking frazzled.

"That was fast," said Mattie.

"Empty," Mulan said. "This place he led us."

Grabbing for his knees, winded, Nick tried to speak. He coughed, spit onto the pavement, and finally managed to say something. "Control room . . . empty."

"The sky fire," said Mulan.

Nick coughed out, "If the fireworks control room is empty, then how is this happening?"

Mattie looked up at the face of the Matterhorn. "I think the answer is up there. With her."

"Her, who?"

"In situations like this, there's only one 'her.'"

"*Her?*" Maybe it was Nick's heavy breathing, or maybe it was his excitement, but Mattie heard something else in his voice: terror.

"Philby's smarter than he looks. Willa, too. The thing is—" Mattie jumped up and over a shrieking firework, its smoking trail fanning out behind it like a gigantic snake. She glanced back; Mickey was well behind. "His father invented the villains, the mortal variety. But it had to involve magic, really dark magic. And after the earthquake, the fire, that battle, the Keepers never could account for—"

"Tia Dalma," Nick said, so red-faced Mattie thought he might pass out.

"How'd you know that?"

"A Cajun witch doctor. Voodoo, and all that? Black magic? Who else?"

They ducked behind a popcorn cart and waited while a stream of park guests poured out of Fantasyland. Some of the little kids were humming "It's a Small World," but their parents looked terrified.

"You're keeping something back," Mattie said.

"The Imagineer archives," Nick said. "A memo between them and Disney animation like five years before *Princess and the Frog*. They had learned of a Cajun witch doctor related to Tia Dalma. They clearly feared his involvement. Hollingsworth had access to that memo."

"How can you know that?" Mattie sharply pulled Nick down to the concrete. A firework streamer zoomed over his head and smashed into the popcorn cart. They brushed hot sparks off their bare arms and Nick smacked Mattie's hair, which was smoldering.

"They're aiming at us!" he panted.

"Yeah . . . I kinda got that," Mattie said.

Mickey caught up to them both, wheezing. "Gee willikers! What in tarnation is all this fuss about?"

Another smoking streak aimed for them. Nick and Mattie both pulled Mickey out of the way. But the smoke wasn't smoke at all. It was Dash.

"It's not good," the boy said calmly, not the least bit out of breath. "But while the rockets are scaring most of the people away, some guests are pitching in and fighting the fires. I saw some hurt people being helped as well. It's pretty amazing, really. People are being so nice to each other."

"The gate?" Mattie asked.

"It's bad. Super crowded. Scary."

"There're two Cast Member exits. One's by the firehouse. There's another on the entrance side of Town Hall."

"And another," said Nick, "just past the Opera House."

"You'll need to divide the guests into three groups," Mattie explained. "Keep them calm so no one gets trampled."

"I can tell them," Mickey volunteered. "They'll listen to me, by golly!"

"Great idea!" said Nick. "Dash, can you get Mickey to the front safely?"

Mattie whispered in Dash's ear, "He may need a little help not getting hit by the fireworks."

"No problemo!" Dash said. "Leave it me. Your Highness?" he said, motioning in a low bow.

"Well, I'll be dashed! What kindness."

"Dashed!" Nick barked. The three kids laughed hard, leaving Mickey looking confused.

A thunderous boom exploded only yards away. All four were blown off their feet. Mickey looked singed on his right side; fear snaking through her, Mattie asked if he was all right.

Mickey smiled. "Maybe it'll burn off some of the gray hair!"

Mattie said to Dash, "You take care of him."

"Don't you worry about that! Good luck, Mattie, Nick."

Dash took Mickey by the hand and the two headed for Main Street.

"He knows my name!" Nick said excitedly. "Dash Incredible knows my name!"

"Easy, boy!" Mattie said, shoving him away as yet another charge struck the cart in a shower of smoke and sparks. "A big head is a way to get us both into serious trouble."

Nick thanked her, nodding vigorously. "That was close."

The stream of guests fleeing Fantasyland had thinned to a few stragglers. It was time to make their move.

"The fewer targets, the more we're in trouble," Mattie said.

"Yeah, I think I just figured that out." The number of rocket strikes around them was noticeably increasing. "And you think if we climb the Matterhorn, we're going to find Tia Dalma up there directing the Air Force?"

"Tia Dalma?" Mattie said, resisting the impulse to smirk. "Who said anything about Tia Dalma?"

"We were just talking about her!"

"Not me," said Mattie. "That was a conclusion you jumped to. She isn't the 'her' I was talking about."

"Then who?" Nick sounded almost angry.

"Philby said witch doctors don't actually do things themselves. They do things *to* people, to animals and trees and plants, he said."

"I suppose," said Nick. "So who could she control? Who would do this kind of thing? You don't mean Joe, do you? Did Tia Dalma take over Joe Garlington, or Bruce, or some other Imagineer?"

"No! She'd want someone, something, far more powerful."

"What the hello are you talking about?" Nick's eyes had widened to the size of golf balls, his eyebrows jammed into his hairline. Despite the few burns glowing on his neck and cheeks, he looked about as pale as powdered sugar.

Mattie pulled him close, and the next firework charge missed. Their time was up. If they were going to scale the Matterhorn, it had to be now.

"Who would you bring back if you were ordered to destroy Disneyland once and for all?"

Nick went even whiter.

78

CHARLENE PRIED THE JAWS of the chair open, freeing Amanda, who seemed to be in shock, staring blankly at the two tables smashed together before her. Charlene didn't have time to think about that. She cartwheeled through another pair of approaching tables, turned, and tossed a snapping chair into the middle. The tables banged together, crushing the chair, and teetered.

The tables fell.

"They're like bees!" Charlene called to the recovering Amanda. "One sting and they're dead."

The front of the dining area burned. On the stage, a charred Witch Hazel staggered, off-balance, still stirring an invisible pot with an invisible spoon. At her feet, the Traveler swung his feathery necklace over an oddly green-hued fire. As Charlene and Amanda watched, he glanced offstage.

The trio of teens emerged from the wings, dragging an adult female mannequin.

What were they doing? Before she could make sense of it, Charlene spun and karate kicked the nearer of two tables rolling toward her. It wobbled, causing its twin to do the same. Changing course, the pair wheeled away, heading toward the fire.

A boy her age was busy lifting a fallen projector off the floor and steadying it on a table. He aimed its white beam toward the stage.

The Traveler pulled a cel from a large case.

The boy focused the projector's lens.

The Traveler was speaking to the three teens. They moved the mannequin and squared its shoulders to the screen.

All this, Charlene thought, with fire and a battle raging around them.

Maybeck ran from the opposite side of the room to its center. Only then did Charlene focus on the tables that seemed to be holding Amanda semi-comatose. A pair of fallen tables.

They lay on the floor, but they didn't look like the other tables that had closed like hunting traps.

These two were different.

Then she saw one of Finn's running shoes, empty on the floor.

79

THIS TIME, WHEN THE WIDE blurry streak raced toward them, Mattie said, "It's Dash."

The boy appeared in front of her and Nick. Moving fast, the group hid among the angular rocks at the edge of the Plaza. Before them rose the imposing summit of the Matterhorn.

"All set," Dash reported.

Mattie nearly said *That was fast*, but bit her lips.

"What Mickey says, people do. He's getting them organized. I can go back if you want?"

"No!" Mattie said, a little too sharply. "That is, we need you to do something else for us."

"It's about the ropes," Nick said, impressing Mattie, as they hadn't discussed any of this. "In order to climb the Matterhorn, we need two ropes dropped from that opening there."

He pointed three-quarters of the way up the mountain's face, to where the tracks briefly ran outside the attraction.

"The problem is," Mattie continued, "that the ropes, if they're still in there, will be near the very top. So we need you to get them without being seen, bring them down to where Nick just said, tie them off, and toss them out."

"Why is that a problem?" Dash asked.

"There are probably bad Fairlies inside. We can count on that. Maybe a few Cast Members working for them, too. If they figure out we're climbing—"

"They'll cut the ropes," Nick said. "And, *splat*."

"That would be us, the splat part," Mattie said. Her face was pale and drawn.

"So if I don't do this right, I get you killed?" Dash said. He blinked innocently, suddenly looking overwhelmed. He was just a boy, Mattie thought.

"Something like that," Nick said. "But you can't blame yourself if something happens. No one's forcing us to do this."

Dash appeared both heartbroken and deeply concerned. "Maybe there's another way?"

"Without the ropes, there's no way up," Nick said.

"What if I just go up and do whatever it is you're trying to do?" Dash said. "They'll never see me, you know? They won't know what hit them!"

"This particular . . . person . . . will know," Mattie said. "What she can't see herself, her pet raven will tell her. And if neither of them knows what's going on, there's a voodoo witch doctor who's part of it, too."

"So you're saying we're kinda the underdogs."

"That's putting it mildly," Nick said.

"And you can't go invisible, or whatever it is you do?" Dash asked Mattie.

"DHI? Not without going to sleep, and there's no time for that."

"Plus, it's a little noisy," said Nick. For a moment, the heaviness hanging over them dispersed into nervous laughter.

"Okay. Hang tight." The smear of supersonic movement that was Dash left only a contrail of oily shimmer hanging in the air. It moved, riverlike, between Mattie and Nick and the entrance to the Matterhorn.

The bombardment of fireworks aimed toward ground instead of sky continued unabated, an all-out attack. The explosions grew in volume, brightness, and destruction. More than a few fires raged in and around Central Plaza. Mattie celebrated the various Disney characters battling those flames; they could count on the likes of Mulan and Anna to maintain order and help Humphrey and the others overcome the grown-ups from the Barracks. She wanted in on that fight, badly, but it was not to be.

The first rope uncoiled and cascaded down the side of the Matterhorn.

"That's one," Nick said. "Are you sure you're up for

this?" He sounded afraid, which Mattie took to be a good thing.

"As to that," she said warily, "I don't think we have any choice."

The second rope tumbled down the side of the towering mountain.

80

A ROOM FILLED WITH ROLLING tables and snapping chairs greeted Jess and Willa upon arriving at the hotel dining theater.

Two fires blazed—one onstage, where the Traveler stood alongside a female mannequin; the other, larger and more frightening, consumed a front table in a hot, sparking conflagration. With smoke rising to the ceiling in a noxious cloud, a foglike haze, and a combination of incongruent sounds, the picture before the two girls resembled Hades.

Jess and Willa watched as a white frame of light, centered on the equally white-painted mannequin, changed to something—or someone—completely unexpected.

Maleficent.

Just as quickly, Willa's incomparable mind sought solutions. Her friends were under attack. Something calculating and depraved was occurring onstage.

Three teens encircled Maleficent as the Traveler hoisted an animation acetate and, lips moving silently, held it over the small fire. It lit, a tiny tower of flame. He let go.

"This is it," a transfixed Jess muttered. "This is the moment I saw. This is where it starts."

"Or not," said Willa. "Where's Finn?"

"No idea. But Willa, it's Maleficent! You understand?"

"Yes, unfortunately, I do." Willa grabbed hold of a plastic flower, one of many scattered on the floor like rose petals on a wedding aisle. She bit into a petal, grimaced, reconsidered, and bit into a leaf.

Jess coughed. The smoke was getting bad. "Maybe not the best time for floral arrangements, Willa."

"See that big box on the wall over there?" Willa pointed. "Hurry up and get that open. Start up what's inside—and memorize the location of the projector and the stage. I mean: exactly where they are, so you can tell with your eyes closed. You'll know what to do when it happens."

Even as she began to shred a second leaf, Willa bent the two wires of the flower until they resembled arms, reaching out from a skinny body with a daisy for a head. It looked like a voodoo doll, like something the Traveler might have fashioned.

"We need to *help* them!" Jess pleaded. "What *is* that?"

"Just go!" Willa's strident rebuke sent a jolt through Jess. "And remember what I told you."

Jess took off at a run.

Willa moved toward the wall. She was counting on the fake flower's plastic to insulate her fingers.

A teenage girl—*how many teens were in here?*—ran toward Willa, screaming a wordless screech. The distraction threw her off; she looked up and away from the wall socket. Mentally cursing herself, Willa refocused, concentrating on the ends of Miss Daisy's bare wire arms. Lining the wires up with the slits in the wall socket, Willa looked left: Jess had the wall box open and a fire hose in hand; to the right, the wild banshee, now only a yard away, prepared to strike.

Willa shoved the wire arms into the wall socket. A loud *pop* sounded, followed by yellow sparks and a puff of smoke.

The flower's plastic failed to insulate. A jolt of voltage stabbed through Willa, tensing every muscle in her body. As her attacker made contact, the electricity shot through her as well.

The two girls fell, unconscious, just as the cavernous room lost all electricity, the only visible light coming from the flames.

81

CONSUMED IN INSTANTANEOUS darkness, Jess turned the firebox's old rusted wheel. About the size of a dinner plate, the wheel groaned and strained, requiring more effort than she'd expected. But at last, the flat canvas hose bulged and became tubular. Jess held it firmly and aimed its green brass nozzle, her eyes already adjusting to the low yellow light from the flames.

The boy with the projector never saw it coming. The powerful stream of water hit him like a battering ram, sending him off his feet. He was midair when a figure that resembled Amanda rose from the floor. Amanda lifted her arms and *pushed*, changing the boy's direction and speed. Rolling tables, snapping chairs, and the boy himself flew toward the stage as if lofted high by a tornado.

Amanda looked witchlike, a tormented force of anger and rage. Burning furniture lifted from the dance floor in a debris storm. Jess directed the fire hose at the stage, as instructed, aiming to douse the campfire over which the Traveler squatted.

At almost the same moment, a brilliant flash of

blue light erupted from the imaginary pot being stirred by Witch Hazel. The air filled with a hundred birds of every size, from eagles, hawks, and crows to swallows and sparrows. In a second, the debris Amanda had thrown was gone, replaced by living organisms.

Not a splinter reached the Traveler.

Jess dropped the hose, astonished. Beyond the Traveler, with no electricity or projector, the Maleficent mannequin glowed. The evil fairy seemed caught, struggling between a projected and material existence. Jess forced herself to redouble her efforts; she had to keep Maleficent from forming.

The birds circled overhead, wings stirring the smoke and clouding the vision of the people in the ballroom. The wild creatures cried in anguish, desperate for open air. Crows and hawks swooped low, forcing Jess to duck—and only then did it occur to her that the birds were agents of Witch Hazel.

Maleficent's wooden limbs moved. Jess swallowed back the urge to vomit.

Maybeck rushed the stage. The three teens closest to Maleficent turned, forming a wall that kept him from both the kneeling Traveler and Maleficent's shifting form.

Jess struggled to regain control of the spitting hose, the power of which made it difficult to hold. She shot some birds out of the air; hit a table, and pushed it across the room. Then, with renewed focus, she trained the watery blast on the stage.

She hit Maybeck in the shoulder, spinning him out of the way. Without pause, she sprayed the three teens. They whisked back and into the transfiguring Maleficent. The mannequin went down hard.

The Traveler looked up then. Straight into Jess's soul.

82

HIS SHOULDER NEARLY KNOCKED out of its socket by the water from the fire hose, Maybeck found himself looking offstage at a symmetrical pattern of stage rigging ropes, neatly tied off to belaying pins.

Pain shot through him; a fireball had hit him in the chest. It bounced off and fell to the stage; Maybeck beat down his smoldering shirt, hollering from the sting of the burn. He looked up, searching for the source.

The half mannequin, half Maleficent, her image not yet fully merged with the wood, was looking at him maliciously.

It took a split second for Maybeck to compute that the *would-be Maleficent* had thrown the fireball at him. She appeared to be reloading, her arm cocked back. Maybeck ducked as a fireball the size of a softball flew wide.

The Traveler smiled. He was eerily calm, though the fire hose had left him a curled ball against the screen, covered in wet ash and pieces of burned finger bones.

In a singsong voice, the Traveler murmured, "Dem

children shouldn't play with no fire!" He wrapped his bony fingers around some feathery thing hanging from his neck and squeezed.

Maybeck's insides cramped so painfully he dropped to his knees. Unable to stand, he fell to the stage and rolled.

"We need dem pains so we don'ts forget dem lessons. Huh?"

Maybeck squirmed and groaned, arms crossed tightly around his shins, his tortured belly knifing pain through his whole body, his eyes pasted open in agony. He rolled away from the Traveler, eyes desperately searching the vast space of the ballroom. It was not Amanda or Jess, not Willa or Charlene that interested him. No. It was the object in the dark overhead.

Calculations, strategies, and game design were Philby's, Willa's, and Finn's strengths. Maybeck had been pigeonholed as the artist of the group, a tag he didn't necessarily mind, but one he found limiting. The thing about any artistic project was this: it had to be planned, from having the idea to collecting the supplies and making the art. Just now, in the midst of his painful roll across the stage, Maybeck had envisioned a masterpiece. A piece of performance art to rival *Einstein on the Beach*.

A third fireball whizzed by his ear. This time, Maybeck appreciated it. *Keep 'em coming, Greenie!* he wanted to shout. His courage defeated the Traveler's painful voodoo grip. Even though he wasn't a hologram, by overcoming his fear, Maybeck made the threat powerless.

Maleficent's image strengthened, suddenly more flesh than wood, more mortal than mannequin.

"You three, out of here!" Maybeck shouted at the three teens.

Their impudent expressions suggested a spell or hypnotism, which meant their anger and hatred toward Maybeck was manufactured.

"Jess," Maybeck called across the room, which was now filled with smoke and circling birds of every variety. "When I say so, hit those three with everything you've got!"

"Got it!" she called back.

"Mandy!" he yelled.

But Amanda didn't answer. He glanced over, saw her folded up once again in a heap on the dance floor. Wounded, he thought. Their numbers were shrinking. He still hadn't seen Finn; in the back of his mind, the thought sent worry squirming through him.

But there wasn't any more time to think. Maybeck had to work to keep the fear at bay—to keep the Traveler at bay. He ducked another incoming fireball, backed across the stage and into the wings.

Keep 'em coming . . .

Maleficent, ever more herself, matched his every step. *That's right . . .*

The mannequin-fairy stepped awkwardly forward. A crow arrowed out of the swirling mass and landed on her shoulder; she reached up and stroked it. As she did, the bird's eyes went red.

Diablo! Maybeck thought.

He moved across the stage, continuing to back up into the wings, keeping himself squared with Maleficent. Manipulating Maleficent.

Where was Finn? Now the question wouldn't leave him alone. Why wasn't he helping?

Cursing under his breath, Maybeck slowed, intentionally allowing Maleficent to close the gap. First, twenty feet away. Now, fifteen.

"Being human is more than not being wooden," he said, hoping to goad her. "You've got a lot of work to do. And the green skin? Not so hot, if you ask me."

The dark fairy continued to stagger toward him, eyes squinting. Behind her, Witch Hazel kept stirring space. Above his head, the birds surged and soared.

Maleficent's green skin showed the wood grain within it—a ghostly pattern. She did not look human, but more cartoonish, like the projection that had helped form her. Neither character nor mannequin, Maleficent was a half-formed thing. A horror. A partial sketch with a mind of its own.

The dark fairy stopped her advance, slightly past the middle of the stage, arm winding up once again.

Maybeck saw the Traveler look up. Saw the strange man's bloodshot eyes widen as he, like Maybeck before him, followed the taut lines of rigging.

"Now, Jess!" Maybeck shouted.

"No!" the Traveler called, his voice mixed with Maybeck's. "Fairy! Don't be—"

But he was too late.

Jess struck the three teens with the fire hose's powerful stream. The blast drove them into the screen. They skidded along, rolling like riders on a slippery slide, and were knocked into the darkness backstage.

"FAIRY!" the Traveler shouted. But he was neither in nor out of control of the transfigured form. Maleficent existed in an ethereal space, caught between transformation and puppetry.

She let fly the biggest fireball yet. Maybeck understood that it was all about timing now. He waited to feel the heat of the projectile before moving aside. The small ones had been easy. This one, the size of a basketball, proved too hot. Maybeck endured the stinging pain to his face, arching his back like a player in a game of limbo.

And then he dropped lifelessly, his hair smoldering, forehead blistering.

Maleficent's roiling flame passed beyond his slumped body and smashed into the wall, igniting posters, a curtain, a bulletin board—and a number of the taut stage ropes. Maybeck, eyes stinging and blurry, saw a rope snap as it burned through. Then another, and several more.

The object he had first spotted high overhead, the same object the Traveler had just seen, a metal catwalk used as a working platform for stagehands, jerked sharply, first to the left side of the stage, then to the right.

It fell.

Oddly, for Maybeck, there was nothing slow-motion about it. The falling catwalk more closely resembled a fly swatter slapping a hard surface. One moment, Maleficent was standing, a menacing form stretched far above him. Behind her, the crouching Traveler was coming to his feet.

The next, a loud noise. Dust. Some scattered pieces of smoking wood and charred bone. No Maleficent, no Witch Hazel, no Traveler. Gone. All gone.

Pieces of wood and debris rained down from the ceiling. No birds.

The fire continued to rage, finding more fuel in

its path. Through the walls came the distant cry of sirens.

The Traveler's teens, strewn about the dining room and backstage, saw the carnage and scattered, heading out the main door.

From within the smoke and silence came the sound of Amanda's desperate tears. Jess looked okay, albeit shaken. Willa stood, wobbly, a chair falling off her.

Maybeck had seen the two tables smashed together earlier. They weren't fully closed, the sides hovering near each other like a bear trap that had been tripped.

He jumped off the stage. Knocking tables and chairs, tablecloths, broken lamps, chunks of wood, and coils of electrical wiring out of his way, Maybeck approached the sobbing Amanda . . . and the shoe before her.

"Finn," she moaned.

83

"THERE!" HUMPHREY SAID, POINTING.

"Where?" Mary Ann said, flicking her blue locks out of her eyes. "All I see is smoke."

"Base of the people mover," Humphrey said.

"I was looking over at the Buzz Lightyear ride."

"No. Closer than that. To the right."

"It's him."

"It is," Humphrey said. "The Dogcatcher."

"I hate that man," Mary Ann said in a gravelly whisper. It caught in her throat. "He made a friend of mine . . . She bumped a table in the kitchen when she was carrying a big pot of soup. It slurped over the edge and spilled. He made her *lick it up*. All of it! I don't know if you ever saw the kitchen floor . . . but I've seen bathrooms that were cleaner."

"He caught Billy, the guy who could make people say things he wanted them to say? Remember him? Anyway. Billy was trying to escape. The Dogcatcher put him in 13 for three weeks! Three weeks! I don't need to tell you how he came out."

"Enough of back then," Mary Ann said. "We need

to focus! Why does anyone care about the people mover?" she asked.

Humphrey studied the empty overhead track encircling Tomorrowland. "We may be dumb, but he's just plain stupid!"

"Humphrey?"

"Don't you see? Whoever controls that track—just look up there!—has the battlefield advantage over Tomorrowland. How many other Barracks stooges like Dogbreath are there? Five? Ten? Without us working for them, they're toast. So they're taking up strategic positions to keep us from gaining the advantage while they try to empty the place with this shock-and-awe fireworks attack."

"Which is working."

"Clearly."

"So we take out the Dogcatcher—*Dogbreath*! I like that!—and gain the high ground. Then what?"

"We put some of ours up there, maybe some Disney characters, too, and we capture any Cast Members or kids the Barracks guys have compromised. The fireworks aren't going off by themselves. The Barracks obviously had a backup plan if we didn't get the job done."

"So, let's get it done," Mary Ann said, face tightening with determination.

"He's powerful, Mary Ann. Let's not forget that." Some of the Barracks grown-ups had once been Fairlies themselves. Though they'd mostly grown out of their abilities, a few like the Dogcatcher still possessed considerable powers. "His thing is pain."

"Yeah," she said, "I know."

"He can throw it."

"Right. Make you howl like a poked dog." Mary Ann shivered. "I heard all about it. He's right-handed, and before he throws the pain he places his left hand over his heart. I don't know if that's for show, or part of his ability, but that's his deal."

"Distance?"

"I've heard everything from ten yards to a hundred. Don't think I'd like to find out."

"And you? The cold? The way you make everything so cold?"

"You mean how far? Forget about me, Humphrey. I'm the Ice Queen when I'm inside a place, but I'm no Elsa. I need small spaces. A room. A hallway."

"But you've got me," he said.

"Mr. Turbocharge. Right. I know what you can do! But consider this: let's say you can touch me and increase my power? Okay. But now my power increases and I freeze you, way colder, way deeper than I mean to. I'm immune to the cold, Humphrey. Maybe by touching me, you are too. But maybe not. That particular test has never been done, and this seems like a pretty pathetic time to start experimenting."

"Have you ever ridden piggyback?"

"Say what?"

"If I'm carrying you, we're touching," Humphrey said. "Once we're touching, I can triple, maybe quadruple your ability. So, I run. You take your best shot at Dogdoo over there. Whaddaya say?"

Mary Ann giggled. "I like you too much to let you do this, Humphrey. But thanks for the offer."

Leaving Humphrey flat-footed, she broke away from their hiding place—behind a trash can, next to a metal bench—and took off running for the Dogcatcher.

A second too late, Humphrey started off after her.

84

MATTIE REACHED HER ROPE before Nick and, taking hold, immediately sank onto her bottom as it stretched. She stood, pulled the slack out of it, and reached overhead. Nick arrived several steps behind her and flew to the wall, taking the rope in both hands. Working hard, he began walking up the face of the mountain, his back parallel to the asphalt. He looked like a Marine.

Mattie's approach was to hold on overhead while wrapping the rope around one leg and clamping it tight at her ankles, exactly like she'd learned in P.E. class before P.E. class had been renamed Activity Hour, which amounted to sixty minutes of sitting in the shade and gossiping.

Above her, Nick began to lose his traction, causing him to put his feet higher than his head. He appeared dangerously close to falling headfirst.

Mattie, the tortoise to his hare, happened to look up the length of his rope to see little puffs of dust, like heavy raindrops exploding on packed dirt. At first she took this phenomenon to be the old rope shedding some of the dust from storage. But then, she understood.

"Nick!"

"Don't worry! I got it! I'm getting the hang of it."

"Nick! The rope!"

"I said I've got it."

"Yeah, but I don't think it has you." Even as she spoke, Mattie felt her own rope weakening, the aged fibers stretched to snapping. *Pop, pop, snap*: the ropes were fraying. Coming apart.

The fireworks charges that had been trained to their positions on the ground had followed Nick and Mattie up the mountain, striking all around and showering them in painful sparks. Colors flashed blindingly: blue, red, white, green, purple. Enveloped in an acrid smoke that tasted sour and made her nose twitch, Mattie climbed steadily up her rope, trying to ignore the repetitive drops, a fraction of an inch at a time, that signaled the rope above her coming apart.

"Nick!" Mattie screamed over the cacophony of the explosions. "Here!" She let go of the rope between her ankles and stretched like an acrobat to reach for him.

"I'm fine!" the inverted boy shouted. "Race you to the top."

"Nick! Take my hand! Now!" Mattie had not wanted to tell him his rope was on fire for fear he'd panic and fall. They had to be thirty or forty feet above the concrete, she reckoned. Any fall would likely be disastrous . . . if not fatal.

Nick dropped in three pronounced sequences—a rope stretch, a taut bump, a fall. The first two were warnings. The third was the act itself, the cleaving of the rope by the fire. To Nick it was slow, faster, fastest. He fell.

Mattie caught his flailing forearm. Nick grabbed hold and together they swung him beneath Mattie and onto her rope. His rope fell away soundlessly, like a squirming snake.

A fireball erupted, precariously close. Mattie's shirt-sleeve caught fire. She pushed against the wall, carrying Nick with her, and angled to smash the smoldering fabric against the mountain, snuffing it out. Her arm stung.

"Cripes!" Nick shouted, struggling to adapt to Mattie's way of climbing and having a devil of a time with it.

Elevated, Mattie got a brief look at the park. Her heart cramped. The scene was chaos: fires, people running, three rivers of guests retreating from the entrance. Somehow daylight made it all the worse, leaving nothing to the imagination.

Fireworks continued a near-finale rhythm from several locations: Tom Sawyer Island, where guests were swimming for safety; New Orleans Square appeared to be caught in a human traffic jam; the Castle, aiming its ordnance into the Hub and up the wall at the two climbers; and from somewhere behind Tomorrowland, an area not associated with any fireworks display. Thousands of escaping guests flowed outward, the groups like a person's middle three fingers extended. Teams of Disney characters battled various small fires while distinct skirmishes broke out around them, the participants too distant to identify.

Mattie and Nick felt it at once. "It's going," Nick shouted from below. Well below. He clung to the rope firmly, but he was making no progress climbing it.

Mattie watched, terrified, as the strands of her rope split and untwined under the burden of Nick's added weight. Some small, some large, the breaks only increased.

"Nick! Bend your knees. Grip the rope with your ankles. Stand up, sliding your hands higher. Repeat!" Mattie moved quickly, inchworming her way steadily higher. She'd crossed the halfway mark, but a good distance remained. She willed herself not to look down or out into the park; the height was beginning to make her woozy.

"Okay. Better. That's better!"

With no slack, Nick's weight on the rope made

Mattie's ankle-lock impossible. It forced her to squeeze the soles of her feet against the braided rope, nowhere near as safe or functional. She slipped too often and too far, her ascent slowing.

"Hurry!" she cried.

Nick caught an angry spark between his sock and shoe. He kicked with his other foot to put it out, but failed to support himself with just his hands. Crying out, he slid like a fireman down a pole, the rope burning his palms, shredding his flesh. He only stopped because the toe of his right shoe hit a bulging seam in the mountain's gnarly "ice-covered" surface. He wrapped his arms around the tight rope to free his hands.

"No good!" he hollered.

Even from a distance, Mattie could see the burns on his hands. He wouldn't be able to climb; he wouldn't be able to let himself down. Having stayed to the left of the mountain and away from both the stone arch and the waterfalls for fear of being intercepted by Fairlies—*or worse*—she guessed the rope didn't have more than a few minutes left in it.

"Wrap your arms with the rope and swing!"

"Wh . . . at?"

"We're going to walk as far that way as we can. When I say so, we push off the wall together."

"But won't we—?"

"Ready?" Mattie started moving without him. Nick had no choice but to follow and line up with her. They stretched the rope far to the left, the popping and fraying continuing above. Mattie counted down out loud.

On "three" they pushed off the wall together and soared, swinging far to the right. The tension on the rope was too much. As they reached the apex, Mattie stretched, reaching for the edge of the waterfall. The rope broke from above. She let it go, her fingers grasping for anything to hold on to on the wet, slimy surface. She heard a *thunk*. Nick! He might have fallen a few feet, or possibly to his death.

Her fingers found an edge, then a slick pipe. But just when she thought she was safe, the pipe tore loose from its anchors, bending and pushing her away. She worked her hands up it quickly as a succession of anchors broke free. At last, she kicked a leg up, caught something with her ankle, and rolled into a pool of tepid water no deeper than a bathtub.

The pipe had broken off cleanly. She held a section in her hand. She tucked it into her waist for safekeeping as she clambered to the edge—partly because her hand refused to let go, partly because it felt good to hold on to something solid.

Nick waved up to her, prone and splayed on a ledge. Mattie let out her breath in a whoosh. He'd survived.

Not one single thing that had happened in the past few minutes was part of her plan. She looked higher, to what remained of the dangling ropes. Dash had tied them off very near the top, easily within reach of a stair step of rocks to reach the lip of the platform hidden there. Nick's burned rope was longer than hers. She motioned for Nick to get inside the attraction and to meet her up where she was.

A few minutes later, she saw him walking the stairs along the edge of the Matterhorn track. She waved for him to stop and get down.

At that moment a firework streaked in through the mouth of the waterfall and ignited, filling the ride's interior with an enormous, blinding ball of burning white stars. In its coruscating light, Mattie saw a figure way up inside the cone of the mountaintop's peak. A woman in rags, seashell necklaces and bracelets, with dreadlocks and a tattooed face. She was climbing a metal ladder toward a trapdoor.

Tia Dalma.

85

HUMPHREY KNEW WHEN he was needed. Down, but not out, he stumbled in the direction of Mary Ann just as the Dogcatcher's left hand slid across his chest toward his heart and his right arm bent at the elbow.

For a nearly infinitesimal moment, Humphrey allowed himself to see the pavement between him and Mary Ann as coral-blue water, a placid and inviting bit of ocean. He dove, hitting so hard it tore the front of his shirt and ripped up his chest. His elbows and forearms, knees and thighs fared no better.

Wincing at the pain, he smeared himself across the short distance and latched on to the back of Mary Ann's right ankle, clamping down like a snapping turtle. He pushed his ability through her, his cheek burning from the effects of contact with the pavement.

Humphrey saw it all from ground level.

The Dogcatcher raising his arm.

The man's arm starting forward.

A look of calm confidence and grim superiority filled the Dogcatcher's face, a kind of smug indifference, like a man about to swat an annoying mosquito.

Then fog, followed by a sugarlike frost, followed by ice crystals. The icy effect unrolled toward the Dogcatcher like a red carpet.

Humphrey felt his limbs chill, as if he'd jumped into a winter lake. He couldn't see Mary Ann, only the Dogcatcher, but the man's arm never passed its zenith. It stuck straight up, making him look foolish. His expression changed as well, from an arrogant control freak to a stunned and helpless victim. As his face froze, his brow furrowed, his lips pursed.

With her ability magnified tenfold by Humphrey's, Mary Ann watched as what should have been a simple freezing turned into a subzero arctic blast. The Dogcatcher wasn't merely stunned by her blast of cold. He froze solid. Solid ice. Like glass.

Fragile glass, at that. The man's right arm snapped off, fell to the pavement, and shattered into a thousand pieces. The loss of the arm threw the chunk of human ice off-balance. Its left leg cracked at the thigh. The knee gave out. Then the Dogcatcher teetered, vibrated through a thousand sudden cracks, and splintered into a pile of crushed ice.

Behind and below Mary Ann, his hand still holding her ankle, Humphrey felt his lungs freeze. He couldn't breathe. Couldn't think. And, as his world turned to darkness, couldn't see.

86

"**D**ID YOU SEE THAT?" Mattie couldn't find her breath, and it had nothing to do with physical exertion. "Did you see her?"

"Her?"

"Up there!" She pointed.

"I hit the deck, as you might remember."

"Tia Dalma, climbing a ladder up to the top."

"You're sure?"

"Oh yeah. Positive."

"But if she's the Grim Reaper like you said, then wouldn't she leave the heavy lifting to others? Like Maleficent, for instance? Doesn't that make more sense?"

"I think we're about to find out. And just for the record, Nick, when it comes to making sense, there's not a lot of that going on around here."

They crept up the track's side stairs, slowly and quietly, ever alert. At the highest waterfall opening, they found both ropes within reach.

"No, not really," Nick said. He looked vaguely sick.

"Oh yes. Really. If we try to go through that trapdoor,

we'll be smacked down like Whac-A-Mole. The only way we have much of a chance, and it's not a great one as is, is taking advantage of the element of surprise. If they don't see us coming, maybe—just *maybe*—we get them before they get us."

"Meaning?"

"Whoever's up there . . . I need to touch, to come in contact with, whoever's up there."

"Whoever's up there goes over the side, Mattie. Don't kid yourself." Nick suddenly looked much older than his years. "It's not like there's going to be a lot of talking going on. This isn't a negotiation. If whoever, whatever, is powerful enough to be running this junk in the park, then he or she is too much for us. This is a street fight! You don't play nice in a street fight."

"I can use my ability against them. They won't be expecting it. They won't have ever experienced anything like it, so they won't know how to fight it. At the very least, Tia Dalma is up there. I *saw* her."

"And she can turn us into spaghetti."

"Not without a curse or conjuring. And those take time. You help me make contact, Nick. I know what I'm doing."

With that, Mattie took hold of the burned rope and began to climb. Nick tried to grab ahold of the rope, but dropped it immediately, wincing in pain.

Reluctantly, Mattie climbed back down to Nick.

"Then we'll find another way," she said, turning to go back into the cave.

When they turned around, Dash was standing there. Startled, Mattie almost cried out.

"I thought you might need some help after that last bit," Dash said. "Another few inches and Nick was a goner. Lucky that ledge is wide."

"The park?" Mattie asked.

"You can hear the fireworks."

"Hear?" Nick said. "We nearly ate one!"

"Chaos," said Dash. "Losses on both sides."

"What kind of losses?" Mattie sounded desperate.

"Losses, Mattie," Dash said, hanging his head. "Better to focus on stopping this, I think."

"Dash, help us find another way."

He vanished.

He reappeared.

"You are bizarre," Mattie said.

"Thank you!" Dash said. "I can lead Nick. You climb, just in case things don't work out."

"Agreed! See you up there," she said defiantly, reaching out and hauling herself onto the ice-painted exterior of the Matterhorn peak.

She discovered a number of handholds and toeholds fashioned into the "rocks" and "ice." They seemed to have been built into the surface intentionally. Deeply recessed and easy to use, the ladderlike grips let Mattie climb nearly fearlessly. She did not look down, except to ensure the rope tied to her ankle would not snag.

A moment later, she was crouched just below the lip of the Matterhorn's hidden deck. Above her, the sunlight bent and shimmered in the air, like oil in water. It took a few seconds to realize the energy the phenomenon represented was traveling from the deck and moving out into the park in three directions: the castle, Frontierland, Tomorrowland.

Whoever was up here was directing the fireworks and the attack on Disneyland.

Mattie knew what had happened to Finn up here. He'd nearly died. She knew the power of the magic he'd faced, too, knew it to be far greater than her own ability.

But Chernabog was dead. Destroyed. Could Tia Dalma have brought back the beast with her black magic? Was such a thing possible? Was it *impossible*?

Only one way to find out. She pulled herself up and vaulted the wall, landing atop the deck's spongy rubber flooring.

What she saw there nearly caused her to throw up. Again!

A flowing, evaporating, reforming, grotesque shape of green, purple, and black wavered before her. It looked like a giant, undulating greenish flame, with a head that appeared intermittently. Shoulders. A skirt? A dress? And the head again. Dark horns.

Only then did Mattie locate the figure in the mountain peak's harsh shadow.

Cackling with glee, Tia Dalma stepped out into the bright sunshine. Her lips already moving, the witch doctor reached for something hairy in her chest pocket.

Whatever Mattie did next, she wasn't going to look at that thing. Nor was she going to allow the witch doctor to chant a curse. Mattie began singing at the top of her lungs, singing the only song she could think of:

> *It's a world of laughter, a world of tears.*
> *It's a world of hope and a world of fears.*

Mattie would neither look at Tia Dalma nor listen to her. Instead she focused on the ethereal, twisting, genielike green shape at the center of the deck, a *woman*, who as she turned revealed herself as Maleficent.

But not like any Maleficent Mattie had ever seen. More like an incomplete Maleficent. Malformed. Unfinished. A Maleficent trapped between two worlds— the world of Tia Dalma and wherever it was that creatures like this one went when their purpose was finished. The place where Finn had sent her: the end of the road; the hole in the ground; the place of devils and pitchforks. There.

Whatever existed of Maleficent was enough to continue emitting an oily bolt of energy from her open palm. It was no fireball, more like a wave of raw energy, a string without the fibers.

Mattie thumped her heel on the deck's spongy surface. She moved toward Maleficent, determined to touch the thing. The shifting image slowly rotated to face her, the dark fairy's visage appearing and disappearing amid the braided swirl of color. The thing looked more energy than body, more oozing spirit than corporeal reality. Mattie didn't dare try to make physical contact. She stomped hard for a second time.

The trapdoor lifted a matter of inches, Nick's wide eyes peering out cautiously. Mattie was well into the second verse at the top of her lungs.

Mattie moved another step closer to the phantom, working hard not to look in Tia Dalma's direction nor stop her own obnoxious singing.

A blur caught her eye. Dash, circling the deck. Nick stood, his feet straddling the open trapdoor, Tia Dalma a yard or less to his right. He jumped across the trapdoor. Maleficent *and* Tia Dalma turned toward him.

The distraction couldn't have been better. Mattie lunged for the wraith, focusing on her evolving *reaching* ability. She plunged her hand into the swirling goo of colorful light—

And flew back, lifted fully off her feet. She smashed into the deck's low wall and onto her bottom. Her brain felt fried.

"Mattie!" Nick shouted.

"Madeline?" Tia Dalma inquired, as if they were long-lost friends. Inwardly, Mattie cursed. Nick should not have mentioned her name.

Now the witch doctor turned her full attention to the fallen girl. "Friend of the Children of Light? Sister of the White Witch?" Mattie had never heard Jess described this way—though if it was a reference to her snow-white hair, it seemed somehow appropriate.

It seemed Tia Dalma had mistaken her, Mattie, for Amanda. Not that they were exactly interchangeable, but still . . .

Reaching for a peaceful outcome seemed unlikely. The flamelike Maleficent arched and extended in Nick's direction. The boy looked about to faint from fright.

But in turning to Nick, Maleficent lost track of her open palm. A shower of fireworks sprayed overhead, blasting and detonating in explosions of color, sparks, and fire. A "bang ball" narrowly missed Nick and blew up.

For a moment, the kind of all-encompassing white light that Mattie took to be heaven.

Black. White. Splashes of shapes. Something green. Tia Dalma behind the light.

Mattie could hear nothing. Her ears filled with a shrill whine, like an injured cat, her head a painful mass of compression.

Nick somehow managed to remain conscious, tucked into a ball, hands over his painful ears.

Dash stopped circling and helped Nick to his feet, pulling him away from the pipe spitting sparks of electricity. It ran to a light tree used to illuminate the Matterhorn at night; the blast had disconnected it.

Tia Dalma jumped back at the sight of Dash materializing. "You! The wee little ghost! Announce yourself. The ether welcomes you!"

Dash zipped to the opposite side of the deck. Then back, immediately next to Tia Dalma. By Nick again. Tia Dalma did not appreciate or understand him. She didn't like him, especially when he stood close to her. Waving her hands, she jumped back and attempted to shake a talisman in his direction. But Dash had no direction, no location. He was a whirling dervish. He was some form of spirit Tia Dalma had not seen. He baffled her. Angered her. Won her attention.

Nick caught Mattie looking in his direction and worked to hold her gaze. He purposefully eyed the sparking pipe and mouthed some words, but she couldn't hear. He cocked his head at Maleficent, who seemed to have suffered from the explosion as well. Her bits and pieces of color were less distinct and not at all congealed. They swirled, snapping together like puzzle pieces, the whole of her form beginning to re-form.

Nick patted his own waist. Mattie didn't understand. He did the same thing again. Belatedly, she checked her waist—the length of pipe from the waterfall was missing. Nick's eyes found a spot on the deck; Mattie's followed.

There it was, having fallen from her waistband. Mattie didn't understand: no piece of pipe was going to clobber Maleficent. But the boy was insistent with his eye movement.

The electric wire mounted to the wall, violently spitting electricity.

The swirling, re-forming Maleficent.

Mattie's thin length of pipe on the deck.

He repeated.

Electric wire.

Maleficent.

Pipe.

His next move said it all. Nick waved his hand in a shaking motion toward the deck.

Lightning? Mattie thought, the signal unmistakable.

She looked overhead: blue sky.

Nick made the lightning gesture a second time. But he also shook his head and held up two fingers. Mattie was lost; she had no idea what he was trying to tell her. He must have suffered a blow to the head when the firework exploded.

But there was Nick, reaching for the fat wire mounted to the wall. And there was Dash, helping him to pull it free.

Electric wire.

Maleficent.

Pipe.

Idiot! Mattie thought. Nick knew exactly what he was doing!

As the two boys tore the live wire from the deck's low surrounding wall, Mattie dove for the length of short pipe and, her eyes on Nick, waited for his signal: a slow closing of the eyes.

Lightning . . . no . . . two fingers. That had been Nick's signal: lightning never strikes the same place twice. Lightning had killed Chernabog on this very deck. But with a blue sky, there wasn't any lightning, so Nick—with Dash's help—was going to make his own. He was going to make lightning strike twice.

Mattie tossed the length of pipe at Maleficent's swirling force field. Just as it entered, Nick swung the thick electric wire in the direction of the dark fairy. The electricity arced and jumped from the broken wire to the piece of metal pipe. It looked like a giant Fourth of July sparkler: a fiery white spray of electricity, thick as water, catching hold of the pipe in midair. The blast was so intense, it jumped from the insulated rubber deck into the sky, erupting forty feet into the air like a Roman candle. A torch of exquisitely hot, brilliant energy.

And then it stopped.

Just like that.

The fireworks stopped, the park sky suddenly empty of explosions.

On the deck, a black doughnut of scorched plastic smoldered. It smelled disgusting. No Maleficent. No Tia Dalma either, though an ugly black vulture with a naked pink head soared off into the sky, heading away from the Matterhorn. A vulture Mattie did not remember seeing.

Nick seemed to be cheering, but Mattie heard only the whine in her ears.

Dash buzzed around in circles, a grin on his face.

Mattie stared at the vulture as it grew smaller and smaller, moving farther and farther away.

Then she realized what had seemed impossible only seconds earlier: it was over.

Her lips were still moving, mouthing words: *it's a small world after all*.

She smiled.

87

MAYBECK LOOKED AT THE TABLES. He looked at Amanda, who couldn't tear her hands away from her face.

He thought of the first time he'd seen Finn Whitman. They'd been on a Disney soundstage in Disney Hollywood Studios. All five of them were there that day, with a guy named Brad.

Finn and Philby had quickly stood out, like overachievers on the first day of school. Philby understood the technology that all five Keepers had individually been part of for the past six weeks. Finn seemed to see a bigger picture, to already grasp what lay ahead.

Of course, none of them could have foreseen the adventures to come, except maybe Jess, whom they knew at the time as Jezebel.

A listener, a quick study, a not-so-special athlete, a pretty boy with an inner confidence that made him special, Finn took on the leadership of the group from the start. They didn't vote for a leader. They just found one among them. The kid everyone liked enough to complain to, the kid without an agenda.

Maybeck handed out criticism and jabs like the guys

giving away pamphlets on street corners. He teased and mocked. He thrived on projecting a don't-care attitude, the Han Solo macho-me that girls liked, that made other boys step away. He'd hit Finn with endless rudeness, knowing Finn could take it, knowing it would form a bond between them.

And he'd needed that bond. Philby? Too smug. Willa? Too lost in her own head. As for Charlene, her beauty had been almost too much to take, her athleticism too great a challenge for someone as competitive as Maybeck.

No, Finn made himself the perfect target. Maybe, Maybeck thought, his mind spinning, it was the way he never called out others in public. He might pull you aside to complain—always gently—or ask advice, and only later would you realize he'd been directing you to a certain conclusion. Maybe that was it.

So how had he ended up here? How could this be the end of his story? Here, in front of Maybeck, tipped over and leaning like a temple offering to the kneeling Amanda.

Maybeck threw a few choice words to the ceiling. His belly hurt far more than anything a stupid witch doctor could concoct. It was the pain of loss, of friendship broken, of a string of years more wonderful than any he'd ever known come to an end.

He backed up in staring disbelief, withdrew until he was side by side with Amanda, and fell to his knees beside her. Felt a sobbing Jess lie atop them, her hand finding Maybeck's shoulder. And then Willa. Together, a pile of grief.

No dramatic words were spoken by the boy at the end. No speech about the meaning of life. No fluttering eyelids or hand gone limp. Just the damn tables, too close together to allow life. The tomb of a witch doctor's insanity, and the boy's final instinct, his willingness to stop the threat to the kingdom by pulling Hollingsworth down with him.

In the end, as in the beginning, for Finn Whitman, it had all been about self-sacrifice.

88

BUSINESS MOGUL FOUND DEAD
IN LIKELY SUICIDE

Amery Hollingsworth Jr., chief executive and board chairman of Renatus, LLC, was pronounced dead at Surgeon's Hospital just after 4 p.m. this afternoon. He was the oldest son of embattled former Disney executive Amery Hollingsworth.

A staff member found the 57-year-old unresponsive in his Westwood home early Thursday morning, according to law enforcement officials.

Sources who wished to remain anonymous due to the ongoing investigation reported the cause of death as self-inflicted asphyxiation. A full medical examiner's report is expected within three weeks.

The elder Hollingsworth died in 1955 after falling from a balcony, which news sources at the time reported as a suicide. The financially troubled business executive engaged in numerous failed legal battles with the Walt Disney Company for more than a decade before his death. Those efforts, which sought to clear his name and reputation, led to repeated bankruptcies in the early 1950s.

Hollingsworth Jr. is survived by his brothers, Rexx and Ezekiel. There will be no service. In lieu of flowers, the family is requesting donations be sent to the Save All Children Foundation in Hollingsworth Jr.'s name.

Joe reread the obituary three times. His office door was closed, his right leg bouncing rapidly, causing a spring in his office chair to repeatedly squeal.

It had been more than thirty hours since Joe had slept. In that time, he'd visited Zeke Hollingsworth at the area hospital where he was being treated for dehydration, interviewed four Fairlies, who'd been caught dragging an adult backstage, spoken with local police and Disney security, and sat in on a conference call with Baltimore police, who'd raided the Barracks facility based on his testimony. He looked as exhausted as he felt.

Mattie was asleep on his office couch in Burbank, as she had been for the past fourteen hours straight. She'd refused medical attention; the doctors said she'd be fine with rest.

He looked over at her, sleeping peacefully, and wondered what might have happened had he managed to grab hold of her ankle.

Some things were meant to be, he thought, closing his eyes and fighting off the temptation to sleep.

Joe's worry now, as it had been for some time, was

the safe return of the Keepers, and of Amanda and Jess. Presently, he had no way to judge if Amery Jr.'s death would affect the creation and eventual rise of the Overtakers.

Joe frowned, searched for another name. It should be five, not four, Kingdom Keepers. He was sure of it. But he failed to find the name he sought. He must have dreamed the fifth.

Mattie snorted and woke, her eyes coming open abruptly. "Good grief. I feel like lunch meat left in the sun. How'd I get here?"

"Do you remember the Matterhorn at all? You were turned over to my care. They told me the bump to your head might cause some fuzziness."

"Fuzzy? I hurt like someone used me for a punching bag."

"Tell me what you remember."

Mattie walked Joe through everything she could recall about the meeting in the Tower, the Fairlies' leader's decision, speaking to Teresa, the train, the fireworks, the attack.

"The Fairlies went after the Barracks adults pretty violently," Joe said, watching her with tired eyes. "Only a few Fairlies were caught."

"Thank goodness."

"That's what you say."

"They've been through too much, for too long. They could use a safe place to live for a while. *Without strings.*"

"I understand what you're suggesting, but I don't see how I could get word to them, to say we might shelter them."

"I can," Mattie said. "You find them a safe place, and I can get the word out."

Joe nodded. Scribbled a note. Looked up and met her eyes.

"And you? I owe you more than I can ever repay, Mattie, including an apology. This company, every guest from here on out, thanks you. If there are parks going forward, that's thanks to you, too."

Mattie sat up and locked eyes with him. She felt undeserving of the praise in so many ways. She'd reacted defiantly. Uncooperatively. She'd disobeyed and gone rogue. If she'd failed, she could only imagine how Disney would be treating her.

"I want to be a Kingdom Keeper," she said. "That's what you can do for me. Amanda and Jess, too. Maybe Nick. Maybe some of the other Fairlies, if they agree. An army of us. Why not? I want to mean something, Joe, to make a difference like Maybeck, Charlene, Willa, Philby, and . . ."

"What is it?"

"A name. I can't remember . . . Never mind. It's nothing."

"So you're obviously thinking there's still a reason for the Keepers to exist. Why is that?"

"I don't know exactly. A hunch?" Mattie twisted her hands together, stared off into space. "But now that you mention it . . . do you think it's over? Really over?"

"It depends on whether or not the Keepers return, and what happened while they were back there."

"Do you think changing the past changes the future?" Mattie's eyes were wide and surprisingly earnest. "Or is everything that happens going to find a way to happen no matter what we do? Like water running downhill: you can put stuff in its way, but it's just going to run around it."

"Interesting." Joe looked up at the ceiling. There was nothing there but lost time and wishful thinking, random ideas stuck like pencils flung by aimless boys.

"That's all you've got?" Mattie sat up farther. Her whole body hurt. "Your take on whether the past changes the future is 'interesting'?"

"Philosophy can wait, Mattie. We'll never know the answer to that, not until they come back. *If* they come back."

89

O<small>N AN OVERLY CHILLY NIGHT</small> in Anaheim in 1955, a red Ford half-ton pickup truck idled noisily alongside the westernmost, darkest wall of Pacific Hospital. Four dark figures slithered over the rails and moved as swiftly as shadows into the dark. It absorbed them like a sponge, and they were gone.

In the Ford, a young guy wearing overalls grabbed the wheel with both hands, staring straight ahead. Next to him sat a beautiful young woman with Asian eyes and warm olive skin. Next to her, a nervous-looking young woman, a little too thin, with dyed white-blond hair.

At first, no one spoke. It had all been discussed an hour earlier, amid a storm of tears and grief. As a group, they were talked out, cried out, burned out. The events in the Tower Hotel's dining room had created a kind of crust over them all, slowing and fogging them till it seemed as if nothing remained.

Jess asked Wayne, "Can this possibly work?"

"If you think about it, as Charlene clearly did, why not? Something that never existed in 1955 in the first place can't be changed sixty years later by events in 1955.

I think it was Philby who said there's nothing to lose by trying. Nothing to lose, Jess, and everything to gain."

"Everything," Amanda mumbled. "Absolutely everything."

Philby's news of the successful crossing and return of a tailless cat named Max—collected from beneath an area of park construction and sent into and back from the future—went uncelebrated. No cheering. No pats on the back. Just a sense of passive inevitability, as if the Keepers had assumed Philby and Wayne would figure it out all along. It upset Philby to no end. Even in the midst of his grief, he'd worked tech miracles. He felt greatly underappreciated.

If the three in the truck cab had been able to clear their throats of tears, they might have discussed the fire at the abandoned hotel, which left the building with scars and markings resembling those of a certain park attraction. An attraction that would not be imagined or built for decades to come.

Or they might have discussed how the radio was already reporting Hollingsworth's death as suicide. According to press reports, he'd jumped from a hotel balcony. This deviation from the facts suggested a staging of the body, either by his own people or the police, a worrisome development that, at best, showed the early reach of the Barracks.

So much to say, and yet they discussed nothing. Just shed a few more tears. The chill in the air seemed symbolic—part Maleficent, part despair.

The four figures emerged less than fifteen minutes later, the tallest—Maybeck—carrying something large and saggy in his arms. The figures to either side of him kept checking the sidewalk behind them, as if expecting trouble.

Wayne checked and adjusted the mirror as the figures flowed over the truck's back rails, returning to their original position in the bed.

"Do they have him?" Amanda asked, her head bowed. "It?"

A knock came sharply against the cab's back window. The three in front flinched.

"It would seem so." Wayne goosed the accelerator, shifted out of neutral, and rolled the truck slowly down the street. When he next looked at the rearview mirror, he saw only darkness. It would have appeared to any other driver that the bed was empty. But Wayne knew his passengers remained, facedown, dissolving so deeply into the shadows that the truck bed seemed suddenly bottomless.

The ride back to Disneyland was bumpy and long, anything but comfortable. Streetlamps cut their harsh glare across the legs and chests of the three in the cab, like knife blades endlessly slicing, trying to reach the depths of their emotions. But just like the truck bed, there was no bottom.

It seemed like Amanda would never stop crying. She would grow old quickly, wrung out, and twisted dry. Existing only to hope and wish, to pray and ache.

This was the life Jess had foreseen. This was not the first time Jess had hoped she was wrong.

90

WAYNE USED HIS CREDENTIALS and company friendships to get his pickup truck through the back gate between Main Street and Tomorrowland, which in 1955 amounted to a single security booth manned by an old guy named Fred. The Ford lumbered onto park property, slipping past attractions with a muted rumble of the engine. The castle stood dark, its broad shape materializing out of empty sky.

It began raining before the truck pulled to a stop beside King Arthur Carrousel. Though it was light at first, the rain seemed to contain the anger of the six teens, and soon it was coming down in torrents.

There were no hugs or handshakes between Wayne and the others, only a grimace, a shared feeling of past memories and lost opportunities. Wayne did stop to wipe the rain and tears from Amanda's face in a caring, loving way—a mannerism that would carry through the decades to come and still be there sixty years later, if and when they met again.

When the truck had gone, Philby addressed the group.

"We all know what this means, right?" He looked from stricken face to stricken face. "We've stopped Hollingsworth. Maleficent and the others will never be OTs."

"Which means we'll never be Keepers," Willa said, interrupting. "How sad is that?"

"It's true," Philby said, disappointed Willa would remind everyone of the possibility that they might be strangers upon their return. They needed all their focus now. "There's a chance that if and when we make it back to the present, we were never needed as DHIs. That Wayne never created us, never crossed over Finn that first time. That we never met. So I guess, this could be good-bye."

Amanda said, "Good-bye happened back in the hotel dining room. It all ended there." She sniffed and Jess threw an arm around her.

Now, as she had then, Amanda knelt beside Finn's body, which was covered in a white sheet, just as it had been when Maybeck carried it from the hospital morgue to the truck. The Keepers and the Fairlies had agreed not to pull that sheet back. Maybeck and Amanda had already witnessed what Finn had endured. They didn't want anyone else to share that burden.

"We could stay," Willa said, grasping Philby's hand and squeezing it bloodless. "Why don't we just stay?"

"Because we aren't from here. We've already changed so much. Who knows what damage we might do to the present—or the past, for that matter! This isn't our place. We owe it to the lives of everyone else to get out of here. Besides," Philby said, "what if Charlene's right?"

Charlene, arguably the least academic of the Keepers, had been the one to present a theory of quantum physics that had taken Wayne and Philby a good measure of time to comprehend. But once they'd processed it, they'd grown excited and demanding. She, too, knelt by Finn, her hand on the sheet covering his bare chest.

"I think," she said, "that if we're going to try this, we should all be connected, all touching him. He kept us together. He never liked to be called the leader, so I won't call him that now, but we all looked to him. We Keepers all became who we are because of him."

"We Fairlies, too," said Jess, struggling not to burst into another bout of tears. "We'd never have been here without Finn."

"'All for one,' and all that," said Maybeck. For once, there was not a hint of sarcasm in his voice. "I'm in." He kneeled, taking hold of Finn's foot. "Whitman, listen to Charlene, would you?" His voice broke. "Don't be so wickedly stubborn. Let her be right."

Philby and Willa joined the others, forming a

circle around Finn's prone form. "If the past no longer exists . . ." Philby said.

". . . then there's only the present," Charlene completed the thought.

The carousel music sounded.

"They're playing our tune," Maybeck said. The huge wheel began to rotate; the horses started to move up and down in steady rhythm. "Somebody click their heels three times, for cripe's sake."

"I'll do even better," Philby said, withdrawing what looked like a mousetrap tangled with a hundred colorful wires. Beneath was taped a phalanx of batteries.

At the very center of the device was a single black button.

Philby pushed it.

91

A CIRCLE OF OVERLY BRIGHT lights atop tripods illuminated King Arthur Carrousel. Fat black cables ran from all sides to a portable generator, while other cables stretched to antennas, also placed around the carousel in a perfect circle. Seven ambulances waited, the motors running. A Disney fire crew stood by.

The carousel was slowing.

Joe was there, as was Mattie. A man named Brad. Kim Irvine and Teresa. They stood watching from beyond the lights as, amid an oily swirl of time and dimension, a group of teens appeared between the moving horses. The teens shimmered, dissolved like smoke, and reappeared, taking on an ethereal quality.

On the next revolution they were gone. A collective sigh of disappointment rose from the crowd, breaking the intense energy that pervaded those in attendance.

"Come on . . ." Joe muttered under his breath. Then, into a walkie-talkie, "More amplification. We're losing them."

The small radio squawked. "Risky, chief."

"Now or never."

"Roger Rabbit," said the Imagineer on the other radio.

Kim Irvine grinned and murmured, "I love this company."

Joe nodded.

The following revolution brought more clarity to the images. Around once again, and they actually looked . . .

"Opaque!" Joe said. He shouted into the handset: "Keep that. Right there! You've got it!"

Another revolution, the carousel winding down to a crawl.

"No more fluctuation," gasped Brad.

"What's that in the middle?" said Teresa.

"You mean *who's* that?" The words were barely out when Mattie collapsed, caught by Joe at the last minute.

"Finn," she said, looking up at Joe. "The name I couldn't remember."

"Finn!" Joe said, nodding. For the past twenty-four hours, the name had escaped him as well. "How could I have forgotten Finn?"

Mattie wobbled. Joe helped her to her knees. "Why is that sheet over him?" she asked.

"Let's not jump to judgment." Joe took a wary step toward the carousel. His knees also gave out, and he dropped as well. "No, no, no!" he mumbled.

454

"Medic to the platform!" shouted Kim Irvine in a calm, professional voice.

The fuzzy DHIs on the platform moved.

"Let's go, people!" Brad shouted.

From behind him emerged more than two dozen Disney security guards, Cast Members, and paramedics. The team swept up onto the carousel, each first responder assigned to a particular Keeper. Individually, the dazed teens were encouraged to their feet as their DHIs prevented anyone from physically helping them. The Keepers staggered off the attraction.

Joe, Brad, and a full team of engineers had discovered how to keep Max alive after failing with some caged butterflies and a pair of lizards sent across time by Philby and Wayne. It hadn't been easy; Max had left the carousel barely able to stand, and had fallen into a deep sleep within a few minutes of the return. The Cryptos and Imagineers had anticipated a similar reaction from the Keepers.

But as the teens stepped down onto firm ground they looked each to the other and smiled widely.

"Where are we?" Charlene said.

Philby looked up at the sky. "Looks like Disneyland to me. *Our* Disneyland."

"You're home!" Mattie stepped forward as if to give Philby a hug, but Joe stopped her, reminding her that the Keepers were holograms.

Barely able to walk, Maybeck tried to lean on the shoulder of the man helping him, but his DHI passed through, forcing him to find his own balance. "Home," he muttered. "But if this is home, where've we been?"

"Their memory," Joe said to Mattie, the two of them standing again. "We don't know how this will affect their memory of the past few weeks."

Amanda's anguished cry pierced the air. "No!!!" Amanda's rescue team was trying to tell her to get off the carousel—and away from Finn. "I won't leave him!"

As she raised her arms toward the team, Joe shouted, "Everybody back!"

Amanda *pushed*—not only her handlers, but also much of the surrounding equipment—lights, antennas included. The lights exploded as they struck the ground, throwing a shower of sparks twenty feet into the air.

The carousel began moving again. It rotated faster and faster, Amanda's pushes responsible.

"Do something," Joe ordered into his radio. No voices replied, the antennas down. Joe hollered. Brad barked orders. The crew ran around trying to fix things.

The carousel continued gaining speed. Amanda had one arm around Finn, one holding on to a carousel horse pole.

Charlene smiled and said under her breath, "That'a girl!"

Maybeck saw a blur of color running from the crew side toward the carousel. "What's that?" he asked his handler.

Philby overheard and looked in the same direction.

Willa, too. She saw the form clearly. "Not what," she said so the boys could hear her. "Who!" Adding, "That's the Dillard."

Joe overheard her. He saw the blur along with the others. "DILLARD!" he cried. He threw his unresponsive radio to the pavement in disgust. "Who authorized that DHI?"

The Keepers and Jess looked on as the carousel's next rotation revealed that Amanda, Finn, and the Dillard were struggling to hold on against the centrifugal force.

When the carousel came around again, only a few of the gathering, including Maybeck, saw Finn's arms wrapped around Amanda.

"See that!? He's *alive!*" Maybeck called out.

The Keepers cheered.

Another blurring revolution of the carousel. Only the bedsheet remained, wrapped around a horse, fluttering like a fallen flag.

"Oh no!" Jess said. "Where are they? Where did they go?"

"Sir?" one of the crew called.

Joe and the Keepers saw the man kneeling by a boy's blue-outlined image lying on the asphalt.

The Keepers rushed to help them.

"It's Finn!" Jess shouted.

"Careful!" Joe called, as the Keepers reached the hologram.

The kids skidded to a stop. It wasn't Finn. It wasn't Amanda. It wasn't the Dillard.

Jess felt drawn toward the facedown boy. He wore strange old-fashioned pants with wide suspenders. Jess didn't understand her attraction to the boy, but she couldn't stop herself either; something felt weirdly familiar about him. One of her future dreams? she wondered. She kneeled, despite calls not to touch what was clearly a patchy and faltering DHI. Willa joined Jess, and together they tried and failed to roll the boy over. Half his face was visible. Jess tried to touch him gently. "I know this kid . . ." Willa said.

"Me . . . too," said Maybeck. The others nodded in agreement. "But how? How's that possible?"

Joe was with them now. He, too, studied the unidentified boy. He asked Maybeck, "Do you remember nothing about where you've been?"

"Where *have* we been?" Maybeck asked, perplexed.

"And for *how long* were we there?" Philby said.

"Where are our parents?" Charlene asked. "Our

families?" She looked around. "What's going on, anyway?"

"I'll be darned," Joe said. "Nothing?"

The Keepers didn't bother to answer.

"What happened to Amanda and Finn?" Mattie asked.

"And the Dillard?" Willa said.

Joe looked up at the empty carousel. "I think we may have lost them."

"What do you mean?" Philby complained, and he shuddered head to toe. "Anybody just feel that?"

All the others responded, nearly simultaneously. "Yes! Tingling."

Philby reached and touched Willa's shoulder. "We're weakening."

Joe's cell phone rang. He carried on a brusque conversation with whoever was unfortunate enough to be on the other end the call.

"We're going to return you," he said, addressing Philby. "All of you."

"Meaning?" Charlene asked somewhat rudely.

"To the Central Plaza," Philby said. "Our DHIs are degrading." He half stated this, half proposed to Joe, who didn't contradict him. "The Cryptos want to return us as soon as possible."

"Sir!" With the degrading of the holograms, some

physicality had returned. Two of the crew had managed to roll over the DHI of the boy. "He's wearing a Cast Member pin. One of the old, metal ones."

"Nineteen fifty-five," Philby said as if remembering the name—or trying to—of a long-lost friend. "Why do I know that date?" he asked.

"The name?" Joe called over. "The boy's name?"

One of the attendants called back. "The name on the tag is Wayne."

92

THE KEEPERS COULDN'T CONTAIN themselves. "Wayne? Alive?" "He's our age!" "Can't be *our* Wayne!" They collected around the shifting DHI as it was transferred to a collapsible ambulance bed.

The Keepers, aware of the omnipresence of magic in the parks, secretly knew that this Wayne was somehow the same Wayne Kresky who had created their DHIs. The man, in boy form, responsible for the Kingdom Keepers.

"What . . . about . . . them?" Willa asked, pointing to the empty carousel, which was noticeably slowing. The momentary high of celebration collapsed. The emptiness of the carousel fell heavily upon them.

"You mean us?" came a boy's voice. A familiar voice. Helped on one side by Amanda, and on the other by a young Dillard Cole, Finn Whitman limped as he struggled to walk on his own. "Somebody might have thought to look on the other side, you know."

"I tried to hold on, but we flew off," Amanda said.

Looking confused, Dillard added, "All of us."

Arms swung up onto shoulders as the circle closed,

tightening its grip around the three surprise arrivals. Words were spoken. Tears were shed. Hugs were shared, even though part hologram. A sense of everything having purpose overcame the group. Years of effort. Tears of joy.

In spite of their limited memory their words included "safe," "all over," "finally." They had started when younger than Dillard. They were older now. More experienced. More damaged in some ways, more themselves at the same time.

"Head to the Hub, we'll return you," Joe said. They walked through the castle drawbridge together; they were not letting go of one another anytime soon. Laughter jumped out from the group. The professing of love, the kind of deep love that took years to form, lifetimes to find. Finn tussled Dillard's cropped hair.

"You're here! You're really here!" Then Finn looked up . . . right at the Partners statue. Something in him vaguely remembered that statue not being there the last time he'd stood in the Hub. Not that it made any sense.

"We're back!" Maybeck said euphorically. "We . . . are . . . back!" He started jumping up and down. The others joined him. A group of kids, unseen by anyone.

Dancing in the dark.

93

JOE GARLINGTON STUDIED DILLARD at an arm's length, the boy's mother in a chair next to the hospital bed that Dillard had been in and out of over the past several days.

"We don't know more than what we already know," he said to the boy. Dillard nodded. "The good news is you check out fine. Healthy as any boy your age."

"About that," Dillard said.

"Yeah. The way it has been explained to me is that we designed your DHI when you were fourteen. That was nearly five years ago. When you jumped onto King Arthur Carrousel with Finn and Amanda, when the three of you were spun off, you returned with them. But as your fourteen-year-old self. We assume, and we can only assume, you will continue to age and grow normally." He said this as much to Dillard's mom as to the boy himself.

"But five years younger than my best friend!"

"You're five years behind in school as well. They've all graduated high school."

"But how?"

Joe shrugged. "Dillard, a terrible thing happened to you."

"Finn stabbed me."

"Well . . ."

"Not that he knew it was me. I'm not saying that!"

"No, he certainly did not! And the point is—"

"He killed me."

"He killed, or thought he killed, Tia Dalma. It was a spell. The point being . . ."

"You're alive!" his mother said for something like the hundredth time since the family had arrived from Florida. At least, Dillard thought, she isn't still crying about it.

"I guess it's better than the alternative," Dillard said, sounding disappointed.

Joe chuckled. "I'm told you're free to go. There will be regular checkups, of course. In Florida, I assume. We'll arrange everything."

Dillard's mother thanked Joe repeatedly and sincerely. "I'm sorry for all those things I said back when—"

"I would have said them too," Joe confessed. "Completely understand. Now, if you'll excuse me."

"How is he?" Dillard asked. "Wayne, right?"

Joe nodded. "It's getting interesting," he said.

* * *

The doctors huddled with Joe for several long minutes before admitting him to the room three doors down. The first day there had been partial evidence. On this day, the aging was far more pronounced.

The way it had been explained, Wayne had created his own projected image in 1955 with the help of Philby's small laser pointers. He remained a DHI because the Imagineers lacked the necessary personalized algorithms and imaging data to return him. With each day, his projected image aged another ten or more years. He already looked like a man in his thirties.

And there was nothing anyone could do to make him human.

Having lost him once, Joe was determined not to allow it to happen again. But for now, the same 1950s clothing had stretched and ripped as the image had aged. It was one of the more bizarre phenomena Joe had witnessed—and he'd seen plenty!

"You'll be happy to know," he told the unresponsive DHI, "the Keepers' memories of 1955 have returned along with them. They remember you as a young man and they said how great you were to them, how you saved them."

A sharp rap on the door startled Joe. He had to check his watch to see he'd been standing there looking at Wayne for nearly thirty minutes.

"I've got it!" Brad said, coming inside. Brad had overseen the original DHI imaging of the Keepers.

"Got what?"

"We're wrong! I mean, it's true *we* don't have any of the necessary DHI imaging data to return Wayne. I get that! I realize that."

"Focus."

Brad's breathing was frantic, his face flushed. "*WE* don't!" he said. "That's been our problem, Joe. We know we never imaged Wayne. We know the data that came through when he returned to the carousel was lousy, corrupted data—that he was lucky to return as any kind of image. But here he is!"

"All of which I know. Tell me what I don't know."

"The Overtakers."

"Are gone. Once and for all. Gone."

"Think!"

"Do not test me, Brad. I've barely slept in three days. I'm about to lose a close friend, *a Disney Legend*, for the SECOND time! I'm running low, friend."

"Fantasmic," Brad said excitedly. "The stage. Remember? Who showed up on the stage?"

"W . . . a . . . y . . . n . . . e."

"Yeah, Wayne."

"That was the Overtakers' doing. They're the ones who imaged him, turned him into a DHI."

"Right," said Brad. "But they projected him—"

"—using our projectors!" Joe said, finishing for him. "The Overtakers hacked us and projected his DHI over our systems!"

"The Cryptos, the Imagineers, capture all that data, Joe. All of it. We save all the data from every show. Been that way as long as I can remember."

"So we must have captured Wayne's DHI data." Joe could barely speak the words.

"We did! Absolutely! I'm going to search our digital archives. It's in there somewhere."

"We extract the data—"

"—and we then have code that is a Version 1.6 of Wayne. We can return him."

"Get on it!"

"I'm on it." Brad seemed to be floating. "Just one thing. We're going to have to match his age to his same age of the data we have."

"At the rate he's aging, that's only a matter of days."

"Yeah."

"Can we do it that fast?"

"We have to, right?" Brad asked.

"Yes, we have to!" Joe heard his voice tremble.

"Then we'll do what we have to do." He reached out and the two men shook hands.

"Yes, we will. We absolutely will!"

94

LATE ONE NIGHT, slightly chilly winds blew out of the north stirring the palm fronds like long hair held out a car window. For over three weeks the Keepers and Fairlies had been soaking up their bedrooms—their real bedrooms at home in Florida. Their books. Their posters. Their music.

Jess and Amanda, guests of Charlene and her mom, shared a room as they always had and hopefully always would. Like sisters.

No one could remember whose idea this night had been. Philby's probably, though Finn was more sentimental, more likely to think of the group.

But here they were, a small team of DHIs, bigger than the five who had started. Alone in the Magic Kingdom. Surrounded by darkness, empty streets, and silence. They rode attractions like Haunted Mansion, Splash Mountain, and Big Thunder Mountain Railroad, remembering a time years before.

They stole glimpses of characters like Mickey, Minnie, and Elsa, spying on them, giggling, and then darting away. "The Children of Light!" the characters gasped as they encountered the group.

The Kingdom Keepers were famous. Celebrities to what many believed were fictional characters. The whole thing seemed upside down.

As DHIs the Keepers, Fairlies, and Dillard watched as Finn approached the Goofy bench outside the Exhibition Hall and the older man sitting there. A man with a wide smile and wise eyes. White hair and red nose. A man to whom they owed everything. All the extraordinary experiences they'd lived for what felt like an eternity. One man. One dream.

He patted the bench and Finn sat.

"Remember?" Wayne asked.

"Like it was yesterday. Yes, sir, I do."

"You didn't believe."

"I did not."

"You do now."

"I do. Yes."

"And you, all of you, have had a good night?"

"The best ever. We've been on most all of the rides. Telling stories. Remembering. I couldn't go on Small World, couldn't bring myself to do it. The others did. I'll have to take their word for it that the dolls didn't come alive."

"Good times," Wayne said.

"Not that one! But, yes. Yes, sir. Exceptional.

Extraordinary. The best." Finn's throat tightened and he looked up at the night sky to keep Wayne from seeing the tears in his eyes. "I don't want it to end. None of us wants it to end."

"It's not as if they're destroying the technology."

"They're destroying the Keepers software. That's the same as destroying us."

"You have college ahead. You have lives to get on with, son. No one can take away what you've had. But we need to take away your thinking it's going to go on forever."

"But it is."

"No, your job is done here. The kingdom, the characters owe you all . . . well, everything. We owe you everything."

"I'm sorry to contradict you, sir. But we . . . owe . . . you everything." His stupid throat wouldn't let the words out smoothly.

The other Keepers stood right in front of the bench now. Finn had no idea for how long they'd been standing so close, how much they'd heard. But their wet eyes answered that for him.

"A real fairy tale has no ending," Wayne said, looking at each one of the kids. "You all remember that. Hold that in your hearts."

The kids nodded.

"So, who's it going to be?" Wayne opened his clenched fist. In it, a small plastic fob, like a garage door opener. Small and unassuming. The Return. No one wanted to touch it.

Finn carefully took it from Wayne, studied it, and handed it to Philby.

"I suppose you'll be an Imagineer someday," Finn told his friend. "Seems only right that you be the one to end this chapter."

"Or start the next," Philby said, accepting the Return from Finn. "Are we ready?"

Finn stood to join his friends.

"You've been ready for a long, long time," said Wayne, wiping the corners of his old blue eyes. "And I'll be seeing you soon."

"To the best ride ever," Philby said, raising his hand, holding the fob to the sky. The other hands joined his, like a sports team ready to start the game.

"The best ride ever," the group echoed.

And he pushed the button.